DAVID'S
VINEYARDS

DAVID'S
VINEYARDS

Bruce Lee Givens

DAVID'S VINEYARDS

iUniverse books may be ordered through booksellers or by contacting:

iUniverse
1663 Liberty Drive
Bloomington, IN 47403
www.iuniverse.com
1-800-Authors (1-800-288-4677)

ISBN: 978-1-5320-0470-4 (sc)
ISBN: 978-1-5320-0471-1 (e)

Library of Congress Control Number: 2016913199

Print information available on the last page.

iUniverse rev. date: 03/30/2017

This book is dedicated to Darlene, my beautiful loving cousin, and Mark, my handsome straight Brother in Christ.

PREFACE

The museums, hotels, bars and restaurants in San Francisco, London, Amsterdam, Paris, Rome and New York, were actual places in the 1970s. The characters portrayed in this book are fictional.

CHAPTER ONE

The smell of eucalyptus mixed with cypress and wildflowers created an atmosphere unique to this particular locale next to the peaceful Pacific Ocean at the entrance of San Francisco Bay. It seemed to David that he was the only person traversing the isolated footpaths and trails that wound through the trees and shrubs along this northwestern corner of the city.

People ostensibly came here to discover stunning glimpses of the Golden Gate Bridge and secluded pocket beaches that could be seen from the rocky ledges with cloistered trees and bushes. He knew, however, that there were more than a dozen cars already sitting in the remote parking lot; owners of those vehicles were not here for the view.

These individuals had an alternate motive in visiting the wild park, especially at this early hour. They were adventuresome men looking for instant acquaintance and immediate sexual satisfaction with another of their own gender. *Land's End* was a notorious haven of daring gay activity both day and night.

David was among those who knew the complex layout of the land and he traversed the narrow trails with nimble dexterity. He always left his search to fate hoping to find a rousing, stimulating encounter; he was confident of finding success in this morning's deliciously impure quest. This was 1970 and the sexual revolution was in full swing.

He was under a slight disadvantage on this particular morning. He had driven his beloved sister, Patricia, to the nearby museum of art, and timing was essential if he wished to indulge his desire for sexual activity before retrieving her.

He really didn't like the feeling of being rushed, so Fate would have to step in this morning if he were to *'have his cake and eat it too.'* That's what David truly wanted out of life...pleasure...fun...play. Aside from being somewhat shallow, he really didn't see anything wrong with his goals.

* * *

Patricia sat poised on a stone bench with her lovely long legs crossed as she overlooked a stunning vista of green eucalyptus and Pacific blue water...another unique view of San Francisco that could only be seen from the *Palace of Legion of Honor*. She had been inside the museum for most of the beautiful April morning searching for rare books illustrated by "modern" artists such as Pablo Picasso, Juan Gris and Andre Derain. She had learned that a French art historian named Daniel-Henry Kahnweiler was known to have published such books, but she also ascertained that the best assortment rested somewhere in Chicago with art collectors Reva and David Logan.

Patricia impulsively considered hopping a roundtrip flight SFO-ORD that weekend, to conclude her project, but decided against it remembering the Saturday night birthday celebration that she had planned for her boy friend Stephen. Besides, she thought, it would be much easier to find a project closer to home that could satisfy the requirements for the advanced Art History class she was taking at San Jose State University. She started to think maybe she would write a short dissertation on illustrated scrolls and artifacts from the *Rosicrucian Museum* in San Jose...it would certainly be a more accessible undertaking for her project rather than embarking on a trek to Chicago.

Patricia abruptly stood up when she saw her brother's white Alpine Sports convertible approaching the entrance to the museum...at that same moment two young men in uniform walked by and simultaneously nodded with appreciative grinning smilles. Patty instinctively tossed her head showing off her beautiful thick chestnut hair as she also straightened her shoulders to emphasize an alluring model's figure. Both of the soldiers whistled as they watched her slip gracefully into her brother's sports car.

Smiling broadly, she waved to them...and quietly whispered an aside to her brother,

"Dirty warmongering aggressors."

David broke into hearty laughter as he often did when an 'untoward' comment was advanced in humor...especially by his sister. He knew that her comment was not serious.

"Patty...Patty, you sound like too many of our war-protesting hippy brothers and sisters at school. We really shouldn't be laughing...we should be more serious and support our armed forces guys... even if they are unpopular."

"Don't preach to me, Poopsie," Patty broke in, "You and I would indeed be unpopular if the majority of our peers had the least inkling of our political inclinations. Don't lecture to me about supporting our military in Vietnam. You know that I love our boys who are in uniform, even if celebrities like Jane Fonda do not. You also know that I believe that just one single solitary life of a USA soldier is worth a hundred lives of those smarmy Viet Cong scum-bags they're fighting."

In a more serious tone David said "I know how you really feel sweetheart, I was only being facetious; we both know better than to take each other literally. I can't help thinking about all the people we know who feel so differently. Yes, it's a very unpopular stance to openly support our American troops in Vietnam...somehow...I wish we could enlighten those people and change that mindset. Most of our friends don't have a clue how we really feel about the war. I often pray for all the guys we personally know in Vietnam...many of our closest friends won't be coming home...I pray for all our soldiers who are deployed there."

Patty glanced at her brother and said, "And to think that many of our closest friends are pot-smoking addicts who play their lives away protesting against the war, while good guys lose their lives in a conflict nobody understands. Our friends of both political persuasions don't have a clue what's happening. A lot of the blame goes to LBJ for using Vietnam to advance his own political agenda with his '*Great Society*.' He's creating the largest possible government under the auspice of providing prosperity and *progressive* social benefits for the American people...and at the same time he's escalating an unpopular war under the pretense of advancing and protecting *our* precious democracy. Much of the younger generation just wants to drop out of the mainstream establishment, sit back, and enjoy 'peace and love' while they smoke dope and let LBJ's big government take care of all their needs. No wonder we're surrounded by a world of unmotivated hippies! Take drugs, screw your brains out, sleep, eat and do more drugs. No need to work for the establishment...let the establishment work for you...'the peace and love flower children!' Meanwhile, LBJ and his band of progressive fiends from Washington are gaining *all* the power and making *large fortunes* at the expense of our soldier's lives."

"Patty, you and I have always had the same point of view about politics, religion and society. Remember we're not totally alone in our sentiments," David said, "What about other people like Vicky and Nancy?"

"Vicky is engaged to that law student from Santa Clara University whose studies were interrupted by the war...and Nancy's brother was also drafted about the same time. It's a little tough for either of those girls to be active protesters. Vicky and her family sincerely believe that South Vietnam is just a cork in a monstrous bottle that keeps the Chinese Viet-Cong puppets from spilling out into the world."

"What can we do about it that will actually and practicably support Democracy in our world? Counter protests to our colleagues would only exacerbate the situation and start a bigger war right here in the Bay Area."

"We can keep our faith and pray for peace. There's a lot of evil in this world Poopsie, and we have compelling reason to believe that much of it festers in Washington, D.C, where bureaucrats and politicians are benefiting from this despicable war. Our personal contribution is quiet prayer. We should stay out of the storm and enjoy the lives God gave us to the fullest possible measure. When it comes to the Vietnam War we can only be innocent witnesses to the insanity both here at home and abroad."

David smiled knowingly and said, "What about your hippy artist boyfriend Stephen, how does he fit into all that's happening?"

Patty responded, "His dad had enough influence to keep him out of the draft, and it's too much of a temptation for Steve not to join the 'hippy movement'. It's more a matter of fun for him. He's convinced that he and his hip colleagues are redefining the art world during the latest renaissance. Steve is talented...but he also subscribes to the emerging philosophy that 'the Great Society' will take care of everything while he develops his reputation as a world class artist."

David added, "It also doesn't hurt that Stephen's dad landed a $25,000 grant from LBJ to assist in that support. It's just another small perk for having two Berkeley professors for parents."

They laughed out loud as they breezed past *Land's End* where David had spent most of the morning while Patricia researched at the museum. The Alpine convertible slipped down the Great Highway past the old *Sutro Baths* when he automatically pulled in front of the famous Cliff House, turned off the motor and said, "How's this for lunch, I'm starving."

"Oh Poopsie," Patty pleaded, "Can't we please go to the *Gold Mirror*? I'm dying for their cannelloni."

David immediately started the engine, backed out and headed down the hill. "We're on our way. Ummm...I think I'll have what Dolly refers to as the *x-rated* dessert, the big mushroom shaped cannoli stuffed with ricotta cream, you know...it's listed on the menu as a Chocolate Mushroom."

"Didn't you already have your dessert at Land's End this morning?" Patty mused.

"I have no idea what you're trying to imply," David replied sardonically.

* * *

The Gold Mirror was not busy when the siblings arrived...it was still well before the noon hour when David found parking right in front of the establishment. They parted the long heavy drapes that led from the front door into what seemed like complete darkness. A dim glow from behind the bar emitted the only visible light at first. Two shadowy male figures were washing glasses and preparing for the busy lunch hour to come.

One of the shadows sang out in a baritone voice with a heavy Italian accent, "Patricia... David... *como-stah. hows-ah* you *familia*? Everybody okay? Always *glad-ah* you come. Sit wherever *you-ah* want...we *tell-ah* Dolly you here."

"*Gracia Guiseppe*," Patty and David rang back in unison as they groped their way to a table against the wall. When their eyes became adjusted to the darkness they could see the huge signature gold mirror with its decorous ornate frame looming above the room. The tables throughout the parlor were relatively small...each one with four prominent straight backed chairs covered in deep red suede.

A tuxedoed figure magically appeared and guided the chair for Patty while David quickly seated himself at the same table. "*Buon journo*" the waiter said familiarly, and Patty and David answered in unison again *"Buon journo!"*.

"It's a delight to see you" the waiter replied.

Patty smiled, "We're very happy to be here."

"Your mom and dad were here two nights ago."

"Yes," David said, "They like *The Gold Mirror* almost as much as we do."

"What can I get you kids to drink while you wait for Dolly...she *be here'a* soon," said the server in his thick Italian English.

"I'm here now you big ape! I'll take their order," barked an appreciatively heavy set female dressed in a man's tuxedo.

Dolly was a healthy looking woman...marginally attractive with fire-engine red hair, too much make-up, and long false eyelashes. She was well known by the locals who ate at *The Gold Mirror*...and she lived in a monstrous Victorian flat just a few blocks from the restaurant. She doted on her regular customers... and the Wellington family members were definitely among her favorites. Everyone who came here regularly knew Dolly...and everyone who knew Dolly loved her.

"I think we'll both have Negronis for starters...we'll decide on a bottle of wine in a few minutes," David said.

"Gotcha," Dolly said as she scribbled a note on her pad. "Got the new wine list right here," as she laid it on the table.

"And Dolly," Patty added, I know I want the cannelloni... David hasn't made up his mind about an entree...but you can save a chocolate mushroom for his dessert."

"You mean the x-rated dessert that's in the shape of a...a..." Dolly couldn't bring herself to say the word...so Patty helped her out by whispering the word "Penis".

Dolly laughed heartily and said, "That's not the word I was thinking of honey...do you want me to save one for you?"

"No thanks," Patty said laughing, "I think I'll pass on x-rated substances for today."

"Speaking of x-rated things," Patty continued as Dolly left to get their drinks, "did you have any success at Land's End on this gorgeous April 11th morning in 1970?"

"It wasn't very active this morning...and why are you making such a point of the exact date?" David asked hoping to change the subject.

"I'm simply tactfully reminding you that my Aries boyfriend, Stephen, was born on April 13th and *our* Aries father, Richard was born on April 16th, and *we* really should remember both guys...especially Daddy who will be exactly fifty years old...and Daddy deserves extra special acknowledgement. Now, back to my original question, I'm curious, did you find any satisfaction at Land's End this morning? I know it doesn't have to be crawling with activity for a good time...it only takes one person to make it fun."

"You know," David said, "You'd make a perfect 'fag-hag' because you want all the explicit details...and you act like you don't have a sex life of your own...it's almost as if you have to live vicariously through my experiences."

"You must not have found any of your type, otherwise, you wouldn't be so crabby about confiding in me. Usually, you're more than willing to give me the sordid details of your cruising escapades. I know my little brother very well. We're inveterately connected personally as well as spiritually."

"Sometimes I almost regret how well you know me." David said with a grin. "There was one kid that kept following me around...he was college age...nice looking but much too young to be a person of interest. When it was time for me to pick you up at the museum, I was desperate for some kind of action, so I gave in to him."

"How did you give in to him?"

David finally blurted out "I got a blow job...all right?"

"Well," Dolly said as she instantly appeared with two Negronis, "Sounds to me like you must have had a good time...you kids let me know when you're ready to order a bottle of wine...meanwhile, your salads are coming up."

Patty laughed out loud, "Thanks Dolly, you are the best!"

* * *

"You know, Poopsie," Patty began a new train of thought as David was gulping down the last of his *chocolate mushroom*, "We're living in a pretty exciting time when you think about it. Just look at what we've been through the last couple of years."

"Are you having espresso with me?" David interrupted his sister.

At that very moment the busboy appeared to clear their table and Patty said "I'll have a Chambord over ice and my brother would like a double espresso."

"Hold the espresso," David interjected as he wiped his mouth and folded his huge red linen napkin. "Make mine a *double* Chambord over ice."

"Make mine a double as well," said Patty, and she went on... "Just think...we were right here for the summer of love...peace...and flowers. History was made once again in San Francisco...and it's still being made...we're in the middle of a revolution. We are here witnessing what is happening right now! We're at the center of the world!"

David offered his sister a cigarette and she waved it aside as he lit one for himself. "What world are you referring to...the art world...the music world...the gay world? I know that unlike many of our acquaintances we made it through the summer of '67 without completely blowing our minds on drugs, sex and acid rock concerts. We even participated in some *establishment-like* activities with our family. We went to the opera...Oakland Raiders football games, shopping at *Gumps* and dinner at *Ernie's*... and we attended church on Sundays seeking remission from our sins from the week before."

Patty threw back her head and laughed loudly, "You crack me up Poopsie...there is absolutely no one as promiscuous as you have been. I was not referring to the sexual revolution or the use of mind-expanding drugs. I'm thinking more specifically of notable events that are having political as well as social implications on our entire culture...most notably from our earlier discussion, the Vietnam War."

Her tone became more serious. "You remember what happened at school that fall after the *summer of love and peace*. The college administration permitted Dow Chemical to carry on recruiting sessions on campus and everyone went berserk."

"Yes," David said, I remember. "It was all because Dow Chemical makes napalm to put in the bombs they're using in Vietnam. Everyone was protesting except the two of us and Nancy and Vicky from the Drama department. It all happened just a few blocks from our house on Ninth Street. You and the girls were sitting on the porch swing and I was on the steps playing with Vicky's dog. We didn't even know what was happening. You and I both have done a pretty good job dodging the effects of Vietnam."

Patty picked up on David's narrative, "We were all stoned and watched as people were rushing by us toward the Administration building on Seventh Street...I was just about to float into the kitchen and make some *Constant Comment* tea when the landlord walked up with his wife."

"How could I forget," David giggled. "My mouth went as dry as the Sahara Desert when they stopped right in front of me sitting on the porch steps...Mr. Anderson said 'I need to speak with you Mister and Miss Wellington'... and all the while Nancy was fumbling to put out the joint and hide her roach clip...that was a groovy roach clip, it was made from a M-16 bullet shell.

"Do you remember what else the landlord said," Patty encouraged David to continue.

"Oh yes," David feigned a hard swallow. "He said 'I wasn't born yesterday, and I know what you kids are up to...everybody can see the tops of your marijuana plants over the fence growing in my backyard...I must have counted sixteen or seventeen plants that I can see from the street. I want those things cut down and hauled off my property. I will not be part of your illegal shenanigans."

"But his wife was so sweet," Patty added to the story. "She nudged her husband with her elbow and said, 'Don't be coming down so hard on the kids, Harry...don't you remember when we used to smoke that stuff during prohibition.' Then she nudged him again a couple of times."

"Right," said David continuing the story, "But he completely ignored his wife and demanded that we have those plants cut down in the next twenty-four hours. I was freaked out...I couldn't talk because my mouth was so dry...and you were so cool. You just kept gently swaying on the porch swing and told him not to worry... the plants would all be gone by the same time tomorrow... and his wife winked at you as they walked off..."

Patty said "We did a pretty good job of clearing out the crop, especially with Stephen's help. I still have a lot of that stuff stashed away."

"Yeah," agreed David, "Steve did most of the work... he was certainly motivated...and he took at least a kilo's worth of grass home for his efforts."

Patty laughed, "We all did our share of the work...I remember you and I strung up the clothes lines in the garage so we could hang the plants to dry...and Vicky made those cute little curtains to cover the windows so no one could see inside. It was definitely a team effort."

"Our landlord never did say anything more, did he?" David asked rhetorically.

"In retrospect, I don't think he ever really cared very much...he just wanted to make sure no one got in trouble with the law. It cracks me up... that all happened on 'Bloody Thursday'...the administrators should have been smart enough not to allow Dow Chemical to recruit from our campus," Patty said.

"Didn't you know the guy who threw the bucket of blood...or whatever it was...against the door of the Administration Building?"

"No," she answered, It's just that someone said he was from the Art department...I don't know who it was... but didn't the riot take place in front of the Chemistry Building."

"I don't know...I was with you...just a couple blocks away...and none of us knew anything about the whole incident until the following Monday. We were being authentic hippies that day...just lay'in back grooving on our pot...away from the combat."

Laughing Patty said, "No trouble for us that day..."

"Yeah," David said, "no trouble until the landlord stopped by and made my mouth go drier than the Sahara Desert."

* * *

CHAPTER TWO

T he day following their lunch at The Gold Mirror Patty declared to her mother, "I'm on my way to the Vineyards...any messages for Nanny and Poppa?"

"Give them our love and tell them we look forward to see them on Sunday. When will you be back to the city?" Sylvia asked.

Patty answered, "I'm thinking of spending the night with Nanny and Poppa...I'll drive back to San Jose tomorrow, sometime. It's Steve's birthday and we have reservations at *Paolo's* for his celebration."

"Will your brother David be celebrating with the two of you?" Sylvia asked.

"Oh yes," Patty responded "And Steve's little brother Paul will probably tag along for the meal."

Sylvia thought for a moment and said, "You children are like a close-knit family when you're in San Jose. You live with your brother in that cute little house on Ninth Street, and Steve and his brother are just a block or two away in their house on....is it Tenth or Eleventh?"

"It's Twelfth Street," Patty corrected her mother, politely, "and it's not a house, it's an old two bedroom duplex that desperately needs painting. Steve's dad bought it for a song, and they rent the other side to four of Paul's friends who on the college baseball team with him." Patty added, "It's not a particularly attractive building, but those guys are happy as pigs in mud to live there. One of the guys next door has a motorcycle that he parks in the living room. No one seems to mind, but it annoys me whenever I have occasion to see it."

Sylvia mused as she meticulously arranged long-stemmed gladiolas, "I don't want to think about the dirt and grime that those boys must wallow in."

It's not as bad as it sounds," Patty said while picking up one of the flowers and began peeling the stem for her mother. "They're all good boys, just a little socially/emotionally immature. They all think it's groovy to have a Harley sitting in the living room."

"Well," Sylvia laughed, "Steve's neighboring tenets do indeed sound like typical college boys... not at all like your brother."

"My brother" Patty retorted, "is *the* consummate gentleman."

"And a scholar," Sylvia added.

"I wouldn't go that far," Patty said. "David is really more of a pseudo-intellect."

Sylvia said, "How can you say that...you know perfectly well that your brother is very intelligent and earns great grades in all his classes, doesn't he?"

"Oh yes!" Patty explained. "But, he doesn't really earn his grades by being studious or resourceful in research. He just charms his instructors into believing they're great scholars and the object of adulation and admiration. David cuts more classes than anybody I know...he's a bull-shitter when it comes to snowing his professors."

Sylvia froze from arranging the flowers and looked directly at her daughter...she often marveled at the closeness of the relationship between the siblings, and she was truly grateful to God for her exceptional children...but she wished Patty wouldn't speak that way about David...even if it was in levity.

"Patricia Kay Wellington, I'm not quite certain what you're trying to say." Sylvia used her daughter's full Christian name as a reminder to keep aplomb when making reference to her brother, "and I sincerely hope you don't use that kind of language around other people when you speak about David."

"Of course not Mother...I wouldn't think of it, but the truth is the truth, even if it's not always felicitous. You know that I love my little brother with all my heart... even if he is a con artist."

"Well," Sylvia said as she put the finishing touches to a flower arrangement, "I sincerely hope you don't use those distasteful expressions and opinions in front of people outside our family."

"What opinion?" asked Patty, "That David is a con artist, or that I love him."

"The former opinion," Sylvia retorted. "Now, if you're going to the Vineyards, you'd better start moving, it's almost ten o'clock and the morning is vanishing...my Bridge club will be arriving soon. Give my love to Nanny and Poppa and tell them we look forward to Sunday."

Patty hopped off the ornate bar stool where she'd been sitting and started to exit the spacious sunny room where Sylvia was still arranging the fresh flowers. Almost as an afterthought, Patricia stopped and suddenly kissed her mother passionately on the cheek.

"I'll be back here Sunday in time to accompany you and Dad to visit Nanny and Poppa. I can't speak for David...I don't know his plans beyond our party for Steve's birthday dinner tomorrow night."

Sylvia said, "Tell your brother we're hoping he will join the family on Sunday, and remind him of his father's birthday dinner on Tuesday. Keep your mind on the road, and don't drive too fast."

"You're thinking of David," Patty said. "I'm not the one who drives fast, it's your son."

Then to reassure her mother, Patty turned toward Sylvia blowing a kiss and said, "God Bless, we'll see you on Sunday. Enjoy your Bridge luncheon. By the way...are there any notables coming like the mayor's wife from down the street?"

"Not this time, but there will be two ladies from the Board of the *San Francisco Opera*, and the Vice-President of the *San Francisco Women's Club*."

"Are you still the president?" Patty asked as she nibbled on a piece of dark chocolate bridge-mix on her way out.

"No...I am the president emeritus...thanks be to God." Sylvia answered.

"Oh Mother", Patricia called from a distance, "I think your caterers are here, I'll have Brenda answer the door."

* * *

David arrived home in St. Francis Wood later that same afternoon. The Bridge ladies had just left, and Brenda, the main house maid, was directing the caterers in clearing. Sylvia was sitting in a dainty French provincial chair rubbing one of her feet gently in lady-like manner as David entered the room. Twin miniature poodles that had been sharing a matching chair next to Sylvia joyfully bolted to the floor and ran to David.

Sylvia sat straight, "What a pleasant surprise, I didn't expect to see you home today."

"I guess Dad forgot to remind you that he and I were meeting for early lunch in Santa Clara," David lifted a poodle in each of his arms and allowed them to wash his face with kisses and licks.

"Oh that is right" Sylvia stated wearily. "How was your lunch with your father?"

"It was okay; Dad entertained one female typist and one male artist who were with him from Lockheed. She seemed real uptight and he was somewhat boring...but they were pleasant enough."

"Where did you have lunch?" Sylvia asked.

"The *Velvet Turtle* in Santa Clara, it wasn't all that terrific. You look sleepy Mom...or are you just a little bit tired from your bridge party"

"It's been a long morning," Sylvia answered. "I'm glad you're home. Your sister went to the Vineyards for the day." (*Vineyards* being the family term used to refer to Sylvia's parents winery estate in Sonoma.)

"Will Patty be coming home here tonight?" David asked.

"I don't think so. I believe she's planning on staying with Nanny and Poppa John until sometime tomorrow, and then she'll be driving to San Jose for Steve's birthday dinner."

"Oh, yeah," David said. "I'm glad you reminded me. We're supposed to be dining at *Paolo's* in San Jose tomorrow night."

Sylvia said, "Speaking of dining, will you be here for dinner with us? Your father said he was cooking or providing, or something. He knew that I wouldn't feel like preparing anything after my luncheon today...so I suppose I'll rely on him for dinner."

David laughed, "I think grilling steaks and waiting on you is one of his favorite projects."

"Your father enjoys serving his *entire* family, not just me." Sylvia asserted.

"Of course you know, that I know, that is not true, Mom. You're his *numero uno* on a pedestal...and...no, I won't be dining with you love birds tonight. I'm meeting friends for cocktails and I'll eat somewhere afterwards...I may even have dinner with George."

Sylvia did not ask for details regarding the agenda, but she did say, almost pleadingly, "If you dine with your friend George, remember to say 'hello' for us...but I hope you'll be home tonight...perhaps have breakfast with us in the morning?"

"Sounds like a plan, Mom."

Sylvia continued her plea, "You won't stay out too late, will you? I hate to see you groggy eyed and tired in the morning. I try hard not to pry into your private life, but I disapprove of any activity resulting in your stupor the following day."

David knew exactly what his mother referred to... she more than strongly suspected that he frequently indulged in what she considered to be corrupt behavior. She was probably right, but being the son of socially prominent parents and the presumptive heir to Nanny and Poppa's successful winery was a challenge. He never denied to anyone that he was gay, but he also did not publicize the fact.

He tried to be as unobtrusive as possible, but even the greatest discretion couldn't mask all his gay activities. He was often delicately reproached by his mother who simply could not accept the fact that her son was a homosexual. She had no idea that he was constantly being pressured from the gay activists at San Jose State who had discovered his private life in San Francisco. He simply refused to join the flamboyantly aggressive society of '*marching queens*' as Patty called them.

He was sick and tired of the aggressive coercion to take part in the liberalization of gay men who were supposedly *suppressed* by society. David had never felt suppressed from his social/sexual activities in San Francisco, and he wasn't going to enlist his support for any of those annoying college activist groups. To this day they had no real success in their militant messaging other than making a nuisance of themselves. He felt the same way about his mother's subtle complaints and objections, it was all a nuisance in his life.

"No, I'm just going out for a little socialization. I'll be home by midnight at the latest."

As soon as David had spoken, Brenda came into the room and announced "I just saw Mr. Wellington coming up the drive."

"Hi Brenda," David called out as he ran past her and his mother. "I'll go greet him at the door!"

David reached the front door just as his father was pulling up the circular drive in the family Town-car sedan. Richard gingerly hopped out of the driver's seat, tossed the car keys in the air and caught them in his left hand as he proclaimed, "Hooray, it's Friday!"

"TGIF!" David rang out as he gave his Dad a hefty bear-hug and then held the front door.

David watched his Dad stride through the cavernous entrance of their beautiful San Francisco mansion and had a rushing feeling of pride for his family. He watched

Richard stoop over Sylvia's chair and practically lift her to an embrace that was inspirational to witness. The poodles were running wildly around them.

"How did things go with your luncheon today?"

Sylvia answered, "Oh just fine; and I heard that you had an early lunch with your son and some of your work related associates. How did that go?"

"Routine," said Richard, "I'm afraid David may have been a little bored with my two colleagues; but of course he would never show it."

"Dad," David said, "You either read me too well or you're projecting your own feelings."

"Probably a little of both young man," Richard said as he playfully threw a punch toward David's stomach.

David immediately covered his body with both hands feigning injury as he limped away.

"I'm going upstairs for the 'Full Monty'," he announced. Then as an aside to his Dad, "Shit, shower and shave."

"I heard that!" Sylvia exclaimed as she put on her shoe.

"Sorry Mom," David said unremorsefully as he left the room. "I'll leave you guys to the perfect happy hour."

Richard slipped behind the enormous hand carved cherry wood bar and began gathering ingredients for his regular Rob Roy cocktail. One of the six ornate barstools seemed out of place because a fluffy white angora sweater hung over the decorous back of its seat.

"Patricia was here today?" Richard asked with a tone of surprise in his voice.

"Yes, she stopped in on her way up to the Vineyards. She's planning on spending the night with Nanny and Poppa."

"Does she know we're going to be up there on Sunday?" Richard asked.

"Yes dear. She and David have the schedule all figured out. It includes a birthday dinner for Stephen tomorrow night in San Jose, and back here the following morning in time for church before we all drive up to Sonoma for Sunday dinner."

Richard chuckled, "Those kids have a more active social schedule than anyone I know. They're like two raging tornadoes flying all over the Bay area."

"I know" Sylvia commented, "But you need to include Monterey, Big Sur and Wine Country as well. I never know where they'll be at any moment."

"Yes," Richard reflected, "Our children sure have a love for staying active."

"I guess it's largely our fault," Sylvia sounded a little wistful. "We certainly gave them a very hearty appetite for the good life."

"Yeah, but they sure are happy" Richard said as he handed Sylvia her glass of champagne.

The couple clinked glasses and exclaimed in unison, "Thanks be to God!"

* * *

David soon reappeared wearing a medium green gabardine dress jacket with ecru trousers that flared slightly at the cuff. His shirt matched the color of the slacks with the same ecru shade and his tie had wide stripes of forest green that complemented his very green eyes. Sylvia thought her son looked exquisitely handsome...Richard proudly inspected him as he adjusted David's gold tie chain.

"This is the tie and chain you gave me for my birthday, Dad. It makes me feel..." David hesitated, "...so grown-up."

Richard laughed, "I hereby declare that you **are** grown up, son!"

David reacted with a warm smile, "That makes me feel good, Dad."

"Perhaps a little too much cologne?" Sylvia suggested.

"Too late now Mom. It'll wear off fast enough if I keep the top down on my convertible."

"Have a good time, stay safe, and remember to put up the top when you park downtown," Richard called out as David trotted down the massive hallway of the Wellington mansion."

By the time David reached the front door Richard had replenished Sylvia's glass of champagne. She looked pensively at the bubbles in her elegant crystal flute. "I don't know why I worry. Even if he's grown up I can't help feeling like a concerned mother."

Richard looked at his beautiful wife and soul-mate. In his eyes she was almost perfection both spiritually and physically. Her delicate creamy complexion and ebon black hair made a surreal portrait in the late afternoon light that filtered through the enormous glass French doors and ceiling-to-floor windows of their family room. Sylvia seemed so fragile and delicate...she brought to Richard's mind an image of some forlorn Oriental princess with jade earrings and matching jade necklace. She was as stunning as any famous beauty he could think of, and certainly more charismatic. Merle Oberon...Claudette Colbert...

Richard put down his drink on the counter and walked around and behind Sylvia's chair. He reached over with his long arms and began to gently massage her shoulders. "What is it that's causing your concern, Mother?"

"Oh I don't know," Sylvia responded, "It's just that, I wish we could keep him away from San Francisco's gay bars."

Richard broke into laughter, "Oh-h-h, is that what's bothering you, *again*? You have to realize that David is in control of his own sexuality, and it's not our place to interfere with nature. He has to make his own decisions about his personal sex life."

Before Sylvia could make any further comment, Patty appeared at the back entrance to the family room from one of the gardens. Sylvia's eyebrows arched in surprise as her daughter sailed across the floor into Richard's arms. "How's my baby girl," he asked as he planted a lusty kiss on her forehead.

"I'm fine Daddy. Just a little tired, it's been a busy week for me."

Sylvia looked at her daughter intently and said, "I thought you would be at the Vineyards by now. What happened? Do your grandparents know where you are? What's going on?"

"Yes, yes Mother" Patty said impatiently as she gave her father a final squeeze. "Everything is just fine. I stopped at the *De Young Museum* in *Golden Gate Park* and tried to locate a notebook I left there the other day. I met a couple of friends from school and socialized too long at the *Japanese Tea Garden* next door. I telephoned Nanny when I realized it was so late. I didn't want to fight commuter traffic across the bridge through Marin...so I came back home... I hope you don't mind."

Richard jumped into the conversation, "I don't know about mother, but I'm delighted you're here for dinner. May I fix you a drink?"

Before Patty could answer Sylvia interjected, "My poor *neglected* daughter, I'm as happy as your Dad that you're here at home with us. I'm just surprised to see you when I was so sure that you would be at the Vineyards with Nanny and Poppa."

"Well, here I am Mom. Nanny didn't seem to mind at all when I phoned...she's looking forward to seeing all of us the day after tomorrow. Poppa John was out somewhere on the property putting up new fencing or something, and yes Daddy, I would like to have a drink. Would you make a Negroni for me?"

"Do you want a traditional one with orange peel, or do you want it your brother's style?" Richard asked.

"I'll go traditional," Patty said as she started out of the room. "I'll be right back, just going to run upstairs and refresh my *neglected* self," she said laughingly.

Richard began preparing the Negroni for his daughter; equal parts of original Bombay gin, Campari and sweet vermouth, well shaken with ice and strained into a martinis glass topped off with a thin slice of orange peel. 'David likes the same drink but topped off with a maraschino cherry,' Richard thought.

While he was mixing the Negroni, Sylvia commented... trying to keep a casual tone, "You were saying that our son is in control of his own sexuality, and I perfectly agree, but..."

"But...what?" Richard interrupted, trying not to sound too sharp.

"But," Sylvia continued, "I simply do not approve of him going to gay bars. It's just so difficult for me to understand why he keeps looking in all the wrong places for an answer to his... *dilemma*? You have to agree that homosexuality is not natural, and I just don't believe that our son was born that way. He's so masculine and manly in every detail. It just baffles me."

"What I don't agree is that David sees his homosexuality as a dilemma," Richard said as he put the final touches on Patty's drink. "Our son is intelligent, thoughtful, loving and caring. And, yes, he's very much a man. But his *natural* sexual inclinations are toward other men, and I believe it's not something he chose, any more than he chose the color of his hair and eyes. I don't know exactly what David does when he goes out with his buddies, and I don't want to know. It's none of our business any more than it's his business what you and I do when our bedroom door is closed. Our son is very happy in this world, and I have a great deal of faith that he is doing what is right for him."

Sylvia sounded slightly irritated as she tried to explain "I know that David is a good faithful Christian, and as his mother I'm not concerned for his immortal soul. God loves him, God loves our family. We're very blessed in this life. It's just that..."

Richard broke in, "It's just that you don't like the fact that your son is *queer*?"

"Oh, please," Sylvia tried hard to keep her voice low, "Please do not use that word. I hate that word, I really hate that word.

"What word?" Patty said as she reappeared in the doorway.

"Queer." Richard said blithely as he handed Patty her drink. "Salute." He said with a forced Italian accent as he raised his own glass.

"*Salute-ta,*" Patty responded in perfect Italian and turned toward Sylvia for a second "*Salute-ta mama mia.*"

Sylvia raised her glass "*Alla salute-ta.*" Then after a short breath, she said "*Amore*", and raised her glass a little higher.

Patty and Richard both responded in unison "*Amore.*"

After another short breath Richard moved closer to his wife and daughter and clinked their glasses as all three shouted "*Monet-ah*".

They each took a sip and Patty said, "*Salute* is for health, *Amore* is for love, and *Monet-ah* is for money. What more could one ask for in this life?"

"It's the perfect toast," Sylvia agreed as she took another small sip of her champagne. Thanks be to God we have an abundance of all three!"

'Patty took a sip of her drink "Umm, Daddy, this is a great Negroni!" After a short pause, "So you guys were talking about David while I was upstairs."

"What makes you think that?" Sylvia asked a little defensively.

"Didn't Daddy say someone brought up the word *queer*?"

"You don't have to repeat it again," Sylvia sounded like a mother reprimanding her child.

Patty and Richard both giggled which infuriated Sylvia more. "I don't see what's so funny. You both act as though David's *dilemma* is a joke."

"I'd hardly call it a dilemma...homosexuality is not a problem or quandary for David, Mother" Patty asserted, "It's only a puzzle for you. I am proud of the way my brother deals with being *gay*. I'm thankful that he grew up here in California and didn't have to face real problems trying to deal with his sexuality somewhere in middle-America where they still burn faggots."

"*Really,*" Sylvia said indignantly, "I'd rather you used the word queer."

"It doesn't matter what word you use Mom," Patty went on patiently. "David is David; he's an extraordinary individual who is not defined by being a queer or a faggot. You wouldn't believe the way the gay organizations on campus constantly hound him to be an open participant. He may happen to have been born homosexual, but that's not the sole purpose of his existence in this society. He doesn't need to march and flagrantly fight for his sexuality in society. He deals with life fantastically, in a beautiful way. The world could sure use more just exactly like him."

"I don't see what is so beautiful about hanging around in sleazy, smelly homosexual bars filled with nasty lechers and child molesters. It's just so demeaning and unnatural," Sylvia argued.

Richard cleared his throat, "Let's all agree to make a concerted effort to use the word *gay*, shall we?"

He went on, "I've worked with some great men who are conservatively gay, and not the least obnoxious about their sexuality. I'm certain they don't lurk around in sleazy bars. Some of them are ranking servicemen with families, and others are respectable citizens who contribute their talents for the protection of their country. I have to admit Sylvia, you do have a naïve perception of men with… shall we say…alternative sexual persuasions."

"Dad's absolutely correct, Mother," Patty interjected. "Your view of David's sexual preference is completely naïve. It's not that you can't understand; it's just that you haven't been exposed to what's really happening. Your life is sheltered. By choice you focused your entire existence mostly on Daddy. Yes...you're a fabulous wife for your husband and a sensational mother to your children...but you live in a big pink bubble filled with tea parties, bridge luncheons, and the Women's Club. You're in the perfect role, playing your part perfectly, but you're still unaware of what is transpiring in this world. I might have trouble convincing you and the rest of the world, but I honestly believe that David's sexuality is genetic."

"I just wish you could help keep you brother out of gay bars, right now." Sylvia said quietly.

Patty giggled marginally, "It's easier to keep Elizabeth Taylor away from Richard Burton."

Richard chuckled slightly and said, "I don't know where David is actually going tonight, but I'll wager it's not any sleazy gay hangout...not the way he was dressed."

"Oh-h-h," Patty said as though a lighted bulb had suddenly appeared over her head. "It's Friday...Friday afternoon...Happy Hour...Happy Hour at the infamous *Sutter's Mill*. I'll bet David was dressed to the nines in coat and tie. You can't get into *Sutter's Mill* without a tie and jacket. I'm sure he looks stunning."

"And just what is so special about Sutter's Mill and on a Friday afternoon?" Sylvia inquired.

"It's a huge gentlemen's establishment located downtown in the financial district," Patty answered. "And I do mean huge. It holds five or six hundred people."

"It caters to all the prominent executives and financial wizards who work in banks and top notch organizations in the financial district." Richard answered.

"Why do *you* know anything about it?" Sylvia inquired. "Have you ever been there? As I recall, you're usually with me on Friday afternoons."

"I read about Sutter's Mill in the Examiner just last week." Richard answered. "There was an extensive article that began on the front page. It explained how popular the place is on Fridays packed with successful local stock brokers, bankers, lawyers and business men...all dressed up in their expensive three piece suits."

"Why would David go there?" Sylvia asked, "He's not a banker or a fancy financier."

"No," Patty interjected, "But he's a *financier fancier*... he enjoys hunting for the cream of the crop. David has a penchant for sophisticated men of taste who will fawn over him. It's largely an ego trip when handsome, successful, older gentlemen find him attractive. They like to buy him drinks, take him to dinner, invite him for a cruise on their yacht, or whatever might allure his attention. David really enjoys the game of being *lured*."

"It all sounds too *lurid* for me," Sylvia stated.

"Now Sylvia," Richard said, "You should be somewhat assured that David is not in a sleazy gay bar." Richard added, "At least, not tonight."

* * *

CHAPTER THREE

Sutter's Mill was already bustling by the time David walked through the impressive hand carved mahogany and beveled stained glass doors. The place was huge with stairways going up and stairways going down, three story ceilings, enormous bars on all sides, and quickly filling up with men. All the guys were wearing *coats and ties* and the majority were dressed in three-piece suits. Most of them were chatting in groups of three and four and many were laughing boisterously.

At least it's not crammed shoulder to shoulder, *yet*, David thought as he ascended a few stairs to his favorite spot at the upper part of the longest bar. He liked the fact that this position provided enough height to offer a bird's eye view of almost the entire establishment. It was also a somewhat protected niche because of the wall directly behind that particular portion of the bar, which made it impracticable for other customers to crowd in behind. There were no stools for sitting...the setup was strictly *SRO*, standing room only.

The army of bartenders could effectively serve gentlemen on two levels of the bar. The amount of activity the servers were going through was already at an insane pace. The length of the main bar on both levels was about one hundred feet. There were already twenty or thirty guys standing on the upper level where David insinuated himself at his favorite end. One of the huge wooden pillars that supported the ornate counter was directly on his right side. Three guys in deep conversation were clumped directly to his left. He staked out a claim at his corner of the bar with a pack of Benson Hedge cigarettes and a shiny gold lighter that Patty had given him for Christmas..

"You want gin and tonic with a wedge," the bartender at David's end said as he reached up with a drink all prepared. "It's Bombay, your brand."

"Thanks Pete," David said in a louder than usual voice to compensate for the noise which was beginning to reach decibels too high for normal conversation. David tried to offer Pete a twenty dollar bill but the he waved it off and said,

"The first one's on me...signal when you're ready for another."

David just nodded and offered a salute as Pete whipped back around to customers who were crowding the lower level. It was amazing how quickly the population had increased within just a few short moments of David's arrival. He looked at his watch; it wasn't even 4:00 P.M. yet. The place was swarming with men who kept pouring in like synchronized arrivals deplaning from a 747 at an international terminal.

David squeezed the lime wedge in his cut glass tumbler and took a hefty sip. Before he could put down the drink Pete whizzed by and plunked a shot glass down on the counter in front of him. "From an admirer," Pete chirped as he dexterously pivoted around to face the lower level and continue to mix drinks at a furious pace.

David saluted not attempting to ask Pete who the admirer might be. It was too late for any conversation with a bartender... Sutter's Mill was in high gear. It would have been impossible for Pete to point out David's sponsor among the waves of suited men who were now cascading against the bar. In future, he would have to remember to be here no later than 3:00 P.M.

Where he was standing the memorable scene from the movie "*Snakepit*" came to David's mind. All the movement and noise of hundreds of bodies pushing around below reminded him of the inmates who were moving and writhing like snakes at the bottom of a big well.

David laughed out loud, getting the attention of the guys next to him. Somewhat embarrassed by his impromptu outburst, he took another sip of his gin and tonic. That same moment Pete slammed down two more shot glasses with one hand. The first guy standing next to David stated "You seem to be a very popular fellow around here today."

"I don't think it was anything I said," David responded, trying not to shout. "I can barely hear myself talk."

"Did you hear yourself laugh a moment ago?" The second guy shouted.

"I did!" David laughed again getting the full attention of all three of the guys next to him.

David went on to explain, "I just flashed on that scene from the movie *Snake Pit* where the camera focuses on all the patients squirming around like snakes in the bottom of a big barrel."

All three of the guys laughed and the one furthest from David said, "I love that movie. Olivia de Havilland is fabulous in that part."

"Oh I know," said the second guy. "She was nominated for an Academy Award, you but she didn't win."

"Who was the best actress that year", said the third guy.

"What was the year?" said the second guy.

"And who did win the Oscar for best actress?" chimed in the guy next to David.

David said, "I believe the year was 1948, and I'm fairly certain it was Jane Wyman who won for *Johnny Belinda*. But, Olivia came back the following year and was awarded the Oscar in 1949 for *The Heiress.* The best actor award in '48 went to Lawrence Olivier for *Hamlet,* although a lot of people thought that Humphrey Bogart was overlooked in *The Treasure of the Sierra Madre.* He didn't even get nominated."

"Wow," the second and third guys said in unison.

"You really know your movies!" said the guy closest to David.

David took advantage of the lull in conversation to look over his three new admirers. Not one of them was unattractive, but none was David's type. David was attracted to men who were more naturally masculine in an unpretentious way. All three of these guys had, as his sister Patty would have said, "*Dropped beads.*" To drop beads meant that a guy revealed a feminine trait of his character through a hand gesture, slightly drawn out inflection of words, or an overly animated facial expression.

'All three of these dudes are dropping beads left and right,' David thought. 'They are nice guys, well groomed with neat coiffures, but not for me.'

He figured all three were probably accountants or clerks at one or another well-known financial organization like Merrill-Lynch or J.P. Morgan. They most likely *hung out* together at some little trendy neighborhood bar like the *Lion's Pub* on Divisidero Street. They were too flamboyant and not sophisticated enough for a more conservative spot like *Dori's*.

There was no need to make homosexuality a driving issue. It was absolutely his God-given nature to be attracted to his own sex...he knew who he was and he accepted it. He was in life purely for the enjoyment at this point in early adulthood. He loved to explore the myriad gay establishments in town, but he certainly wasn't addicted to any one place.

David's thoughts were interrupted as Pete plunked down three more shot glasses on the bar.

"Good grief, *girl.* You're really piling 'em up high," shouted the third guy next to David, and getting the attention of the nearest ten or twelve men who were now along the bar.

David hated that kind of gay talk where the guys referred to everybody and everything in the female gender. David believed that *she, her, lady, girl* were not attractive words to apply when describing a boy or man. Unfortunately that type of language was undeniably part of the gay scene.

David said "I want each of you to have a drink on me," and he pushed three shot glasses toward the guys on his left.

"Just do me a favor and save my spot!" he shouted starting down the stairway on the other side of the pillar next to the bar.

"We've got you covered!" shouted the guy who was closest to David.

David disliked having to push and fumble his way through hundreds of bodies across the wide expanse leading to the grand stair-well that went down to the restrooms. He blamed himself for not going sooner before the crowd got impossible.

Everyone seemed to move in different directions at once. There was very little standing still in this heaving and pushing mass of humanity. Thankfully, the expansive stairway that led to the men's room was moving more freely. There was enough space for twelve people to march in horizontal military formation up and down the stairs. It was very similar in size to the grand staircases at many of the older elegant hotels and theatres.

David moved nimbly once he got to the stairs. He quickly descended and took care of business looking neither left nor right. He ascended less quickly on the return because of a somewhat large delegation of guys which had formed to hold conversation at the first landing of the stairwell. They didn't seem to mind impeding the flow of traffic for those going up or down the stairs.

Back on the main floor, David was slowed to a near stop. He tried politely to nudge and guide bodies aside so he could make headway toward his place above the grand bar.

"Oh," cried a heavy set guy in the crowd, "I just got groped."

"Did you enjoy it," another voice shouted out.

"I think I just got goosed," a third voice screamed joining the inane conversation.

"Was it good," one of the other guys, shouted.

"Just okay" came the answer from somewhere in the voluminous crowd.

"Do it again, do it again," someone squealed, causing a ripple of masculine giggles.

David continued persistently moving slowly toward his destination when his progress was blocked by a body that confronted him face-to-face. He came to a dead stop.

"Can you direct me to the *head*?" the guy said in a very deep barely audible voice.

David literally had to step back in order to separate his body from the tall handsome stranger that had confronted him. The man was astonishingly gorgeous! He was slender and very well built in his gray Italian custom made three-piece suit. His face had a striking resemblance to Joseph Cotton, although more handsome, and his premature white hair was thick and lustrous, like Peter Graves who played Jim Phelps in the television series *Mission Impossible*. Yes, he looked a lot like Peter Graves.

"Yes, yes of course," David shouted. "I just came from there. You'll have to plow through the herd in that direction," David said as he gestured over the crowd. "When you come to the stairs go down to the bottom and hang a right. You'll find it."

"Thanks," the exquisite man said as he nodded his splendid head.

David reflected on the passing momentary encounter as he began the trek back to his place at the bar.

"Wow, what a rare beauty," he said out loud. That man was absolutely gorgeous by all classical standards. "Wow!"

"Thank you," said a cute guy that was just pushing by David going in the opposite direction.

David ignored the comment and kept moving toward the bar. He was thinking only about the resplendent figure that he had just briefly met. He wondered if he had been singled out by that sublime creature who asked him for directions to the men's room. It was a slim chance in this mass of humanity, but David liked entertaining the thought he had somehow attracted the gorgeous man from afar. 'After all,' he thought, 'other guys have been sending me drinks this afternoon.'

"No, no such luck," David again spoke aloud as he pushed his way back to the bar. The three original guys had left and were replaced by five men who overcrowded his former spot. There was a small area on the bar counter next to the pillar where David saw his cigarettes and lighter now sitting on top a stack of seven or eight shot glasses. At just that moment, Pete the bartender reached up and slammed down a fresh Bombay gin and tonic, and shouted "Here you go, Honey."

Two of the new guys who had their backs to his spot whirled around and stated concurrently, "Sorry," as they both nudged their acquaintances to make space for David at the bar.

"Thanks," David said to the community including Pete, the two guys who said they were sorry, and all the subsequent guys who were slightly inconvenienced while making space at the counter.

David squeezed into the bar with his right shoulder and took a hefty sip from his fresh drink before reaching for the unopened Benson Hedge menthol cigarettes that sat atop the stack of shot glasses still piling up. He didn't smoke very much, but he did enjoy a cigarette after dinner and when he was drinking socially, but never during the morning hours, and rarely before 5:00 PM. Friday at Sutter's Mill was one of the few exceptions.

He tamped down the pack with his right hand and opened the cellophane covering by using his perfectly straight white teeth. He turned his body just enough to push his left arm on the counter to complete procurement of a cigarette and place it to his mouth. Before he could reach for his lighter two guys from the near group thrust flames in his face while a third was struggling to strike a match.

David lighted his cigarette from the two burning flames and said with a manly smile, "Thank you."

He turned slightly away feigning interest in trying to get the bartender's attention. Pushing a half dozen of the stacked shot glasses forward, David shouted in his deep masculine voice, "Hey Pete, get these guys a drink."

Pete did a pirouette and pointed to the group of guys counting aloud, "One, two, three, four, five...six!" He then gathered three shot glasses in each hand and set them on the bar in front of the men...he glanced up to take a mental note of what each person was drinking.

"Thanks," said the guy closest to David, and the only one of the men who heard or saw what was transpiring.

"My pleasure," David said

"What you say? I can't hear you," the guy shouted.

"You're welcome!" David roared.

The guy just nodded his head in appreciation while David turned back to look over the entire scene at Sutter's Mill. It no longer reminded him of the Snake Pit... that film scene was subdued compared to this setting. This popular establishment had reached a fevered pitch. There couldn't possibly be room in this magnificent structure for one more body or soul. "It's packed to the tilt," David said to himself.

Pete reappeared and began distributing drinks to the group of guys just above his work station. "These are on David," he yelled as he pointed.

Every recipient turned toward David and made a comment or gesture of thanks with peace signs, salutes, nods and approving smiles.

"You're welcome!" David boomed.

The bar became abruptly and unexpectedly dispiriting for David. His enthusiasm for Sutter's Mill on this afternoon had suddenly diminished and was rapidly dwindling. His immediate impulse was to leave, so he tucked his cigarettes and lighter into his jacket pocket, pushed the remaining shot glasses toward the bartenders and shouted for Pete.

"Here's for you, Pete. Thanks for everything," he thundered as he handed down the twenty dollar bill that was originally intended to pay for the first drink.

Pete smiled and cried out, "Hope to see you next week, Babe."

David was already halfway down the steps from the upper level and preparing himself for the pushing and shoving of the crowd. He really didn't like operating among multitudes of people, but he made an exception on Friday night at Sutter's Mill. He had attended a few major rock concerts and happenings in Golden Gate Park and around the Bay Area, but he really disliked the crowds.

"Thank God I missed the free concert at Altamont," he said to himself, "I still can't believe Patricia let Stephen drag her to that debacle."

David took a deep breath and looked down toward the floor as he pushed his way through the throng. He seemed to be making fair progress toward the door when someone grabbed the back of his arm just above the elbow. David made a half-turn and for the second time that afternoon faced the most handsome man he had ever seen.

Once the imposing stranger knew that he had David's attention he focused his startling blue eyes just slightly away and said in a low baritone voice, "Thanks for the directions to the restroom...you weren't one hundred percent accurate."

"I'm certain I did not intentionally give you a bum steer," David replied somewhat tersely. "It may have been your inability to accurately follow directions."

"Sorry," the man went on to say "I meant no offense whatsoever. How about allowing me to take you to dinner, and give me the opportunity to apologize."

Not hesitating for a fraction of a second, "Do I get to choose where we go?" David asked excitedly like a child going to the circus.

"Of course," the man answered. "You lead."

David turned in the direction of the door and thought to himself, 'He did handpick me to ask for directions.' Again, he took the back of David's arm as they now seemed to glide through the hoards and out the front door of Sutter's Mill.

The fog was just beginning to sift into the streets of the financial district. It usually didn't get too thick this time of the year, but there was enough to comfortably cool the air. The two men walked side by side.

"I'm David."

"Hello David, I'm Hank."

"I'm parked around the corner," David said, and immediately added "I'll drive."

"Great!" Hank said. "I don't have a car...I just flew in from L.A. for the weekend."

"Terrific," David resounded. "I'll be your chauffer and tour guide. Where are you staying?"

"I took a room at a small hotel downtown in what I believe is *the tenderloin*...it's on Turk Street near Mason..."

"Well that's definitely the Tenderloin," said David, trying not to sound disappointed.

"It was suggested by a friend of mine in LA who knew it would serve my purpose for this weekend. I'll tell you more over dinner."

"This is it!" David said feeling enthusiastic again as they approached his car and he ran spryly to open the passenger door for his new acquaintance.

"Where are we going?" Hank asked.

"Do you like Japanese?" David inquired encouragingly, hoping for a positive answer.

"I'm not sure," Hank said, "But I'm certainly willing to try."

"We're on our way to the *Bush Garden* on Bush Street. Even if you're not crazy about the food, you'll have no complaints about the service or the atmosphere."

Hank laughed reassuringly, "I'm sure I won't."

* * *

The Japanese Bush Gardens Restaurant was located on Bush Street in the Bush Hotel. Entering the building was like taking an excursion to Japan. There were lush miniature gardens with streams and tiny waterfalls that bedecked the lobby. An impressive walking bridge crossed directly over the aquatic scene to an elevator where a pretty Asian attendant dressed in a colorful kimono was waiting. She was there to greet and receive the dining guests.

Hank and David walked straight to the elevator where the girl bowed slightly and said. "*Konnichiwa*," which means good *afternoon* in Japanese.

David looked at his watch and then corrected the girl by politely nodding his head saying "*Konbanwa*," which means good *evening*.

The girl giggled and twittered as she escorted the men into the elevator which took them a few floors upward. The doors opened to a spectacular scene that looked like it a setting from the 1957 Technicolor film "*Sayanora*", starring Marlon Brando.

David glanced at Hank's face which reflected a slightly surprised, but approving grin. The atmosphere was too much to take in all at once. There were beautiful carved teak wood screens in-laid with ivory and precious stones, rice paper paintings that were true works of art, ornamental statues and intricate dioramas with bonsai trees. Further into the restaurant they saw more paintings, elaborate ice-carvings, embossed lanterns and girls wearing Japanese kimonos that looked as colorful as flamingos in flight. It was an enchanting scene.

David and Hank were led by a beautiful Geisha-style lady down a corridor with dozens of secluded *tatami* rooms. Every room was partially obscured by hand-painted sliding doors that matched the encircling walls. Each room was different, but they were all elevated a couple of steps above the main floor which was lined with a display of the guests' footwear. Hank quickly noticed as he glanced through the cracks in the doorways that the rooms were quite private, and the customers were seated on the floor around low hand carved cherry wood tables.

The hostess turned down a smaller corridor and led the men to one of the quiet *tatami* rooms where David immediately sat on the first of two steps outside to untie his shoes.

"Footwear at the door," he said, leaving his shoes on the first step.

He jumped into the room, rearranged a couple of huge cushions for lots of back support and took his position at the table, back to the wall so he could face the sliding doors. He stripped off his jacket and tossed it carelessly next to a bamboo mat on the floor.

Hank followed David's lead, slipped off his shoes and entered to sit at the table with his new friend. He was grateful to find that the table was strategically placed over a carpeted sunken well that permitted diners to drop their feet in a sitting position rather than requiring them to fold their legs in the authentic Japanese style.

"This is comfortable," Hank sighed as he slipped off his suit jacket and carefully folded it on the mat next to him. When dining at Bush Garden, men were expected to wear coats and ties, but it was customary for them to remove their jackets once they were privately seated. Hank also noticed that there was a telephone resting on a small stand next to their table... it was obviously there for customers to conduct business during long dinners.

"I love this place," David declared as two lovely girls appeared and began setting their table.

One of the girls gracefully entered the room and placed a small tray holding rolled scented steaming hot towels in front of each man. She said, *"O-genki desu ka?"* how are you?

David nodded an approval as the other girl set down a delicate bowl of fragrant floating gardenias at the center of their table. Both girls slipped out of the room, sliding the door behind them for the guests' privacy.

"Wash up," David commanded as he unraveled his steaming towel and placed it on his face and then on the back of his neck. "Our server will be here in a minute."

"You mean those girls weren't our servers?" Hank asked.

"No," David replied as he finished wiping his hands and folded his towel. "Those were supposed to be just our greeters."

Hank unfolded his towel and finished performing the same ritual, the door opened and three more girls appeared. They were all quite lovely and as one took the towel trays she said "*Dou shiteru*", how's everything?

The second one said "*Kawatta koto aru*", what's new?"

The third waitress, who also obviously recognized David said in a louder voice, "*Nannika atta, David-San*?"

David laughed and said "What's up with you, Wendy-San?" and then he added politely

"*O-genki desu ka*", how are you?

"*Aikawarazu desu*", as usual, she replied, "but not too busy yet, David-San, to make you *Ichiban...* number one customer."

The first waitress gracefully knelt down with serving bowls of hot *misou* soup while the second girl knelt and placed tiny hand painted ceramic cups in front of them.

"Sake?" she asked David serving it from a small pitcher that matched the cups. She poured it before David could answer.

"*Hai*", he said. "Hank, I usually have hot sake when I'm here, but you might prefer some other cocktail. They have anything you'd like."

"When in Rome," answered Hank and clinked David's sake cup with his.

The original girls who had greeted them again appeared at the doorway carrying trays filled with various Japanese appetizers. All the waitresses moved in and out noiselessly kneeling, serving bowls and plates of delicacies that were all foreign to Hank. David felt a rush of delight as he watched Hank's chiseled face take in the curious spectacle.

One of the girls presented plates that contained artistic arrangements of shaved radish and carrots in long strips that coiled around lemon wedges cut in the shape of swans and birds. There were small tempting pieces of meat that looked like very rare slices of filet mignon in the center of each dish. The main plate also held a tiny saucer with some kind of green paste that had been designed in the shape of a lotus flower.

Another girl put down delicate teak chopsticks on large linen napkins. She also presented porcelain holders to rest the chopsticks when they weren't in use. She knelt next to Hank and gently picked up his chopsticks pointing to the slices of meat in front of him saying, "*Sashimi*, very fresh raw tuna...very good."

Then she picked up the green paste flower with Hank's sticks and pronounced the word "*Wasabi*."

"Very hot and spicy," David warned while vigorously diluting his own wasabi with soy sauce from a ceramic bottle. He then delicately handed the bottle of soy to Hank.

The server who had placed Hank's wasabi in a tiny saucer, now offered him the chopsticks.

"You okay with chopsticks?" David asked.

"No problem," Hank said taking the sticks, pouring soy sauce on the wasabi and stirring the concoction.

"This is my first authentic Japanese meal, but I learned to use chopsticks eating Chinese food in L.A... this will, however, be my first raw fish," he added blithely as he dipped a small corner of tuna in the wasabi and bravely downed the entire slice.

The lavish Japanese feast continued and they sampled other traditional entrees such as perfectly cooked teriyaki steak, tempura lobster, and fresh raw Pacific oysters sautéed in seasoned rice vinegar. The food was superb as the two men smiled and laughed their way through a glorious dinner while drinking ample amounts of sake.

The cavalcade of Geisha-style waitresses and food finally began to slow after the men had been eating and drinking steadily for two and a half hours. David began fumbling through his jacket on the floor next to him when Hank reached deftly across the table with a gleaming cigarette case and said, "Have one of mine."

David took one of the unfiltered cigarettes between his thumb and finger and gently rolled it back and forth like testing a cigar. "They're oval!" he blurted.

"Yes," said Hank, "exactly... they're English Ovals... made by Phillip Morris," he added reaching again across the table to deliver a flame from his unadorned lighter.

"Thanks," David said while playfully French inhaling a hearty puff of smoke. He and Patty had practiced French inhaling together for many hours when they first smoked as teenagers. Patty always said it was "...a true sign of sophistication, especially among the elite 'Jet-Set' who traveled the world in luxury while *French inhaling* cigarettes."

David smiled to himself and took another drag from his English Oval.

"You like those," Hank said almost triumphantly. "A lot of people don't care for them because of their flat shape," and he quickly lighted his own cigarette.

"Yes, I like them," David said as he studied the lit end of his cigarette. "It's good tobacco."

After a moment of pause, he said, "Hank, I was hoping that you would tell me about the purpose of your trip up here from Los Angeles."

Hank grimaced slightly, "It's not a real easy thing to talk about, but I do need to discuss it with you."

"Do you need to discuss it with *me* in particular, or do you just wish to talk about it?" David inquired.

"I suppose I really want to do both," Hank spoke in a low voice, "I want to talk about my reason for traveling out of town, and at this point I really want to share it with *you...* in particular."

David felt a little rush of excitement eager to continue the conversation. Unfortunately the men were interrupted by two of the servers bringing delicate finger bowls and fresh napkins. David put out his cigarette and Hank placed his still burning smoke on a large ornate ash tray nearby.

"Would you like tea, or an after dinner drink?" David asked.

"How about having a *stinger* with me?" Hank replied.

"Sure", said David, "Just tell me what's in a *stinger*."

"It's usually made with about two parts cognac or brandy and one part white crème de menthe," said Hank.

"Two stingers, please, Wendy-San" David requested the waitress as she was on her knees rearranging items on the table.

"*Hai,*" she answered. "Would David-San and his friend like desert?"

"Not for me," said David, "Ask *Hank-A-San*."

Hank shook his head deliberately from side to side and said, "No thank you, not for me."

"Tea...coffee...?" she offered.

"Just the stingers for right now," said David.

"*Hai*!" and she was gone.

Hank flicked the ash from his cigarette and took a final draw before he put it out. There was an ominous silence for what seemed like many minutes. Hank just looked down bashfully at the table... David sat politely quiet.

It occurred to him that Hank might be waiting for the server to return with their drinks before beginning his story. There was an extreme sense of mystery that surrounded Hank, and David suddenly realized that he actually knew very little about this very reserved handsome stranger with whom he had just shared a Japanese feast.

Almost reading David's mind Hank said, "I'll continue the conversation as soon as our drinks arrive."

"Sounds good to me," David said as he gestured toward the door where Wendy-San was just entering with a tray that contained two tumblers and a fragile bowl filled with *okashi*, a variety of traditional Japanese snacks.

As if she knew there would be a serious conversation she carefully placed a drink in front of each man and said "Please take your time...take your time."

"Thank you, Wendy-San," David said as he raised his glass across the table to clink a toast with Hank.

David took a deep breath and Hank looked down at the table as he began speaking again in a very low voice.

"I'm a surgeon," he began. "I have a clinic in Huntington Beach, it takes up most of my life. I have a family...wife and three children...I'm in the process of finalizing a divorce and just moved out of our home to a bachelor apartment in West Hollywood. I guess I've always been attracted to men, especially a guy with a handsome face. My best friend is the family's lawyer and my fraternity brother from college. We went to Stanford. He suggested that I should come up to San Francisco... alone."

"My mom and dad met at Stanford," David interrupted.

"Didn't you mention something about still being in school, yourself?" Hank was thankful for a break from his own story.

"Yes," David answered. "My sister and I attend San Jose State... she's just finishing her second Master's degree in Art History and I'm finishing my first in Theatre Arts...but please go on and tell me about *you*. Your friend told you to come up here alone?"

"Yes," Hank began again. "Richard has always been somewhat of a confidant for me, but there's never been anything...you know...sexual between us. He is much more knowledgeable about *ulterior* lifestyles than I am. He suggested I come to San Francisco for a weekend and explore my *inclination* toward...you know... my own gender."

"He does sound like a lawyer," David laughed lightly, "and incidentally, *Richard* is my dad's name."

Hank smiled slightly, "I also call him *Dick*, especially around our casual acquaintances. He's discreetly introduced me to some of his friends... but I'm just not attracted to them...you know...in *that way*. It's kind of difficult for me to explore my *inclinations* in my own neighborhood...so I came to San Francisco."

"Richard, or should I say Dick, suggested that you begin your *trek* at Sutter's Mill?" David asked.

"Oh yes, he said it was the '*In*' place to go on Friday, and there'd be very little chance of running into anyone from L.A., especially in the afternoon."

"I'm really glad that you literally ran into me," David blurted out.

"It wasn't by accident," Hank said in a very low barely audible voice as he looked down bashfully.

David tried hard not to blush as he fumbled around with his jacket. "I think I'll have a menthol... it goes with the crème de menthe," he said as he found his pack of Benson Hedges. "Would you like one," he offered the pack to Hank.

"Sure," Hank said, relieved that the most critical part of his story was over.

Right on cue their server returned with two fresh stingers on her serving tray. "These as you say in America '*on the house*'. Please take your time."

David pushed his drink aside and stood up bowing to Hank and said "Will you excuse me for a moment, I'm going to... as Americans say...visit the *head*."

"That's a good idea, where is it?" Hank asked starting to get up.

"There are several," David answered. "I'm using the closest one which is just around the corner...only enough room for one person. Do you want to go first?"

"No, I'll wait until you return," Hank answered slipping back into his seat.

David slid back the door of their *tatami* room and stepped into his shoes without bothering to tie them. He turned right at the first corridor and immediately saw his girl.

"Wendy-San," he cried out, "Please take this from me...I don't want my friend to pay," he said as he handed over a Diner's Club credit card...it had a thousand dollar limit and David said a silent prayer that he was still well below the maximum for the month.

"*Hai, arigato!*" she answered taking the credit card, as she continued down the colorful hallway.

David quickly finished his mission in the restroom and returned to slip off his shoes and slide back the door just in time to see Hank draining his glass.

"Were you thinking of having another one here or would you like to move on to another spot for nightcaps?"

"Let's move on," Hank said as he stood up from the floor, "just point me to the *head* and I promise to follow your directions exactly this time."

David gestured toward the door and waited for Hank to step down and put on his shoes.

"Here," David said handing over the jacket of Hank's beautiful gray suit, "It's easier to take it now so you don't have to remove your shoes again to come in and retrieve it."

David stepped halfway out the door and pointed the direction of the restroom and said, "You can't miss it."

Hank went down the hall and David popped back into the *tatami* room to gather his cigarettes and coat. Wendy-San once again appeared right on cue with the check and David's card on a little tray. He signed it standing up, returned the tray and gave her a side hug as she looked at the tray.

"*Domo Arigato,* David-San give too much tip," she said returning his hug.

"You deserve it Wendy-San, *Domo Arigato.*"

David sat down on the step to tie his shoes and stood up just before Hank came down the corridor.

"The check," Hank called out. "Where is the check?"

"All taken care of," David answered brightly.

A very serious, sullen expression darkened Hank's face. David didn't like seeing it.

"That's not right," Hank said in his deep quiet voice. "I thought we had an agreement."

David took a deep breath, "Look Hank, I couldn't help myself. San Francisco is my town, and you're a visitor from Los Angeles. It's sincerely my pleasure to escort a distinguished handsome man from out-of-town. No body could have enjoyed the dinner more than I... if you promise to forget it...I'll let you buy me a nightcap."

To David's relief, Hank smiled slightly and said, "The rest of the night is on me."

"Agreed," said David, "What kind of place would you like to go? I know most of them."

"Do you know of somewhere nice where we can have a conversation without shouting."

David said, "I know a lot of places like that...let's do it!"

David headed for Grant Street first; there was always a lively carnival of people parading up and down the street in and out of the myriad restaurants, shops and clubs. *Katie's Opera House* was probably the most reserved gay bar on the street. Gentlemen rarely walked through the door without being formally attired or at least wearing a tie. It wasn't that the place had a strict dress code; it had simply evolved into that type of gathering. It was also not rare to see a man escorting a lady. People actually stopped by *Katie's* before and after a night at the opera or other dressy affairs.

The large room was softly lighted and contained a main bar, booths, and tables for two set along the walls covered with signed photos of famous sopranos, tenors and baritones, who had, ostensibly, visited the establishment. The place wasn't very crowded, two or three couples of the same and mixed genders were seated at booths or tables. Joan Sutherland's voice could be heard singing the famous aria from Puccinni's *Madame Butterfly.* Hank was surprised that the music was coming from a huge elaborate jukebox.

"The most classical jukebox in all of San Francisco," David declared.

No one was sitting at the bar which had cushioned swivel seats with comfortable arms and backs. Hank assessed the scene and asked, "Can we sit here at the bar?"

"Sure", replied David, quickly interjecting himself into the first seat, closest to the door.

"Good", Hank replied taking the next seat and reaching for a cigarette.

There were two middle aged bartenders wearing waist length Eisenhower jackets with pleated backs, slash side pockets and epaulets with brass stars. David seldom came to Katie's and didn't recognize either of the servers. The eldest one approached and set down embroidered linen napkins and lead-crystal coasters on either side of a matching heavy lead crystal ash tray that lay between the two men at the bar.

"Shall we stay with stingers," Hank asked David in front of the bartender.

"Oh, yes...that's fine," David said as he nodded to the server. "Where's Katie?"

The bartender responded with an expressionless face and a monotone voice, "She is not here tonight," as he stepped away to complete making their drinks.

"When was the last time you were here?" Hank asked.

"It's been a while," David said. "My last time here I think I was with Patricia...my sister. We were at the Opera...it was Wagner's <u>*Der Ring des Nibelungen*</u>, ...we decided to leave after the first act and go eat. Patty was hungry for *Paella* so...even though we were formally dressed, we went 'slumming' and ate across the street on Grant at the *Savoy Tivoli*. They have long wood tables with mismatched wooden chairs. It's sort of set up like a high school cafeteria, but the food is great...afterward we came across the street and had a nightcap here at Katie's."

Hank rose from the bar and stepped out the front door for a moment to check the exact location of the Savoy Tivoli across Grant Street. There were small groups of people everywhere strolling along the sidewalks. There was a foggy mist in the air. He could see a huge steamy picture window under the bright sign of the Savoy Tivoli. People were inside eating and talking at the tables. There was also a long line outside on the sidewalk made of small groups who were patiently waiting for available seating at the restaurant.

"The Savoy looks like a popular place," Hank said as he returned to his seat at the bar next to David.

The bartender also returned to serve their stingers in generous tub glasses made of the same cut glass design as the ashtrays and coasters. Hank quickly pushed a twenty dollar bill on the bar and the server snapped it up and opened a large gingerbread cash register to deposit the bill and retrieve change.

"Do you attend the opera often?" Hank asked.

David scratched his head as if to jog his memory, "I guess it's been seven or eight years that my Dad has maintained a box for the family. Prior to that, my sister and I attended as children with our grandparents. In a way, we were raised on opera. We spent a lot of our years growing up surrounded by classical music. Nanny and Poppa, who are very Italian, have had Gian Carlo Menotti and Samuel Barber as guests at their home in Sonoma."

"I think I know some of Menotti's work, but I can't recall who Samuel Barber is," Hank said.

"Oh-ho," David sounded amused. "Notorious...Barber and Menotti are well known for their collaborative work on opera, most notably *Vanessa* where Barber did the music and Menotti wrote the *libretto*. But, even aside from many successful professional affiliations, they're also known for having been lovers for many years."

Hank raised his eyebrow in interest as David continued, "Menotti is probably best known for his opera *Amahl and the Night Visitors.* I saw a live production in New York a few years ago... the same one NBC often shows on television with Kurt Yaghjian...but that's another lengthy story. My point is that Barber and Menotti are still making great contributions to music, and they are also partners for life."

"That's interesting background information," Hank said, "But it sounds to me that you and your sister don't appreciate Wagner very much. He's one of my favorite composers."

"Wagner is not my favorite composer; *Tristan and Isolde* is palatable even without a great cast, but I am only sold on one of his Operas when there are truly great performers. I admit that I'm inclined to favor the Italian composers. Rossini, Belinni, Donizetti...and especially *Giuseppe Verdi*," David said with an Italian flourish. He's probably my favorite of the Italian composers. I'm also a fan of Mozart. I love his *Magic Flute, Don Giovanni* and *Cosi van Tutte.*"

"Which of Verdi's operas do you prefer?" Hank encouraged David to continue.

"That's really hard to say," answered David. "They're all grand. *Aida*, of course is well known by everyone, and I love *Rigoletto*... *La traviata* and *Il Trovotore* are magnificent, and of course there is *Don Carlos* and *Otello.* Right at this moment we're listening to the duet *Libiamo Brindis* from *La traviata,* it's my mother's favorite."

* * *

David took Hank to three other San Francisco bars and they finally walked out of the last one and headed toward the hotel. The sidewalk was wet from the heavy mist that now engulfed the city. The air wasn't moving at all, and the cool humidity just sat over most of San Francisco and the bay.

Hank put his hands into the pockets of his trousers and David did the same. David didn't feel the least bit tipsy or tired, and it appeared that Hank was in the same condition as the two briskly walked side-by-side toward the hotel.

The small *Tenderloin* hotel was tucked between two shabby buildings on Mason Street. It was one block and a half from where they had their final nightcap at the *Landmark* on Turk Street. David's mind unexpectedly became devoid of thoughts or feeling as Hank led him through the tiny lobby furnished with a couple of well-worn wing-back chairs and a blotched library table. There were a couple of old magazines stuffed in a marred rack next to the table.

David blindly followed Hank to an old rickety elevator where they ascended upward a floor or two. He followed Hank down a narrow hallway with a very thin worn carpet and just a couple of low burning naked bulbs to light the way.

David still didn't feel drunk or tired, but he couldn't think of anything to say or do except follow Hank into the dingy hotel room. There was enough light coming through the scraggy muslin curtains that covered a weather beaten window. Hank took off his jacket and placed it over one of two disfigured wooden chairs that sat next to a dented metal table. David robotically followed Hank's movements and took off his own jacket.

Hank walked over to a scarred brass bed and sat down on its sagging mattress covered by a gnarly chenille spread...he immediately lowered his head and stared at the floor. Without saying a word David sat down gently next to this exquisitely statuesque human being.

David was not thinking about sex, he just wanted to get past this awkward moment and move on to something else. He would have been happy if Hank suggested playing a game of cards or going out for another nightcap...lighted a cigarette...anything. It didn't matter to David.

'Let's do something!' David thought to himself.

Hank just continued to sit in his frozen position looking down at the floor. David began to think maybe Hank didn't want to consider sex right now; he certainly wasn't making any moves.

It wasn't in David's nature to be the aggressor in his affairs with other men. He liked to be sure that everything was consensual. There was rarely a question

59

of masculinity or femininity in David's perception of homosexuality. He just wanted everything to happen spontaneously as it frequently did when he and a partner were excited and ready together.

David looked at Hank and felt nothing. Hank was gorgeous...Hank was intelligent... he was masculine...he should have turned on David's desires to the maximum. Half the gay men in the world would have been ecstatic just to be sitting where David was at this moment, yet, Hank just sat in his frozen position.

"Maybe it's best that I go," David said in a soft voice.

Hank looked up startled, "No...no, please, no!"

David didn't know what to say, he just looked at Hank who had folded hands with fingers intertwined. Hank took a very deep breathe as though he were preparing to dive into a pool of frigid water.

"I'm a little embarrassed because I've never had sex with a man before."

David promptly felt the blood rush to his own face and groin. He was going to have sex with Hank... it was going to happen...here...now...tonight! David was thrilled, happy and excited. He took the lead.

"Why don't we start by taking off our clothes," David said quietly, as he stood up and began with his own tie.

Hank stood up and began unbuttoning his own vest. David gently turned Hank's body toward him and said, "Here, let me do that." They both continued to unbutton the vest and Hank let it fall to the floor. David immediately picked it up and folded it carefully over a chair with Hank's suit jacket.

David turned back to Hank wordlessly and began removing Hank's tie...at the same time Hank deftly unbuttoned David's shirt and peeled it off sending it flying over the other chair at the table. David finished doing the same with Hank's shirt.

The two bare-chested men stopped and looked at each other silently. Both men stared approvingly at each other's chiseled physique and narrow waistline. David could detect a swelling at the crotch of Hank's tailored trousers, and he knew that his own ecru slacks were beginning to bulge somewhere below the waistline.

They looked intently at each other face to face, and unexpectedly Hank's lips touched David's. Somehow they were now naked and lying closely against one another on top of the bed.

'My socks are still on,' David thought, not caring at all.

Hank kissed David with aroused ardor as he moved to the perfect position that allowed each body to feel his own manhood lying firm and swollen next to the other. David felt indefectible happiness at this moment...he was in paradise as Hank's lips stayed on his. David conceded to Hank lying over him...mouths together...Hank gently undulating in a seamless indefectible cadence as their bodies rubbed coincidently and in silken harmony.

Hank lifted his lips from David long enough to breath a silent 'Ah,' before resuming his caress.

David ejaculated feeling a complete felicity that he had never experienced in his twenty-three years of life. Hank's jaw dropped slightly and he gently lifted away from David's lips. Swallowing uneasily he said, "You didn't *come* did you?"

David answered, "Oh yeah...of course I did...what makes you think I didn't?"

Hank pushed his naked body up from David's and looked down toward their crotches.

"You mean that's not all my chaos down there?"

David laughed out loud as he rolled Hank over and nimbly jumped to his feet. "You lie right there...I'll be right back," he said on his way to get a warm wash cloth and towel.

Hank could see copious amounts of gleaming white semen that had splashed on his body along the stomach and around his crotch.

"I guess you're right, it's not all mine," Hank said with a tone of wonder in his voice.

"I've never heard anyone refer to *cum* as chaos," David shouted over running water from the tap. "I'll remember that term."

David returned to the bed bringing a warm moistened washcloth and a towel. He began intimately wiping all the private portions of Hank's amazing physique. Hank was obviously pleased as he commented rhetorically "Where did you learn to do that? I mean it as a compliment when I say you'd make a great nurse."

"Coming from a doctor, I'll take the compliment" David said...then added further, "What is the *métier* at your medical clinic? Maybe you can get me a job there."

"I don't think you'd be interested," Hank inwardly laughed, "We specialize in Gynecology and Obstetrics."

David laughed out loud, "I have to admit that I'm not really very familiar with genitalia of the female anatomy...do you ever have to perform surgery?"

"Surgery is... as *you* would say...my *métier,*" Hank said somewhat mockingly. Then on a more serious note he added, "My practice usually includes surgery involving Cesarean sections and pregnancy terminations."

"You mean *abortions*," David nearly shouted the word.

"Yes," Hank said, "But, don't be concerned, everything I do is necessary for the patient's health, and it's all legal...well within existing laws...I'll tell you about it some other time."

David felt a small degree of shame that he had bellowed out the word abortion. He must have sounded like a naïve kid just realizing the facts of life. Hank really didn't seem to mind at all, but David wanted to make a good impression. He wanted to learn everything about this spell-binding man. David wanted to know all about Hank's profession...his politics...his philosophy... everything that was important to him including all the significant events of his life.

David folded the washcloth into the towel he had used to dry Hank's body. The two men stared at each other momentarily. Hank was still stretched out and David was sitting next to him on the side of the bed. Hank sat up and very tenderly kissed David before they both rose from the bed and Hank stated, "It's time for a cigarette."

"I'll get them," David said as he started for the table, "Do you want one of yours or a menthol?"

"It doesn't matter," Hank said, "either is good."

David took the pack of English Ovals from Hank's coat pocket, removed two cigarettes putting them both in his own mouth. He found his own lighter in his pants that he'd tossed over the back of one of the chairs. He walked over to Hank who had just put on briefs and stood next to the bed. David tried successfully to recreate the scene from *Now Voyager* where Paul Henreid lights two cigarettes and gives one to Bette Davis.

David and Hank both took a satisfying drag from their respective cigarettes. David walked back to the table, put his cigarette in an ashtray and quickly begin to dress. He tried to sound casual, "I really enjoyed our time together this evening. I don't know if you have plans for tomorrow...but if you don't...I'd be honored to pick you up first thing in the morning for breakfast...brunch... whatever; and continue the tour of San Francisco."

Hank slipped on a white t-shirt from his duffel bag and stepped next to David, "Sounds good to me." They touched lips.

David finished dressing leaving his tie undone around his neck. Hank walked him to the door as he said, "What time tomorrow?"

"Would ten o'clock be too early," David asked as he started for the door.

Hank walked over and opened the door, "Make it nine-thirty?"

David saluted as he walked out the doorway, "I'll see you at nine-thirty."

* * *

Most of the main lights in the Wellington Mansion were out when David drove up the driveway and got out of his car to open the gate. Soft night lights were gleaming along the pathways the wound through the gardens and along the house.

He moved quietly to the door that led into an impressively large gourmet kitchen. Patty was totally involved in a project as she sat at a huge island counter with copper pots, pans, and various gourmet utensils hanging overhead. She was wearing a dainty filmy negligee embroidered at the sleeves and hem of the garment.

Zachary, one of the family miniature poodles, had been placed on the counter next to Patricia and also seemed included in her project. The two of them wouldn't have noticed David's entrance if he hadn't cleared his throat.

"Poopsie!" Patty squealed out her delight while Zach began beating his tail on the countertop like a drummer at a jazz concert. Patty strained to turn her head, but kept her hands on the counter, receiving her brother's kiss on her forehead.

"You're just in time to help me...you know I can't do this," she pleaded.

"What in the world are you trying to do?" he asked.

"I've been trying to roll a joint for the last half hour," she said throwing up her hands in a gesture of defeat.

David laughed as he moved closer to his sister, "Here sweetie, let me help you."

He instantly received two kisses, one from her and one from Zachary who had stepped right in the middle of Patty's marijuana paraphernalia. Brother and sister laughed as Patty lifted the dog off the counter and David picked up the pieces of her project and resumed rolling.

"Is this the stuff we grew on Ninth Street?," he asked as he continued with the operation.

"Of course it is, Poopsie. We had *kilograms* of it hanging in the garage drying out. You couldn't take a breath in there without getting high. There was enough grass to keep the entire Art and Drama departments at San Jose State stoned for a year."

David laughed as he produced a perfectly rolled marijuana cigarette.

"Lovely!" Patty proclaimed. "Absolutely perfect in every detail. Light it up!"

"We'd better take it outside in the garden...don't want to leave any tell-tale odors."

"Good thinking, Poopsie," she said, "Let's hit it."

"Wait a second," David said cautiously, "You need a wrap."

He took off his jacket and placed it lovingly over his sister's elegant shoulders.

Knowing she might object to his gesture he said, "Don't worry, I'll be fine in my long sleeved shirt."

They passed through the doorway into the softly lit garden. Zach wagged his tail happily as he dashed out in-between the siblings.

"He enjoys getting high too," Patty announced as she slipped her arms into the sleeves of her brother's gabardine coat.

The night was cool...but not too cold to step out of the house for a few minutes to smoke a joint. There was no wind and the fog now formed a stationary blanket about a hundred feet over their heads. The shroud of haze had lifted to produce a night sky of solid luminescent gray. There was no mist in the air now, but they could feel the tranquil humidity in an unmoving atmosphere.

"How was your Friday afternoon and subsequent evening out?" Patty asked as she drew in a hefty puff of marijuana...held it...and passed the joint to her brother.

"Ohh-h-h," David groaned as he took a *drag* and looked up at the starless barrier of fog.

"Is that orgasmic sound you just made a personification of your evening...or is it a comment reflecting on the toke you just took from that joint."

"Both," David said as he exhaled smoke and handed the burning *joint* to Patty.

"Are you going to tell me about *him,* or are you going to leave it a mystery for me to trip off on now that I'm stoned," Patty said as she took another puff and bent down to gently blow it in Zachary's eager face.

"His name is Hank...he's a doctor...a surgeon from L.A...married with three kids...just finalizing his divorce... came up to San Fran for his first gay experience."

"Did he consummate the exploit with you?' Patty asked warily.

"Oh yes...and then some," David answered.

Patty inquired, "Were you gentle with him for his first experience?"

"*Tender* is a better word," David answered.

"*Tender!*" Patty said cunningly as she raised her brow.

"But it was also fervent...impassioned...and romantic," David added.

"Oh good Lord help us," Patty said. "It sounds like you might be in love."

"I think I am," David said with a tear glistening in the corner of his eye.

"Oh Poopsie, my little Poopsie...you're really serious... you really fell in love," she said as she put out the joint on the back of a nearby wrought iron chair.

David smiled sheepishly holding out his arms in a sign of surrender. "It's true, I am in love."

"Oh, Poopsie... Poopsie," she repeated as she engulfed her younger brother in a long sisterly hug.

The siblings were absorbed in the moment, oblivious to their surroundings, until Zachary started prancing about. He was trying to join in on the celebration as he danced around Patty and David's legs in a frenzy of delight.

Patty leaned down and took Zach into her arms. Holding the *puppy* close to her firm well-developed breasts she asked, "Is he handsome?"

David laughed "Are you referring to the dog you're holding, or are you asking about Hank?"

Ignoring her brother's attempt at humor Patty said, "I shouldn't even have to ask...of course he's handsome... you couldn't possibly be in love with him otherwise. How handsome is he?"

"Unequaled in handsomeness...I've never met anybody like him...and not only is he the uttermost handsome man in the world, he is the consummate gentleman".

"That settles it Poopsie! You've found your soul-mate!" Patty shouted as she put down Zach.

Zachary began barking and again started dancing around the two siblings.

"Shh, Shh...hush," Patty warned. "We're getting much too loud."

"We'd better go in the house," David said.

Patty picked up Zach in her arms, "When will you next see Hank?" she asked as they reached the doorway to the kitchen..

"I'm meeting him at his hotel first thing in the morning."

"Good," Patty said, "That means you'll be with him all weekend and won't attend Stephen's birthday dinner tomorrow night."

"Ooops," said David.

"Oh no, honey," Patty said with a sigh. "I'm relieved that you're not coming tomorrow night. I'm hoping Steve's brother Paul won't be there as well. It'll be a much more pleasant evening with just the two of us. You know how Stephen and Paul always end up squabbling about one silly thing or another. Besides, I'm picking up the tab for the *birthday boy* and it would probably cost a small fortune to feed all three of you guys."

Once inside the kitchen Patty said, "How about a cup of Sleepy-Time Tea...it'll make your *dope* induced dreams of Hank much more pleasant."

"I won't argue with a cup of tea," David said smiling "...and I'm definitely high...but my dreams of Hank won't be 'dope' induced...they'll just come naturally. I'm so excited about the prospects of getting to know him...he seems too good to be true."

"You know Poopsie," Patty articulated, "You...are...a...very...blessed...young...man!"

"You know...that I know...that we know...how very blessed we both are," David whispered.

"Oh yes Poopsie...it's disturbing to think we can't really share our faith with the rest of the world. Sometimes I have the urge to become a 'prophetess' and spread the word like a missionary going into darkest Africa."

David laughed boisterously, "You'd undoubtedly have more success in Africa than you would with some of our hedonistic friends who cringe at the mention of God or Jesus, or even religion!"

"Sh-h-h Poopsie...I know this is a big house...but Bogey has big ears...and we don't want him to wake Mom and Dad."

"I don't know why we call them 'Mom' and 'Dad' David said in a quieter voice.

"Well Poopsie...we can't very well refer to them as 'the monsters' like we used to when we were little kids."

David put his hand to his mouth and stifled a laugh, "I remember so well when you used to say 'It's us against the *monsters,* Poopsie, we have to stick together."

"Well, you know that we love them both...but they were way too strict when we were growing up. Wherever we lived you and I were in bed by six o'clock while all the rest of the kids in the neighborhood would romp and play until well after dark."

"I know," David agreed, "But I still think their strictness bothered you more than it did me."

"That's because you were much younger, Poopsie, and much less aware of how unrelentingly stern and hard-line our parents really were."

"I guess they were just 'over-protective' with us... yeah...I'm sure the strictness was tougher on you being the eldest."

Patricia poured boiling water over two mugs holding Sleepy-Time tea bags, "But thanks to the good Lord for Nanny and Poppa John...if it weren't for our long summers in California at the Vineyards...I don't know how we would have made it through childhood."

"You're right about that," David concurred, "I spent grades three through twelve just counting the days until summer vacation...I don't think that Mom and Dad really understand the toll it took on us to change schools so often."

Patty finished preparing their tea and passed a mug to her brother. "Yes...those were hard times absorbing all those experiences that we were *forced* to endure. I think often of those tough days just in Maryland. We were *forced* to learn about places like Mt. Vernon, Lincoln and Jefferson Memorials...Fort McHenry."

"Yes," David said, "...and we were *forced* to spend days, almost weeks over time at the Smithsonian

Institute...and don't forget weekends when we explored the Arboretum and Theodore Roosevelt Island."

"I remember," Patty said, "...and don't forget those arduous walks the *monsters forced* us to endure through the White House and the Capitol Building."

"And you remember waiting in line at the Supreme Court? How many days we went through that..."

"I know," said Patty, "Daddy used that Albert Trop case as a model for us to understand how the Supreme Court works. I gave a report on Chief Justice Earl Warren's decision to my Social Studies class when we moved to Hagerstown."

"I remember your report," David said, "That's the case where Trop was denied a passport because he had been a deserter back in World War II. The old *Nationality Act* said that soldiers in the armed forces who deserted had to lose their United States citizenship. Trop filed suit and lost in a U.S. district court."

"That's right, Poopsie, but Justice Warren said that 'denationalization as a punishment was prohibited under the *Eighth Amendment*...loss of American citizenship was a punishment more primitive than torture."

"Yeah," David said, "...and who was the guy on the Supreme Court who argued against Warren and said that desertion was punishable by death?"

"Frankfurter...Justice Felix Frankfurter...an easy name to remember. He argued that the loss of citizenship is *not* a fate worse than death."

"What else did the monsters *force* us to go through just because it was supposed to be educational?"

"Don't forget when you and I tried climbing the stairs of the Washington Monument...we didn't even make it half way...and oh, yes...in addition to Mount Vernon they threw us in the *George Washington Masonic Memorial Museum* while they went shopping somewhere in Alexandria."

"I know how much you really hated that memorial Patty...you were just like Uncle Remus *'Br'er Rabbit'* who didn't want to be thrown in the briar patch."

They both laughed loudly then and stopped just short of hysteria. Patty and David each took a sip from their mugs to quiet themselves.

"I specifically remember you saying that day, 'Thank God, we're rid of the monsters for a couple of hours."

The brother and sister giggled again as they reminisced under the influence of marijuana and took sips of their tea. Patricia walked to the double door refrigerator and pulled out a tray with chocolate éclairs and cream puffs and placed them in front of David. Zach had been sound asleep in one corner of the counter sat up to full attention as David started to devour one of the pastries.

"I guess we'll shift our agonizing thoughts of Washington D.C. to a food-trip," Patty said as she put an éclair on a plate and delicately sliced it into four pieces.

She was just having her first bite while David nodded his head, grunted approval and started in on his second pastry.

"My poor little Poopsie...when I think how much we suffered during those years of hardship...we were literally *forced* into learning about all those stuffy historical things and places."

"Yeah...it was really tough...probably the only fun we got out of those days was eating...we really went to a lot of great restaurants," David said licking Bavarian cream off his fingers, and noticing a glob of chocolate icing on his shirt.

The siblings both started to chortle with hands over mouths to keep from horse laughing too loudly. They didn't have to say another word to each other because they were both thinking identical thoughts...reflections of their childhood... being loved and nurtured by parents and grandparents who were fervently devoted to understanding and adoring Patricia and David.

* * *

CHAPTER FOUR

David didn't have to look for a parking place the following morning. He found Hank standing in front of the hotel with a duffel bag leaning against his leg. He looked astonishingly aristocratic even though he was wearing a regular pair of light gray wool slacks and a dark blue cashmere sweater over a white shirt. The streets were fairly quiet and the misty fog from last night had burned off leaving a few white wispy clouds overhead in a baby blue sky. David made a mental note to recapture this wonderful image of a classically handsome nobleman standing in the morning sun...in front of an old run-down, sleazy, shabby hotel in the *Tenderloin District.*

'What an oxymoronic picture,' David laughed to himself, as he drove to the curb and reached across to open the passenger door for Hank.

In what seemed like a single agile movement Hank athletically tossed his bag behind the driver's seat and bounced into the sports car as though he'd done it many times before.

"Good morning. Why all the smiles?" he asked.

"I don't know," David answered. "I guess I'm happy... why are you smiling."

"I guess I'm happy too." Hank said. "Where are we going?"

"Oh, I thought I'd take you on the thirty-five cent tour of San Francisco. It includes a quick drive to Fisherman's Wharf...then a trip across the Golden Gate Bridge...turn around in Sausalito and back across the bridge to the Presidio...Baker's Beach... past the California Palace of the Legion of Honor... maybe brunch at the Cliff House and then to Golden Gate Park to check out the latest fine arts display at the de Young Museum. If there's time we can stop by the Steinhart Aquarium and the Japanese Tea Gardens. They're practically right next door to each other. We'll figure on dinner when the sun starts to go down... so-o-o many great places to eat," David declared excitedly.

"Really sounds enjoyable...I'm ready for the day. Let's start the tour!" Hank exclaimed.

* * *

David faithfully followed the itinerary he had described to Hank. When they drove down to Fisherman's Wharf the vendors were already selling fresh crab and shrimp that were being served directly from the boiling cauldrons in front of tourist shops that lined the walkways. There were mixed scents of lemon, and tartar somewhat like the smell around the wine casks at the Vineyards.

It was still too early in the day for the major restaurants to open, but the two men strolled past famous places like *Fisherman's Grotto*, *Alioto's*, and *DiMaggio's* peering through windows and reading menus posted outside the doors.

They walked by *Sabella* & *La Torre's* where a boy had just finished hosing off the sidewalk in front of the establishment. David told Hank the brief story of Luciano Sabella and Antoine La Torre who had started the business.

"They were basically a couple of crab catchers who fished for their families. They caught so many Dungeness crabs that they opened a stand and started selling the overflow to locals. These were two guys from Sicily who are credited for starting the trend of cooking the crabs right on the wharf and marketing to hungry tourists. My maternal grandfather, who is Italian, knows their families."

"So, that makes you, at least partly, of Italian descent," said Hank. "I'd never have known with your light hair and very green eyes...you look almost Nordic or maybe a little Scottish."

David was glad that Hank had noticed the color of his eyes. "Yes, my grandfather is from northern Italy, a town called Bergamo. It's in the foothills of the Alps, where you'll find many blond haired people. The composer Donizetti was from Bergamo."

"My grandmother, Nanny is Romano," he continued. The majority of my relatives on her side of the family are red-heads with green eyes. My sister Patty has very dark chestnut hair with the same green eyes exactly like mine, and you're right about the Scots, that's from my Dad's side of the family...mostly blonds... blue eyes.

"Was your maternal grandfather involved with fishing," Hank asked as they walked by *Alioto's*.

"Not ever," David replied with a laugh. "He's strictly involved with wine. Bergamo is in a region of Italy called Lombardy. Lombardi spelled with the letter '*I*' is Poppa's last name. Lombardi, of course, was my mom's maiden name. Have you ever heard of *Lombardi Champagne*? You can find it in a lot of restaurants throughout the United States."

"Of course," Hank answered, "Anyone who knows wine knows the name *Lombardi*; it's like *Mondavi* or *Gallo*."

At this point, David wanted to avoid further conversation about his own family. "We can talk about wines later; it's time for a ride across *the* Golden Gate Bridge."

"I'm ready, let's go," Hank said. "I forgot where we parked."

"Just follow me," David said taking the lead again.

* * *

David drove the car slowly down Sutter Street, and up a ramp into a parking garage next to the *Olympic Club*. He jumped out of the car and dashed around to the passenger side to open the door for Hank, who stepped out with a stretch and a yawn...it had been a long day of sightseeing.

David reached to the back seat and grabbed Hank's duffel bag. "Oh, I've got that," Hank said as he took the bag from David.

David walked around to the back of his sports car and opened the trunk. He brought out a smart-looking overnight leather case not much larger than a briefcase, the kind often seen with professional businessmen in the Financial District.

"Hi Jack," David greeted the parking attendant as he took David's keys.

"Look's like it's gonn'a be an overnight stay, Mr. Wellington," the attendant said eyeing the luggage.

"Yes sir, Jack," David said, "Appreciate if you park it somewhere out-of-sight."

"No problem Mr. Wellington. You'll be staying at the *Marine's Memorial Club*?"

"Yes," David *lied* as he took the claim ticket in his left hand, "We'll see you in the morning."

"I won't be here tomorrow," Jack said remorsefully, "Chuck will be on duty in the morning."

"Oh, here...then let me give this to you," David said as he handed the attendant a ten dollar bill.

"Thank you Mr. Wellington, you know you don't need to do this, your dad always takes good care of us." Jack said as he climbed into the driver's seat, "Enjoy your weekend."

He started the motor and drove up an alternate ramp and out of sight. The two pleasantly tired men walked down the first ramp to Sutter Street.

"We'll be staying at the Marine's Memorial Hotel?" Hank asked.

David tried to keep from blushing for having made a *disingenuous* statement in front of Hank.

"No, but I feel comfortable when Jack associates my parking here with the Memorial Club. Other members of the family park here...and I just didn't want any confusion on anybody's part. My Dad gives them a monthly fee for us to park here at any time. My sister Patty visits the Academy of Arts across the street, and Mom goes to the Woman's Club...it's just a few doors from here on the corner of Sutter and Taylor streets."

"Then this is familiar territory for you and your family," Hank interjected looking around the street.

"Yes," said David… "And, we *all* visit the Marines Memorial frequently for dinner and drinks and other activities. The club has a great swimming pool and gym, where I occasionally meet my Dad… the building also holds one of the most popular theatres in town."

"This looks like a great neighborhood," Hank said as they came to a Victorian style establishment with a sign that spelled out *The White Horse Pub* under a green canopy.

"Do you ever go here?"

"Yes," said David. "In fact, this is where you and I will be staying tonight," as he moved down the same green sidewalk canopy that announced *Hotel Beresford*.

The face of the building consisted of large stone blocks painted white with the same green and gray trim on the hotel as the pub. *The White Horse* was very obviously part of the same establishment as the *Hotel Beresford*.

David led them into the small quaint lobby with large white wainscoting panels and textured wallpaper in soft gold. They walked straight to the old-fashioned check-in counter that was perfectly sized for one employee at a time.

"Good evening," said a handsome young man dressed in a white shirt and tie that matched the gold color of the wallpaper.

"How may I help you gentlemen," he asked cheerfully.

"We'd like a room for just this evening," David answered. "We need to clean up for an affair we're attending in the vicinity…and we don't want to have to drive anywhere afterward."

"Of course," the clerk agreed, "I understand precisely what you mean. I'm the same way; I don't like to drive late

on a night when I'm out for an evening of entertainment...
if one of you would sign the guest register...I have a
splendid room for you gentlemen...it's just two floors up
so you can either take the stairs or the elevator as you
prefer."

Hank politely brushed David aside positioning
himself to sign the register.

"Check-out is at noon...but of course since this
is Saturday night so if you require more time in the
morning, just call down to the desk," the clerk said as
he handed a key to David and a key to Hank who had just
finished signing.

"I'll be here till midnight, but there is always
someone on duty...twenty four hours...let us know if you
need anything."

"Thanks," Hank said. "Do you need a deposit or a
credit card?"

"Oh, no," the clerk answered. "You gentlemen can
settle-up in the morning."

* * *

When they went to their room David slipped off his
shoes without untying them. He stretched out on the
bed nearest to the only large window covered in rich
embroidered ceiling-to-floor drapes.

"Ah-h-h," he moaned softly, crossing his legs at the
ankle and wiggling his toes. "This feels good," he sighed
placing his hands directly under his head.

Hank was lighting a cigarette looking for an ashtray
when he noticed a small clock radio on the stand that
separated the beds. Without sitting down he clicked the
radio on and instantly Chopin's piano composition of
Fantaisie Impromptu in C-sharp minor could be heard.

David sighed again… Hank put out his cigarette and grabbed a pillow from the other bed.

"Mind if I join you?" he said as he kicked off his shoes and tossed a pillow right next to David's head. David answered by scooting over a few inches and patted the mattress for Hank to join him.

Hank moved lithely onto the bed, knee first, kissed David fully on the mouth and said,

"Let's take off all our clothes and get under the covers."

* * *

The two men were once again dressed in coats and ties. Hank was wearing a classic gray herringbone blazer with a light blue shirt complemented by a blue and white silk *Wembley Jacquard* tie. David had on a Pendleton brown windowpane sport-coat with a white shirt and solid coffee brown tie. They both looked conspicuously handsome and masculine.

The elevator attendant was a short little fellow, one of many Filipino employees at the establishment dressed in a uniformed vest with shiny brass buttons.

"Good evening, gentlemen. Welcome to the Marine's Memorial Club."

Looking directly at David he asked, "Skyroom?"

"Yes sir," David responded with a smile, "Please."

Checking his watch David said, "It's a little later to have dinner than I'd planned, but I'm sure the kitchen will still be able to rustle up something for us to eat."

"They'll be no problem at all sir," said the attendant, "It's Saturday night and the restaurant is prepared to be serving late."

David turned to the attendant and said "Thank you, and good evening," as the elevator door opened to reveal an extremely distinguished couple waiting just outside.

"Good evening," said Richard who was standing next to his radiantly smiling wife.

Sylvia was dressed in a luxuriant green jade gown with breathtaking décolletage highlighted by a dazzling diamond necklace. Her ebony hair was swept up in a magnificent mass of ringlets and curls that fell softly around her face. The diamond earrings were just the right touch to her exquisite countenance. She was absolutely stunning to behold.

"Mom...Dad!" David cried out as he exited the elevator and embraced Sylvia, "You look positively gorgeous... what are you doing here...I thought you'd be having a quiet dinner at home."

"It was a last minute invitation from the Burke's... it's their anniversary tomorrow and they wanted a quiet celebration with us tonight. They've left...but your father talked me into staying for a nightcap."

"I'm so happy to see you guys... I never expected to run into you *tonight*."

Richard guided all of them a step away from the elevator into the foyer, "We're happy to see you too... hello...I'm Richard Wellington," he said extending his hand to Hank, "and this is Sylvia...we're David's parents."

"Hank Stafford," Hank said as he firmly shook Richard's hand.

David jumped in, "Hank and I have been sightseeing today...he's just in from L.A., for the weekend."

"Welcome to San Francisco," Sylvia said graciously, "You have a fine tour guide."

"I'm finding that out," said Hank with a genuine smile.

"I'm sorry we can't stay and socialize a little...but we need to be off," then looking at David, "Church in the morning...brunch...dinner with David's grandparents in Sonoma...you're more than welcome to join us Hank...if any of that interests you."

"I'm sure these fellows have their own plans for the weekend...Patricia warned us that we probably wouldn't see David until Monday morning. Perhaps we'll meet with Hank again on his next visit to San Francisco," Richard said extending his hand.

"Nice to meet you," Hank said shaking his hand and bowing very slightly to Sylvia.

"Glad to meet you Hank," Sylvia said stepping toward the elevator door just as it opened on cue. "You gentlemen have a pleasant evening."

As they walked toward the reception podium to request a table, Hank commented, "Your mother is a beautiful woman."

"What'd you think of my dad?" David asked.

"He is an exceptionally distinguished gentleman."

The hostess approached the podium with a broad smile and said "Hi David...you just missed your mom and dad...you're here for dinner, right?"

"Yes, please Susie," David said as he peered around the hostess to check out what table might be available.

"I know where you like to sit," said Susie, "but it may be a few minutes...they're not quite finished eating."

"No problem Susie...we'll just hang out at the bar."

"I'll come and get you when the table is ready."

David escorted Hank to the bar which was empty except for a tired looking bald-headed man at the far end in a gray flannel suit. As soon as they sat down a

Filipino bartender dressed in uniform trotted over to take their order.

"Good evening Mr. Wellington...you just missed your mother and father," he said putting down a couple of coasters in front of the men.

"I know Arthur...we actually saw them on their way out...and please, call me David. What would you like to drink Hank?"

"Hank looked at David and asked, "What are you having?"

"Bombay martinis straight up...well chilled with an jalapeno stuffed olive!" Arthur stated.

Hank smiled, "Sounds good to me."

"I didn't know you liked gin," David said offering Hank a cigarette.

"Gin's my number one drink," said Hank as he accepted a cigarette and snapped out his lighter, "usually with tonic and a lime wedge."

"Yeah...for me too," said David as Arthur was shaking the first batch of martinis.

"It didn't seem to bother you that we ran into your folks tonight."

David replied, "Not at all...why should it? They know I have friends from all over California...it's not surprising to them that they saw us here tonight...but it was surprising to me."

"Why would you be surprised? You told me that your entire family comes here frequently."

"They do...we do...it's just that when I saw them yesterday they seemed intent on staying at home Saturday night. I guess I shouldn't be so surprised...but I just never expected to see them here tonight."

"Are you sure it doesn't bother you?

"Oh no...I'm glad they met you...they're always delighted to see me with someone who has a haircut and isn't dressed in a *tie-dye* shirt with beads. I'm proud they saw you with me tonight."

"I gather they know you're gay?"

"They know...it's just something that they don't discuss...at least with me."

"You've never talked with your parents about the fact that you are gay?"

"Nope," David said grinning, "and I don't ask them about their sex life. They have spoken about my sexual preferences among themselves...but they've never broached the subject directly with me. The only family member that I share secrets with is my sister...Patricia."

"Is she...,"

"No," David finished Hank's sentence, "She is not... gay. She's a totally beautiful heterosexual woman who enjoys having stimulating affairs with remarkable straight men."

"She discusses her exploits with you?"

David threw his head back and laughed, "Not exactly... we don't discuss the precise details of our escapades... but we do talk about emotions and feelings regarding our attachments and infatuations. We love each other... we trust each other...we are very close to one another."

"That's *top-shelf*," Hank said, "Sounds like you have a very special relationship with your sister...but getting back to your parents...how do you know that they discuss your sexuality between themselves?"

"My sister Patty is often there when they do...she tells me about all the conversations that take place when I'm not around...and there have been quite a few."

"What do they say about you?"

David hesitated for a moment as Arthur placed their martinis on the bar in front of them. They clinked glasses in a toast and each took a sip. Hank offered David a cigarette but he waved it off as he continued the discussion.

"My dad and sister do not have *any* issues with the fact that I'm gay...my mother, however, does have issues. She worries...I think...more from a social point of view... and somewhat about hygiene."

"Hygiene?" Hank asked as he lit an English Oval.

"Yes...she knows I go to gay establishments around town, and her impression is that they are all dirty, diseased ridden pools of corruption."

"Heh, heh," Hank chuckled, "That's certainly a vivid description."

"That's exactly how she sees it...she's really quite naive and unknowing about gay life anywhere in the world...and especially in the city where she lives...and loves. Oh, I don't mean that she's not totally unaware that San Francisco, aside from being *'everyone's favorite city*,' is a gay Mecca. She simply chooses to ignore that side of this town. There was a big spread in Life Magazine when I was a senior in high school. It characterized gay life in San Francisco as 'sad and sordid'...I'm afraid my mother will always see it that way. Patricia keeps telling Sylvia that what's happening in San Francisco is just the beginning of a *sexual insurrection*...what we see now is just the tip of the iceberg. One example that brought Patty's point home was when Sylvia found a *SIR* flyer in my jacket."

"Is SIR one of the city's notoriously known gay bars?"

"Not exactly," said David, "The flyer was from S.I.R. which stands for *Society for Individual Rights.* Some really nice folks belong to S.I.R. Sometimes I still go to the dances on Saturday night at their community center down on Sixth Street. That one time I made the mistake of keeping their announcement bulletin in my coat pocket."

"So, SIR is a gay club?"

"Yes...but it's a lot more than a club...it's an association that advocates for gay men and women... they have parties, celebrations, bowling groups...just about anything you can think of... S.I.R. is not in the least militant...but they do advertise themselves as the first gay community center in America...they just started a few years ago...they do a lot of good things for the gay guys and gals in San Francisco."

"What sort of things?" Hank asked.

"Social service stuff for 'gays in trouble', legal advice and medical assistance for venereal diseases, you know, things of that nature. S.I.R. also advocates conservatively to eliminate victimless crime laws... they're trying to promote a feeling of a unified gay community. I think that they may play an important role in developing civil rights legislature in the future. They are not an obnoxious or offensive organization. They even sponsor theatrical musicals, usually with an all male cast performing in *drag*."

"How did you find out about this consortium?" Hank asked.

"Whoa...ho," David said, "That's another story in itself...my wonderful friend George who takes me to S.I.R. from time to time...actually he's a close friend of Patty's as well. Both of us were introduced to him when we attended a spiritualist service a few years back. He 'read' for us."

"What did he read?" Hank asked wonderingly.

"He read the spiritual aura emanations that he saw surrounding my sister and me." David said rolling his eyes mysteriously."

"Is he a truly a psychic with extraordinary powers?"

"Not so much when you get to know George...he's more fun than a '*barrel of monkeys*' as my sister would say. There's really nothing that mysterious about him...it's just that he's in training as a spiritual medium. It's almost like a hobby for him."

"You mean like talking to dead people?"

David laughed, "I don't know if he has actual conversations with people who have died...from what I understand he acts more as an intermediary between this world and the world of spirit. He's not one of those *physical mediums* who hold séances and make spirits materialize through ectoplasm to rap on walls and ring bells. George is a *mental medium*; he 'tunes in' and interprets through sensation, listening or seeing symbols from emanations and lights that surround living people. He interprets the lights and auras that he sees. He's really extraordinarily intuitive."

"Fascinating," said Hank eating the olive from his martini, "What's he do for a living?"

"Yes, he is fascinating...and it's a lot of fun to have George read for you. He is a senior editor at the *San Francisco Examiner*...he always claims he's nothing more than a glorified proof-reader. I'm sure that you'll have the opportunity to meet him. I know that he's going to love you the moment you're introduced."

"Why so?" Hank asked.

David put his hand on Hank's knee and said, "Because you, sir, have a fantastic aura."

* * *

It was close to midnight by the time David and Hank finished their steak dinner at the Marines Memorial Club. The bar was now crowded with people who had finished their meals and were having nightcaps. There was only one other table where a group of four were still eating. David got up and walked over to the piano player, put a $10 bill in the glass jar, conversed a few minutes and requested a tune...before he got back to the table the lady was playing the theme song from the movie '*The Sandpiper.*'

"*The Shadow of Your Smile,*'...I'm really partial to this song," Hank said.

"So am I," David agreed...the movie was okay...kind of a corny soap opera...but the background scenes of *Big Sur* were spectacular."

Hank said, "I've always wanted to do that drive all the way up the coast from L.A. to Big Sur country...I've only been as far as San Simeon...I spent a full day there with my family taking the tours of *William Hearst's Castle* and estates. One day I'd really like to drive up the Pacific Coast Highway to Bodega Bay."

"The Pacific Coast Highway has to be one of the most beautiful stretches of road in the entire world," David said, "I've done it at least a dozen times in my lifetime...and I plan on doing it dozens of times in my 'golden years'...the actual state Highway # 1 begins in Orange County at Dana Point and goes all the way up to the Redwoods of Northern California ending at Legget.

"Sounds like you're really familiar with the coast," Hank said.

"Oh, yeah," David said, "I know scores of beaches up and down the California coastline. My grandmother always says that I grew up swimming in the Pacific Ocean. My grandfather on my dad's side of our family has property in a place called *Dillon Beach*...we went there all the time in the summers when I was a kid growing up... we still go whenever we wish...as a teenager I explored all the beaches in Sonoma county."

"Do you have a favorite beach that you especially like?" Hank asked.

"I can answer that positively...no...I do not have a favorite...I do enjoy the beaches where the water is easily accessible...but I also love places like Big Sur where the *Santa Lucia Mountains* from the *Los Padres National Forest* plunge right into the ocean. I've never seen anything so beautiful. We drive down there regularly when we cut classes at San Jose State. If we just want to go for a quick swim we can be in Santa Cruz in less than ½ hour...everything else is just minutes from there including Monterey and Carmel. We go hiking along *Point Lobos* or at *Jules Pfeiffer State Park*. It's certainly a lot more exhilarating than taking notes in a stuffy university classroom."

"I've been to Monterey and Carmel," Hank said, "It was when I came *down* the coast from *Half Moon Bay*.'

"What in the world were you doing in Half Moon Bay?" David asked.

"My sister-n-law's wedding...she's a History teacher at the high school...she married an infantry sergeant she'd dated for years...he was from *Fort Ord* in Monterey. My wife and I flew up from LAX to San Francisco and rented a car. The wedding and reception was actually in Santa Cruz, but we stayed at her sister's home in Half Moon Bay."

"That's when you visited Monterey and Carmel." David said.

"Yes...good guess. We stayed in northern California for three or four days...it was a pleasant trip."

This was only the second time Hank had spoken about his wife and having a family. David wanted to know more, but he wasn't sure this was the right time to pry. He thought it would be best not to press for information about Hank's *straight* life...it could be hurtful or uncomfortable to talk about it so soon after a major separation. This was Hank's first weekend away from married life...and David wanted it to be a memorable and very positive experience.

"Patricia and I had a favorite restaurant in Monterey," David said to keep the topic away from Hank's personal life.

"You said *had* a favorite restaurant?"

"Yes," David went on, "*Neil De Vaughn's*, a delightful French Seafood restaurant right on the beautiful Monterey Bay where you could see the sandpipers on the sand and the seagulls flying in the sky. It was a great place... fantastic menu...everything gourmet right off Cannery Row. They served *Monterey Jack* fondue with homemade sour dour bread cut in big squares...it wasn't even an appetizer...it just came as standard fare with the salt and pepper shaker at every table. The freshly sautéed sand dabs were the best ever...and the delicately poached filet of sole...um-m-m."

"You just ate a half pound of charred rare filet mignon and you're sitting here, right now, talking about food?"

The two guys started laughing just looking at each other completely enjoying the moment. The music stopped and Hank got up to put another bill in the piano player's jar. David jumped up behind Hank and followed him to the piano.

"Hi David," the entertainer said, "When your folks were here earlier tonight I sang a lot of the old songs."

"Hi Helen, this is Hank...he's up for the weekend from L.A."

Helen immediately hit the piano keys and sang,

> *L.A. is a great big freeway*
> *Put a hundred down and buy a car*
> *In a week, maybe two*
> *They'll make you a star*
> *Weeks turn into years, how quick they pass*
> *And all the stars that never were*
> *Are parking cars and pumping gas*

"Hi Hank, I'm Helen...Helen Tweedy...and I'm glad to meet you."

"Hi Helen...Dionne Warwick's song...Burt Bacharach wrote the music and Hal David did the lyrics...you make it sound good."

"Well...thank you honey...I only wish I had some of the money that Dionne and Burt made on that song."

They all laughed and Helen said, "Would you gentlemen like a song before I'm on the road again? I'm ready to quit right after one last tune."

"That would be a good one, Helen," David said.

"What would be a good one?" asked Hank shaking his head as though he missed something.

David didn't have to answer because Helen was already playing and singing:

> *On the road again*
> *Just can't wait to get on the road again*
> *The life I love is making music with my friends*

And I can't wait to get on the road again
On the road again

Goin' places that I've never been
Seein' things that I may never see again...And I
can't wait to get on the road again

* * *

The following morning David and Hank got showered, shaved and dressed for brunch at the *Redwood Room* at the *Clift Hotel*. It was off Geary Street, just a very short stroll from the Beresford Hotel where they were staying. There were plenty of places to have brunch, but the Redwood Room was one of the best in San Francisco on Sundays.

The buffet spread was filled with eye-opening dishes and foods...many which were being served by men wearing tall white chef's hats. They were creating fresh omelets on demand and carving from huge roasts of prime beef, golden braised turkeys, and real Virginia baked hams. David and Hank were escorted to a table by a cheerful lady wearing a straight low cut black gown and black onyx jewelry.

"If you wish to give me your drink order, I'll have Andy, your waiter, bring it from the bar," she said as she held the chair for Hank to be seated.

"Ramos fizz, for me," David said as he seated himself.

"Ramos fizz," Hank echoed.

"Andy will be right over with them," she said.

"My dad says they make one of the best Ramos Fizzes in town here...the secret is to use genuine orange flower water and not orange 'anything else.'"

"Good gin, heavy cream, egg white, lemon, lime juice and powdered sugar," Hank said licking his lips...one of my favorite drinks for brunch. There are a few places in L.A. that know how to make good ones."

The waiter soon arrived with their drinks. "Hi Andy...I'm Hank...no...I don't know why I said that... I mean this is Hank, and I'm David," he said laughing.

"Hello David and Hank...welcome to brunch at the Redwood Room...just give me the high sign when you want more drinks or coffee or anything. You can jump into the buffet whenever you're ready. The chefs will make you any kind of omelet you can think of and the seafood buffet is filled with large boiled tiger prawns, fresh raw oysters, clams, along with poached or smoked salmon, and steamed Alaskan King Crab legs that were flown in early this morning. The rest of the food speaks for itself...enjoy!"

* * *

David and Hank relished their Sunday brunch at the Redwood Room of the Clift Hotel. The establishment never became overly crowded and there was no waiting in line to get a fresh slice from a perfectly cooked roasted pork butt or leg of lamb that was served with homemade mint sauce. The pastries were all from San Francisco's famous *Victoria Bakery*...miracles of flaky dough and custard creams of irresistible textures and flavors.

A trio of musicians kept playing the same Bach sonata for flute, cello and violin as the two men ate and drank for more than three hours. They both felt a little melancholy and regretted that the morning had slipped away so quickly. David consoled himself with the idea that he would see Hank again...but when...where?

There was barely time enough to check out of the Beresford Hotel and get Hank to the airport for his 2:00 P.M. flight back to Los Angeles. As they raced down the 101 Freeway David wanted to say so many things, but didn't know where to start. Hank was preoccupied in the passenger seat shuffling through his travel documents and changing his tie that was sprinkled with seafood marinara sauce. David just couldn't think of anything to say as they headed for the main terminal at SFO. They drove to the main entrance and Hank hopped out of the convertible and reached for his duffel bag.

"Egad, I didn't even give you my phone number... here," he said flipping through his wallet and producing a business card. "That's my number at the clinic...call me tomorrow morning...maybe we can make plans for you to come down to L.A. next weekend."

David put the card in his top left jacket pocket. They shook hands and Hank jogged into the terminal. David hadn't even said goodbye. As he drove away from the terminal he turned on the radio and heard Willie Nelson singing *On the Road Again*. David wondered how early in the morning he should call Hank.

* * *

CHAPTER FIVE

After dropping Hank at the airport David headed straight for the Vineyards. Once he got to wine country he drove along the Sonoma County country road passing miles and miles of neatly rowed vineyards until he came to the familiar landmark sign pointing the way to half a dozen of the local wineries. Among the family names David could see the familiar letters LOMBARDI VINEYARDS out of the corner of his eye. He turned off the highway and onto the secondary road that took him toward his grandparents' estate.

The Victorian Gothic structure was surrounded by more than five acres of perfectly manicured lawn with inlaid stone walkways lined with trimmed hedges, flowering bushes, and gushing fountains. The Sonoma Mountains made a picturesque background for the imposing structure with its multi-gabled rooftops and cathedral windows. Patty used to say it reminded her of *Mandalay House* from the 1940s movie *Rebecca* with Joan Fontaine and Lawrence Olivier.

David drove around to a side drive that led to the garages. There were several cars parked back here including Richard Wellington's town-car, Nanny's new salmon colored Imperial, and a couple of vehicles he didn't recognize.

He pulled up next to Patty's two-tone brown and cream Chrysler Cordoba and parked his Alpine. He hopped out and jogged up some stone steps to a porch... he entered a side door that led onto well worn faded Persian carpeting lying on a cool marble floor that ran half the length of the house. Going down the hallway he passed several junctures connecting to other rooms and corridors with spiral staircases.

David turned at a large intersection that led toward the front of the house. He passed more decorative archways with ornately hanging crystal chandeliers and walls filled with antique collector's paintings lighted by grand Victorian candelabras. He heard the chatter and laughter of his family in the distance before he found them gathered in the grand salon.

David entered the room noting that every person in the parlor was holding a glass of red wine. He walked straight to his grandmother for the first of his greetings. She laid down her wine glass and started to get up for a hug.

"Don't get up Honey...stay right where you are," David commanded.

"Oh-h-h," she said falling back to her seat as David embraced her, "I like to get up to hug my favorite grandson."

"Your only grandson," Sylvia added and everyone in the room laughed or grinned as David turned to his grandfather.

"Poppa John...my Poppa John...*dimmi a cosa stai pensando*...what are you thinking about?"

"*I'ma* think *dat'a I'ma* glad to see my grandson," he said in a very heavy Italian accent.

David leaned down to passionately hug and kiss his grandfather on the cheek and forehead."

"Um-m-m-ma, *thank'a* you my boy...my *grand'a son*... heh heh heh...*my grand'a* son!"

Patricia, Sylvia and Richard were just on the other side of the room sitting comfortably in antique Victorian period carved rosewood parlor chairs. There was also a somewhat elderly man and woman who were seated in a Victorian tete-a-tete conversation chair that shared a matching hand carved tea table holding a colorful plate filled with Italian biscuits and cookies. David did not recognize the couple.

"Poopsie!" Patty squealed with delight, "You're here...how delightful!"

David blew a kiss to his sister and parents then walked up to the older couple and said,

"Hi, I'm David," and he extended his hand for a shake.

Nanny said to David, "*Ti presento mio cugino Alfonso di primo grado.*"

"I'm your grandmother's first cousin...Alfonso...no handshake from me...I want a hug," the older guy said standing up. "I know who you are young man, I met you when you were about two years old," he said grasping David around the waist and kissing him on the ear.

"I just gathered that from Nanny," David's ear was still ringing from the kiss as he bent down to hug Alfonso's partner.

"This is Mary, she's my wife."

"Mary! Just like me," Nanny exclaimed from the other side of the room, "They're here from Providence, Rhode Island...you remember me telling you about Alfonso."

Alfonso broke into the conversation, "Yes, I own three liquor stores in Providence...I sell lots of your grandfather's wine. Everybody in Providence drinks Lombardi Champagne. My stores are very successful. I'm a very rich man...no *Mafioso*...everything's legal."

'I'll just bet it is' David thought as Patty handed her brother a glass of Lombardi's Beaujolais,

"Yes of course...I'm sorry I didn't recall you...that was a rough year for remembering things when we last met... if I'd been three or four years old instead of two...well that's a different story."

Everyone in the room laughed except for Richard who disliked small talk and inanities. He could enjoy a good joke, or even a pun or witticism...but this kind of conversation was shallow almost to the point of being absurd. He didn't like seeing his son interacting with Alfonso socially...and he especially didn't like the fact that Alfonso was really pushing the 'related cousin routine.'

"May I pour you some more wine Mary or Alfonso," Patty said graciously holding a crystal decanter of the ruby red liquid.

"No thanks Hon, I'm fine," Mary said.

"Sure!" Alfonso blustered, "Fill 'er up!"

"Questo vino è un omaggio del signore seduto là in fondo...mi cugino di secondo grado," Patty said as she filled Alfonso's glass.

Poppa John spoke up, *"No cugino di secondo grado... cugino terzo classe."*

Everybody laughed loudly except for Richard who didn't speak Italian and Alfonso who didn't like what he heard. Just at this point the Lombardi's chief male servant Leonardo walked into the room. He had worked for the Lombardis over the last 45 years and had watched Sylvia, Patricia and David grow up. He was much more than just a butler at the mansion...he was a cherished family member to both the Lombardis and the Wellingtons.

"The table's all set and Mary's ready with Holiday Wedding soup!" he announced to Nanny.

"Mary, Mary...how can that be?" Alfonso bellowed, "Mary's here with her husband Giovanni...and I'm here with my wife Mary...there can't be another Mary in this house."

Nanny chuckled at her cousin and said, "Oh yes there is another Mary...as a matter of fact there are two more! Mary Rubino is our cook and Mary Gaudio is the head housekeeper."

"Too many Marys," Alfonso shouted as everyone stood up to go into the dining room, "I'm getting confused."

Patty and David eyed each other both trying to stifle a laugh. Alfonso saw them grinning and said, "You kids go in first...everything for youth... it's all about youth. The young people we like to spoil."

Patty and David walked into the elegant foyer that led into the grand formal dining room. Nanny and Poppa directed Alfonso and his spouse to walk in front of them. Sylvia and Richard stayed behind.

"We'll be right there, Mom, just give me a minute," Sylvia said picking up her purse and feigning going through it as Nanny left the room.

"What did Patricia and Poppa John speak in Italian that made everybody laugh with the exception of Alfonso?" Richard asked.

"Oh, it was nothing much, dear," Sylvia answered as she took a handkerchief from her purse. "Patty said something to the effect that the wine she poured was courtesy of Poppa John and than she referred to Alfonso as being her Second cousin...that's when Poppa said that Alfonso wasn't a second cousin...he was *cugino terzo classe*...interpreted as a *third class* cousin."

Richard laughed this time as he and Sylvia walked toward the dining room.

* * *

David telephoned Hank very early Monday morning hoping to talk with him first thing. Hank answered the phone.

"I had a feeling you'd call first thing this morning," Hank said.

"I had a feeling you'd be there first thing in the morning. How are you feeling?"

"I feel great   probably because I had a great weekend thanks to you...and probably because I got back early enough for a good night's sleep. Did you go up to wine country and have dinner with your grandparents?"

"I did," David answered, "I went straight to the Vineyards after I dropped you off."

"Good," Hank said, "When will you be coming down to L.A. and visit me?"

David could feel his heart beat faster...he was truly excited to hear these words over the phone. He had to think quickly for an answer...he was ready to fly down to LAX tonight.

"I'm...I'm not sure...I hadn't thought about it," David said honestly.

"Think about it," Hank said, "Call me back tomorrow and let me know when you'll be here."

David laughed, "Okay, I'll think about it and call you back...but not tomorrow...I'll phone you on Wednesday or Thursday morning."

"Make it on Wednesday, I won't be here at the clinic on Thursday."

"Where will you be on Thursday," David asked.

"That depends on you, my handsome new friend."

"I understand," David said feeling more confident, "I'll phone you there at the clinic first thing Wednesday morning."

"Good," Hank said, "I have to go now...looking forward to your call on Wednesday...hope to see you on Thursday."

"Talk with you on Wednesday," and David hung up the phone.

* * *

CHAPTER SIX

During the months that followed, David and Hank enjoyed numerous rendezvous in Los Angeles, Santa Barbara, Catalina, and, of course, San Francisco. The relationship was satisfying for both men who were very involved with their lives respectively in Northern and Southern California, but who were grateful for the blissful trysts away from routine obligations in their hometowns. David's only regret had been that he had not found occasion to introduce Hank to Patricia. There always seemed to be an obstacle of scheduling in the active involvement of one or the other's busy lives.

The opportunity for them to meet finally arrived when the siblings cashed in on their graduation gift from Nanny and Poppa John. They were given a long promised trip to Italy, and they were thrilled. It was unfortunate that neither of the grandparents would be going along... but the "kids' would still have a good time on their visit," Nanny had said.

"Patricia's been abroad before and she can show her little brother the ropes."

Patricia and David were scheduled for their European trip to begin the day after Christmas. Their itinerary took them from San Francisco to Los Angeles where they would have a short lay-over then fly non-stop to London on Trans World Airlines. Their stop at LAX International would be just long enough for Hank to drive from his clinic in Huntington Beach for a quick introduction to Patricia and a bon-voyage drink.

* * *

Hank stood outside the gate as he watched Patty and David hurry down the boarding bridge to their Boeing 707. Their *layover* in Los Angeles had been one hour and fifteen minutes...just enough time to meet for farewell cocktails and see them board the plane for London. David had been very anxious to show off his beautiful sister to Hank. The introduction had gone splendidly. Patty had Hank charmed from the moment he saw her, and she did look lovely in her attractive *Norman Norell* camel skirt suit and belted jacket.

Patricia was always steady in her carriage and posture and *for the most part,* so was David. He usually had to make a conscious and disciplined effort to keep his composure in moments of excitement. He knew there were times when his eagerness or enthusiasm for a person, place or thing would overcome his equilibrium. It was sometimes difficult for him to keep from shouting or jumping with exuberance when he was encountering an incentive for jubilation...and those incentives seem to come frequently in his happy life.

The moment he and Patty sat down and buckled their first class seat belts he wanted to rejoice. This was his first expedition to Europe, and he felt sufficiently prepared for whatever would develop during his travels. He had his sophisticated sister (who had previously toured Europe)...he had packed everything he knew he would need for many months...he had thirty thousand dollars in traveler's checks...he was a healthy handsome American man of twenty-three years...*and* he had the passport to prove it.

"Passport!" he screamed over the take-off roar of the Boeing 707 engines.

"What's wrong Poopsie?" Patty asked as she watched her brother frantically dig through the pockets of his Pierre Cardin suit.

"My passport! I was sure I just had it? Where is it?" he said trying to control his voice.

Patty sat back relaxed in her seat, "Too late to worry about it now, Poopsie...we're in the air."

"Oh my God," David cried in near despair. "This cannot be happening."

"There, there Poopsie," Patty said as she maternally patted her brother's knee. "We'll do whatever we have to do when we reach Heathrow...there's always a solution."

Patty turned toward the window to watch LAX and the surrounding area shrink as their airplane rose higher and higher. David huddled in his seat, eyes closed with head resting in both hands. No one spoke as their craft made a gradual ascent turning high above the blue Pacific Ocean and the *somewhat* green San Gabriel mountains.

"May I offer you a beverage," the silence was broken by a stewardess who leaned over David's seat and spoke directly to Patty.

"Yes...please", Patty answered, "I would like a glass of champagne...*Lombardi* champagne if you have it...and a double gin Bloody Mary for my brother...he's just had somewhat of a shock."

"Oh my," said the stewardess with a sincerely concerned tone of voice. "Is there anything I can help with?"

to satisfy requirements for the special syllabus that Dr. Brooks devised for our study. She is brilliantly intelligent...speaks five languages fluently...and she is marvelously flamboyant."

"Who? Dr Brooks?" David interrupted.

"No Poopsie...you're not listening to me. Magda! Magda is brilliantly intelligent and flamboyant...Dr. Brooks doesn't speak any language except English...oh, she might know enough Spanish to order a burrito in a Mexican restaurant...but Magda speaks English, Italian, French, German and Russian!"

"Russian!" David echoed, "How did she learn Russian? That's a complex language to know."

"She speaks, reads and writes Russian fluently because it is her native language...she is a Russian Jew," Patty said.

David was intrigued at this point in the story. "How fascinating," David said, "I didn't remember you telling me that Magda was a Russian Jewess."

"Yes," Patty went on, "...and not only is she a Jew, she has experiences to tell about her family's persecution by the Nazis during the war. Her stories sound like something from *The Diary of Anne Frank.* Magda and her sister Sonja had to spend literally days hiding under floor boards while they waited for the enemy to vacate their aunt's house somewhere in Czechoslovakia. She's gone through inconceivably incredible experiences in her life time."

"How old is she?" David asked.

"Who knows," Patty shrugged her shoulders, "She alluded to being somewhere around thirty eight...I suspect she's older...but it doesn't matter...Magda is ageless...I never met a person quite like her. You'll find out for yourself, Poopsie ...she's difficult to describe."

"Is she pretty?" David asked.

"Oh yes...and much more...she's absolutely seductive...she has a magnetism that captivates everyone she meets. People always think she's a famous stage or screen star...I've been with her when she was mistaken for Maggie Smith...I think she looks more like Greer Garson in Mrs. Miniver. You'll be fascinated by her, Poopsie..."

Patty was interrupted by the stewardess who appeared with a fresh drink for David. She took the empty glass and put it on her serving tray which also held a small leather folding case.

"Oh," she said handing the case to David, "By the way, Mr. Wellington, I think we found something that belongs to you."

"My passport!" David yelled out as if he were going to cry, "Where did you find it?"

"I didn't find it," the stewardess said as she stepped back and pointed down the aisle.

"It was the lady in the last row in First Class...she sighted it next to her foot...apparently it slid back a few rows on our take-off."

David stretched his head over the aisle and looked back at a sweet little lady who was waving to him...she wore an old fashioned floral hat and had a very happy smile on her face. David blew a kiss to her and turned back to the stewardess who was leaning over to refill Patty's champagne glass.

"Please," David stated, "Give that sweet little lady my eternal thanks."

"I certainly will," said the stewardess cheerfully bouncing down the aisle.

David picked up his glass and turned to his sister who was prepared to clink glasses for another toast.

"Cheers, Poopsie...here's to our fabulous trip!"

* * *

David hadn't realized that the ten and one half hour flight would take such a toll on his body. Once they landed at Heathrow Airport and were walking through Customs, the jet-lag hit him... all he could think of was a warm shower and nice clean sheets in which to rest his nagging body. Everything around him seemed to take on the unreality of a dream.

He hardly noticed how efficiently they had passed through Customs as his passport was stamped for the first time. Thankfully, Patty seemed to have taken the lead and did all the talking as she artfully guided them through the procedures. David just followed like a stooge...dumbfounded...tired...and aching all over.

"My body is in distress," he heard himself say, "My body is waving white flags...it's surrendering...it wants to give up...I feel like I've been gravely wounded."

"You be okay Poopsie," he heard his sister say, "Just have a little courage...don't give up...you'll feel fabulous again in the morning."

"Oh-h-h..." he groaned carrying his luggage in both hands, "I wish it were morning now."

Patty didn't respond...she had stopped walking, dropped her luggage and was hugging an attractive woman with flaming red hair. All David could think of was '*The Queen of Technicolor*' Miss Rhonda Fleming.

"Dah-h-ling Patricia...you're more beautiful than ever I could have remembered. Welcome...welcome back to London" she said in an accent that sounded like Eva Gabor.

"Magda...what a surprise! What are you doing here...I thought you'd meet us at the hotel?" Patty said.

"Well dah-ling I couldn't remember if you were staying at the Kensington or the May Fair..." Magda said using a more British tone, "You know I never pay attention to details."

Patty snickered and said "We decided to act like Americans and stay at the Hilton."

The two beautiful ladies laughed heartily and embraced each other for what seemed like an hour to David. Magda broke from her hug and looked directly at him.

"Well...well..I know who this must be," said Magda completely letting go her grasp on Patty.

"You must be David," Magda declared as she held out both arms and moved toward him.

David gathered all his composure to respond to his greeter who now reminded him more of Rosalind Russell in the film *Auntie Mame*.

"Magda...I'm truly honored to meet you in person."

As David and Magda hugged, she looked over her shoulder at Patty and said, "Patricia dahling...you didn't tell me your brother was so...so...so..."

"Charming?" Patty said.

"Yes dahling," Magda continued, "So charming...and handsome...and virile...and so American...I love it!"

"Stop it...you'll give him a swelled head," Patty said picking up her luggage. "I'm delighted that you came out to the airport to greet us...as I said we weren't expecting to see you before were arrived at the hotel."

"We do have time for a welcome cocktail here at the airport," Magda said taking the smallest of Patty's bags.

"Just a quick one...or two... before Sonja chauffeurs us to the Mercedes dealer downtown."

'*Oh God...please don't let this be happening now...I just want to go to sleep.*' David thought to himself.

"Sonja has come with you to the airport? Where is she?" Patty asked in a puzzled voice.

"Yes, dahling, Sonja is here," Magda said, "She's double parked right outside the door."

David jumped in "Oh...I would feel very uncomfortable having a drink when your sister is parked outside waiting for us."

"Yes, Poopsie," Patty agreed, "We can't just leave Sonja parked outside waiting for us while we celebrate without her."

"I stand corrected,' Magda said lightheartedly as she breezed toward an exit that she designated with a theatrical wave of her hand. "Poor Sonja is just puffing on cigarettes sitting in the car waiting for us...follow me children."

She was shorter than Patty...but somehow Magda seemed to make up the difference in height with her bodacious figure and her conspicuous posture. She was wearing an eye-catching tweed coat with billows of silver fox fur flowing at the neck, arms and hem. Her brilliant red hair cascaded over the back of her coat like a series of crimson waterfalls. Yes... David had now finally met Magda...and he knew that she was going to be a riotous tornado of entertainment.

* * *

Sonja was much more modest and sedate than David would have expected. She was simply beautiful and demure sitting behind the driver's wheel of the 1968

Humber Super Snipe sedan. He got a really good glimpse of her as he crawled into the back seat after depositing luggage in the trunk, and he could see that she was absolutely stunning.

"Salutations and many greetings," Sonja said in a very British accent, "I'm Sonja...Magda's sister...and I'm here for your pleasure," as she offered her hand to David over the front seat of the vehicle.

"I'm David," he answered taking her hand to his lips, "...and I'm thrilled to meet you."

"Not so fast, please," Magda said as she pushed her way into the back seat with David, "I've already claimed him and now I catch him kissing my sister's hand. It's not fair."

"Who said anything about being fair," Sonja laughed, "You weren't here to chaperone us...what can you expect?"

Patty slid into the front seat with Sonja and said, "I won't have you girls fighting over my little brother...just flip a coin and get it over with."

Patty and Sonja hugged and giggled...but Magda, *noticeably*, did not laugh.

David had to fight to stay awake on the drive into downtown London. He had no concept of the time of day, and he didn't really care...he only wanted sleep. The three women kept talking and chattering. '*Yak, yak, yak,*' thought David, 'God please let them *shut up* for just five minutes.'

Magda kept her jewelry adorned hand on David's knee through most of the ride...he was almost past the point of being *charming*...it was a great effort on his part to remain cordial... but fortunately his genteel manners prevailed.

"David," Magda caused David to pay attention, "David...you're nodding to sleep. Us girls didn't mean to bore you."

"He's not bored," Patty interceded, "He had no rest on the plane, and I'm afraid the jet lag is catching up with him."

"No...it's not catching up," David said with his eyes closed, "It's completely over taken my body, mind and soul."

"We're almost at the car dealer," said Sonja encouragingly, "I am certain that you shall be able to wait comfortably for a bit while your sister takes care of the dreary business."

"Thank God," David said aloud as he rolled his eyes to the back of his exhausted head.

"Don't be too thankful just yet, Poopsie...you'll have to stay alert long enough to drive us to the hotel...I'm certainly not prepared to drive in London traffic on the left side of the road."

"All right," David said with a resigned sigh, "I'll get us to the hotel...but then I'm going to sleep for at least twenty four hours."

"David...David," Magda lamented, "Don't you want to 'break bread' with us tonight somewhere *special*...or at least have a cocktail to help you sleep?"

"Not this day Magda...we have weeks ahead to party and play...but right now it's imperative that my body gets rest."

"I have a suggestion," said Sonja cheerfully, "Why don't I drive you lovely children directly to your hotel... Patricia, you don't have a specific appointment to claim your new vehicle...I'll be happy to take you there tomorrow...or whenever you wish."

"To the hotel it shall be," said Patty turning around to look at her brother's face.

David's eyes were closed, but he wasn't asleep. He was thinking about how much he was going to love his new friend...*and his savior from exhaustion*... Sonja.

* * *

David made good on his promise to sleep for twenty four hours. He was awakened by the jangle of an old fashioned porcelain telephone with a delft blue pattern and a rotary style plate.

"Hello," he said sleepily blinking his eyes on and off while answering the call.

"It's your sister Poopsie...do you have any idea of the time?"

"No," he answered dreamily as he stretched, "and I don't exactly know where I am or why I'm here...where are you calling from?"

"You, my dear, are at the London Hilton in a suite on the twenty-second floor...it's past seven P.M., that's in the evening, and I am in the suite right next door to yours. Actually, it's a very cozy arrangement. If you get up and open the door you'll find yourself in a private alcove shared by three royally grand suites...I don't think any one is occupying the third set of accommodations...but it doesn't matter...I have on a slip."

"Patricia, my lovely sister," David said, "I have no intention of moving my body from this bed for at least fifteen minutes...no...make that ten minutes...my body has been accumulating fluid for the last twenty four hours and when I do arise in ten minutes I'm going to take a ten minute piss."

Patricia laughed and said, "Okay, Poopsie...go take your piss and when you're finished, clean yourself up and get dressed for dinner. Magda and Sonya will be picking us up around eight thirty to take us somewhere special."

"Ugh," David responded "Eight thirty...won't that be a little late for dinner by the time we get to where we're going?"

"Get used to it Poopsie...this is London... no one dines in London before ten p.m....and besides, we need to get downstairs pronto."

"Why?" David asked. What do we need to do downstairs?"

"Poopsie," Patty said in a joyous voice, "I want to show you the new Mercedes...it's parked in the garage underneath the hotel."

"Wow," David said, "You've been a busy lady while I've been sleeping."

"Yes, indeed," Patty said proudly, "You're going to love the car...better get dressed, Poopsie, so we'll have time to look it over before the girls get here."

"How dressed do I need to be," David asked, "Do you know where we're going?"

"It's some fun place called the *Elizabethan* where we sit around a big table like in the times of Henry VIII. We'll eat fowl and other meat with our fingers and throw the bones over our shoulders onto the floor."

"Sounds charming," David said, "I'd better wear a raincoat with a big baby bib."

Patty laughed again, "Sonya said something about the dinner guests at the restaurant select a King and Queen from the group...and you know Magda...she'll have to be the Queen...better wear your tux, Poopsie...

there's a good chance you'll be playing the role of a King tonight."

Patty could hear David groaning loudly as she hung up the telephone.

* * *

Patty and David's acquaintance with *The Elizabethan* would be their first, and last experience at the restaurant... but the evening turned out to be a truckload of fun.

Sonja, who was driving, arrived at the hotel slightly tipsy from earlier cocktails she had with Magda. By the time the four of them polished off a few more at the Hilton bar...they were absolutely drunk...and no one was the least bit apologetic about being intoxicated.

When they finally arrived at the restaurant they stumbled down a wooden stairway that led to a great dining hall. There were two oversized blazing fireplaces on each side of the great room. In the center was a massive rustic table that seated twenty people... sixteen of the chairs were already occupied. It was quite evident that the other patrons had been waiting for the arrival of these last four guests because Sonja, Magda, Patty and David sat down to rowdy shouts and applause.

"Apparently," Patty said in her deep cool voice, "We're fashionably late."

A stout square shaped attendant dressed in medieval apparel materialized and cleared his throat heavily. "Lords and Ladies...welcome to *the Elizabethan*. Before we begin the feast, it is customary to select a King... this person will not only be your King for this evening... but he will also be the spokesperson to give approval... or disapproval of the cookery and serviceableness throughout the evening."

"Serviceableness? David asked rhetorically. "Well... such an erudite word coming from a *peasant.*"

Several of the dining guests giggled at David's comment as the attendant continued with his extravagant spiel,

"May we please commence with ladies offering their nominations for our King," the server continued trying to ignore David's comments.

Magda took over shouting, "Yes dah-h-ling...it's abundantly obvious that David is our King! He is the most debonair of all the men at this table...and besides... he's from America! Every colonial should have an opportunity to be King of England for at least one night."

Patty jumped in, "I'm not certain that I completely understand your line of reasoning...but I second the nomination and ask everyone to toast my brother David as your handsome King for our festivities tonight."

She raised her wine filled chalice and said, "Here's to King David...long live the King!"

Eager to commence with the banquet, every guest at the table responded with a raised chalice as they chanted "Long live King David...Long live the King!"

The attendant made no effort to hide his disapproving rolling eyes, "Very well," he snorted, "Long live the King... might I now ask the King if we may proceed with the feast?" he said in a rankled voice.

David, who had just finished draining his chalice answered, "Just remember Beau Brummel...it's King David to you...and before you begin the dinner...more wine for everybody!"

Some of the other guests applauded loudly while two or three shouted "Long live the King!"

The attendant headed toward what was obviously the kitchen as he passed a procession of servers carrying more wine and steaming hot plates of food. He was shaking his head at the servants and mumbled, "This is going to be a very long evening."

The servers began refilling the goblets and Sonja helped herself to steaming cabbage from one of the plates, "I am glad that bit of business is over."

"It's not over yet," Magda whipped back, "We still haven't selected the Queen..."

A very heavy set man wearing a three piece business suit across the table said in a mid-western American accent, "I think that business is already settled, *maam*, it's up to the King to pick his queen...and you're already sitting on the King's right hand side."

For a moment Magda smiled broadly at the heavy man, but her grin quickly diminished when Sonja could be heard saying, "Doesn't the Queen sit to the King's left... actually?"

"Oh shut up, Sonja," Magda snapped, "It's been decided...I am the queen! Here's to the Queen...long live the queen!"

"Long live the Queen," said the heavy set man admiringly as he lifted his chalice and the much younger girl he was escorting did the same.

Unfortunately, no one else at the table was paying attention to the coronation of 'Queen Magda.' The rest of the guests were too involved in eating and drinking to reaffirm their latest monarch.

The servers from the kitchen continued the parade of steaming bowls and plates of food, new silverware, glasses, and condiments. It seemed to David that everything being served was extraordinarily ordinary. Boiled potatoes...more boiled cabbage...peas and carrots...slices of what appeared to be canned ham...

overdone roasted chicken with no flavor...some kind of bland porridge made of oats or barley...hard tasteless bread with a particularly tough crust.

"This is more like food you'd expect to find in a high school cafeteria," he said as an aside to Patty.

"Good analogy, Poopsie," Patty whispered back, "...but we're not necessarily here for the cuisine...we're here to have a good time with our friends."

Patty always had a sobering way of putting things into perspective for David. He suddenly didn't care about the food...he made up his mind to have fun...after all, he was already hammered.

"More wine!" he shouted above the noise... "More wine for everybody!"

The diners sitting at the table were oblivious to David's command...they were all guzzling from their own chalices and chatting while busily tossing chicken bones over their shoulders. Fortunately, the floor was made of dark polished concrete and there were several boys dressed as pages constantly scooping up the discards with brooms and brush pans.

A pretty young girl dressed in a peasant's gown with laced bodice brought a large tray of some kind of meat, and a vessel containing gravy. She offered some of the contents to David who inquired "What is this that you're serving to your King?"

"This is," she stated proudly, "Lamb...with lovely brown gravy to accompany it...we hope it pleases his majesty."

"And his majesty's Queen," Sonja added to assuage Magda who put on a tolerant smile to show her appreciation for being recognized as a monarch.

The original attendant of the feast reappeared for the first time since his portentous departure to the kitchen. "Is his majesty's dining going well?" he asked timidly.

"David slammed down his chalice and shouted for all to hear, "The King is not fond of this lamb fat covered in shit sauce!"

There was an immediate and dead silence at the large table which Magda broke after a short pause, "It's not the lamb fat I mind so much as it is the shit sauce."

Every person at the table howled with ruckus laughter and no one laughed as hard as David. His stomach hurt more than anytime in his life, and he had to remove himself from the table and sit on the staircase to control his cachinnate outburst of hilarity.

"I'll bring out the cook, immediately," said the flustered attendant as he scurried back to the kitchen.

Patty, Sonja, and Magda were still laughing uproariously creating pandemonium at their end of the table. The revelry persisted until the cook finally appeared. He was very somber in demeanor, and also very big and menacingly serious. "The King has a comment regarding tonight's feast?"

The entire table fell silent again as all attention turned toward David who was still sitting on the wooden stairs holding his stomach.

Without flinching but staring right at the man David laughed and roared, "I have no comment, just a command; *off with the cook's balls!*"

Patty broke the dead silence in a coquettish voice saying, "Poopsie...don't you think that castration is a bit too severe even if the food is hideous?"

"Then off with his head!" David commended, "That way he won't be able to think about the disposition of his discarded testes."

Everyone in the room laughed robustly...except the cook who retreated to the kitchen mumbling obscenities to himself. Patty, Magda and Sonja raised their chalices and shouted in unison "Long live King David...Long live the King".

* * *

CHAPTER SEVEN

Patty and David's sojourn in London proved to escalate in amusement and festive conviviality with each day that passed. Magda and Sonja arranged countless entertaining lunches, dinners and receptions to celebrate the visitation of their two American friends. Each day was like a joyous holiday crammed with fun and enthusiasm...and every day ended with eagerness and an appetite for the next day to come.

Sonja was not always able to join Magda and her American friends...she had daytime responsibilities to established publishing companies in the United Kingdom. She was well known in London as a top literary agent who marketed works of mostly established authors to various book publishers. Many of these organizations maintained a strict policy of "no unsolicited manuscripts...and it was Sonja's job to intercede on behalf of her clients.

Tonight, however, it was Sonja's turn to provide the evening's entertainment and dining for her American associates, and she felt confident that Patty and David would approve of her choice in both categories. On this particular evening Sonja was looking forward to treating the group to the theatre and a late night supper.

She had obtained tickets to one of London's most iconic and longest running theatrical productions, *The Mousetrap,* Agatha Christie's intriguing tale of murder and suspense. In all the years she had lived in London, Sonja had never seen the play and was looking forward to finally enjoying it with her friends.

Sonja had also made late dining reservations at the *Kalamaras Greek Restaurant* which was also located in the West End of London. She had eaten there with clients, and she'd had some memorable dates with interesting beaus who had wooed her in the three years since her divorce.

The restaurant had actually been opened for the last four years and was already famous for feeding patrons such as Mick Jagger, Peter Sellers, Dusty Springfield and even Telly Savalas. Sonja couldn't guarantee that there would be any famous entertainers dining at *Kalamara'sTavern* tonight...but she could guarantee that everyone would love the food and the trip to *Notting Hill.*

* * *

The play produced much fun and laughter that the author had *not* intended...the main catalyst was the pint of vodka Magda had brought in a sterling cask hidden in her purse. The four friends giggled and talked through the entire play disturbing everyone sitting anywhere nearby in the loge.

The last scene of the *Mousetrap* was finally over and the quartet of disrupters led by Magda gathered their coats and stood up to leave. A very distinguished older gentleman who had been seated behind the constant interruption from the assembly sitting in front him stood and directed his comment toward Sonja.

"Let us hope that the next time the Americans attend our theatre that they will behave themselves," he said in a slightly reproachful tone of voice.

Applying her most British accent Sonja replied, "I do beg your pardon...I certainly am not an American."

The gentleman bowed his head in a gesture of submission and responded by saying "It is I who beg for your pardon."

Patty, David and Magda laughed clamorously as they exited the theatre. They were all having a wonderful time together in spite of the harshly cold air that greeted them as they walked along the Bayswater avenue. Patty and Magda got into the backseat of their car and huddled together for warmth...David jumped into the passenger side next to Sonja.

"Br-r-r-r," David said, "Turn on the heat please."

"Yes dahling," Magda chimed in, "The heat...I think it's more frigid in here than it is outside."

Patty let out a frozen laugh and said, "I can't wait to get to the restaurant."

"Yes-s-s," Magda and David agreed in unison.

"Oh dear," Sonja whined as she began driving.

"What is it dear?" Magda asked with an anxious detonation in her voice.

"I can never remember quite the best way to negotiate these silly streets," Sonja replied.

"Look," David offered pointing to a sign, "It says Way Out...or does it mean as we say in Haight Ashbury *'far out'*?"

"Either way," Sonja said as she made a very sharp u-turn that took the car over a sidewalk and in the opposite direction, "We're definitely not on the proper course."

Sonja stepped on the gas and headed up the street at an unnerving speed. She came to an intersection and made a squealing right hand turn up another street that had no visible signs of nightlife.

"Sonja, dahling," Magda offered, "I still don't believe you're going the correct direction."

"Oh-h-h," Sonja complained, "This is maddening."

David felt a little uneasy with the speed and Sonya's frantic driving. He wanted to tell her to pull over or at least slow down. With every wrong turn she became more agitated and continued to blunder through the Bayswater neighborhood. She was just short of losing control of both her composure and the car.

"Oh look," Sonja cried out in a high pitch, "We're on a circle."

"That is not a circle," Magda corrected her, "It's a roundabout, and you are going the wrong way on it."

"What is the difference between a roundabout and a circle?" David asked nervously grabbing his seat tightly.

"It's too complicated to explain right now dahling," Magda replied, "Just suffice it to say that at the moment Sonja is driving like a wild woman from Borneo."

Sonja went back down the street they had just driven up...and she resumed her erratic driving, partially on and partially off the sidewalk, trying to make up her mind which direction to take.

"Oh God, no," she said as she finally pulled over and stopped with the Humber sitting half on the sidewalk and half on the street.

"What's wrong Sonja?" Patty asked innocently having been oblivious to their close call with death.

"Bloody bobbies," Sonja stated in a resigned tone. "Roll down your window please David...he wants to speak."

David rolled down his window on the passenger side and said to a smiling face "Good evening, constable."

"Yes," the bobby answered, "A good evening to you sir...you are American are you not?"

"Yes, sir," David answered, "My sister Patricia and I are visiting your wonderful country and we're being escorted by two beautiful British subjects." David nodded first to Patty, then indicated Magda and Sonja.

"Ah yes," said the bobby as he stuck his head further through the opened window, "The driver."

He went on, "You realize...of course madam...that you are driving rather poorly this evening."

"Yes," Sonja said slumping back in the driver's seat, "I'm afraid I've lost my direction."

"I see," said the bobby tolerantly, "Exactly where would you like to take your American friends?"

"We are trying to find our way to Kalamara's Tavern," Sonja said.

"You are actually not far from your destination," he said calmly. "Please *carefully* make a turn and drive to the roundabout...take the second exit and you will be on course to the restaurant...and please be more mindful of your driving."

"Yes...thank you," Sonja said starting the car and recapturing her composure.

"Thankfully there's no traffic," Patty commented as the car proceeded at a safe pace. "David, how did you know to refer to him as constable? I would have addressed him as 'officer'...sir."

"Well...I wasn't going to call him 'bobby' which is British slang. It's obvious he carries a truncheon...the officer is unmistakably from London, England where British officers are known as constables."

"Sonja...I told you it was a roundabout and not a circle," Magda said.

David said, "Magda...nobody likes to hear the words '*I told you so*'...and..." he went on... "I'm beginning to believe that there's not much difference between a roundabout and a circle."

"I'll explain all about it during our supper," Magda said.

* * *

The Kalamaras restaurant was nestled in a little corner of Bayswater and David thought the ambience and decor to be reminiscent of the Savoy Tivoli in San Francisco. The lighting was very dim and the wide plank wooden floors matched the oaken table and chairs that were cleverly arranged to maximize privacy. The enticing smells and odors wafting around the large room made David realize his intense hunger level.

Their group of four was escorted to a large table for six...which turned out to be ideal with the two extra chairs providing space to drape their bulky coats. The headwaiter assisted Patty and Magda with their seats and David pulled out a chair for Sonja.

Magda, who was seated directly across from David leaned across the table, showing off her plummeting décolletage, and said, "A great many celebrities are known to come here regularly."

Sonja, who was seated next to David, said "I think we have some celebrities arriving now," as she pointed toward the side window where a limousine had just driven up. "I wonder who it might be."

Then, as the waiter lighted the one candle lamp at their table, and distributed menus, Sonja said "We'll have one bottle of red and one bottle of white to start with, please."

"May I suggest *Makedonikos* for both bottles," the waiter said.

"No," Sonja averred, "*Damakinos* for the red and *Dogmatikos* for the white."

"Excellent choices, madam," said the waiter.

As she looked across the table and past her brother and Sonja's shoulders Patty said, "I think we know the identities of the celebrities that just arrived in the limousine."

"Who is it?" David asked in a whisper.

Magda looked up from her menu and announced in a bored tone, "It looks like Ringo Starr and John Lennon."

"Is George with them?" David asked eagerly.

Patty, who was still watching while the two artists were being seated at a remote table, shook her head and murmured "Uh, uh...it's only John and Ringo."

"How disappointing," David said, "I had hoped to see George Harrison in person."

Patty explained to Magda and Sonja, "Everyone in America has a favorite from the *Fabulous* Four...I would liked to have seen Paul McCartney."

"I think Paul is the cutest of the four," agreed Sonja.

"I don't think any of them is particularly 'cute'," said Magda. Then turning her full attention to David she fawned "But David...David is extraordinarily handsome... David is sexy."

"You've had too much to drink Magda...you'd best slow down on the wine," Sonja said reaching across the table as she moved the bottle of white wine away from Magda.

Magda grabbed the bottle of red that was easily within her reach and poured a generous glass for herself, "David is sexy," Magda continued, "He makes me secrete."

Sonja, elbows on the table, put her head in her hands and grimaced, "Oh, God, here we go."

Patty looked on in great amusement and sipped her wine. She was very interested in how David would handle the situation. She turned her head, sat back in her chair and looked at Magda sitting next to her.

"David and I are going to make wildly passionate love together...not once...not twice...but over and over again until he falls completely in love with me."

Patty and Sonja were now both completely attentive to the conversation.

"No...we are not going to make love together," David said calmly.

"Why not dahling," Magda demanded. "I want one reason, just one reason that we will not make love."

"I'm homosexual," he said in a normal tone of voice.

Magda glanced at Patricia, who pretended to yawn, then turned back to glare at David.

"I don't believe you!" Magda declared.

"It's true, Magda," Patty intervened, "My little brother David is as queer as a three dollar bill."

Magda's jaw dropped almost to the rim of the glass that was sitting before her, "I simply don't believe it."

"Oh you can believe it Magda...David is homosexual...I knew it when he was just three years old. He was a little princess even back then. I remember well that we had gone to see *King Kong* with our parents...just before we went to bed that night, David had one his first homosexual *episodes* with our father."

"Oh no, "David protested, "You're not going to tell that story are you?"

Patty went on, "He...David that is...had been told it was time for bed...and our father offered to carry him on his shoulders...I remember it like it happened yesterday...David ran to our father and begged... 'Please daddy, pretend that you're the big gorilla and I'm the lady with the long blond hair hanging down, and you carry me off to the jungle'."

"How embarrassing," David said as he covered his eyes with one hand.

"What did your father say?" Sonja asked curiously.

Patty went on, "Our father picked David up and growled like a gorilla and tickled David's tummy with his nose...I'm not certain of everything that transpired when they got to David's bedroom...but I presume that my father put his son to bed and listened to his prayers."

"That doesn't make David a homosexual," Magda protested.

Patty proclaimed a bit too loudly, "He's always been queer for his own sex...we grew up together...we know everything about each other. I love my brother more than my own life...but he is definitively a homosexual!"

"Here, here," came a shout from one of the tables nearby, and someone clinked his glass with a utensil, and several other people in the restaurant joined in clinking their glasses.

"Here here," Sonja said as she clinked her water glass with a spoon.

Magda sneered, "Oh shut up Sonja."

* * *

CHAPTER EIGHT

The London trip turned out to be more fun for both Patricia and her brother David than ever they had envisioned. Every day, every night was filled with escapades and noteworthy adventures. David particularly relished his experiences now that the pressure from Magda's sexual attentions had abated... or at least somewhat *de-escalated.*

Magda still continued to dote on David with her preponderance of attention directed toward him. He knew she was attracted to him, and his best defense was to treat her equally to Patty and Sonja. He played the role of male escort to all three ladies...assisting them by opening doors, helping them with their coats, pulling out their chairs to be seated...and appositely commenting on their choice of clothing and jewelry.

The jovial quartet of friends energetically bounced through a sequence of museums, shops, boutiques, famous landmarks and *restaurants* during the day... and enjoyed classical concerts, theatrical productions, pubs, bars and *restaurants* at night. There seemed to be no end to the delights that London provided for their entertainment week after week. The city seemed to be theirs exclusively. They explored Soho, Carnaby

Street, Chelsea and Kings Road. Delectable divergence and indulgence gratified them day after day, night after night...until David got sick.

He came down with symptoms and infirmities that would persist on and off for weeks to come. The first malady was a rash...a nasty rash that covered most of his body. The Mayfair physician that attended him in the hotel surmised it had been brought on by the enormous amounts of oysters that David had consumed at *Wheeler's* seafood restaurant the night before.

The oysters were fresh from Scotland and as delicious as David had ever tasted. They were not as large as Pacific oysters but every bit as flavorful as Chesapeake oysters. The ladies in his group were not as disposed toward the oysters, but had their sights on other seafood dishes such as Dover sole, crab bisque, fresh sea bass, scallops and smoked haddock.

Patty was the only other person at the table to sample the oysters...she had a half dozen as an appetizer. David had a half dozen *six* times over...a grand total of thirty six oysters. Sonja and especially Magda were made uneasy with the way David was eagerly swallowing them down.

"Too many oysters cannot be so good for you," Magda cautioned.

"Don't worry about David," Patty defended her brother, "I've watched him swill down huge amounts of massive oysters for hours at a time at *The Tides* in Bodega Bay."

"Where is Bodega Bay," Sonja asked. "Is it off the Pacific Ocean somewhere near San Francisco?"

"Yes," Patty answered, "About sixty miles north of the city."

David stopped eating long enough to ask, "Did you ever see Alfred Hitchcock's The Birds?"

"Of course, dear," Sonja answered, "It's one of Hitchcock's best...and very unsettling."

Patty picked up the conversation because David was too busy squeezing lemon on another of his freshly shucked oysters. "*The Tides* is the restaurant where some of the citizens took refuge during a seagull attack in the movie. It has become quite well known since that film came out. Our grandparents on both sides of the family are from the same county in Sonoma...we've been going to *The Tides* since we children...long before the movie made the restaurant famous."

"You and David are very blessed being from such a beautiful place in the world," Sonja said.

"Oh yes, we are blessed. We've covered much of that gorgeous area on horseback."

"You like to ride?" Sonya asked.

"Like to ride?" David joined in, "She's a master at handling horses! She is the personal owner of the best known stallion in Sonoma County. His name is Majestic Genius, her twenty-first birthday present from Poppa John. Nobody else can even get near that spirited steed."

"That's not quite true, Poopsie, You know that Majestic also adores you, and you've exercised him and even assisted in breeding other horses in the county when I wasn't there."

"Yeah...he'll let me handle him, but I sure can't ride him the way you do."

"Your sister is a wonderful equestrian...I know... we've been riding in Hyde Park," Magda interjected.

"She's the best!" David avowed, "Everyone in the county has watched her gallop and jump Majestic all up and down the Sonoma Coast...I know...I've plodded along on several different American Saddle horses we have in the stables."

"Oh, that settles it, we must all go riding in Hyde Park one of these days soon before you depart from London," Sonya said with finality.

David had finished his sixth round of oysters when Magda said in a startled voice, "Dahling David, your scratching your arm as though it belongs to someone else!"

"I know," David answered unalarmed, "It's just that it itches." He rolled up the sleeve of his shirt and continued to scratch.

"Oh dear," said Magda, "I hope this compulsive scraping is not the result of an allergic reaction to the oysters."

"I don't believe so, Magda," David answered. "I've never had a reaction to shellfish during my entire lifetime."

* * *

David's rash cleared almost immediately after the doctor gave him a big shot of cortisone...however just a few days later David was annoyed with a light but chronic cough. It was especially annoying because he was unable to smoke. He felt lost not enjoying a cigarette during the evening hours of cocktails or promptly after supper.

Patty was concerned about her brother. Magda and Sonja didn't seem to realize that David uncomfortably was not up to his usual speed...but Patty knew her little brother all too well. She knew that his immunity system was working overtime. She also knew that his physical resistance had been lowered following the outbreak of rash.

* * *

The quartet of friends experienced a strenuous day at the *Tate* where Magda was one of the museum's star curators. She had arranged for them to participate in a much anticipated interactive exhibition... *Bodymotionspacethings*...by the American artist Robert Morris. The London Times and the BBC had heightened the excitement of the exhibition which catered to large crowds of enthusiastic art lovers.

To be fully enjoyed the exhibit required physical participation of those who came to *experience* it. The properties of the exhibit were massive and incorporated platforms, walls, tunnels, ramps, rollers and dangling ropes. The materials included everything imaginable such as stone, steel, wood and aluminum. It was an exuberant escapade for everyone who ventured to explore this unique work of art in Turbine Hall of the Tate Museum.

It was especially an exceptional trip for the four friends. Sonya had procured psilocybin for an enhanced *trip* to the Robert Morris' exhibition. She gave Patty, Magda, and David a large capsule and had each take it with a mimosa immediately during breakfast at the Hilton.

"These look a lot like the ginseng tablets we take with our vitamins," David said swallowing his down with a gluttonous gulp of mimosa as Patty winced at her brother's lack of table manners.

"Do you take magic mushrooms in America?" Sonja asked taking her capsule with an intentionally reserved sip from her drink."

"We do psychedelics in moderation," Patty answered. "The students at San Jose State would call these capsules *shrooms.* I've not seen it in such a civilized form before this morning...usually we eat them fresh or dried in their natural form."

"Fresh?" Sonja asked in wonderment, "Where do you get them fresh?"

"The best place is our Granddad's farm...there is a large pasture next to his apple orchard where the mushrooms are at their peak late in February and early March toward the end of the rainy season in California. David and I have taken friends from school there to hunt for *shrooms* under the pretext of fishing. The pasture is in an isolated spot and we've been there when the grass and surrounding ground was covered with mushrooms."

David added to the story, "Last year when it was drizzling we went out with fishing poles with two of our friends...and I remember Vicky fell in the water when we crossed the swollen stream."

Patty laughed, "Yes...I remember...we laughed for hours that day. Fortunately we had the foresight to bring towels and an extra set of dry clothes in the Jeep Cherokee...I'll never forget the scene of Vicky standing butt naked drying herself behind the jeep."

"Oh, oh," David interrupted, "I think the magic mushroom that Sonja gave me has already begun to kick in."

That day at the Tate Museum was one of the most memorable in the lives of David, Patricia, Sonja and Magda. David especially tripped out on Robert Morris' experiential exhibit when he saw the bigger than life photograph of the artist with a beard and mustache wearing a black Nazi helmet, dark glasses, and heavy chains hanging around his steel collared neck down a buff naked torso. It was one of the most provocative portraits David had ever seen. He had first seen the picture in the publication *Artforum* and would never forget the image.

The actual exhibit was an overpowering deluge of surfaces that splashed, swirled and gushed around them. Substantially enhanced by the psilocybin, the entire sculpture gallery of the Tate became a psychedelic experience within itself. This was a living, breathing, manifestation of textured cubes and ramps that shimmered and rippled. David warped, *morphed* and melted into an environment created by an artistic genius...even his beloved sister and friends became an intricate part of the adventurous happening...their every movement vibrated in a sensational psychedelic phenomenon.

When they left the museum that afternoon David had only one thought. "We've must go back and do it again before we leave London."

Unfortunately, David's wish to re-experience Robert Morris' *Bodymotionspacethings* never transpired. Magda announced at tea just two days after their visit that the interactive exhibition had closed. Apparently the Board of Trustees at the Tate had decided that the public's response was "unexpectedly and overly too enthusiastic". It had been the first time in the museum's history that the viewers were permitted to interact physically with an art work...and it could quite possibly be the last.

"You don't think that our over exuberant participation had anything to do with the board's decision to shut down the exhibit...do you?" Patty had asked Magda during the late afternoon tea.

"I don't know dahling Patricia...it may well have been...I don't care...I don't think that we were the only persons to be high on something other than a seesaw...I'm just glad we were able to participate and have a splendid day. I sent Robert Morris a personal note with flowers from all of us thanking him for our delightful adventure."

Magda's connection with the Tate Museum also afforded Patty and David the opportunity to view Andy Warhol's tribute to Marilyn Monroe which was supposed to be displayed concurrently with Robert Morris's exhibition. David wasn't very impressed with Warhol's work, and much to Magda's disappointment he had refused the opportunity to meet personally with the artist who was in London.

"I've already been introduced to Andy Warhol," David had announced at tea. "In fact I've met him on two separate occasions. Once at *Pearls* in San Francisco...the second time was with Patty at a party we both attended in Hayward, California."

"What's *Pearls?*" Sonja asked, fingering one of the pearl stud earrings she was wearing.

"It's an after hours cabaret that operates behind the *Gilded Cage*...a popular gay bar in the city," Patty answered. "I've only been there a couple of times...but I know David goes frequently on weekends for the shows. The last time I was there Charles Pierce did his imitation of Janette McDonald. The crowd was hysterical when he flew in drag over the audience in a big swing covered with roses. He lip synced the song *San Francisco* and everyone sang along."

"David, how did you happen to meet Andy Warhol at Pearls?" Sonja asked.

"It really wasn't my design to meet him there...it just happened," David said. "I was at Pearls to see a new show with Charles Pierce and his talented pianist named

Sabu. It was Patty's colleague, Bruce, a professor of Art at California State College in Hayward, who saw me sitting at a table just before the show. He came over to say hello and told me that there was someone I just *had* to meet...so I went over to his table and he introduced me to Andy Warhol."

Patty jumped in, "David didn't even know who Andy Warhol was...and he still wouldn't know if I hadn't enlightened him."

"I was not in the least impressed," David said. "The man was sitting there in some kind of stupor...and I remember thinking he was not very attractive...very pale, wan, unhealthy looking with terrible pock marks on his face."

Patty resumed the story, "Later that week, Bruce, our professor friend, had a reception party for Warhol at an old farmhouse he rents behind the hill of Cal State. David and I were both there, although we had not driven together on that particular evening. I was with Stephen... we had come in his station-wagon with some friends from San Jose State University...I didn't stay very long."

"Neither did I." David added. "Our colleague Bruce became a little too highly strung out that night...and I remember leaving just moments after Patty and Steve.

"What happened," Sonja wanted to know.

David continued, "Apparently Andy had given Bruce an idea for a new art project that required collecting pubic hairs from his guests. He put up a sign over the toilet in the bathroom and a large jar with a pair of scissors sitting next to it. The sign said *'Please contribute some of your pubic hairs for Bruce's project'*. Of course I did not support the cause, but washed my hands and opted to depart for the city. There was still plenty of time that evening to enjoy something more entertaining than that ridiculous party."

"Why didn't you leave some of your pubic hairs in the jar?" Magda demanded. "I insist on knowing why you refused to cooperate...it was such a simple request..a few snips here and there..."

David ignored her question and went on with his story. "Just before I left the party...still saying my good-byes...there was a blood curdling scream...Bruce came rushing out of the bathroom holding the jar of hair and shouting 'You've ruined my project, someone has deliberately sabotaged my art project!'

"Andy Warhol jumped in and grabbed the jar and starting examining it like there was a living fetus inside. '*What happened...what happened*?'..." he asked.

"Bruce hollered out, 'Someone cut regular hair from their head...they contaminated my project.'...David continued.

"How did he know it wasn't pubic hair," Magda inquired.

David answered, "I didn't hang around long enough to find out...I left and it seemed that the majority of guests were doing the same thing...filing out of that farmhouse behind me. I could still hear Bruce raving and screaming as I drove away."

Patty added thoughtfully, "I haven't seen Bruce since that night at Andy Warhol's gala reception in Hayward...I'll have to remember to ask if there were any significant consequences to the evening. Meanwhile," she continued as she extinguished a cigarette, "If you'll excuse me I'd like to bathe and rest a bit before this evening's activities."

"Sounds good to me," David agreed rising from his comfortable chair in the lobby.

He couldn't remember what theatre they were attending or what restaurant they were going to, and he didn't care. He was tired from the rigorous escapades of their day which included horse back riding in Hyde Park. David felt like he'd spent the whole week at giant playgrounds for adults. He definitely wanted a little rest and recharge for his body before facing the evening's activities.

Magda made no attempt to get up from her chair in the lobby. She set her teacup on the crystal table between her and Sonja. "Patricia and David, go rest and change...Sonja and I may still be here in the same riding clothes when it's time to leave for the theatre."

"Oh, good," Sonja agreed, "I didn't feel like getting up from this glorious chair."

Patty and David just nodded as they walked toward the elevator. The last thing Magda could be heard saying to Sonja was, "Honey...I think we should have something a little stronger than just another cup of tea."

* * *

When Patty and David reached the twenty-second floor they went immediately to their suites. They had duplicate keys to each others suite on the twenty-second floor of the London Hilton. She felt somewhat peaceful knowing her brother was so close...she was in Suite 2203, David was in the center Suite 2205, and Suite 2207 was supposedly vacant.

"Poopsie," Patty said as they opened the doors to their respective rooms. "I'll come over to rouse you after I'm dressed...you go straight for a nap."

David nodded his head and opened the door to 2205. He went directly to his bed and threw himself fully dressed on the mattress. He managed to kick off his shoes and promptly closed his eyes. Three breaths later David was in a dreamless sleep...the next sound he heard was his sister's voice.

"Poopsie," she was saying, "It's time to get up...you've been asleep for over two hours...you haven't even taken off your clothes."

"What time is it?" he asked in a scratchy voice.

"It's past seven...you need to get dressed," she answered.

"Are the girls still in the lobby?" he asked as he began preparing to bathe by stripping off his clothes.

Patty gathered the shirt and pants her brother had indifferently thrown on the floor. "Magda phoned about an hour ago and said she would pick us up at eight o'clock...I'm not certain if they went home to change or if they're still in the hotel lobby swilling down drinks."

The very moment that Patty stopped speaking, the chimes to David's suite sounded.

"That is probably Magda and Sonja at the door now, Poopsie...you'd better jump in the bath and get dressed."

David had already started running the water in the marvelous marbled bath and wondered what he would wear as he stepped into wash his somewhat weary body.

Patricia went to the foyer and opened the door to find a very stately couple standing in the alcove.

"Good evening," the very distinguished man said in a familiar British accent. "Is this David's suite...we really weren't certain."

"Yes," Patty said wondering 'who are these people...the man looks so familiar.'

"Yes," Patty said again with more commitment, "This is David's suite...I'm his sister Patricia...call me Patty if you like...I have the suite next door," she said pointing to the number 2203.

"This is not 2207?" asked the lovely lady who was hanging on to the arm of the gentleman.

As if to verify where she was, Patty looked at the number 2205. "Oh," she said realizing that the couple had come to the wrong suite. "I guess that you have come to the wrong door."

In validation of Patty's comment the door to Suite 2207 popped open and David Niven appeared...he looked at Patricia and said "Good evening."

"David,"...the other handsome man said, "We rang the wrong suite."

Patty blithely said "Dilemma solved!"

"Sorry about that Larry," David Niven looked at Patty and said "So sorry maam...I hope you're not disturbed again...I'm having a cocktail party...you may find a stray guest or two ringing your suite by mistake."

"Not at all a problem," Patty said reassuringly as the couple went into Suite 2207 and she closed the door to Suite 2205.

'I wonder,' she thought 'just who was that distinguished man? There was no doubt that David Niven was definitely David Niven...and she knew that the other man was Larry...but Larry who...Larry...Laurence...

"Laurence Harvey!" Patty said out loud.

"What about Laurence Harvey?" David asked as he stepped out of the bedroom partially dressed.

"Poopsie...Laurence Harvey was just here."

"What?" David cried.

"You heard me," Patty said. "Laurence Harvey was just here with a gorgeous female model"

"Why didn't you ask *him* in for a drink?"

"Believe me, I would have if David Niven hadn't turned up at the door of Suite 2207." Patty said.

"David Niven!" David shouted in dismay.

"Yes," Patty answered "David Niven! He's having a cocktail party right next door to us!"

"Weren't you able to wring out an invitation? What did you say...what did they say?" David implored.

"It all happened so quickly," Patty said. "I didn't have enough time to ask anybody anything."

"Not even Laurence Harvey for his phone number for me? Do you know how much I love Laurence Harvey? Damn...why couldn't I have answered the door...bloody damn!" David rasped.

"You better calm down and save your voice, Poopsie," Patty said. "Just finish getting dressed and give me a minute to think while we wait for Magda."

There was a knock at the door and David lunged to answer it first, "I'll get...I'll get it," he said eagerly.

David flung the door open hoping to see Lawrence Harvey. Instead, he beheld Magda standing there in all her glory. She had a burning cigarette on a holder in one hand and an open flask of vodka in the other hand. She was wearing the heavy tweed coat with the fox fur and two little heads were poking out of the pockets on each side of her wrap. They were perfectly beautiful little miniature poodles...one black...one white.

"What is this thing called charisma?" Magda cooed as she took a swig from her flask and a puff from the burning cigarette. Little beads of perspiration were beginning to form on her forehead as David tried not to look too closely.

'Well dah-h-ling...answer me...what is this thing called charisma?"

"I don't know," David said grouchily as he waved Magda into the suite. "There doesn't seem to be any charisma around here at the moment. I just see booze, smoke and sweat."

Magda gave David a nasty look as she walked silently into the suite.

"Magda," Patty said in an urgent voice, "Sit down dear...we have something to tell you immediately."

Magda pulled the two miniature dogs from her coat pockets and sat heavily on one of the grandiose divans that adorned the suite. She quickly got over her irritability from David's reprimand and gave her full attention to Patricia.

"David Niven is having a cocktail party," Patty began.

"When...where!" Magda interrupted.

"Right here in the hotel...right now in the suite next door." Patty said.

"And," David added, Laurence Harvey came to our door by mistake...and Patricia failed to acquire his telephone number, for me!"

"Don't worry Dahling," Magda said as she rose from the couch, placed the dogs back in her coat pockets and headed out the door, "I'll manage the situation."

* * *

Magda was gone for about twenty minutes which gave David enough time to finish dressing into his *Jones of New York* dark blue wool suit complemented with a fresh white shirt and dark blue tie. He thought that one of the best perks of staying at a four-star hotel was the laundry and dry cleaners, and at that moment he also appreciated the fact that he was standing in clean underwear and a freshly pressed suit.

Patty looked strikingly beautiful in a sleek black dress that exposed her lovely shoulders. She had opted to fashion an upswept hairdo that displayed a pair of handcrafted earrings made of black onyx and shimmering diamonds. The earrings matched an eye-opening necklace that embraced a five carat diamond. Patricia had matching bracelets that she decided not to wear because she didn't want to be *overdressed.*

Magda swooped back into David's suite through the door that had been left ajar, "Dah-h-lings...come immediately...we've been invited to David Niven's cocktail party...and you won't believe who's there."

"Where are your puppies?" Patty wanted to know.

"They're entertaining everyone until we get there... we must hurry...all the celebrities are having a quick cocktail before they depart for some big affair at the *Dorchester.*"

"Who's there?" Patty asked.

"Everybody famous...there are scores of limousines just outside your hotel...I had wondered why they were here...it's for the cocktail party," Magda said as she beckoned for Patty and David to proceed out the door. "Prepare yourselves...it's a big crowd packed into a rather small space."

'It can't be any worse than Sutter's Mill on a Friday afternoon in San Francisco,' thought David.

But he was wrong...the throng of people was more crushing than Sutter's Mill at peak cocktail hour. Magda led the way into the moving mass of humanity. The scents of perfumes and cologne were overwhelmed only by the cigarette smoke that moved through the suite of rooms like a San Francisco fog. Magda was lost almost immediately in the crowd...she could last be heard saying "Mingle dahlings...mingle."

Patty figured it made sense to hang on to her brother for protection. She was grateful that she was wearing high heels, which made her almost as tall as David. Their height delivered them from being totally obscured by the mob. The party looked like the cocktail party scene from *Breakfast at Tiffany's* where Audrey Hepburn plays Holly Golightly.

The large suite was tightly packed with a sea of famously luminous heads and faces...it was impossible to see what anyone was wearing unless you were standing right next to the person. The majority of the men were obviously in tuxedos as evidenced by the formal bowties that could be seen bobbing up and down throughout the suite. Looking mostly at the men, David recognized many handsome faces like Peter O'Toole, Richard Harris and Trevor Howard.

"This is unbelievable," Patty said as she and her brother pushed through the multitude of swarming celebrities. She thought she spotted Peter Ustinov chatting away with Christopher Lee in a crowded corner of the suite...and there was also a shorter guy who looked just exactly like James Mason.

David wanted to find someplace where he and Patty could sit and watch the show. He also thought it wouldn't be a bad idea to find a drink and some hors d'oeuvres... but he had no inkling where he could find either in this massive hoard of famous people. He stopped abruptly in front of a divan much like one in his suite next door.

There were two women talking side by side...each one was holding one of Magda's poddles. David heard himself say "Holy shit!" and Elizabeth Taylor looked up and smiled.

"Aren't they darling...I just love toy poodles," she said.

David could not speak but simply nodded his head in agreement as he stared in awed amazement at his very favorite female actress in the whole world! She was too overwhelming to absorb. She was wearing a wide strapped low cut white chiffon dress...sparkling diamonds adorned her resplendent neck and wrists...her piercing eyes emitted a lustrous reflection of light that was enhanced by glittering diamond earrings dangling on each side of her exquisite face. This was Elizabeth Taylor!

Patty smiled and inclined her head toward the woman sitting next to Elizabeth Taylor...then taking her brother by the hand she guided him back into the fray of talking smoking confabulation. David felt immediate remorse at having produced no contribution to the conversation other than the words "holy shit."

"It's okay, Poopsie," Patty said as she squired David toward the front door. She knew exactly what her little brother was thinking. "This isn't the right time or place to make introductions and exchange dialogue," she said as the two of them moved away from the pandemonium into the foyer of the suite. Magda was there chatting with a supremely dignified lady.

"Dahlings...there you are," Magda cooed. "I want you to meet Dame Edith Margaret Ashcroft."

"Please call me Peggy," the elegant lady said.

"I'm Patricia Wellington," Patty said extending her hand. "This is my brother David...and I'd like you to know that our entire family comprises just a few of your many great admirers."

"Oh, how kind of you," Dame Edith Margaret said as she clasped both hands over Patty's. "Welcome to England...I know you're in good hands with Magda. Now if you'll pardon me I must find Noel...he's my escort for the tribute dinner."

Magda gave the Lady a tender embrace and said, "I hope you enjoy your evening at the Dorchester."

Peggy Ashcroft energetically pushed back into the chaotic revelry as Magda, Patty and David made their way through the door to the alcove outside their suites.

"I have one word...whew!" Patty said in a half formed whistle as the three adventurers slipped back into David's suite.

"I know what you mean when you say whew!" David exuberantly agreed. "Who was that woman holding one of Magda's puppies...the one sitting next to Elizabeth Taylor"

"Poopsie," Patty said with a hint of alarm in her voice, "You mean you didn't recognize Hermione Gingold?"

"Dahling," Magda said in a scolding tone, "You didn't recognize Hermione Gingold?"

"Yes, of course now that you've told me, if she had spoken a word or two with her distinctive voice that I could hear, I might have distinguished her. I suppose that when Dame Edith Margaret Ashcroft said Noel was her escort that she meant Noel Coward?"

"Very clever of you Poopsie, to figure out that one," Patty taunted her brother.

"There was much too much to immediately assimilate in just a few minutes," David said in his own defense.

"Yes dahling," Magda said sympathetically, "You saw a lot of astonishing celebrities tightly stuffed into one small space...did you happen to notice James Mason?"

"Yes!" Patty said emphatically, "He was right next to Peter Ustinov!"

"I can't wait to tell everybody back home," David said. "I only wish I could have taken pictures."

"If you'd like," Magda said casually, "We can use the camera in my car and go crash the tribute dinner at the Dorchester."

Patty said, "Oh...you drove tonight...I didn't even think to ask...where is Sonja?"

"She ended up having to work this evening," Magda said. "We'll see her tomorrow."

David said in a panicked voice, "The puppies...where are your puppies."

"They'll turn up somewhere," Magda said nonchalantly, "They've been abandoned before...they love meeting new people. I'll ask at the front desk when we get back later tonight.

"By the way," David said, "Did you know who is being honored at the tribute dinner?"

"Oh, just another of our British actors," Magda said. "I believe it's Sir John Gielgud."

"I don't think it's a good idea for us to crash the party at the Dorchester, Magda," Patty advised as the three headed toward the elevator.

* * *

The following morning David arose in his baby blue silk pajamas and put on the luxuriant comfortable robe that Mr. Hilton had provided as a perk of the suite. He found the key to his sister's suite and went directly to it thinking they might order a continental breakfast to eat in Patty's rooms. He let himself in and heard her call from the bedroom.

"I'm in here Poopsie."

He walked into the back rooms and found his sister dressed in a slip sitting in front of the dressing table mirror. She was applying her mascara. The grandiose dressing room had two magnificent provincial chairs and she indicated for her brother to be seated in one of them.

"Poopsie," she said in a no-nonsense tone of voice that David did not usually like to hear, "Poopsie...we have to leave London...we have to leave right away...today."

"Why?" David asked with a note of grave concern in his voice.

Patty knew her brother would not be pleased if he thought he was the reason for the sudden change in itinerary. "We both need some rest," she said succinctly. "The pace has been much too strenuous...even for us."

David let out a long breath as Patty continued the discussion.

"Are you disappointed in leaving London...we'll be back in a few weeks...I just believe that both of us can benefit from a change of pace...for a little while. There's so much for us to see in Europe and we've already been in London for almost six weeks."

David let out another long breath and said, "Where would you like to go...Italy... I suppose?"

"No Poopsie," Patty said a little more cheerfully. "Not Italy, not yet. We have that beautiful new Mercedes just waiting for us downstairs. That poor car hasn't gone anywhere since we drove it from the dealership and parked it in the garage of this hotel. I thought we could head north...go up the coast to one of the little townships and take the ferry across the channel to Holland."

David agreed immediately. "It sounds good to me! It would give you a chance to drive on the left side of the road...and you're absolutely correct about both of us needing a more restful environment...I'll go pack right now...Amsterdam here we come!"

* * *

CHAPTER NINE

The drive out of London was made easier by the fact that it happened to be Sunday and the streets of the city were relatively quiet. The concierge had hastily thrown together a small packet that included a simple map of the roads to take. Their immediate destination was Harwich, England where they would book passage for themselves and '*Big Red*' to cross the English Channel to *Hook of Holland*. Big Red, the name Patty dubbed her new car, also happened to be the name of David's favorite saddle horse at the Vineyards.

He was grateful that Patty didn't want to keep the automatic hard top of the convertible lowered. He was also glad that the heat worked so effectively in the new car...furthermore he was having fun playing around with the radio. It didn't take long to find familiar tunes for a sing-along as they drove down the road. David sang word for word and mimicked playing the guitar right along with George Harrison...Patty sang all the *hallelujahs* and *hare krishnas* along with the chorus.

My sweet lord (hallelujah)
Hm, my lord (hallelujah)
My, my, my lord (hallelujah)

I really want to know you (hallelujah)
Really want to go with you (hallelujah)
Really want to show you lord (aaah)
That it won't take long, my lord (hallelujah)

"Oh-h-h Poopsie" Patty said freshly inspired, "Thanks be to God…"

"Thank God for what?" David chuckled as he searched the airwaves for another song.

"Thank God we're alive!" Patty responded happily. "Thank God we're traveling down this road in a beautiful new car! Thank God for everything! Thank God for God!!"

"Listen," David interrupted as he turned up the volume on the car radio. What a perfect song for driving down the highway in England!"

The long and winding road
That leads to your door
Will never disappear
I've seen that road before
It always leads me here
Lead me to you door
Why leave me standing here
Let me know the way

"I love the Beatles, Poopsie!"

"So do I," said David looking for another song. "I just wish it had been George Harrison and Paul McCartney we'd seen at *Kalamara's* that night instead of John and Ringo…I would have jumped right on George Harrison's bones."

Patty laughed, "I'm sure you would have, Poopsie… along with half the people in the restaurant…the other half would have been all over Paul."

They both laughed as they sped down the old English highway in Patty's candy apple red Mercedes with its sporty white bucket seats. Magda had insisted that the color of the leather interior was bone, not white. She wouldn't specify the exact shade of red that glistened on the exterior of the car...possibly because it too closely matched the color of her hair.

"I think I'm getting a sore throat," David said. 'It hurts when I swallow."

"Oh, oh," said Patty, "I was just about ready to ask you to light me a cigarette."

"I will...if you'd like," said David as he rummaged through his pockets.

"No, no, no..." Patty said, "Not if you're beginning to get a sore throat...I was hesitant to smoke in my new car, anyway. That clinches it...I'm making a rule...no smoking in this vehicle...at least until it arrives in the States. How much farther before we reach our destination at Harwich?"

"It's hard to tell," David answered. "We haven't seen any signs lately and when we do they're confusing because they always show the distance in kilometers instead of miles."

"Well Poopsie...what else would you expect in Europe?"

"Sonja did say that these days a lot of signs indicate distance in kilometers and in miles."

"I think that's true only around the larger cities...it seems to me that we're pretty far out in the boondocks." Patty said, "We've been on the road for about an hour and a half...shouldn't be much longer before we get to Harwich...the concierge said the drive shouldn't take more than two and a half hours."

"I hope we don't have to wait too long for the ferry once we get there...I'm a little tired...guess I didn't get enough sleep last night," David said.

"Buck up Poopsie, I think we'll have a little bit of a wait before we're on the boat. It doesn't look as though we'll be in time to take the morning ferry to Holland."

"There's a ferry leaving in the afternoon sometime, isn't there?" David asked a little anxiously.

"Im afraid not Poopsie...from what I understand there are only two ferries that cross from there...one leaves in the morning and arrives in Holland at night... the other leaves at night and lands in Holland in the morning. It looks like we'll be making the night trip."

"Oh no!" David whimpered, "Will we have to sleep in the car?"

Patty giggled, "I don't think so Poopsie, I already asked about that...we should be able to get private rooms with beds. Listen! Turn up the radio!"

> *And when the night is cloudy*
> *There is still a light that shines on me*
> *Shine on until tomorrow, let it be*
> *I wake up to the sound of music,*
> *Mother Mary comes to me*
> *Speaking words of wisdom, let it be*
>
> *Let it be, let it be*
> *Let it be, yeah, let it be*

"Everything's going to be okay Poopsie! There's always an answer...we'll just rely on the Big Guy," she said pointing to the sky. "This is going to be a great trip... even if we do have to sleep in Big Red once in a while."

* * *

Patty was right...the siblings had missed the morning ferry to Holland by less than twenty minutes. They'd have to spend the day in Harwich waiting for the eleven p.m. boat to take them across the channel. David was in near despair...more than anything else in the world...he hated having to wait.

What made the situation more unbearable was the fact that they had no where to pass time pleasantly. They had to queue up with the other cars to wait in line for the next ferry...they were number four in the row of vehicles waiting for the boat. The line quickly started to fill up behind them, and Patty was pleased that they would be among the first to get Big Red on board. She urged David to sit behind the wheel while she went inside a dingy office right next to the wharf from which they'd leave that night.

She returned to find David hunched over the car radio singing along with B.B. King's *The Thrill is Gone.* "This song says it all," he said wearily turning up the volume.

"My poor Poopsie," Patty commiserated, "There's good news and there's bad news..."

"Give me all the good news first," David pleaded, "I really need to hear some good news."

"Well, Poopsie, the good news is not all that bad...I have the tickets for our voyage tonight. It includes first class passage for Big Red you and me. We have a private rooms with our very own beds...and we can sleep and dream for the better part of ten hours until arrival at the Hook of Holland around nine a.m. tomorrow morning."

"Rest and sleep...how good that sounds," David agreed weakly. "What's the bad news?" he asked fortifying himself for the worst.

"The bad news is that there is no place particularly comfortable for us to pass time as we wait for tonight's ferry...and we cannot stay in Big Red."

"Why not?" David growled.

"I don't know...some silly regulation...and we'll also have to turn over our passports to the official once we board the boat...we'll get them back when we arrive at the other end of the channel."

"What a pain in the a-a-a...my eye!" David complained trying to be a gentleman.

"I know Poopsie...but let's not ask for trouble...we'll just follow procedure until we're all rested up."

"Can we complain and be intently obnoxious again when we get to Holland?" David asked half seriously.

"Of course Poopsie," Patty said in a placating tone. "We'll go directly to the American Consulate and make a fuss about how disrespectfully we've been treated as American Tourists."

"So in the meantime where are we going to wait while we're waiting?"

"Good news and bad news, again, Poopsie."

"Better give me the good news first..."

"Well Poopsie...there is a lounge for passengers with vehicles...it's not much but we'll find a place to sit while we're waiting."

"What's the bad news?"

"The bad news is that there is no restaurant...just a sandwich stand where we can buy coffee or hot chocolate and plastic snacks."

"Oh damn," David said, "I was looking forward to a good meal and some fine wine."

"There is supposedly a restaurant on the ferry... maybe we can have a midnight supper before we turn in tonight. Right after we get the car on board we'll head for the lounge Poopsie and I'll buy you a nice cup of hot chocolate."

They drove Big Red onto the ferry's parking deck as soon as the ramp was lowered for vehicles to be boarded. Except for their travel bags they left the bulk of their luggage locked in the trunk. As Patty gathered her few personal items from inside the car David turned up the volume to the radio. *The Thrill is Gone* was playing again.

> *The thrill is gone*
> *It's gone away for good*
> *All the thrill is gone*
> *Baby, it's gone away for good*
> *Someday I know I'll be open-armed baby*
> *Just like I know, I know I should*
>
> *You know, I'm free, free now, baby*
> *I'm free from your spell*

Well, Poopsie," Patty said as they left the car and walked down the passenger ramp in the dark chilly air. "We'll just say a silent prayer that the *thrill* will be back tomorrow morning when we're in Holland"

"Right now," David griped, "I don't feel like I'll ever be thrilled again about anything."

Patty knew for certain that her little brother must be sick. She again promised herself that she would find a good Dutch doctor tomorrow when they arrived in Amsterdam in the morning. She knew that David's resistance to illness was strong, but she was especially concerned he was struggling with a sore throat. In the past when he came to the point of complaining about pain when he swallowed, it meant that he had acquired an infection.

They entered the large waiting area which looked like a sleazy bus terminal one might find in the slum area of a large American city. The air was stale with smoke and the floors were filthy. Grime seemed to be on everything including the people who were milling around the establishment.

"This place looks like a scene out of a movie about Hungarian refugees being evacuated from a concentration camp." David whispered to his sister.

Patty led her brother to a couple of half broken chairs that sat next to a very small table with a dented ash tray sitting on it. David wearily sat down and surveyed from his seat looking to find the concession that might sell hot chocolate. He was really too tired to care...and his throat still hurt every time he swallowed.

Patty reached over and patted her brother's knee, "Look Poopsie," she pointed to the ashtray sitting on the tiny marred table next to them. In big white capital letters it spelled C-O-U-R-A-G-E against a dark green background. "Take heart, that's a message from the Big Guy," and she pointed somewhere beyond the ceiling conceivably toward heaven.

* * *

David's first trip across the English Channel was an agonizing blur. His private room was nothing more than a cramped cubicle with bunk beds. To make the situation even more gruesome was the fact that no late supper was being served and he was starving. Escape through sleep seemed to be his only recourse.

Everything in the cell-like room seemed to be made of metal including floor, walls, the door and the bed. There were no amenities that one usually found in the cheapest of motels in America. Even the toilet paper was too hard to use for blowing his nose. David felt like he was in a torture chamber. He was so tired that he threw himself on the lower bunk and decided to sleep with his clothes on, coat, shoes and all. The pillow was so thin it provided little cushioning even when it was doubled. The bunk above was stripped and provided no extra bedding; so David used the sheets from his bed to pad his puny pillow

"I hope I can sleep," he said aloud, "what I really need is a valium."

David knew that Patty carried all types of painkillers and goodies in her travel bag, but now that his body was finally reclined, he didn't have the energy to grope his way down the corridor to his sister's *cell*. "I'm just going to close my eyes and pray for sleep," he thought.

He fell immediately into a deep dreamless sleep that allowed him to avoid further stressful mental activity. Impulsively he felt his body drop and was awakened by a loud sound...Boom. He felt ill. For an instant he couldn't remember where he was...then Boom...that sound again.

David had never been seasick in his entire life, but for the first time he felt nausea overtaking his body... Boom...the sound that woke him were waves crashing against the hull of the ferry. Boom...Boom...Boom. "I think I better stand up," he said aloud.

Once on his feet the wave of nausea passed and David collected his thoughts. "I wonder how long I've been asleep." He tried to look at his watch, but it was too dark in the room. He grappled around looking for a light switch, but there was none. 'This is ridiculous,' he thought as he tried to keep his balance. He found the handle to the door of his dinghy cell and threw it open. There standing before him in the dim light was his beautiful sister.

"Oh Patricia, thank God."

"Come with me Poopsie," she said guiding him into the hallway and down the corridor.

"What's happening," David said trying to adjust his eyes to a little bit of light.

"We're in the middle of a storm, Poopsie," Patty said calmly, "But the consensus is that we're not going to sink."

"Thanks to God for small favors," David was able to say. "Ugh...my mouth is dry."

"How about a cold bottle of Perrier, Poopsie?"

"Sounds good to me," David said, "It doesn't even have to be cold as long as it's wet."

Patty led her brother up a set of narrow metal stairs...as they reached the landing David said, "I don't remember going down any steps when we boarded."

"We didn't Poopsie...we came up a flight to get to our rooms...now we're going up another flight to get to the main deck."

Patty threw open the door at the top of the next landing and the main deck was alive with scores of people walking around...sitting... chatting...eating...and some hippy dude wearing a colorful poncho was playing a guitar as three admiring girls hummed along resting their haunches on the floor.

A middle aged woman dressed in wool slacks and a tie-dyed knit sweater appeared and said in a heavy

German accent, "There you are Patricia...this must be your little brother."

"Hi...I'm David," he said extending his hand.

"This is Ilsa...she's from Munich."

"I am happy to meet with you," she said holding out an unlit poorly rolled joint of marijuana."

"I think we'd better get David some water before he lights that,' Patty advised.

"My goodness" David said, I know that you make friends fast but this is ridiculous."

"Yes, yes, your sister and I were very fast to make good friends. She is a woman that is rare to find. She is very beautiful and very intelligent."

"I think," David said, "that you must be a lady with many of the same qualities.

Ilsa giggled and offered David some matches, "You smoke while I get you a bottle of water."

Ilsa disappeared some where through the lobby and Patty said, "Light it up Poopsie."

David did not hesitate to light the joint and take a deep hit holding the smoke in his lungs. He passed the burning ember to Patty and exhaled saying "How did you find time to do all this," he said waving his arm as Ilsa magically appeared with a bottle of Perrier.

Patty passed the joint to Ilsa and said, "I haven't been to bed. I went exploring and met a few new friends along the way."

"David," Ilsa said indicating for him to take the joint, "You are having a good time?"

"I am now," he answered as he inhaled deeply.

* * *

David was deeply appreciative that Ilsa was so generous with her grass...it kicked in after his third toke...miraculously everything seemed comfortable once again. He found out that there were seven hours left before the ferry docked...maybe longer if the storm had delayed their journey across the Channel. He left Patty chatting with Ilsa and floated down the stairwell to his room.

This time he didn't notice the movement of the vessel or the pounding of the waves against the hull. He didn't even care that he was in a claustrophobic cube with only a make-shift pillow to comfort his head. He fell into a restful sleep and dreamed of nothing until once again he heard his sister calling in the distance.

"Poopsie, we're docking in Holland...Poopsie, I have your passport...Poopsie, open the door."

David didn't bother to yawn or stretch. He threw his legs off the bed, landed standing on the floor, and flung open the door. Patty was there with her travel bag and purse in one hand and David's passport in the other.

"You ought to hold on to this Poopsie," she said playfully, "You don't want it turning up under someone's seat."

David took his passport and knelt down to put it in his travel bag. "I'm hungry."

* * *

CHAPTER TEN

Patricia and David were welcomed to Holland on a mostly sunny morning. The sky was filled with big puffy white clouds that moved slowly against a medium blue background.

"Remember what Sylvia used to say," Patty remarked, "If there's enough blue in the sky to dress a Dutchman... it's not going to rain."

The brother and sister team quickly found their Mercedes sitting among the myriad other vehicles on the parking deck. David grabbed the keys and made a cursory check of the items they'd left in the car. He checked the trunk and counted the pieces of luggage. Patty had already made herself comfortable in the passenger seat when David got in the driver's seat and reached over to open the glove compartment.

"It all seems to be here," he said as he snapped the compartment closed."

"Good," Patty said, "Let's start moving, Poopsie."

David started the engine, turned on some heat and put his hands on the steering wheel.

"Looks like we're not going anywhere, yet."

He pointed to the triple line of cars in front of them. The engines were all going creating small clouds of exhaust in the chilly morning air...and they were disembarking at a snail's pace rate.

"Oh Poopsie," Patty said, "Do you suppose if we hadn't been so eager to get the car on board that we might have parked in a better position to drive Big Red off this tub?"

* * *

David was glad to be traveling from Hook of Holland to Amsterdam; it was suppose to be an easy ride and by all calculations would not exceed an hour travel time. The sun seemed to prevail over the clouds and there was minimal traffic going into the city. David pulled the car to the side of the road, put the gear in neutral and made an announcement while the motor hummed.

"You make take the wheel of your own car because you may now drive on the right side of the road."

"Oh Poopsie, how exciting to drive this wonderful vehicle for my first time in Holland." Patty said as David hopped out of the car as she scooted into the driver's seat.

The previous concierge at the London Hilton had given clear-cut directions that led them directly to the Park Hotel where they would be staying. *Stadhouderskade 25* was pretty much within walking distance of all the places they would be visiting in Amsterdam. Patty was especially eager to drop-in to the *Rijks* and *Van Gough* museums, and maybe do a bit of shopping along *De Negen Straatjes*, The Nine Streets.

David hadn't discussed it with Patty too much... but he would like to spend a little time exploring the notorious gay-life in Amsterdam...after all, the city did have a reputation for being as "queer" as San Francisco...

if not more so. He didn't expect to fall in love or even find another rare beauty like Hank Stafford...but he was more than ready for an interlude with some charming European.

Growing up in San Francisco afforded David a great deal of experience with men who were committed to their own sex....he vividly remembered informing his sister how jaded he felt about sex when he was only nineteen years old. She had given him good advice back then. He silently reminisced as he drove.

"It's okay to be queer, Poopsie," she had said "...just don't live your life in a cock trance. There's a lot more to who you are than being just another pretty faggot," she had warned.

"Remember the Ancient Greeks who recognized the power of moderation...avoid the extremes especially when you really enjoy or love a person, place or thing. *Do not overindulge.* Don't believe Mae West when she said 'Too much of a good thing is wonderful'. It's a cute line, but it's not true. Learn to be prodigious and temperate with all things; you'll be much calmer and happier in life."

Five years almost to the day had passed since Patricia enlightened her brother with that little speech. He had taken every word to heart knowing that his sister's prescription to happiness was absolutely correct. There had been many over-indulgent days and nights of debauchery that had left David devoid and depleted of feeling. It was an utterly empty sensation and he really didn't like it.

David had learned to apply checks and balances to sating himself with food, drink, drugs, and sexual activity. He recognized that his disposition had matured and his passions had softened like the tannins in an eleven year old bottle of Cabernet Sauvignon. He gave Patricia most of the credit for his guidance into adulthood...she'd never been judgmental or really critical when he made mistakes...she was like his personal angel.

As Patricia drove along the highway David allowed his mind to wander back to the one and only ugly night they had experienced in London. Magda had been eager to explore gay night in her city, especially after David's pronouncement of homosexuality at the Greek restaurant. Patty and Sonja weren't particularly fond of the idea, however, they did visit one private membership club that served cocktails and provided music with a small floor for slow dancing. They went as guests of one of Magda's colleagues from the Tate Museum...a *very* flamboyant black man with a *very* British accent named Michael Smith.

David had been very uncomfortable around Michael who tried relentlessly to get him on the dance floor. The more that David refused to dance, the more Michael would persist. With every drink Michael became more and more obnoxious...and it didn't seem at all to bother Magda who was enjoying the whole tug of war show.

Patricia had finally stepped in and said, "Michael, sweetheart...I know my brother is gay, but he doesn't *ever* slow dance with men. You are just wasting your time."

"I won't accept hearing that...he has an obligation to dance with me," Michael said belligerently. "I was kind enough to entertain him at *my* private club...David needs to have at least one dance with his host."

"Michael, didn't you hear what Patricia just told you? David does not dance with men," Sonja intervened.

"You keep out of this you bloody whore," Michael screeched at Sonja.

Magda promptly stood up and forcibly smacked Michael in the face, "That's enough Michael," she said in a threatening low tone of voice that Patty and David had not heard before this moment. "We're leaving...and we're leaving without you."

"Oh God, how I hate scenes like this," Sonja said as she arose and put on her coat."

Patty and David were on their feet almost the same instant as Sonja. Michael began to rock back and forth growling in his seat...fists opening and closing...staring angrily at Magda who now seemed very composed as she put on her coat and picked up her purse.

"There's no scene, dahling," Magda said to Sonja, "We're leaving and Michael *will* take himself home where he *will* go to bed and sober up."

"You mother fucking bitch...you pig whore...you scum sucking cunt," Michael expectorated with saliva shooting from his mouth.

Magda nudged her friends and indicated for them to move toward the exit. "Michael," she said in a superior tone, "I'll see you next Tuesday for the staff meeting at the museum...and I'll expect a sincere apology for your disgusting words."

"Get fucked!" Michael screamed as Magda followed her friends toward the exit.

The conversation seemed to have gotten the attention of everyone in the club. As Patty, Sonja and David passed a table with four gentlemen one of the men said loudly enough for the club to hear, "Oh dear, it seems as though the Colonials have started another war."

Sonja had paused long enough to say in her British accent, "Sir...you are gravely mistaken if you think that any of us are Colonials."

* * *

David's drifting thoughts came back when Patty abruptly pulled the car over to a curb. The reminiscences of London had preoccupied his mind and kept him from even noticing where he was traveling. They were now somewhere in the city of Amsterdam near a picturesque canal with sightseeing boats and people walking briskly along the adjoining streets.

"Poopsie...I'm going to let you take the wheel. I'm not quite certain how to get to the hotel from here," she said jumping out of the car indicating for David to take the driver's seat.

"No problem," David shouted as he scooted behind the wheel and looked over the simple directions they had been given in London.

Checking in at the Park Hotel was trouble free. They had made the selection based on the Hilton concierge's recommendation...and the fact that the hotel could accommodate parking for their vehicle. David had already decided they would not be driving around in Amsterdam. Most of the locals didn't have cars, and transportation in the city was readily available from public transit and taxis cabs.

Everyone at the Park Hotel spoke English. Check-in went swiftly and the siblings were happy to find they could easily trade American Express traveler's checks into cash for Dutch Gilders. Their rooms were on the same floor, but at opposite ends of the hotel.

The hotel attendant loaded up a cart with Patty and David's luggage and directed them to the elevator. David couldn't help but notice the handsome face and tall firm body that fit nicely into an appealing masculine uniform with epilates on the shoulders and brass buttons on a manly chest. David admonished himself for his calculated thoughts of persuading this man into a discreet rendezvous...perhaps that night...in his room.

'Stop it!' David thought to himself. 'Slow down! I'm in Amsterdam...the gay capital of Europe...there'll be plenty of time for self-indulgence after I'm settled.'

* * *

The first thing Patty insisted upon, after checking into The Park Hotel, was that David needed to see a doctor. The hotel attendant escorted them to her room first where he quickly unloaded her luggage from the cart. When he had finished he bowed and held the door for David.

"After this handsome man unloads your luggage I want you to go directly downstairs and meet me in the lobby," Patty said as she stepped into the hallway with the two men.

"What for," David protested, "I was hoping to order breakfast in my room and then put myself to bed."

"You and I are going to visit a Dutch doctor before we do anything else," she ordered forcefully. "I'm on my way downstairs to see about it right now."

"No use arguing with her," David consigned himself to her as he looked at the attendant more closely. The man was startling imposing in his handsomeness...he could have played the prince in Cinderella.

"It's no good to disagree with the boss," the hotel employee advised in a deep accent.

"...and Poopsie, please tip the young man for both of us," she said as she closed her door and headed for the elevator.

David turned to follow the man who had started down the hall to the other room to unload luggage. "Follow me please 'Poopsie'..." the attendant said with a grin.

"My name is really David...what is your name?" he said laughing.

"My name is Chandler...and I am at the hotel everyday except Sunday. I am assistant manager four days a week."

They came to David's room and Chandler opened the door and allowed the new guest to enter first. "You can just put everything on the floor at the foot of the bed," David said, as he withdrew his wallet and took out a handful of colorful bills. He knew the tip was extravagant, but he wanted to make an impression on Chandler.

"You gave me too much," Chandler protested as he counted out several bills trying to hand some back to David.

"Oh no, Chandler...my sister and I are very happy that you are taking care of us...so we want to take care of you."

"Thank you so much...you can ask for me at any time," he said grinning from ear to ear and extending his hand.

David grasped Chandler in a solid handshake as they looked directly into each other's eyes.

"I'll go down on...the elevator with you," David said with a hint of suggestion in his voice.

Chandler, once again held the door for David and the two sauntered toward *de lift*.

David put his hands in his pockets and Chandler pushed the cart to the elevator door. They took the lift down to the lobby smiling at each other the entire ride. David knew that he and this provocative man would be good buddies.

They found Patty conversing with the concierge who was apparently offering directions to the doctor's office. They turned to face David and Chandler who were still smiling as they approached the counter.

"Poopsie," she said, "We're going to walk to the doctor...he's just around the corner and he's waiting for us now."

"You guys really worked *fast*," David said politely.

Chandler made a brisk military bow and said to Patty, "Thank you so much for the generous tip, Madam."

"You're very welcome," Patty said graciously.

"His name is Chandler," David interjected.

"Let's go Poopsie," she said as she guided her brother toward the front doors of the lobby."

She took David's arm and said in a low whisper as they exited the lobby, "Talk about *fast* work."

* * *

The Holland sun appeared in and out of fast floating billowy white clouds. "Look Poopsie....it's a good omen," she said reacting to the large expanses of blue sky, "There's enough blue to cover *three* Dutchmen."

The concierge had written the name of the doctor and address on Park Hotel stationery just in case they got lost. Patty was good at following directions, but even a child would have understood the simple path that had been laid out for them. The medical office was right off the same canal that could be seen from her room. All they needed to do was make a left turn and follow the water.

The sidewalks and streets were not very busy and the doctor's office was closer than Patty had originally thought. "I've been very worried about you Poopsie...I know that you don't complain about your health very much...but when you do there is usually something major gone awry with your body."

"I hate being sick," David agreed, "and I'm sure it's an infection... I checked out my throat in the mirror and could see those hateful white spots on my tonsils. Those spots have always meant time for penicillin."

"Well this is it, Poopsie," Patty said as she turned off the main sidewalk to a cobblestone walkway that led to the door of a large brownstone house. They went up a few steps and verified their destination by reading a small brass sign with the doctor's name next to the door.

Patty rang the bell and a dowdy older woman dressed in black and dark gray said sourly in a heavy accent "Come in...my English is not so good...sit and I will tell doctor you are here."

The decor in the foyer was as drab as the woman who walked over to a pair of old fashioned doors on wooden runners and slid them open...moved to the other side...and slid them closed.

"How mysterious Poopsie."

"Yes, she could have at least said '*please*' sit down."

"Sh-h!" Patty whispered, "She might hear us."

At that moment the sliding doors opened and a pleasant looking man in a vested suit appeared. The front of his open jacket revealed a gold chain that was hanging from his vest. He had very dark gray hair that was tipped with white at the sideburns.

"Come this way," the doctor said indicating another set of sliding doors on an adjoining wall.

Patty and David stood up to follow the doctor who abruptly turned around and said brusquely, "There are two of you to see me?"

Patty said, "Yes, doctor...I would like to stay with my brother while you examine him."

"Come in...sit down." The doctor pointed to two huge polished wood chairs that sat in front of a massive polished antique desk.

The siblings sat down and the doctor positioned himself behind the desk and said, "Why do you want to see a doctor?"

David and Patty already were not impressed with the doctor's humorless, almost impolite bedside manner. They wanted to get down to business and get out of there.

David thought he'd get right to the point. "I have an infected throat...I know the symptoms...and I'd like a prescription for penicillin."

The doctor arose from his chair and walked around and placed one hand on David's chin and said "Open your mouth."

The doctor put on a pair of glasses with fatigued rims and firmly moved David's head from side to side checking his throat, "You Americans are all alike," the doctor laughed smugly, "You want to kill a fly with a cannon."

"You don't think that his throat is infected Doctor?" Patty asked. "I am concerned that he has been running a low-grade fever...I know my brother well."

"No penicillin is required," said the doctor sternly."

David tried to sound as polite as possible, "What would you suggest doctor?"

The doctor was already in his chair opening one of the lower desk drawers. He fumbled around awkwardly for a few moments and finally produced a small box containing two foiled wrapped disks the size of a silver dollar. Then he reached across to a tray and poured half a glass of water from a pitcher that was sitting on the desk. He opened one of the foiled tablets and dropped it into the glass.

"This is a sulfur tablet," the doctor announced as he stirred the glass with a silver spoon from the tray. "Drink this now and in two days take only one half of the second tablet...count two more days and take the second half."

David promptly downed the contents of the glass and tried not to burp.

"Are you certain that will be enough to knock out the infection?" Patty asked skeptically.

The doctor answered confidently, "Oh yes...I have said there is no need to kill a fly with a cannon. Eat beefsteak, take the sulfur, rest and you will be well. You will feel good in one or two days...but remember to take all the sulfur as I have given to you."

The doctor stood up and handed the remaining foiled tablet to David who also stood up and assisted his sister with her chair. The doctor wrote a quick note and said, "Give this to my assistant...it is the bill for your visit and the sulfur."

"Thank you," Patty said taking the slip of paper from the doctor's hand as she and David walked through the sliding doors back into the foyer.

Once they were outside on the street heading back to the hotel David said, "I didn't like his bedside manner... but I feel better already."

"You know, Poopsie...I thought about something during our visit to *doctor grim-face*. When he said...'Eat beefsteak,'...I was reminded of something I read in the book that Daddy gave you, *Europe on $5 a Day.* There was mention of a restaurant here in Amsterdam called *The Five Flies*."

"Oh yeah," David said with great interest because he was getting hungry, "What did it say about the restaurant?"

"It said...and I quote...*This restaurant is the antithesis of everything my book stands for'.*"

David said, "So the author of *Europe on $5 a Day* is saying that The Five Flies is a very expensive restaurant, so stay away."

"Yes, and no," Patty said musingly, "I think that the author is saying even though the restaurant is expensive, it's worth the splurge for the specialty of the house."

"What is their specialty?" asked David.

"Well, the book makes the statement that the Dutch love big juicy beefsteaks...and the best you'll find anywhere is at *The Five Flies*."

"Let's go back to the hotel...unpack...rest up for a while...cleanup and take a taxi forthwith to *The Five Flies* for an early dinner."

"Poopsie, that sounds like a good plan for our itinerary today."

* * *

The siblings traveled to and returned from *The Five Flies* in a taxi. They rode with the same driver in both directions. David figured that the driver was impressed with his tip enough to arrange for the head waiter to call him back when the siblings were finished eating their unexceptional steaks. On the return to the hotel, David looked more closely at the driver who was somewhat attractive...but not quite appealing enough to pursue for a tryst.

"Do you know anything about the gay clubs in Amsterdam?" David asked.

Before the driver could answer Patty announced, "I'm going to have a cigarette...may I offer one to anyone else?"

"Do you have American cigarettes," the driver asked eagerly.

"Yes," Patty said extending her pack to the driver. "These are made by a British company using American tobacco from Virginia...Benson Hedges."

"Oh, thank you so much," said the driver pushing in his lighter of the car's ashtray. "Yes," the driver continued addressing David's questions, "I know where to take you to the most popular gay bar in Amsterdam...*De Odeon Kelder*...the D.O.K...it is not too busy until after dark."

"Is it far from our hotel," David asked.

"It is not far...if you want to walk your concierge will tell you how to get there. Anybody in Amsterdam knows how to find the D.O.K. You can always take a taxi."

"Thanks for the information," David said.

The taxi driver continued the conversation, "You will find many young men there who like to dance...but there are also older men who go to drink and talk. You will find many people there to tell you about other gay clubs. The D.O.K. is new...it was opened by the C.O.C...the *Center for Culture and Recreation*...you will go there too, but first you must go to the D.O.K."

"Thank you, again," said David as he got out of the taxi and held the door for Patty. "I appreciate all the information."

"It is my pleasure," the driver said as he pocketed the fare and generous tip in gilders that David handed to him.

"Good night," Patty said as she and her brother strolled up to the hotel entrance..."and Poopsie, don't even think about going anywhere tonight except to bed. You need lots of rest, peace and healing time for your medicine to kick in."

David and Patty hugged each other in the hall in front of her room.

"God Bless you Poopsie, pleasant dreams...and don't plan on seeing me anytime before 2:00 P.M. tomorrow afternoon."

David turned down the hallway to his room. He had hastily unpacked his things earlier and his luggage had been shuffled around the room. He straightened up a bit by tossing almost everything in the hotel room closet where he had to again muddle through the hodgepodge of things to locate his toiletries. He took off his coat, threw it on the bed and headed to the bathroom where he looked in the cabinet mirror.

His tonsils were still noticeably swollen, but the white spots were gone. "It's either the sulfur or the dinner I swallowed," he said aloud still examining himself in the mirror.

He took a bottle of Listerine from his case and mixed a capful with some very hot water from the tap. He loosened his tie and after a significantly long gargle, brushed his teeth.

David then reached for his bottle of Abercrombie Fitch Woods cologne and generously applied it to the back of his neck and to his hands which he ran threw his thick perfectly trimmed sandy blond hair. He straightened his tie, grabbed his cashmere camel over-coat and rushed out the door.

David jumped into a taxi that was waiting right outside the lobby doors. "D.O.K.," he said a little bit sorry that it wasn't the same driver that had taken them to the *Five Flies* earlier in the evening. That first driver had been right...it wasn't too far to walk, as David made a mental notation of the route.

The driver pointed to a dimly lit doorway and David paid his fare and gingerly jumped out of the taxi. He ambled across a small yard and stepped up to the door where he rang a bell. The door attendant greeted him with a smile and a request for cover charge... "*Drie gilders, alsjeblief,*" he said holding out a hand.

The music was not overly loud but David politely said, "I only speak English...did you just ask me for three guilders?"

"Yes...three guilders...welcome to the D.O.K."

David gave the effeminate boy/man a five guilder bill and said, "Please keep the change."

"*Dankzegging,*" said the guy flirtatiously batting his eyelashes.

'Oh brother!' David thought as he strolled to the bar removing his coat which he folded over a stool and sat on it.

One of two unattractive bartenders approached and said in a friendly manner, "You are American?"

"How'd you know?" David asked.

The bartender giggled and said, "You hair is cut short...and you wear a tie."

"Do you have any after dinner liquors," David asked.

"*Pas bier,*" only beer."

"Only beer...no gin...no wine?" David asked with alarm.

"No gin...no wine...*pas bier.*"

David sighed heavily, "What kinds of beer do you serve?"

"Heineken, Grolsch, and Amstel."

"I'll have a Heineken," David said resignedly.

"Okay!" the bartender said nodding his head in approval.

David swiveled around on his barstool to survey the scene. He was not captivated with what he saw. He thought 'These are dismal pickings' as he looked around.

There were a half dozen guys dancing on the floor to Santana's *Black Magic Woman. All* of the participants were dressed in disco shirts and bell bottom pants with big wide belts...*all* the guys had shoulder length hair...all the guys were well under six feet tall...and *all* the guys were very effeminate as they danced.

David swiveled around to pick up his bottle of Heineken and found the bartender staring at him. David smiled slightly and the bartender said, "My name is Hans, please tell me your name."

"David."

The invisible disk jockey was now playing Freda Payne's *Band of Gold.* "Good name...I like the name, David. Where did you live in America?" the bartender asked.

"California."

"Hollywood?" the bartender asked, "You look like an actor from Hollywood."

"No, no" David laughed, "San Francisco."

Hans yelped loudly enough for the entire establishment to hear. "San Francisco...hey... everybody... San Francisco...right here!" he screamed repeatedly pointing at David.

"Everybody loves San Francisco," Hans said excitedly.

'Oh brother,' David thought silently.

There was a huge burst of applause after Hans' announcement and David sat a bit taller in his seat. The unseen D.J. put on Scott McKenzie's *If You're Going to San Francisco (Be Sure to Wear Some Flowers in Your Hair)*. Another half dozen guys that had been sitting at the bar to the left of David strutted to the dance floor. Almost the entire patronage at the bar abandoned stools and were prancing to the D.J's selection. David looked down the empty left side of the bar and noticed a solitary figure just standing up.

He was very tall compared to the rest of the crowd... and he looked very attractive. David could not see the guy's eyes, but he had short cropped blond hair and a very handsome chiseled face with what appeared to be a muscular firm body. In some ways he reminded David of the film actor George Peppard in the 1966 movie 'Blue Max.' His countenance and demeanor seemed somewhat bewildered as he approached David.

"Howdy," he said extending his right hand.

David jumped up immediately and offered the guy a manly handshake. "Howdy."

"You're American?" he asked still looking somewhat perplexed.

"Yes," David answered, "and so are you."

"Thank God," the guy said and cracked a wide smile showing off perfectly aligned sparkling white teeth.

"My name is David, and I guess you figured out where I'm from."

"You bet...you're from San Francisco," he sang off key with Scott Mckenzies's song which was still blasting over the speakers. "I'm Ronald from Fresno...never been to San Francisco...but I hope to be going there when I get back to the states."

"Well, well," David said still holding Ronald's hand and looking into a pair of twinkling hazel eyes, "How absolutely refreshing to meet up with a fellow Californian, and a very handsome one at that."

"You're telling me *pardner*" he said checking out David's handsome face, "I've been here on leave for three days and haven't met a real man yet. I've felt lost the whole time I've been here."

"I think I can understand exactly what you mean," said David looking across the room. "You said you're on leave...what service are you with...where are you stationed?"

"I'm in the Air Force...I'm not a pilot... I'm with the 52nd Equipment Maintenance Squadron at Spangdahlem Air Force Base near Trier, Germany. I have ten months of duty left before I go home. What do you do in San Francisco?"

"My family lives in San Francisco...I just finished my degree in Fine Arts at San Jose State University...my sister just finished her Master's in Art History...we're in Europe to celebrate. We'll both be looking for jobs when we get back to San Francisco."

"Is your sister in Amsterdam right now?"

"Yes", David answered "We just got here today after five...or I should say...six weeks in London...from Amsterdam we'll probably go to Paris."

"Gee...I wish I'd met you sooner...I have to be back at the Spangdahlem Air Base early tomorrow afternoon."

"Where have you been staying?" David asked.

"At the American Hotel with a couple of my buddies from the base. They've been hanging around a joint called the *Paradisio* where they get all kinds of drugs... they've been high on dope since we got here. They have no idea that I'm in a place like this", he said.

"We're staying at the Park Hotel not far from here", David said. "Do you want to go there and have a couple of *real* mixed drinks instead of this *bier*?

"What would your sister think if she happened to see us drinking together at your hotel?"

"She wouldn't think a thing other than I was sitting at the hotel bar with a handsome American man...besides, she's sound asleep in *her* room...which incidentally is at the opposite end of the hall from *my* room."

* * *

After a couple of stingers at the hotel bar David said, "Would you like to crash here at the Park, there's plenty of sleeping space in my room."

"No pardner, I can't stay...I have to be back with my buddies before long...they'd have a fit if I don't show up before dawn at my hotel, especially on this last night out...but I sure wouldn't mind coming up to see what your room looks like."

"Let's go", said David thinking a 'quickie' wouldn't be all that bad.

The two handsome American men left the bar and walked across the deserted lobby to the hotel elevator.

"The room's nothing spectacular...but it is clean and quiet", David said as they walked down the hall.

David opened the door and was grateful to see that the maid left the light on next to his bed and the sheets had been turned down. He ushered in his new friend and as he closed the door was pushed against it roughly and kissed right on the mouth. His crotch was being tenderly stroked through his pants and he yielded to his rising manhood.

"How about a standing up blowjob"

"So...who's standing?" David asked recovering from the delightful kiss but still enjoying the soft strokes to his now hardened erection.

"You are sir", said the handsome Air Force cadet as he dropped to his knees.

* * *

David slept very well...alone. He woke up feeling good but extremely hungry. He picked up the phone and dialed the front desk. "What time is it please?"

"*Elf,* eleven of the morning," came the curt answer. "You do not have a clock in your room?"

David looked at the stand on the other side of his bed, "Yeah, I guess I do. Is there a menu so I can order breakfast or lunch here in my room?"

"There is no lunch...we only have continental breakfast with coffee or tea."

"Whatever it is...could you please send it to my room right away?" David asked in an irritated tone because there was no menu.

"Do you want one or two?"

"Just one," David answered brusquely and hung up the phone.

David wondered if Patty was still sleeping...she had specifically stated not to be disturbed until after two in the afternoon. He was tempted to call her but he really didn't want to disturb her rest. In direct response to his thoughts the phone rang and it was his wonderful sister.

"Hi Poopsie...are you dressed?"

"No," David answered "but I can be good to go in less than ten minutes."

"Meet me in the lobby, Poopsie, your sister is hungry."

David did a quick mouth rinse and sprayed some deodorant under his arms and cologne behind his ears. He threw on the same collared shirt and pleated pants that he had worn the day before, put on the same socks, tied his shoes and scrambled around for his grunge leather bomber jacket that he finally found on the floor of his overcrowded closet.

Still wrestling with his jacket David ran down the hall to the elevator and restlessly waited for *de lift*. The door opened at the lobby and he dashed out expecting to see his sister impatiently waiting for him. She was no where to be seen.

"Mister Wellington," someone called from the front desk.

"Yes," David answered the stern faced clerk.

"Did you make a mistake to order continental breakfast for your room?"

"No...I did order it...but we're going out for lunch... please put the breakfast on my bill."

"There is another matter to bring to your attention," the clerk said very coldly.

"Yes," David said, "What is the matter?"

At that moment Patty emerged from the elevator and strolled over to the front desk to stand by her brother.

"The matter is that we do not allow our guests at the Park to entertain in their rooms...no one except registered guests are permitted after twenty-one hundred hours or *ten p.m.* as you say in America."

"I've never heard of anything so absurd," David responded in a dominant tone trying to keep his temper.

"I never suspected that people in Amsterdam were so bloody uptight."

"What's this all about Poopsie?" Patty asked.

"It's about last night, I met an American friend and we came back to the hotel bar for a nightcap, he came up for a few minutes to see the room. That's all, he didn't even stay for the entire night."

"This is not permitted," said the clerk shaking his finger.

Patricia arched her eyebrow and took a deep breath, "I really hate arguing on only my second day in Denmark...so I am just going to make a statement and I want no more discussion from you on this matter..."

Patty continued, "... if my brother, or I, wish to entertain guests in our rooms at any hour of the day or night, *we will*. Even if we decide to invite the Queen of England and her entire entourage to our rooms, *we will*...and if you have a problem with that you may ask the management of this hotel to speak with me...Let's go eat Poopsie...I'm starving"

"This is not Denmark...this is Holland!" the clerk shrilled in a squeaky voice as the siblings walked away.

"I bet people in Denmark are more polite," David shouted as he and his sister glided out the lobby's front door.

* * *

"This is the hotel where we should have stayed," said David taking another sip of the *Nouveau Beaujolais* that was being offered *gratis* from a gigantic vat at the back of the immense *Cafe Americain.* "I just don't understand how they can afford to give away such delicious wine."

"It's from France, this hotel has undoubtedly purchased it for a song. The French are such wine snobs; they're completely finished with nouveau wines just a few months after it's release in the third week of November. You know that Poppa has Gamay Grapes in the Vineyards."

"Yes, of course," said David "*Lombardi Nouveau Gamay Beaujolais* is my favorite wine in the entire world...but we have bottles of the stuff at home that are over three years old...it's still great wine."

"But Poopsie...Nouveau Beaujolais does not age well...it needs to be consumed while it's still very young. Nanny sells it very cheaply after three or four years... she and the family use it mostly for cooking when it's been in the bottle beyond that time."

"All I have to say is that the wine in this colossal barrel of Nouveau, here at the *Cafe Americain,* tastes just as good as Poppa's at home."

"It is good, Cheers Poopsie!" Patty said taking another sip from her glass and noticing that her brother was frowning.

"What's wrong Poopsie?"

"Oh nothing much...I was just thinking that I am more disappointed with the burger I just ate than I was with the steak at the Five Flies."

"Poopsie, Poopsie...the steaks last night were not all that bad...but I do agree that your burger didn't look too appetizing...you should have ordered the local grilled Bratwurst and sautéed red peppers. Sylvia warned you that there were no good hamburgers to be found anywhere in Europe, outside of Italy."

"Italy...I'm ready to go right now," David said wistfully, "If for no other reason than the food and warmer weather, I'm ready for Roma."

"There's no reason in the world we can't go to Italy right now...except we have to take the car back to London first, we can't just leave it in Holland...and I don't want to have to come back to Amsterdam just to see Rembrandt's works at the Rijksmuseum and of, course, the Van Gogh museum... actually there are about a dozen museums I'd like to visit, but those two will be enough for this trip. I'd also like to see Anne Frank's house while we're here... and it would be nice to go through at least one windmill."

"How long will it take us to do all that?" David sighed.

"If we really rush it I could satisfy my curiosity within three days or so. I would also like to go to the *Jordann* district."

"I know you told me but I forgot. What is the *Jordann* district?" David asked.

"It's supposedly a hodgepodge of cultures, artists, a few cafes, and some interesting shops crammed into narrow streets and canals. Vicky said that it reminded her of Haight Ashbury. It's a very old section of the city which is just beginning its renaissance like the Haight. It also has a significant gay element which might be to your liking. Vicky said she discovered it when she sailed her Seven Seas Voyage around the world. She also said we absolutely should not leave Amsterdam without going there. Who knows, we might even find an exotic *art deco* piece to ship back home."

"I think I've seen enough of the gay element here to know that I would be attracted to *very few* Dutchmen... but the rest of your itinerary sounds okay. Let's give ourselves until the end of the week to see how much we can get covered. It'd be nice to start with the museums and maybe we can save the Jordaan for last. It sounds like we might be doing some shopping."

"Here's to Denmark," Patty said loudly raising her class for a toast.

David raised his class and said quietly, "This isn't Denmark, it's Holland."

"Well Poopsie...let's just call it 'downtown Europe'," she said raising her glass higher.

They both laughed boisterously.

* * *

It was their last night in Amsterdam and the siblings had just finished eating dinner at a little Northern Italian Restaurant within walking distance of their hotel. It was the third time they had eaten there and it never disappointed their expectations for a good meal. David had been thinking of Rome where the weather would be much warmer.

They walked briskly back to the Park Hotel and caught the lift to their floor. They hugged each other briefly and Patty opened her door.

"If you go *cruising* tonight make certain you get back for a little rest and enough time to pack. Remember that we need an early start to get the car to Hook of Holland in time to catch the morning ferry to Harwich," she said as she blew her brother a kiss and closed her door. David trotted down the hallway to his room.

Four days ago he had taken the last half of the sulfur disk the doctor gave him on their first day in Holland. The swelling and soreness in his throat had totally vanished and he felt fit for travel once again. The only annoying thought to David was his lack of success in finding gratifying sexual activity. Aside from the quick interlude with the American Air Force guy, there had been no other release.

David was determined to at least get a blowjob from a Dutchman before he left Holland. These were his last hours here in Amsterdam and he didn't know anywhere to go to make this happen...except the D.O.K.

"Ooh..." David moaned aloud, "I don't really want to go back to that dump...but I guess it's my only alternative.

He hurriedly changed into his well worn buttoned Levis 501 and a white crew-neck t-shirt. He pulled a blue v-neck wool sweater over his undershirt and put on his black steeled toed shoes. He ran his hand through his hair, grabbed his leather Bomber jacket and headed for the door.

'I'll pack in the morning,' he reasoned with himself as he put on his jacket and walked down the hall to the elevator.

The lobby was empty and David could see that there was no taxi out in front of the hotel. He stopped at the front desk, which was deserted, and rang the bell for the attendant who instantly appeared.

"Would you please call a taxi for me?"

The attendant leaned over the counter and peered toward the lobby door to see if there was a taxi already waiting. He picked up the telephone, dialed a number, and looking at David asked, "Where are you going?"

"The D.O.K," David answered feeling slightly relieved that this was not the same clerk who had made a fuss about having 'guests' in the room.

The clerk put down the phone and said, "There is a taxi now."

David turned to see the taxi that had just driven up to the hotel letting off an older couple.

"Thanks," David said as he trotted to hold the hotel door for the two people who had just gotten out of the cab.

David jumped into the taxi and took a long breath, "D.O.K.," he said.

He was glad he was riding, it saved time even though he could have easily walked.

'I'll walk back,' he thought, 'and I hope I'm not strolling alone.'

* * *

The D.O.K. was crowded and the volume was much louder than the first time David had visited here. It would take a little time to visually sift through the stratum of men both on the dance floor and at the bar. He ordered a Heineken and found a strategic place to stand and survey the crowd.

The D.J. was playing Tony Orlando and Dawn's *"Knock Three Times"* and everyone in the joint stomped his foot three times with the song's refrain. Even the bartenders stopped in the middle of whatever they were doing and pounded their fists on the bar three times. Some of the patrons would clink their beer bottles with the *'Twice on the pipe'* refrain

Although he never liked Tony Orlando, David had to admit to himself that it was a festive scene. Everyone seemed to be enjoying himself and having a good time. It was slightly reminiscent of Pearl's on a Saturday night when all the guys would join in singing *'San Francisco'* with Charles Pierce in drag as Jeanette MacDonald.

Oh my darlin
Knock-three-times *on the ceiling if you want me*
Mmmm **twice** *on the pipe if the answer is no*

*Oh my sweetness (**knock-knock-knock**)*
Means you'll meet me in the hallway
*Oh **twice** on the pipe means you ain't gonna show*

When the song was finally over David took a swig of his beer and noticed an imposing figure standing near the entrance. He had just paid the cover charge and was chatting with the doorman. He was taller that most of the others, and he seemed very attractive, and familiarly intriguing. He was also dressed American style like David, with Levis jeans, and a leather jacket he was just now taking off. He revealed a trim but very muscular torso that filled out a dark pullover sweater.

David positioned himself in a masculine pose with one hand stuffed in his Levis pocket and the other hand casually holding his beer bottle. The appealing man walked directly to him with a captivating smile. David knew he had met this guy somewhere before... 'but where...?' he thought.

"Why don't you take off your jacket," he asked in a deep voice with Dutch accent..

"Chandler!" David said happily surprised, "I didn't recognize you without your uniform."

"Yes," Chandler said still smiling, "I have come here to find you."

"I'm curious...how did you know I was here?" David asked.

"That's easy to answer...Fritz told me...Fritz at the front desk said you had taken a taxi to the D.O.K."

"That little snitch," David said with a laugh as he took off his Bomber jacket

"I like your jacket, it looks like my jacket...see?" Chandler held up his coat for David to inspect.

"They do look alike, except mine is slightly more worn than yours. My jacket was second hand when I bought it in a Haight Ashbury thrift shop."

"I will ask Hans to keep them both behind the bar... Hans," he called over his shoulder as he took David's jacket.

Hans was available straightway and Chandler moved up to the bar handing over the coats. "Keep these for us."

"Of course," Hans replied taking the garments, "I am happy to do this for you," he said fluttering his eyebrows and winking at David.

"We are going to dance," Chandler proclaimed as he took David's hand and led him to the dance floor.

The D.J. had just started to play the Jackson Five's 'I'll Be There.'

> *You and I must make a pact, we must bring*
> *salvation back*
> *Where there is love, I'll be there*
>
> *I'll reach out my hand to you, I'll have faith in*
> *all you do*
> *Just call my name and I'll be there*
> *And oh - I'll be there to comfort you,*
> *Build my world of dreams around you, I'm so*
> *glad that I found you*
> *I'll be there with a love that's strong*
> *I'll be your strength, I'll keep holding on - yes I*
> *will, yes I will*

David was so gratified that Chandler had selected a slow song for their first dance; in fact he preferred slow dancing to jumping around at a disco beat. He loved being held tightly fastened like Siamese twins joined at the heart. He wished that Michael Jackson would go on singing the same song all night long.

Chandler took the lead for every dance and was delightfully graceful. David loved the fact that his partner was slightly taller...and stronger...he could just close his eyes and glide with every movement of Chandler's body. This was the most delectable emprise of the entire trip to Europe; this was like being in paradise. David wanted to go on dancing all night with this man...and he came close to doing just that.

In between slow dances Chandler would lead David back to the bar so they could continue their secondary goal of drinking bottles of Heineken beer. They drank one beer after another and David felt closer to heaven with every bottle...he didn't even seem to mind that the D.J. played *'Knock Three Times'* every third song. It finally reached the point where he was dancing to the 'bloody' tune and pounding his foot on the floor.

But it was the slow dances that kept David mesmerized. The lyrics became more and more meaningful with every song. He was thoroughly and totally falling in love and he didn't care one wit if Chandler felt the same way just as long as they remained partners. on the dance floor.

David rested his head on Chandler's shoulder and Chandler made love to David's ear as they danced. They became so immersed in their closeness that when the D.J. played the Carpenter's *'Close to You,'* David felt a rousing vibrancy pushing against his 501 Levis. He was ready to make love.

Why do birds suddenly appear, ev'ry time you are near?

Just like me, they long to be close to you.
Why do stars fall down from the sky, ev'ry time
    you walk by?
Just like me, they long to be close to you.
On the day that you were born the angels got
    together.
And decided to create a dream come true.
So, they sprinkled moon dust in your hair of
    gold,
And star-light in your eyes of blue.

The men continued to drink and dance...dance and drink...and David was consumed with enchantment. When he danced with Chandler to the Bread's '*I Want to Make It with You,*' he got so uncontrollable hard he thought he might ejaculate. He knew that Chandler was just as excited.

Hey, have you ever tried
Really reaching out for the other side
I may be climbing on rainbows
But baby, here goes

Dreams, they're for those who sleep
Life is for us to keep
And if you're wondering what this song is
    leading to
I want to make it with you

When the song ended David and Chandler broke apart, both guys with fierce erections projecting against their jeans. "We have to get out of here," David said.

"Where will we go?" Chandler asked. "We cannot go to The Park Hotel, and I cannot take you to my home."

"Get our jackets," David said, "We're getting a room at the American Hotel."

As they departed from the D.O.K. the D.J. was playing the Partridge Family's 'I Think I Love You.' Even though they would have never danced to it, David thought it was the perfect song for their exit.

> *I think I love you so what am I so afraid of?*
> *I'm afraid that I'm not sure of a love there is no*
> > *cure for*
> *I think I love you isn't that what life is made of?*
> *Though it worries me to say I've never felt*
> > *this way*
> *I think I love you*
> *(I think I love you)*
> *I think I love you*
> *(I think I love you)*)

*   *   *

Renting an accommodation at the American hotel was easier than ordering fries at McDonald's. David found himself in a blissful state of comfort lying on the bed with this handsome Dutch Adonis kissing his lips, face, and neck.

"Take off your shoes...take off your sweater," Chandler commanded as he pulled his own sweater over his head and revealed a body that looked like white chiseled marble.

David removed his t-shirt and sweater and surprised how dark his own skin appeared next to

Chandler's white skin. David pressed his shirtless forearm against Chandler's to contrast the difference in coloration.

"You're very white," David said.

"I am never in the sun without clothes," Chandler answered, "I do not live in California...but you are very sturdy and powerful...do you go to gym a lot."

"No," David said laughing, "I do isometrics every morning when I get out of bed...my Dad taught me when I was just a kid."

"What is isometrics?"

"Just simple exercises in which you push your muscles against each other or against something else that doesn't move... like a wall or floor."

David flexed his biceps and tightened his abdomen for Chandler to get the idea.

"I go to a very old gymnasium for men near the Jordaan district three...four days a week," Chandler said contracting his pectoral muscles.

"You are beautiful Chandler."

"No...David...you are the one who is beautiful."

David rolled over and straddled Chandler with one leg on each side of his white torso. He gently ran his hands over Chandler's chest and said, "From where I sit it is you who are beautiful!"

"Okay, we are both beautiful," Chandler said pulling David toward him for another passionate kiss.

"Let's take off all our clothes," David said vigorously yanking down the buttons of his and Chandler's jeans with both hands in one simultaneous motion. David rolled over and the men undressed completely, their organs quivering like rising dough. David jumped off the bed and said "I'll be right back."

He jogged to the bathroom and clinked around for a moment and came out holding a small vial. He left the door to the bathroom opened slightly and turned off the light in the bedroom. There was now just a soft glow of illumination.

David jumped onto the bed and again straddled Chandler so that now their manhood was touching, one against the other. David opened the small bottle he had brought from the bathroom, poured some of its contents into his hand and began to massage their large tools together as if they were one.

"Ah-h-h...what is that stuff...K-Y?"

"No," David said pouring a little more out of the vial, "it's hand lotion supplied by the hotel.

"Ah-h-h-h...David...don't stop...no one has ever done this...don't stop...don't stop...ah-h, don't stop."

Stroking their stiffened tools together as one, David leaned down and very affectionately and tenderly kissed Chandler. He never missed a beat but kept rhythmic swipes with his hand...he was in heaven...and so was Chandler.

"I'm close..."

"I'm cumming..."

"So am I..."

David looked down at two enlarged protruding heads as they burst forth like fire-hydrants with white fluid shooting their hot pulsating liquid upward...hard... high! This was that savory delectable instant which was being relished now...and would be remembered for a long time to come.

CHAPTER ELEVEN

David knew that he was late when he saw Big Red sitting in front of the Park Hotel. Patricia was standing beside the passenger door of the car.

"Let's get going Poopsie, everything is packed up and ready to roll."

"You got everything...you got all my things?" David said breathlessly as he hurriedly ran up to the car.

Patricia didn't answer David's question but tossed car keys over the roof of the car and said with annoyance in her voice "You're driving...and I don't think we're going to make the morning ferry...our only hope is if it's running late...and I doubt that."

David caught the keys, and jumped into the driver's seat. He started the motor and the tires squealed as he pulled onto the main street. Patty opened the ashtray and pushed in the lighter as she held a fresh cigarette in her hand.

"You don't usually smoke first thing in the morning," David said quietly.

* * *

They arrived at the wharf and could see that the ferry had not yet left...but it already had plumes of smoke rising from its big solitary stack. David drove next to an empty pavilion and up to a gate that blocked their access to the ramp. A chubby uniformed man who looked very European approached the passenger side of the Mercedes.

"*Goedemorgen,*" he said cheerfully

"Good morning," Patricia said in her officious voice, "We have an emergency...we have to be on that ferry with our car."

The man's face became very grave and said "What is the emergency?"

David listened to Patty as he watched the ramp being removed from the ferry.

"We have to be in London by eleven o'clock tonight to sail to New York...it is a serious matter of life or death."

"I do not understand," the chubby official said.

"Let me explain this way," Patty said in a softer tone, "My father works for the American government. He has the highest security clearance of any civilian or military personnel in the United States." Then, looking directly into the man's eyes she said very deliberately in slow bold words, "We must have this car on the ship from London to New York tonight."

"*Begrijpen*...I see...I understand."

The official dashed around the front of the car and bounced into the open pavilion where he picked up a red telephone. David had been listening to his sister talk as he watched the ferry pull away from the wharf. It had already begun backing into the waterway that led to the channel. It was too late.

David felt as if Kenny Stabler had made a "Hail Mary" pass to Fred Biletnikoff who caught the ball, but was pushed out of bounds one yard from the goal. He was disappointed; but he was proud of his sister's attempt to get them on the boat. He knew that Patricia was capable of miracles, but it didn't look like this one was going to happen.

The chubby man in uniform hung up the phone and disappeared for a moment below the window in his kiosk. His head pooped back in view and he smiled and saluted. The gate was slowly opening in front of them. David watched openmouthed as the ferry moved back to its position on the wharf, and the ramp to the parking deck was put in place.

"*Afscheid*" the man yelled with his hand still holding a salute to the siblings

"I don't believe you just pulled this off!" David whispered as he drove their car through the gate and up the ramp onto the morning ferry for Harwich.

* * *

The next couple of days were spent in London making arrangements preparing Big Red for the voyage to America. The siblings also kept busy with their own plans and preparations to continue their trip to France and Italy. Magda's participation in the itinerary turned out to be an extreme blessing, at first.

The really positive aspect about going to Paris now, was the fact that Magda would act as their guide. She spoke French perfectly. In truth, not even a French National could detect that Magda had not been born in Paris and that French was not her primary language. David thought it would be delightful to have his own private interpreter for his first trip to France.

David was grateful that Magda had insisted on designing their entire itinerary from London to Paris. She not only made all the arrangements, she also purchased their first class train tickets across the channel and she had reserved rooms in Paris at the *Hotel Princess Caroline.* Magda knew that Patty had never stayed at this quaint French Hotel and hoped that she and David would be delighted with her selection.

The train trip from London to Paris proved to be an excursion within itself. David was once again glad that Magda had booked passage on the *train ferry* that took them overnight from London to France. They each had their own compartment and Magda had explained how the trip would transpire.

"We board the train here in London which goes right up to a ship with train tracks. They detach our coach car and push it onto the boat. The ferry crosses the channel while we sleep on the train...and in the morning our car is attached to a locomotive engine in France where we continue the journey to the downtown train station in Paris. *Voila!*"

"Astounding," David remarked, "How long has this been going on? I mean travel by train across the English Channel?"

"Oh Dahling...they've been using the same formula for decades...the whole process started sometime in the 1930s before the war."

"I thought that there would have been a tunnel under the channel by now," Patty said. "This is 1971...weren't there suppose to be plans for a tunnel between England and France decades ago?"

"Oh yes Dahling...there have always been plans for a tunnel. I believe that the first time it was seriously considered was in the nineteenth century long before the first war...that project never materialized. Then, once again, everyone was planning for a tunnel back in the late 1920s. They decided it would cost much too much money. Then there was the world depression. Later, during the *occupation* of Paris, everybody thought that Hitler was planning to make a tunnel with slave labor...and as you now that didn't happen. It wasn't until 1964 that an agreement was finally signed between Britain and France. The two countries are still arguing over political details. I do believe, however, that we most definitely shall ride through the tunnel in our lifetime."

"Magda," David said, "I think you make a wonderful teacher, thank you!"

* * *

Hotel Princess Caroline was in the *Etoile Area* of the 17th District of Paris, just steps away from the legendary *Arc De Triomphe* off the *Champs de Elysee*. Most of what David knew about the Arch of Triumph was from the 1948 film by the same name...it had taken place in pre World War II Paris, starring Ingrid Bergman and Charles Boyer. It all seemed very romantic to David.

The hotel was small, only about 50 rooms, and took its name from Napoleon's sister Caroline Bonaparte. The service was first class complete with a very attractive concierge, elegant bar, laundry/cleaners, and breakfast downstairs or served in the room from 7:00a.m.-10:30a.m.every morning. David was hoping that the hotel itself would have enough charm to entice his sister to spend at least a couple of weeks in France, using this place as their operating base to see the city and some of the rest of the country. However, his wishful *ignis fatuus* did not transpire.

Patricia left for Rome the day after their arrival in Paris, and David was left alone with Magda to show him the city. Patty had said to her brother "Poopsie...you couldn't have a better tour guide and translator...and you know that Magda will be more fun than a barrel of monkeys."

Still...David felt a little melancholy about his sister leaving him behind. Patty had been the center of his existence all of his life. She was not only exclusively his only sibling...she was his best friend. There were other members of his family that he loved and trusted completely...but Patty was the number one person in the world in whom he could confide. He felt diminished knowing he would be even temporarily separated from his beautiful Patricia.

Magda and David rode in the cab with Patricia to see her off at Orly Airport. The concierge from the Hotel Princess Caroline had made a reservation for her on Alitalia...a morning flight that would take approximately two and a half hours. It was the same flight David hoped to take when he left for Rome less than three weeks later.

Patricia was thrilled to be going to Italy for the second time in her life. Her mind was filled with the aspirations and intentions of her arrival in Rome. She must visit all her favorite *piazzas* again...she was already thinking about 'happy hour' in the Piazza di Spagna where she could sip a negroni and envision Vivien Leigh as she appeared in Tennessee Williams' *The Roman Spring of Mrs. Stone*...walking down the Spanish Steps.

"Oh...and thanks be to God," she said aloud, "I'm going back to *Saint Peter's Square* and the Basilica...and this time I promised Poppa John that I would light a candle for him at *San Giovanni Laterno* where he had lit one decades ago during the first war."

"You make me wish I were going with you," David said as they got out of the cab."

"You children go to the gate and say your good-byes...I'll have the driver assist me with checking in the luggage," Magda said as she gestured for the Parisian cabbie to open the trunk of the taxi.

Patricia went right on with her conversation about Rome...half talking to her brother and half thinking aloud.

"The Vatican...ah-h-h...the *Vatican museums*... Poopsie...you won't believe it! *St. Peter's church*... *the Sistine Chapel*...the ceilings. The *Vatican gardens* and *Michelangelo's Pieta*...and I want to go back to the *Colosseum*...you might enjoy that too Poopsie...I understand that there's late night activity for someone of, shall I say, *your* persuasion."

"I get the drift," David intejected.

"Oh...and Poopsie...*Fontana di Trevi*...The Fountain of Trevis...you'll never guess what I did..."

"You pulled an *Anita Ekberg* stunt from Fellini's film *Le Dolce Vita* and took off all your clothes and jumped naked into the fountain."

"Don't think it didn't occur to me Poopsie...but no, that's not what I'm talking about. You remember the movie '*Three Coins in a Fountain*"...the girls throw in coins hoping to find husbands, or whatever, and return to Rome? Well...I threw in three coins...one to return to Rome...one to find a husband...and one for you Poopsie... one for my little brother David so you would be with me on my return."

David turned to Patty and said, "Stop...don't make me cry...hug me, right now."

The siblings stopped right in the middle of the bustling Orly Airport terminal and embraced each other in a crushing bear hug. Tears came to both their eyes as they just held on to each other.

"Sometimes I feel like we're two little monkeys just holding on to each other in a foreign hostile world," David whispered.

* * *

"Don't despair dahling," Magda said solicitously as she and David got into a taxi, "You'll be with your exquisite sister soon enough in Italy...but for the next few days it is my duty to introduce you to Paris...and it is your duty to enjoy my talents as a tour guide."

David smiled, "How could I possibly be in despair if you're here with me, Magda. Patty said you and I would have more fun than a barrel of monkeys."

Magda laughed robustly. "We'll start with the Eiffel Tower...*Tour Eiffel, Monsieur, sil vous plait,*" she directed the driver.

"*De ce pas...Madame.*"

"*Monsieur...est'ce que c'est bien la route pour aller Tour Eiffel?*"

"*Comme de juste...mais oui, Madame! Vous etes francais, cest ca?*"

"*Oui, cest ca.*"

"I won't even pretend to understand what you talked about other than the *Tour Eiffel,*" David mused.

"It's nothing dahling...he just wanted to know if I were French...so I lied and said *oui.*"

Magda and the cab driver continued to schmooze in French. David did understand a word or phrase here and there, but he didn't want to interrupt their congenial conversation by asking for a translation. However, it reached a point where the conversation became more animated...then louder...then there was no doubt that Magda and the driver were in a heated argument.

Magda seemed quite acrimonious, but the driver was down right enraged...foaming at the mouth, bristling beyond aggravation, "*Vous etes fou, Madame...fou etes fou!.*"

Magda said in a very deliberately calm voice, "*Contrairement a certainje m'assure que mes sources sont solides...Eiffel etait juif.*"

"*C'est scandaleux!*" the driver shouted in a shrill piercing voice.

"*Eiffel etait juif,*" Magda repeated in her most composed tone of voice.

"*Vous etes fou...vous etes fou...c'est scandaleux,*" the driver screamed.

"*Il etait juif,*" Magda said with finality, "*Tais-toi...fais ce que dois!*"

"Magda," David said, "What in the world is this all about...it sounds as if you're arguing over the Eiffel Tower."

"Yes dahling...we are...our driver cannot accept the fact that Eiffel was a Jew. This is so typical of the French to argue about something of which they know nothing... in fact, this is a nation of such intelligent people that no one can agree with anybody else. The argument about Eiffel being a Jew is an old one that stirs a lot of emotion... there are those who may wish to deny it, but the fact is that Eiffel was of German-Jewish descent."

David felt a little uncomfortable when Magda made this pronouncement because he heard a long growl coming from deep within the the driver's throat.

"Well, I hope the argument has ended," David said looking at the driver. "Leave it to you to push all the right buttons...or in this case all the *wrong* buttons."

"Don't worry dahling, it's all finished...I told him to shut up and drive."

'Thanks be to God,' David thought.

* * *

His partner was soundly sleeping when David left the *Hotel Troyon* at the crack of dawn and walked the short distance to the Princesse Caroline. He knew that Magda was incensed regarding his escapade with the young Swiss businessman...but it was she who pushed the entire issue by challenging him to have sex with the guy. It was a somewhat gratifying experience...but definitely not one to record as indelibly memorable.

David breezed through the lobby to the elevator and up to his floor. He hesitated for a moment considering going straight to Magda's room to report that he had returned...but, then he thought, 'better not.'

The best tactic would be to clean up with a shave and a quick shower...he also needed to brush his teeth, gargle with Listerine and put on fresh clothes. His breath reeked of brandy and his clothes were inundated with the smell of cigarette smoke. Yes...it would be much better to face Magda after he completed his hygienic checklist...that way he would also be ready for another day of sightseeing and adventure in Paris.

When David was finished with bathing and changing clothes or '*changement de vetements*' as Magda had taught him in the last few days, he thought it best to phone her room before charging down the hall. It was still very early in the morning and she hated to be seen without at least some make-up.

He rang her room directly...and it continued to ring several times before there was an answer... "*Allo!*"

It was a woman's voice but it was definitely not Magda. David thought that perhaps in a state of sexual frustration Magda might have picked up a female trick for the night.

"*Sil vous plait...qui est-ce?*" David asked 'who is this' as politely as he knew how.

"*C'est ce employee de maison, monsieur.*"

"Oh, the maid...uh...uh...do you speak English?"

"*Oui monsieur...*you are the English gentleman in the next room?"

"Yes...yes thank you...*sil vous plait...ou Madame?* Where is Magda?"

"*Elle n'est pas partante...*she is not here monsieur, she has checked out of the hotel."

"Checked out," David said in a panicked voice, "how long ago...where did she go?"

"I do not know monsieur," the maid said in a cool tone, "They can inform you downstairs," and she hung up the phone.

David grabbed his leather jacket and slung it over his shoulder as he dashed out the door, down the elevator and appeared at the front desk. The hotel check-in clerk was ready for him.

"She took taxis to the train station...*Gare du Nord*...she left about one half hour ago you may have time to see her before the train leaves for London."

"Thank you," David shouted as he ran to the front door, "*Gare du Nord!*"

* * *

David wondered how he always found himself in the middle of these ridiculous situations where he was rushing to beat the clock. He knew for certain now that Magda was 'pissed off.' He wasn't sure what he'd say if he got there in time to see her...what could he say?

He really didn't feel that he owed her an apology... if the man from Switzerland had favored being with a woman last night...the shoe would be on the other foot.

'I wouldn't have been in the least upset,' David thought as he stepped out of the cab in front of the bustling Paris train station. She would have run off with him in a New York second... without blinking...in fact... she'd probably still be in bed with him. 'I most likely would not have seen Magda for the next two days,' he thought. No, he didn't owe her an apology...it was she who was acting like a juvenile schoolgirl running off to the train station without saying a word.

David was momentarily taken back to reality as he scanned the immense main hall of the train station. It was enormous...but finding Magda proved to be no difficulty at all. She had, of course, found a strategic spot to position herself so that she could see, and easily be seen, by everyone who entered the main hall. She was wearing a nearly full length scarlet silk cape...and her hair was piled high over her aristocratic face...she was smoking, of course...but this time she was using her *Hollygolightly* cigarette holder which was being clenched ostentatiously in a dramatic pose.

David could not help looking twice at the very tall, suave, silver haired gentleman that Magda must have captured immediately upon her arrival to the station. He was truly handsome and he towered over her like a lighthouse on a hill. He had to be several inches taller than David...maybe even six foot six or six foot seven inches. He reminded David of Clint Walker (only with grey hair) who starred in the black and white television series *Cheyenne* they used to watch as kids back in the fifties and sixties... but it was still Magda who was the center of attention puffing away with her cigarette in a holder.

"David...da-h-h-h-ling...you came to see *us* off," as she threw her arms around him in a theatrical embrace.

"Yes, of course," David said looking straight at the tall stranger who was frowning.

"This is Arin...he is from *Oz-loh*...Norwegian you know."

"Yes," David said, "I've heard Oslo is a very beautiful city...I hope to go to Norway someday. Hello Arin...I'm David from San Francisco," and he extended his hand.

Arin smiled broadly for the first time since David had seen him. He extended his enormous right hand and grasped David's tightly.

"I always want to go to San Francisco," he said looking steadfastly into David's eyes.

'Uh-oh,' thought David...'I'd better make this a quick good-bye and get out of here before I get into trouble.'

"Magda," David turned to face her, "You left without saying good-bye."

"I know dahling...I'm sorry...it's simply that I need to be back in London as soon as possible...and I didn't want to miss this train...do you forgive me?" she asked flitting her eyelashes.

"There's nothing to forgive," David said, "I'm just here to see you off. When is your train leaving?"

"It should depart in less than thirty minutes dahling... but give me another hug and you can be off...I have Arin to keep me company."

"Of course," David said as he hugged her and extended his hand again to Arin.

Magda almost pushed David away from Arin and said "I'll phone you at your hotel when I arrive in London... bye-bye dahling."

David did a half turn toward Arin and said "Glad to have met you Arin...enjoy your trip to London."

"I am not going to London...my train doesn't leave for more than three hours...I am going to Berlin on business."

"Oh-h," David said, "Then, have a good trip to Berlin."

David rushed out of the terminal and hailed a taxi... he didn't want to look back at Magda who had to be embarrassed about the scenario she tried to pull off. 'She wanted me to think that Arin was accompanying her to London.' Once again, David had unintentionally foiled her. They both knew, just like the Swiss businessman from last night, Arin was much more sexually inclined toward men.

There was temptation on David's part and enough time to take advantage of Arin's disguised message, '... *my train doesn't leave for more than three hours*...' but David couldn't trust Magda to leave if she thought for one moment that he and Arin would '*make the scene*' together. No, even a quickie with that Norwegian adonis wouldn't be worth risking more of her wrath.

David skipped into the first available cab and asked the driver, "Do you speak English?"

"*Oui, monsieur*, where would you like to go?"

"Do you know any gay bars or restaurants in Paris that serve breakfast?"

"*Oui monsieur*...of course...I will take you to one of the best gay restaurants in Paris."

David was not in the least perturbed that Magda had left so abruptly...in fact, he felt more relaxed at this moment riding in a cab to a new episode of 'good eating' at a gay French restaurant than he had since he arrived here. Patty would have referred to the occasion as '*adventures in gay eating.*'

He allowed his mind to wander as he comfortably rode through the streets of Paris in his taxi. He looked back on his last days in France. It wasn't that David hadn't enjoyed Magda...she had unarguably shown him Paris. They had spent literally days in the *Louvre*... Magda had even held the museum guards at bay during closing time allowing David to run down the corridor and touch the *Venus de Milo* after visitors were gone... and of course they had to look at the *Mona Lisa*. He was disappointed that Leonardo da Vinci's masterpiece was so small...in his mind it should have been ten feet tall. Poppa John who had seen it years ago would always say '*La Gioconda...que bella!*'

"Why does my Italian grandfather always refer to the *Mona Lisa* as *La Gioconda*?" David had asked Magda.

"There have been many experts and historians that believe a wealthy 16th century Italian aristocrat named *Francesco Gioconda* commissioned *da Vinci* to paint a portrait of his wife *Lisa Gherardini*...the Italians call her *La Gioconda* and the French say *La Joconde*."

One of the great things about Magda, David thought, was her tremendous knowledge. He understood why she was such good friends with Patricia. They were both scholarly, well-read, and well acquainted with all the arts. He loved and admired these women for the academic enlightenment they both shared freely with him, their cohorts and companions. David continue to reminisce.

"How long have you been a homosexual?" Magda asked David as they had drunk wine at a little cafe in the *Place de la Sorbonne*.

David was altogether amenable and open to discuss his homosexuality...and he was enjoying the third bottle of wine they had just ordered after eating a delectable *salade niscois* made with fresh anchovies and tuna, green beans, tomatoes, boiled eggs, green onions, capers and potatoes...the presentation was *recherche*...absolutely exqusite. David was in an amiable mood for any topic of conversation.

"Magda," he said after taking a hefty sip of his *Pineau de la Loire*, "I am a homosexual from birth...as Patty always says, 'my little brother was born queer.'"

Magda threw back her head and laughed, "Dahling... how could she possibly know...you were a baby."

"To be genuine about this conversation...I have to preface it with some background. I have a memory *extraordinaire*...it's phenomenally freakish how far back I can remember things. No, I don't have a photographic mind, but I do have a phenomenal ability to recall incidents and my precise feelings and experiences at they time they occurred."

David went on, "I recall many details from the first Christmas I can remember. I was less than 22 months old when we lived in Gulf Port, Mississippi, not too far from New Orleans. I remember sitting on one of my father's knees while Patricia sat on the other. We were in front of the Christmas tree and he held us as we opened presents. One of the gifts was in a huge box wrapped with blue paper and a gargantuan white bow and my mother helped open it. Inside was a big yellow and green beach ball that Patty and I bounced around in the front yard on Christmas day."

"I remember my third birthday party just not long after that Christmas. Patty was in the first grade and my mother invited two of her girlfriends (and their moms) to help out with my party. There were about a dozen school kids at the party from Patty's class and there were at least a dozen cadets from the Gulf Port Military Academy where my Dad taught English and coached boxing and football."

That birthday party is the first time I remember really being in love. It was with Stanley. He was gorgeous, and he also used to babysit us from time to time when Sylvia and Richard would go out. He had beautiful straight blond hair that fell over his right eyebrow whenever he would bend his head...Patty was in love with him, too. Magda, I remember virtually every significant incident in my life from that point, after the age of three years."

"Do you remember anything...anything at all dahling...before that first Christmas when you were only twenty two months old?" Magda asked.

"There is one thing...no, two events...no three events now that I think about it. I'm sure my very first memory was in the swimming pool at the academy. My dad took me there a lot...he'd just put me in the water and I'd start swimming...I remember cadets who would carefully play around with me. I remember the hot Mississippi sun gleaming on splashing water...I remember the smell of chlorine...I remember feeling happy when I was in the water with my Daddy. When I was much older my parents told me that I was swimming at the age of eighteen months...but I can't be sure if those memories started then or a few months later. I do remember swimming came before I could even talk."

"Fascinating Dahling," Magda said as she poured more wine into both of their glasses. Do you ever remember having an erection in those early years?"

"Yes, indeed...I used to sleep in one of those baby beds with guards all around it. I slept in one of those until I was nearly four years old. It was after my third birthday party that I woke up almost every morning with a hard-on. I remember being alarmed that something was dreadfully wrong with my 'tee-tee.'

Magda let out rowdy laughter, "Dahling...when did you find out that your cock was performing a healthy and normal male function?"

"That's a good point to bring up Magda because I think that may have been the first time I realized that I was homosexual."

"What?" Magda said nearly slamming down her wineglass, "Do you mean to tell me that you were barely three years old and you had homosexual thoughts or fantasies?"

"Exactly...and they started coming fast and furiously."

"Tell me how such a thing happens to a three year old boy," Magda said draining her wine glass and pouring herself the last of the bottle.

David took a deep breath and indicated for the server to bring another bottle.

"So enlighten me!" Magda demanded.

"You know of our American singing cowboy Gene Autry?"

"Of course Dahling...did he molest your little tee-tee?"

"In a way," David said laughing.

"Tell me!" Magda shouted.

David laughed again enjoying the moment, "We didn't have television in those days...just radio and occasionally the movies. We regularly listened to Gene Autry's program over the air-waves and then we saw him in a movie at the cinema. I fell in love..."

"The same way you loved that cadet who would baby-sit for you and Patricia?" Magda interrupted.

"No," David said, "This was really the *real* thing. I starting having romantic, almost erotic dreams about Gene Autry."

"Do you mean that you had *wet* dreams at three years of age?" Magda asked in a serious tone.

David laughed again, "Of course not, I was still a good eight or nine years away from puberty...but I dreamed about Gene Autry...he would sing to me...I could hear his voice in my dreams...I could see him on his horse. One time I dreamed that he was wounded by a bullet...shot in the shoulder. He got off his horse and lay down on the ground...I went to him and put his head in my lap...I held his head and stroked his hair...my tee-tee got bigger and bigger. I would wake up with an erection."

Magda sounded like a psychiatrist, "You are telling me that this was a recurring dream?"

"Yes," David said gulping down more wine, "I dreamed of Gene Autry being wounded many times... but as I grew up my hero would change...I had a long affair holding Roy Rogers in my arms...and then there was Hopalong Cassidy...but it was always the same...I would get hard dreaming about holding those cowboys in my arms."

"Fascinating! When did you stop feeling alarmed about your tee-tee growing big?"

"Oh, I got over that quickly after the first couple of incidents with Gene Autry. I confided in my mother that I thought something was wrong with my tee-tee."

"Your mother...um-m-m...interesting...why didn't you tell your father?"

"I most certainly would have told him before I told my mother...it was mostly a matter of availability."

"What do you mean when you say 'availability' dahling."

"My father wasn't around when this started happening...he was at work almost every morning at 6:00 A.M. while I was still dreaming of Gene Autry. It was usually Sylvia who lifted me out of bed in the morning... sometimes even Patty would pick me up."

"Is that your mother's name, is her name Sylvia? Sylvia," Magda repeated, "What a beautiful name, Sylvia...I like that even better than the name Sonja."

"Sonja, Magda, Patricia and Sylvia all have something in common," David said.

"What's that?" Magda said, "That all four names end in an '*a*'?

"No," David said, "All four of you are extraordinarily beautiful and intelligent women."

Magda reached across the table and took David's hand to her lips. "Oh dahling," she said sentimentally, "You are so wonderful."

"The truth is the truth, Magda, and sometimes it's not so well-favored, but in this case the truth is resplendently exquisite...each of you ladies is a ravishing beauty...and that is not only the truth...it is a fact."

"You are really wonderful dahling...but let's get back to Sylvia. What did she tell you when you expressed concern about your tee-tee growing bigger dreaming of cowboys?"

"Sylvia told me that I had nothing to worry about. It was very normal for a little boy to get excited when he dreamed about his heroes. I remember feeling good about nothing being wrong with my tee-tee, and it was okay to be in love with cowboys."

"Had you told her specifically that you were in love with Gene Autry?"

"Oh yeah...I had reported to my entire family that I loved him. They thought I was slightly fickle."

"Why is that Dahling?"

"Well...I already told you that didn't last very long...I dumped him for Roy Rogers. I remember Patty asking 'What happened to your love affair with Gene Autry?'

"What was your answer, dahling?"

"I said that Roy Rogers was the most handsome cowboy in the whole world when he sits on Trigger."

* * *

Yes, David was now happily heading to places in Paris without Magda breathing down his neck. It felt so good to be free from her clutches. She had been fun...but he was really glad to be in this taxi heading for one of the 'best gay restaurants' in town.

It turned out to be a little neighborhood bistro off *rue Saint-Martin* and he immediately felt comfortable with the old *bartender/waiter/chef* who spoke English and was happy to accommodate David at the cozy relaxing bar. There were a few guys tittering away in French at the other end...but David didn't pay any attention as he ate a lovely plate of sliced roast pork and delightful cheeses with freshly made croissants and creamy butter.

He didn't notice that the three guys from the end of the bar had left their seats and were heading in his direction.

"*Bon jour, monsieur*," said the tallest, who couldn't be more than five feet six inches

"You are American?"

David turned and faced the somewhat scruffy looking fellows who had just approached him. The tallest one who first spoke was the most presentable of the three...and he was nobody David cared to engage in conversation. The other two were pathetic. They looked like street urchins from one of the poorest *banlieues* surrounding Paris. The shortest guy, and the ugliest, had distorted Asian facial features He was a skinny sickly looking creature with dirty straggly shoulder length hair.

Philipe, the bartender, came back toward David's end of the counter and made his presence known by clearing lunch dishes and wiping the bar. He was frowning and looking directly at the tall guy.

"Yes...I'm an American," David answered.

"Hello...my name is Henri," he said extending a hand with long filthy fingernails.

"My name is David...David Wellington," he said with a wince as they shook hands.

"These are my two friends," Henri said as he pointed to the other two, "Ruelle and this is Chien," and he pushed the ugly Asian looking guy up against David. "Chien is Viet Cong...what you think of that...he is Viet Cong...you are American...what you think, huh?

David was repulsed and nearly lost his lunch from the foul nauseating odor that emanated from the Asian's body which was blemished with scabs and scars. He didn't want to be rude to these three guys, but he was ready to dismiss them in one way or another. He could ask Philipe to send them drinks at the other end of the bar...or he might just ask them to go away.

David didn't have to say another word because Philipe took over the conversation,

"*Casse-toi d'ici*! ; *Fiche le camp d'ici*! ; *Barre-toi d'ici*," and for David's sake he added in English, "Get the hell out of here now!"

They quickly dispersed and Ruelle and his Viet Cong boyfriend Chien headed straight for the front door. Henri ran back down to the other end of the bar to retrieve some personal belongings. He bungled around for a minute and then at a Boy Scout's pace headed toward the door.

"No tip for you, Philipe," he shouted as he jogged out of the bistro.

"*Dégage d'ici!*" Philipe shouted back just as Henri stepped outside.

David was pretty sure he understood the words Philipe had just shouted...and he was grateful to feel a little relief that those idiots had left. He still felt a little uncomfortable... it was possible for them to return with a machine gun or a machete...but he didn't want to say anything to Philipe who had just served him a fresh drink.

"Apologies monsieur for those *mauvais garçons*, bad boys. We must forgive them...they are very *enfantine*... you know stupid."

"Infantile, as we would say in America."

"Oui monsieur...infantile."

Philipe continued to wipe around the bar with a rag and then paused for a moment as if he were thinking aloud.

"Monsieur David...I would like to ask a request of you."

"Sure," David said wondering what this guy could possibly want from him, "I can only say yes or no."

"I would like you to return to my bar tonight. I have a very good friend who belongs to the *Brigade Parachutiste* in the French Airborne Regiment...you understand...he is a paratrooper, one of those who wears the red beret."

"Yes," David said intrigued, "I understand...tell me about him."

"He is *un homme dont la beauté attire l'œil... magnifique...masculin.*"

"Yes," David said with greater interest, "He is *very* handsome and masculine."

"Oh, monsieur David, he is as the French say *avoir l'air resplendissant*...he is fabulous to look at...but there is a problem...he is *des bi-sexuel.*"

"That's not a problem...I know many men in America who are bisexual."

"There is a problem because he is sad. He is married and his wife has left him...she did not want to see her beautiful husband go with other beautiful men. She wanted him only for herself. Tonight it is sad because it is Jean-paul's *jour de naissance*, his birthday, and he has no one to celebrate with him. He will come here, sit at the end of the bar and become *bu comme des trous*, drunk as the fishes, and feel sorry for himself."

"Philipe, wouldn't it be better if *Jean-paul* was consoled by someone who spoke French...unless he speaks English at least as well as you, I won't be able to carry on a decent conversation with him."

"*Hélas,* Monsieur David, Jean-paul does not speak a word of English...but it will not be important for conversation. I will be available for any necessary translation at the bar, and when you go to his *appartement* later in the evening...you will both speak the same language."

"I don't know, Philipe...it's a tempting offer...but what if we don't, as the French say *s'entendre*, you know, get along together."

Philipe laughed heartily, "That will be impossible, monsieur, when you see each other it will be *le coup de foudre*...love at first sight for both of you."

* * *

CHAPTER TWELVE

David's trip from Paris to Rome took about two and a half hours. His Alitalia 727 arrived at the *Leonardo da Vinci Airport* after an uneventful flight. The two pretty stewardesses in first class had been filled with warmth and congeniality for every passenger, however, they both flirted outrageously with David.

David found just enough time to relax with a tempting snack and a couple of drinks. He reflected on his visit to Paris which hadn't been all that great. The highlight had been the day he'd left Magda at the train terminal and discovered the delightful gay bistro in downtown Paris. He would always be grateful to the manager, Philipe, for his kindness and especially for setting him up with Jean-Paul, the handsome and masculine *parachutiste* who really knew how to make love.

David only felt disappointed because he was fast running out of money and had no immediate way to contact Patricia for relief. He had telephoned Nanny and gave her his S.O.S., send money story. She was, of course, alarmed that David might starve before he received the funds. He had encountered a lot of problems with the bank in Paris accepting her wire, so he was on his way to Rome pretty much broke.

Nanny had instructed David to 'get his body to Rome' where she knew he could stay at the *Nord Nouva Hotel* where her cousin was concierge and part owner. Nanny also knew that Patricia had stayed there before going on to Firenze...but nobody had heard from her since she left Rome many days ago. David reassured his grandmother that he would phone as soon as he arrived.

Nanny told him to find a bank immediately upon his arrival and get her the address to resend the funds that never got to Paris. He had used up just about the last of his money getting this Alitalia flight to Rome, and now it would be less than an hour when he landed at the Michelangelo terminal. He took a sip of his drink...put on his headsets and sat back in his seat listening to Simon and Garfunkal.

> *When you're weary, feeling small,*
> *When tears are in your eyes, I will dry them all;*
> *I'm on your side. When times get rough*
> *And friends just can't be found,*
> *Like a bridge over troubled water*
> *I will lay me down.*
> *Like a bridge over troubled water*
> *I will lay me down.*

* * *

The passengers exited the plane from the rear stairway of the craft which led directly to the tarmac. There was a short walk to the terminal and as David strolled in that direction his first instinct was to kiss the ground. He had a tremendous sense of relief being here.

The weather felt like San Jose on an early spring morning with a clear and sunny sky. It was a bright contrast to the last few dour and damp days he had spent in Paris. David thought this Mediterranean landscape and environment was *extremely* reminiscent of California. He promptly felt at home in his latest surroundings.

David's joy at arriving in Rome was just slightly diminished by the fact that he was broke. He thought it wouldn't be very much fun being without money his first time in the *Eternal City*. He checked his wallet again and was pleased to find a twenty dollar bill tucked in a compartment with a couple pieces of paper that had notations he had written before leaving home.

After collecting his luggage David went straight to an exchange window to turn his twenty dollar bill to Lira. He was close to jubilant as the clerk counted out more than thirty thousand lira for his American money. "*Grazie, grazie, grazie*" David said enthusiastically, as he tucked the lira in his coat pocket.

"*Prego*," came the reply in a neutral tone from the clerk.

"Oh," David said, turning back to the counter. "*Excusa*...Taxi?"

The clerk smiled slightly and pointed to a nearby sign that said *Parada de Taxis* and an arrow pointing to the street. "Thanks," David said as he picked up his luggage and walked toward the glass doors that led to the taxi stand.

The clerk replied in perfect English, "You are quite welcome."

"Heh," David thought to himself, "It's going to be easy getting around in Rome."

He didn't even have to approach the cab stand because a driver with a waiting orange Fiat reached out with both hands to retrieve David's luggage. The bags hardly fit in the tiny back seat of the car, and David crammed his long legs into the passenger seat next to the driver.

"Do you speak English?" David asked.

"Of course," the middle age taxi driver answered, "I have two sisters in Chicago. I went to visit them a few months ago....where are you from?"

"San Francisco," David answered.

"Hey! San Francisco," the driver shouted excitedly. "*Que Bella* ...the most beautiful city in America."

"You've been there?" David asked.

"Yes...yes!" came the answer. "One time three years ago. I traveled with my sisters on a train from Chicago to California. We stay in San Francisco five days. Beautiful... Ah-h."

"It's a wonderful place to live," David said.

"Where you want to go now?" Driver asked."

"Here, I'll show you," David said as reached for his wallet and pulled out the pieces of paper with notations. He pointed to a small fragment and asked, "Is this far from here?"

"Nice hotel...good place to stay...no too far," the driver stated in an Italian accent.

David was a little concerned that he might not have the money to pay for the ride after he got there. The little scrap of paper had the address of the *Nord Nuova Hotel*. He knew very little about the place aside from the fact that one of Nanny's cousins, Luigi, was the Concierge and partial owner of the establishment.

David planned on having Luigi make a telephone call to Nanny first thing on check-in. He would have to tell her that the money she wired to him in Paris had never arrived. He hoped with all his heart that she would be able to pull strings and have funds sent to Rome within the next twenty-four or thirty-six hours. He did not suspect that he would be in the *Eternal City* for the next several days without financial reinforcement from home.

David knew that Patty was still *somewhere* in Italy, but the siblings had not been in touch with each other for almost two weeks. He wondered if she were still in Rome. He desperately needed to hook up with her so he could replenish his empty wallet. He knew she had the American Express card that Poppa John had given her for her twenty-fourth birthday. She had unlimited access to the world, including the ability to draw as much cash as she wanted at anytime and any place...and all the charges went to Poppa.

As the taxi drew up to the front entrance of the *Hotel Nord Nuova* David awkwardly scrambled out of the passenger seat and reached for his luggage in the back of the little car. The driver also got out of the cab and took another of the suitcases from the far side of the back seat.

"We take you inside," the driver said as he rescued David from carrying the heaviest luggage.

"Grazie," David said as he slung his carrying case over his left shoulder and followed the driver into the inviting lobby of the hotel that would be his new home.

David reached into his pocket and brought out all the Italian bills he had been given at the airport exchange. He calculated the fare would be eleven or twelve American dollars and silently prayed there would be enough left over for a couple of decent meals.

The taxi driver laughed and said "No, no...too much. Five thousand lira is *perfecto,*" as he counted out

'Whew,' David sighed to himself and figured that five thousand lira couldn't be much more than three or four American dollars.

An attractive older man with silver hair and wearing a dark blue suit appeared next to David as he was shaking the taxi driver's hand.

"Buon giorno," he said offering his hand to David.

"Buon giorno," David said trying to emulate the same accent.

"Welcome to the Hotel Nord Nuova," the man said in what David thought was a very appealing voice. "How long will you be staying with us?"

"I'm not certain," David answered, not trying to show that he was a little nervous. "I would imagine at least two weeks, and perhaps longer."

"*Molto bene*," the Italian gentleman said warmly. "Please, sign our book."

Stepping toward a beautiful hand carved library table David presented the tattered note paper he had shown to the taxi driver. "Do you know this person," David asked as he pointed to the paper.

The man put on a pair of glasses which were held on a gold chain around his neck.

"Luigi Andreozzi," he read with a startle. "Luigi Andreozzi...that's me!"

"Oh good," David said, "I believe that we are relatives."

"I don't understand," Luigi sounded perplexed.

"My grandmother is Marietta Lauro Lombardi, your first cousin," David proclaimed.

"Your sister, Patricia...*que bella* she was here...just a few days ago," Luigi declared as he threw out his arms hugging David.

David felt a rush of complete relief as he received kisses on both cheeks from his new found cousin.

"Where is Patty now?' David asked, "Is she still in Italy?"

"Oh yes...she will come back here...we keep her room for her. Right now I think she's in *Firenze*, but she will come back here. We have more than one hundred fifty rooms...we no fill up too much right now. We keep the room for Patricia. She leave plenty in her room...clothes, boxes, suitcases...lots of things."

"I'd be very happy if I could stay in her room," David quickly offered.

"No, no, no, I have a nice room just for you. You will like it my cousin, David."

David was surprised that Luigi knew his name without even looking at the register. Patty must have talked about her little brother enough so that Nanny's cousin had it memorized, he thought.

As if to verify what David was thinking, Luigi said, "Everybody think you sister so beautiful...I have a beautiful daughter too...Tanya. Patricia and Tanya make good friends. They go all over Roma together. You will meet Tanya, *dopodomani,* the day after tomorrow. She works at the hotel, sometimes...Concierge...like her Papa."

"I look forward to meeting my new cousin," David said.

"You find out you have *lotsa* cousins in Roma... come...I'll show you to your room."

* * *

David's first morning in Rome turned out to be exhilarating. He began by having a scrumptious breakfast at the hotel's restaurant and then departed for an enlightening walk through *The Eternal City*. He decided to dress for comfort and put on his travel worn corduroy suit and well-worn walking shoes. He figured that the medium brown fabric went well with the darker brown shoes, belt, and tie. He also thought the clothes were just right for the sunny but slightly cool May morning.

About a block and a half from his hotel on *Via Giovanni Amendola*, he noticed the close proximity of the *Termini Train Station* off *Via Giovanni Giolitti* where he would be kicking off to destinations in Italy once he was more familiar with Roma. He envisioned getting money from Nanny and taking off for cities like Florence, Venice and Milano. He had a slight pang of nostalgia thinking about Patricia and wondered if he might meet up with her in one of those places.

Walking up and down the surrounding streets from the train station David came to the *Hotel Massimo d" Azeglio* where he saw the entrance to the *ristorante* of the same name. He knew it was a favorite of Nanny and Poppa John when they visited Rome.

"I'll remember to come here right after my funds are replenished," David said aloud.

He took a mental note of other locations that were part of his new environment near the Hotel Nord Nuova. He discovered *Museo Nazionale Romano*, *Piazza del Cinquecento*, *Piazza del Repubblica* and the *Teatro dell'Opera Di Roma*. These would be just a few of the places he would explore in depth while he was in Rome... but at this point David was ready to backtrack toward the Termini Train Station for a closer look there before he returned to the hotel for lunch.

The massive modernistic terminal looked more like an American shopping center than a train station. It was surrounded by boutiques, restaurants, and bars for both espresso and other adult beverages. This time of the year it didn't seem too crowded with travelers, but there were plenty of well-dressed locals who apparently frequented the local merchants. David noticed a sign *Mediobanca* that sat next door to the foreign exchange at the station.

"Nanny might be able to wire money to that bank," David thought as he continued his morning walk.

"Stop!" he said aloud and froze in place.

David turned and walked back to the bank where two files of customers were waiting. He stood behind the last person in the shortest line. He was going to ask if money could be wired here from Nanny's bank in California. If so, he would obtain this name and address in order to consummate a transfer of dollars, just steps away from his hotel.

David waited anxiously in line and looked closely at the face of the teller he would be speaking with in a few moments. She was beautiful...she was smiling...she looked like she could have been Sophia Loren's sister! David knew that this lovely creature would successfully assist him in getting his money from Nanny!

He smiled broadly as he approached the teller and asked, "*Excusa*, do you speak English?"

"Of course," she smiled back, nearly laughing. "How may I help you?"

"I need to know if money can be wired to me... here to this bank...from America," he said.

"Of course," she smiled again, looking a little more serious. "You can have money sent to you here from America. Here is the name of our bank and here is the address," she said handing him a card, and added "Where in America?"

"California...San Francisco...and...thank you so much," David sighed as he took the business card and placed it in his corduroy jacket pocket. "May I ask your name?"

"Adrianna," she answered leaning her face closer to David on the other side of the counter. "My name is on the card. You come see me every morning after the money is wired. I let you know as soon as it arrives."

"Grazie, grazie," David sang out. "I'll see you *domani,* tomorrow."

"*Ciao,*" she said.

David walked back to his hotel feeling relieved to have an official place to claim his wired money. He hoped that Luigi would be on duty to listen to his story of financial woe. It wasn't going to be easy to explain why he was unable to pay for the room and meal he had already procured. It was going to be even harder to ask for continued credit for an indeterminate period of time while waiting for relief funds.

Luigi made it easier then David could have imagined. Thankfully, 'Cousin' Luigi was on duty and more congenially cordial than ever.

"Hey, *mi cugino,*" Luigi sang out when he glanced up from a ledger he was reading and caught sight of David. "*Cume stai*...how are you? You've been seeing the sights without my guidance. Good for you...already I can see that, like your beautiful sister Patricia, you are not the typical American tourist."

"I walked around a few streets near the hotel...not too far...I did not want to get lost," David answered.

Luigi laughed, "I am sure you would not get lost...you are too smart to lose your way...but if you have not had lunch...I can recommend many places within walking distance."

"Um-m...that's nice Luigi...but right now there is a problem for me," David said shyly.

"What could that be?" said Luigi in a more solemn tone of voice.

David came right to the point "I was expecting money to be wired before I left Paris...it never arrived. I needed to get out of that city before I was flat broke... so I made one last visit to the French bank before I left. That stupid bank in Paris could find no record of money being wired from San Francisco; so I came here to Roma to contact Marietta and Giovanni to let them know I did not receive the money they had wired to me in France"

Even before David could finish his dismal tale, Luigi reached into his own coat pocket and produced a doe skin wallet from which he was counting out bills.

"No...no," cried David. "I don't want any money from you Luigi."

Luigi continued to count what seemed to be a considerable sum and offered it to David with a pleading look. "Take this...take this...please...you cannot be in Rome with no money. I will not allow it."

"No...no," David repeated. "That is final...I will not take your money."

Luigi tried to reason with David, "Then how you see Roma if you have no money? When in Rome you have to eat at many different restaurants...no money, no *ristorantes*.

"I'll have money in a little while...meantime I can eat here at the hotel, if you accept my credit. The hotel has everything I need...beautiful room...food...*farmacia*. I can see Rome on foot...I'm young...I'm healthy...I can walk...I can even run if I need to run. No Luigi, I will not take any money from you...but if you will help me to make a call to Marietta...she will wire money to me here."

David produced the card that had been given to him at the bank and presented it to Luigi. "I even made a beautiful new friend...her name is Adrianna...she'll be on the lookout for my money when it arrives in Rome... she looks a lot like Sophia Loren," he added.

"Please Luigi..just help me make the telephone call to Marietta."

"Okay...you win...this time. We can no make the call now...it's three in the morning for your grandmother," Luigi said looking at his watch. We'll call after you have supper here tonight at the hotel. Now you go have lunch and no worry about nothing. Everything for you going to be okay. Go eat lunch...take *sonnollino...pisolino*...we will call after your supper tonight...go," Luigi commanded as he directed David toward the restaurant.

David obediently walked to the restaurant thinking to himself, "I know that *sonnollino* is the Italian word for nap...but I hope *pisolino* doesn't mean what it sounds like."

* * *

Supper at the hotel was absolutely delicious. The local white wine, a *Pinot Grigio*, was served with an antipasto of heavenly thin sliced prosciutto wrapped around fresh white figs. Light red *Montepulciano d'Abruzzo* came with the entrée, a delectable veal Milanese served with a drizzle fresh lemon sauce. Dessert was rich homemade *spumoni gelato*.

"A terrific meal," David said to the young male server who cleared the table.

"I am glad you like it," the young man said proudly showing off his English.

"Would you like after dinner drink?"

"Whatever you suggest," David said.

The waiter nodded and happily jaunted off to prepare David's drink. Meanwhile, Luigi appeared in the restaurant walking directly to David's table. He was carrying a small pad and pen which he laid next to David and demonstrably said "This is the time to call your Nanny ... please write the number and I will come for you when I have reached her."

As David wrote down the telephone number he asked, "How did you know that I called my grandmother by the name 'Nanny'?"

"Ah-h-h," Luigi answered, "You forget, my boy, it is not so long that your beautiful sister was here."

"Of course," David said. Then he inquired "Do you know if Patricia telephoned to America while she was here in Rome?"

"I think so," Luigi answered and then he added "Yes, I remember Patricia, she say that she speak with both Nanny and your Mama, Sylvia."

"Once again you have relieved my mind, Luigi. In America, they probably all think I'm still stuck in Paris... but tonight, they will know I am in Roma."

"Remember," Luigi said, "It is still morning in San Francisco. I will come for you as soon as I reach Marietta and Giovanni in California."

Luigi swerved immediately toward his office next to the lobby. David's server returned with *Cointreau* over shaved ice in a tub-like crystal glass. After just two sips of the orange flavored liqueur, Luigi reappeared to escort David to the phone.

"Bring your drink," Luigi ordered David. "Your Nanny is waiting to speak with you."

Luigi ushered David to the ornate, but tastefully decorated office that sat adjoining the lobby. David went straight to Luigi's desk to pick up the telephone and look for a spot to rest his after dinner drink. Luigi plopped down a wooden coaster and pointed to the chair behind his desk where the phone was resting off the hook on a green inkpad.

"She's on the telephone," Luigi announced.

David lifted the phone and said in a bright voice, "Hi honey, how's my favorite lady?"

Other than an occasional 'yes' or 'no' those were the last words that David spoke for the next ten minutes. Luigi stood by silently like a sentry on guard...not moving...only listening to the vague one-sided comments he heard spoken from his graceful young American cousin sitting at the desk.

David finally said "Yes...yes honey...I'll call you as soon as the money gets here...don't worry, I won't talk any longer on Luigi's nickel."

Luigi threw his hands up in the air and said, "Give me the telephone, please."

David quickly finished his conversation with, "I love you too...tell Poppa I love him...and honey," he added "I am in love with Rome, already."

David quickly handed the phone to Luigi who chattered on in Italian for another ten minutes. David gleaned a word or phrase that was being said but really concentrated more on sitting back to enjoy the rest of his *Cointreau.*

Quoting a dozen Italian good-byes Luigi finally finished his conversation with Nanny. David stood up as

Luigi placed the phone back in its cradle and pronounced "You grandmother is a very elegant lady... I think maybe you look like her a little bit."

"Now I have something to tell you," Luigi went on as he reached for his wallet and counted out many bills of Italian lira, "You have no choice...you have to take this money and spend it in Rome. Your grandmother wants you to have a good time...I want you to have a good time."

Luigi took David's left hand and deposited a huge wad of lira smack in the middle of his palm. David shoved the bills into his pocket and threw his arms around Luigi in a bear-hug of appreciation.

"I don't know how to thank you Luigi."

Luigi said, "You let me know *when* you need more... anytime...as much as you want."

* * *

David was really ready to get moving and take in as much of Rome as time and money would allow. He didn't want to take advantage of Luigi's offer to finance *all* his travel needs while waiting for Nanny and Poppa to send the money...but, for the time being he did feel more adequately prepared to enjoy life.

After days of sightseeing and discovering layers and stratums of history everywhere he went in Rome, David was beginning to tire of playing the role of tourist. It was wonderful to discover the myriad exciting aspects of the Eternal City. *The Città del Vaticano* alone was cause for nearly a week of exploration, and he covered all the areas permitted to tourists. He went to the Vatican museums frequently to revisit the amazing sights.

On his treks through Vatican City David never failed to finish his daily cycle with 'standing time' in the Sistine

Chapel. He was always overwhelmed with the grand scale of Michelangelo's *Day of Judgment* that scaled the entire span of wall behind the altar.

The colossal painting depicted the second coming of Christ on *Judgment Day,* and David would literally gawk for hours staring at the characterizations and finding hidden little treasures throughout the mural. He remembered the story that Patty had told him about the genitals in the fresco being covered after the artist had completed the work. The artist commissioned to 'clean-up' the painting was Daniele da Volterra who was given the nickname *Il Braghettone*, the breeches-painter.

David made daily visits to the bank a compulsory component of his touring routine. Every afternoon after a day of sightseeing he would stop at *Mediobanca* for check-in with Adrianna to inquire if finances had arrived from America. It got to the point that he didn't even have to wait in line to ask…as soon as Adrianna saw him she would shake her head 'no' and blow him a kiss and a smile.

The last day of his touring week at Vatican City, Friday, David stopped at the bank not expecting any change in the negative signal he was used to seeing from Adrianna. The moment he walked in the door she called out his name.

"Mr. Wellington…your money has arrived…*Mama Mia*…you have enough to retire in Rome and become an Italian citizen for the rest of your life!"

* * *

David was thrilled as he jogged back to the hotel with a fat new checkbook and plenty of cash in his pocket. He couldn't wait to tell Luigi, and he especially couldn't wait to pack up his gear and head for Firenze to find his sister.

He missed her blisteringly; he just wanted to hug her and cry for happiness, and then laugh out loud with joy, and go eat and drink and catch up on all that had transpired in the last weeks without her.

"Luigi...Luigi," he shouted as he ran into the lobby of his hotel, "I have good news to tell you!"

Luigi who was speaking with one of the maids turned with a big smile on his face and said, "I have big news for you too."

"You go first Luigi."

"Patricia...your sister...she will be here tomorrow morning."

"Yaho-o-hoo!" David could not hold back a howl.

Luigi laughed, "There is more news...she is bringing her new husband."

"What!" David screeched, "*di cosa stavate parlando*... what are you talking about?"

"Yes," Luigi went on excitedly...the beautiful one... *si è sposata* ...she got married in Firenze."

"I can't believe it...I'm shocked...I'm stunned...I'm speechless!"

"Heh-heh-heh, but you are still talking *il mio cugino*."

"When did all this happen Luigi? How long has she been married?"

"Sorry...I know not too much, David...she be married maybe two weeks...she no tell me so much...she come on train and be here ten o'clock tomorrow morning with your two new brothers-in-law."

"Two!" David grimaced, "She got married twice? That's considered bigamy in America...it's illegal to have more than one husband at a time."

"Heh-heh-heh," Luigi laughed, "I no say the right thing...let me try again. Patricia...she married a man of great distinction who is the grandson of a count from Lombardy."

"Oh my Lord," David interrupted, "His last name isn't Lombardi spelled with an 'I'!"

"No...I think the name is only Lombard with no 'I' and no 'Y'. It is a name of great distinction. There is much Royalty in the family. Her husband's name is Angelo, and we will meet him and his brother Salvatore *domattina,* tomorrow morning."

"Ah-h, now I see why you said *brothers*-in-law. Patty is bringing her husband Angelo and *his* brother Salvatore. I wonder what you *do* call your brother-in-law's brother?"

"Call him Salvatore." Luigi answered casually.

* * *

David looked up from his bed and could see light filtering in through the ceiling to floor brocade drapes that hung elegantly from the two windows of his hotel room. He didn't have a hangover but he was still a little groggy from the two bottles of wine and after dinner drinks he had with his supper the night before. He stretched with a prolonged groan and reached for his watch.

"Good grief!" David said aloud, "Patty's train will be here in fifteen minutes!"

He interrupted the feeling of panic just long enough to think calmly for a moment. He was just steps away from the terminal where the newly wed's train would be arriving from Firenze. He could just throw on some clothes and run like hell to meet it on time, or, he might clean up with a much needed shower and shave and make a good impression.

David permitted vanity to win as he calmly headed for the bathroom. He shaved first with his electric razor and then stepped into the shower and scrubbed every inch of his toned body with the fragrant soap provided by the hotel. He vigorously massaged his head with their shampoo and wished he had gotten a haircut. Thank goodness his last haircut had been short enough so it still fell into place dry with a whisk of his long fingers.

He slipped on a pair of navy blue slacks and a white cashmere pullover sweater that emphasized his tanned, trim, buff body. After a splash of Abercrombie Fitch cologne he glided into penny loafers laying by the door... no time for socks. He dashed toward the elevator and stopped halfway down the hall in front of an opened door.

There she was fussing around with her suitcases and clothes. He didn't say anything at first but just drew in a long breath of relief as he watched his beautiful sister unpack both men's and women's articles of clothing. David would have to get used to the fact that Patricia was now a married lady.

"How does it feel to be unpacking your husband's clothes?" David said in a deep voice.

Patty looked up, startled for a second and then smiled with outstretched arms as tears welled up around her long dark lashes, "Oh Poopsie...my little Poopsie...oh Poopsie."

They embraced. David couldn't see...his eyes were running over with tears...he couldn't stop them from flowing...they were streaming down his face. The siblings hung on closely to each other and they cried.

Still crying and holding her brother tightly Patty said, "We're still like two little monkeys Poopsie...it's us against the world."

David held his sister and looked into her face, "Oh-h Patty...I really needed to see you...I can't even begin to explain how much I missed you...oh-h thank God...thank God I'm with you. I missed you so much...I feel like I've been away from you for a life time."

"I know...I know Poopsie...I'm so happy to see you...I'm so happy to see you."

They took turns wiping their eyes and blowing their noses on a dainty handkerchiefs that Patty had pulled out of her purse on the bed stand. They sniffed and smiled and laughed all at the same time. Patty dug through her purse again and walked over to the set of matching Renaissance chairs in front of a window.

"Sit down Poopsie; let's have a cigarette."

David followed Patty's directive and sat in the chair next to hers. She pulled out two cigarettes from a case that he didn't recognize and lit them at the same time. She handed one to her brother and they both took a long drag.

"It's a good thing you remember that scene with Paul Henreid in *Now Voyager.*"

They both laughed hard looking at each other. Everything in the world seemed to be in place now that he was with his sister again. He had the feeling 'all was well' as he studied her demeanor. She was more gorgeous than ever. She seemed to be surrounded by a warm steady light. If their psychic friend George were here he'd say Patricia's aura revealed a radiantly brilliant emanation. David knew that she was also gloriously happy.

"So where's the groom...I want to see him *immediately.*"

"The boys are downstairs having brunch. We were up late last night and there was no time for breakfast; and of course there is no food on the train between Florence and

Rome, and they are starving. So am I come to think of it. We should finish these cigarettes and join them *immediately*."

"Aren't you going to tell me the story of your whirlwind romance and marriage, or do I have to wait and hear it from Angelo?"

"You already know his name, Poopsie...how sweet. Yes...that's a good idea...I think you should hear Angelo's version first...I'll let him tell you the whole story. One thing that I will tell you is that there was no elaborate wedding...we eloped."

"Sounds absolutely like you...romantic and audacious!"

"We were married by a fully ordained Franciscan monk...Brother Thomas...you will be positively amazed at the details."

"I doubt that!" David said. "I just can't get over the fact that your last name is Lombard.

It kills me that your new name is one letter away from Lombardi."

"Anyway, Angelo will enjoy telling you about our wedding. Of course, he's anxious to meet you and get to know you...Poopsie...you're going to love each other beyond belief...but I'm not saying another word about him until you're introduced. We should go downstairs now," Patty said as stood up and put out her cigarette.

"Wait just a minute Mrs. Angelo Lombard...there is one other thing you have to tell me before we go downstairs."

"What's that Poopsie," Patty asked as she reapplied a little lipstick.

"What does he look like?"

"Okay," Patty answered, "Prepare your eyes for an exquisite feast...he's absolutely heavenly...there are not enough superlatives to describe his moral character and individuality...but his physical presence, in my opinion, is unsurpassed. Angelo made the same kind of impression on me as Hank did on you."

"Wow," David interjected.

"Yes Poopsie, it's true, my husband is divine. The only actor I can think of that he somewhat resembles is a very young Louis Jordan. You'll see what I mean when you meet. They have a similar little cleft in their chin, and similar hair and eyes."

"Wow," David repeated himself, "and what about his 'little' brother, does he have a cleft chin too?"

"Yum-m-m, yes...it runs in the family. Salvatore is also a rare beauty. He looks much like a young Alain Delon. He is also absolutely magnetically entrancing. Thank goodness he's *much* too young to be your type. Come on...let's go downstairs and meet the boys."

* * *

The 'boys' as Patty called them were everything she had said they would be in appearance. What she hadn't told David was about their extraordinary enchanting charm and charisma...their intelligence and vast knowledge of the liberal arts and sciences...and their impeccable manners and sensitivity for social graces. The sibling connection that existed between Salvatore and Angelo was congruous to the relationship that Patricia and David had always loved and enjoyed with each other.

The brothers adored and greatly respected each other with what seemed to be a consecrated devotion. It was joyful to witness another family whose members were dedicated to regard each other with such deep and profound love. The real miracle was in the fact that David immediately felt an integral part of these two men, and, he knew they felt the same about him, especially Salvatore.

Angelo was nothing short of a regal patrician. He was noble, gentle and knightly, all rolled into one highbred prince. His marriage to Patricia was no accident; she was the princess who would be queen sitting next to her king. The union of this couple had to be an act of divinity... *it was a match made in heaven*...and the impassioned couple knew it!

David was truly ecstatic about Patty's marriage and there was sheer joy in his heart for her and her indefectible husband. David wasn't the least concerned about Angelo's acceptance into the Wellington and Lombardi families. He envisioned introducing Angelo to all their friends in California; his gorgeous physical appearance and emanating aura would certainly thrill George. This marriage was going to create a lot of delight and electrification back in the old hometown of San Francisco, California.

David's only other cerebral preoccupation was with Salvatore. Salvatore with his vibrant enthusiasm and exuberance for life...Salvatore with his masculine exhilaration and effervescent spirit...Salvatore with his provocative lustiness...Salvatore who could not keep his heavily lashed luminous eyes off David.

David was well aware that Salvatore was instantly enamored with him, but it was disturbing to David who had *never* found a younger man so lustily attractive. Salvatore might indeed become the unique exception to David's repertoire of older handsome men. He was very young, but he enticed David's imagination into visualizing stimulating trysts in lovely Roman settings. David had to admit it...Salvatore was salaciously hot!

* * *

David extended his long arms around Salvatore's sinewy trim body as they glided through the streets of Roma on the back of a large frame *Vespa* scooter. Every breathtaking view they passed escalated David's concupiscence with gripping sensations as Salvatore became increasingly more captivating and mesmerizing. The weather was perfection and the masculine feel of his *brother-in-law's brother's* body was electrifying as well as intoxicating. In David's mind he was in a scene as romantic as the award winning film *Roman Holiday* starring Gregory Peck and Audrey Hepburn.

Salvatore was almost three years younger than David but reflected an omniscient maturity in his countenance. Yes...Hank was statuesque and refined like a classic nobleman...but Salvatore was certainly no less regal or magnificent. His appealing and seductive attributes were completely enrapturing on this early afternoon in Rome. This aesthetically alluring boy/man totally absorbed David's fascination at every level.

He found it challenging to believe a man this age could be so stimulating and magnetic for the libido; but he was holding on to this exciting breathing entity who had become an overwhelming obsession for David. Salvatore was indeed enchanting and tantalizing; he was consuming and enthralling beyond any of David's former perceptions regarding men. Salvatore was hypnotizing and spellbinding winning David's yielding heart as they drove the ageless avenues and streets of Rome.

The scooter climbed a long winding single lane road that took them above the Eternal City and looked down on a magnificent vista of timeless surroundings. Salvatore knew exactly where he was driving, and he took the scooter up a secondary pathway to a secluded locale surrounded by variegated Italian buckthorn bushes and trees. It was the same type of expansion that provided protection for the family's private pool at the *Vineyards* in Sonoma. David's heart started to pound as they parked the scooter and discovered a miniature private meadow of soft green grass surrounded by fragrant flowering shrubs.

Not saying a word Salvatore knelt on the inviting lawn and with outstretched arms he beckoned for David who readily accepted the invitation on the silky green grass. The two young men knelt facing each other looking intensely into each other's eyes. Salvatore enclosed the back of David's head with both hands and brought his face so that their lips touched. It was a gentle passionate moment; it was a kiss to remember for all eternity.

Salvatore unzipped his trousers and revealed his majestic upraised manhood. David did the same and exposed his ardor. Salvatore lowered his lean agile body and kissed the preeminent head of David's trembling erection. Slowly moving sideways on the soft ground, David positioned himself to accept Salvatore's rock hard implement to his warm moist mouth. The two men, still fully dressed, engaged in mutual fellatio.

David cushioned Salvatore's vigorous and intense ardency between the roof of his mouth and his tongue as it slid down his throat...back and forth. One...two...he subconsciously counted every loving downward thrust of his head...three...four...he could do this forever...five...

six. David was so satisfied and involved with pleasuring his counterpart that he was just marginally conscious that exactly the same maneuver was being performed on him by Salvatore. They both subconsciously continued rhythmically in unison, suspended by integral delectation...nine...ten...'God...don't ever let this end.' David felt his own explosive release fast approaching... eleven...twelve...thirteen...when unexpectedly a pulsating warm liquid jetted against the roof of his mouth and streamed down his throat...he swallowed once...twice...three times. He met every surging squirt of fluid like a thirsty boy drinking deliciously from a gushing spout.

Still holding their precious instruments lovingly in each other's mouths, arms wrapped around buttocks and thighs, David realized that his own passion had been discharged at *exactly* the same moment that Salvatore had reached his climatic pinnacle. They lay there recumbent, side by side, relishing and basking in the most satisfying moment of emotional and sexual gratification of their entire young lives.

* * *

Salvatore knelt in front of a chair at the hotel room and stroked David's legs, "I want you to tell me something you have never told anyone else in the world."

"Do you want me to tell you how much I love you and the many ways you delight me?"

Salvatore laughed, "No, I like very much to hear these things, but it is not my meaning."

"What is your meaning?" David said trying not to feel slightly wounded.

"I mean tell something about yourself that you have kept secret; something that you have not told anyone in the world that nobody knows except God."

"I can't recall anything *really* secret; I have to think about it," David said, "What about you? Do you have something you've never told anyone in the world?"

"Yes," Salvatore answered, "It's something I never told anyone."

"Do you want to tell me now?" David asked as he cradled Salvatore's face and looked directly into his eyes.

"Yes, I would like to tell you now. It is about my uncle Vincenzo...*che razza di idiota.*"

"So he's a real asshole," David chimed in.

"Yes...and much more... *è un abusatore di minori*...a child molester!"

"I don't think I like your Uncle Vincenzo, he sounds like a pig."

"Nobody likes him... *Chiamarlo maiale sarebbe un insulto per i maiali*...calling him a pig is an insult to pigs."

"Tell me how he molested you Salvatore."

It was *vigilia di Natale*...Christmas eve...and the family came home late from midnight mass. I did not go because I had *un raffreddore* ...you know...a common cold. *Ho dormito nel soffitta.attico*...you know...I slept in the attic so no one would have the cold from me. It is a beautiful attic filled with a great bed and much wonderful furnishings. Angelo and I slept in the attic often when we were children. It was a comfortable adventure."

"Sounds like fun," David said.

"It was no fun that night. Our house was filled with guests and relatives from all over Italy...it was very crowded...but there was no need for my uncle to sleep in the attic with me...he was supposed to sleep somewhere else in the house. He came up to the attic and he got into my bed...*il bruto*. He is a very strong big man...he said no words...he turned me over like a piece of meat...*me l'ha messo nel culo*...he fucked me in the ass."

David closed his eyes and said, "I hate anal sex, I don't know why but even the thought of intercourse with someone's rectum always disgusted me. This is something you never told anyone...not even Angelo knows about this...this... *violation*?"

"No David, I have told no one in the world but you...it is a terrible secret that I share only with you...and God. I also hate sex with the *culo*. I have wanted to tell somebody for a long time. Now I have told you.

"How old were you when this happened, Salvatore?"

"*Avevo undici anni*, I was eleven years old. I was to be twelve *nona nel marzo* on the ninth of March."

"Hey...you're a Pisces like me...my birthday is March 7th."

"Yes!" Salvatore said, "*Sono del segno dei pesci*."

"We are *fratello dell'acqua*...'water brothers'...forever!" David shouted as he stood lifting Salvatore to a standing position so they could bear hug each other.

"*Ti voglio bene...ti amo!*"

"*Anche io ti amo*...I love you too," David said kissing him passionately.

* * *

CHAPTER THIRTEEN

Patricia, Angelo, Salvatore and David were on their way to one of many Lombard family villas in Italy. This one was about 20 miles outside of Rome. Angelo was driving the *gang* in a leased 1971 Alpha Romeo sedan. It was the first of the Berlina 2000 series with a twin cam engine that was capable of cruising at 140 m.p.h. David and Salvatore sat in the comfortable back seat and struggled to keep their hands off each other. Neither of the boys wanted, *yet*, to tip off the newlyweds about the private and torrid affair.

David believed that Patty had a pretty good idea that something was going on between him and Salvatore, but she hadn't said anything about it, *yet*. Salvatore believed that his brother Angelo was totally oblivious to anything in the world with the exception of his new bride. Angelo was not concerned about his brother's love-life, at least for the moment. His little brother was sitting close-by in the back seat with his wife's brother, they were all on their way to the 'lake'. All was well with the world.

They were driving to *Lago di Bracciano* where their father had an impressive estate he had inherited from his grandfather decades ago. The lake itself was originally formed thousands of centuries ago by volcanic action which left some smaller, still recognizable, craters in the vicinity. Most of the pristine water came from underground springs that flowed outward from the lake to form the *Arrone River*.

The views from the villa were breathtaking to behold. The house was empty except for two or three servants, one who assisted with the luggage when they arrived. It was like checking into an exclusive hotel as they were met with hugs and introductions. Salvatore, however, was almost rude in his eagerness to get David alone.

"Guiseppe... *Le nostre valigie sono nel bagagliaio*....we left our luggage in the trunk. Prepare my bedroom for David and give me the guestroom next to him. I am going to show the lake to David," he said dashing out the door and down steps from the veranda.

"Follow me David!"

Shrugging his shoulders, David felt a little embarrassed as he looked at his sister and Angelo. Although Salvatore wasn't being completely discreet, David was feeling the same enthusiasm for his new lover. It was wonderful to think that they were going to be together in a new romantic setting. Maybe, one day soon, they would tell Patty and Angelo what was actually happening...surely they wouldn't mind...surely.

"Well," Patty said, "You guys must really be bored with Angelo and me. Go have some fun, but don't stay away long, I'm certain lunch will be ready whenever you get back. It would be nice to have our first meal at the lake with everyone present at the table."

"Please honor your sister's request," Angelo reinforced his wife, "Have fun, but bring Salvatore back to the villa soon for our delicious meal. I am hungry now."

They heard Salvatore shouting from afar, "Make haste David...hurry!"

"Don't worry," David said, "I'll bring him back really soon. I'm already hungry too."

All three of them laughed. Patricia and Angelo watched David trying to catch up with Salvatore who was already halfway down the old stone stairway that wound to the lake. The sky was a cloudless startling blue with the lake stretched out in a darker blue expanse. Birds were twittering brightly and fragrant flowers were blooming everywhere around the villa. It was another glorious day.

Salvatore led David to an isolated spot secluded by rocks and trees near the water. There was an intimate stretch of sand that led to the edge of the lake and an old wooden pier a little further from where they were walking. Two engineless boats with peeling paint were tied to the dock. They must have been silently sitting in the water for a long time.

Salvatore grabbed David by his arm and spun him around. They kissed tenderly, gently caressing and carefully fondling one another. They were experiencing exactly the same reverie. They were boundlessly attached and shared their steadfast love for one another. This was another moment that would be remembered forever.

Salvatore walked to the end of the dock and motioned for David to join him. They sat on the pier side-by-side and looked out onto the quietly undulating water the color of lapis lazuli. David placed his hand behind Salvatore's head and softly stroked his hair.

"What are you thinking Salvatore?"

"I am thinking about the love between you and me."

David leaned over and delicately engaged in a long soft kiss as he continued fondling the back of Salvatore's head. When their lips separated Salvatore grabbed David and clasped him in a demonstrative embrace of jubilation. He took David's hands and fervently kissed the palms and the tips of his fingers. David delighted in every touch.

"Hey Salvatore...what else are you thinking?"

"I'm thinking that maybe it is time to tell me something you never told anybody."

"Okay," David said, "I guess it's time for me to tell you about something that happened right after I turned 19 years old."

"Were you *preso per il culo*?"

"No," David said, "I wasn't fucked in the ass...at least not in the way you were by your uncle."

"How?" Salvatore asked giving David his full attention.

"It's somewhat of a long story...you have heard about conscription in the United States?"

"No...what does this word mean...conscription?"

"It is the compulsory enlistment of young men into the military service...it is the law for every boy who turns 18 years of age to register for conscription or drafting into the United States Army, Air Force, Navy... or the United States Coast Guard. In America, all boys are ordered by law to serve a period of time in the armed forces, and during times of war these guys can be forcefully drafted or go to prison."

"*Barbarie!*" Salvatore said sternly.

"Yes, you're right, in a way it is barbarism...not so much because boys are drafted into the military...but more because the way it is done."

"You were drafted?" Salvatore asked with concern.

"A little more than five years ago I was notified by the Selective Service that I must report to the Oakland Army Base for a physical examination. Just about all the guys I knew in high school and college had already been drafted because of the Vietnam War...and as you know... it's still going strong."

"Oh yes," Salvatore confirmed, "The world is not good there."

"Anyway, my dad insisted on driving me to the induction center which is just on the other side of the *Bay Bridge* from San Francisco. It was on a gray overcast day when we drove up to the big brick building where I was to be inspected and scrutinized like an insect under a microscope. I had an appointment for a specific time to undergo the examination and there was a very long line of boys who were in front of me.

I knew my dad felt concern for my lack of receptiveness to being pushed around and probed by uncaring military doctors and draft personnel. It was not a pleasant experience to face. So Dad told me he would stay close to the Army base and drive by about every half hour or so and be there to take me home after the ordeal was over."

"I know that your father, like Patricia, loves you with all his heart," Salvatore said.

"Yes...I have had love pouring from my ears since I was a baby...I'm ready to share it with you," David said kissing Salvatore's hand.

"I will take all that you give me, and I will give you back more," Salvatore said returning the kiss..." Please, please tell me much more about this story of conscription."

"I must have seen my father drive by at least three times while I was still standing in that long line. I finally got inside the building where there were a couple of Army officers shouting and dividing the lines into smaller groups of 12 or 15 guys. They made us take off all our clothes and stand naked on a very cold cement floor...they lined us up and made everyone bend over at once...the stench was awful. The doctor walked behind each guy and spread the cheeks of his ass...he had an assistant that gave him a clean rubber glove each time he probed into somebody's butt...they had a trashcan that they dragged along and discarded the used gloves.

Other doctors came along the line and held our testicles while we were made to cough...we got our ears checked...our eyes...and there was a doctor who even inspected our feet. They looked at our heads, our hands and under our arms. They examined and handled our bodies roughly everywhere. It was awful, Salvatore."

"We also had to complete long-drawn-out forms with tough questions. Many of the questions were very personal and required lengthy essay type answers. There was one question that asked if I was homosexual or possessed homosexual tendencies. I can't remember exactly how it was phrased, but I answered *yes* in my explanation. Patricia had told me that it was just a matter of checking a box...but I remember I had to write it out."

Salvatore's eyes got bigger, "Does Patricia know that you reported to the Selective Service that you are homosexual?"

"No...she does not know...nobody knows except the United States Selective Service...my entire family thinks that the service rejected me because I'm color blind."

"Are you color blind?"

"Yes…one of the eye examinations I had to take on that awful day was for color blindness…I failed the test. At first, the doctor was very grouchy with me because he had to give me the same test two times. He hollered at me and told me I wasn't concentrating hard enough. He finally figured out I wasn't faking it; so he signed some forms and told me to go back out to the front desk and turn in all my papers.

When I gave the papers to the officer at the desk, he shuffled around and gave me another form and directed me through a door to a small office. It was a psychiatrist's office and I was asked to sit down. He was an ugly little man with a crooked moustache and squinty eyes; he wore glasses. He looked through some papers that were lying on his desk, then, he looked up at me and asked 'how do you know you're homosexual.'

I told him that I was born homosexual. I liked men since I was three years old. I told him that I was currently involved in a romantic affair with an older man. I guess that's all I had to say. He didn't ask any more questions. I was out of his office in 5 minutes."

"Was that the finish of your examination?"

"Oh, no," David said, "That's when the real fun began. I had to take my papers back to the main hall where there were still long lines of young men. I was directed to a smaller line of guys, some of whom I recognized as the guys who had started the examination with me when I first had to bend over. A couple of them were quietly bragging that they weren't being inducted, one said he had asthma, one had missing toes from some accident, another had a broken eardrum…you know…things like that."

There was a table at the end of the line with several officers who were stamping papers and releasing the guys for the day. I thought I was finished as I presented my papers from the psychiatrist. There was a handsome officer that looked up at me and said 'I'll take care of this one,' and he asked me to follow him to a private room."

"Oh, oh," said Salvatore, "This is where the trouble comes."

"Not yet," David went on with his story. "This officer was a gentleman. He closed the door and sat in a chair next to mine. He looked right at me and asked if I ever wanted to serve my country by being part of the military. I told him I would be happy to serve my country in some other way. I didn't want to be a part of the armed forces."

"I know that you have declared yourself as a homosexual, but we would still like to have you join... nobody has to know about this...nobody at all" the officer said.

"You know," I said to the officer, "You know about me."

He said "I'm only here to help you. I'm not going to tell anybody," and then he put his hand on my knee and said, "You are very special in a lot of ways. *We* will look after you in the army. I want to give you the chance to join us."

"Look," I said, "I'm not an anti-war protester...my dad was a World War II hero in the Army Air Corps... Distinguished Flying Cross...I love my dad...I love the United States of America...I support our troops...but you found out today that I am a homosexual. The United States Military rejects homosexuals. I cannot change my sexual orientation any more than I can alter my gender. You also discovered that I am color blind which should constitute a completely separate determent exempting me from military service."

The officer told me "Not necessarily, your colorblindness could be very useful in detecting camouflage from Reconnaissance Aircraft. We would apply your minor sight disability to assist us in many different operations."

"I don't understand," I said, "I'm a colorblind homosexual, and the Army still wants me?"

The officer leaned over and clasped his hand over my knee again and clenched his fingers under my leg, "You will serve your time very comfortably and safely. What do you say?

"I didn't have to think for a split second. I looked right in his face and said, "No."

"Good on you!" Salvatore shouted, "I am glad that you refused to join your army."

"Later on I figured out that it must be up to the *commander's discretion* to retain homosexuals. That still didn't end my day at the induction center. I had to jump through two more hoops. The next step was to have an 'exit' interview with an older lady who was some kind of a social worker. I don't think she intentionally tried to humiliate me, but she came off as very condescending. She spoke to me as though I was a person to be pitied and I would be walking away with my life ruined forever. She gave me a card with the name of some social service and told me to contact the people when depression and despair caught up to me. She put all my papers in a folder and said I was to turn it over to the sergeant who was just outside her office.

Then she said to me, 'It's natural that despondency will overwhelm you as you fully realize your mistake. You look and talk and walk like a normal man. Hopefully one day you'll find a beautiful girl who will lead you to the correct and proper lifestyle.'

I told her that I didn't think there was much chance of that happening. She tried to look kindly at me, she shook her head and said 'What a waste.' I left the room thinking how happy I was that conversation was over."

"Amico, queste pollastre Americano del assistente sociale sembrano stupide!" Salvatore said.

David laughed, "Not all female American social workers are stupid, but you're right, this one was pretty dumb. When I left her office my folder was thick with all the papers I'd collected throughout the induction process. I started to hand it over to the really mean looking sergeant who was gathering them from the guys who were leaving. He snatched the folder out of my hand and starting screaming...'I know some of you guys have a legitimate reason for not joining the army... but I see too many here today that look like faggots. I hate faggots...they should all be shot at sunrise...the world has no place for faggots...faggots are worse than maggots...I hate faggots...I've got a steel rod to stick up some faggot's butt...fuck all cock sucking faggots.' He kept on shouting obscenities as he followed a half dozen of us to the exit door. It was especially ugly because he stared directly at me during the entire tirade."

"He probably did want to stick his rod up your ass... and I do not mean the one made of steel." Salvatore said with a smile.

David smiled too, "I never gave it much thought, Salvatore, but you're probably right. Anyway as soon as I stepped out onto the street, Dad drove up...he looked very serious

...I got in the car. I told him everything was all right that I wasn't going into the Army.

They had discovered I was colorblind. I never told my dad that I had *checked the box.* I've never told anybody. My confidant Patricia does not know. You are the only one."

"You did not have to tell a lie...it is true that you are colorblind...you were given a choice to join the armed forces or not to join. You did not disappoint or disgrace your family in any manner. What did your father say when you told him you were colorblind?"

"He said that since we were already in Oakland, just the two of us should go to dinner at *Jack London Square* where there was a new seafood restaurant that had just opened. He said we needed to stop first and call my mom to let her know why we were celebrating."

* * *

That night Patty and Angelo seemed quietly somber as they were being served a late supper by the house servants. Salvatore didn't stop talking about how happy he was to be at the family's summer home in Rome. The food kept coming and Salvatore kept talking and gulping down glass after glass of wine.

David kept up with Salvatore's excitement and immoderate eating and drinking. The two young men appreciably enjoyed the abundant meal and the congenial company. Full of jocundity they both did their best to overlook the repressed participation of their respective siblings. The two boys genuinely savored every bite of their sumptuous meal.

Patricia and Angelo would scantly smile and occasionally glance at each other, but it was evident they were both preoccupied with thoughts less festive than their brothers. David who was usually quite sensitive to his sister's feelings did not acknowledge her unusually introspective disposition until the plates and dishes were being cleared for dessert. He poured more wine into Salvatore's and his glass to offer a toast, hoping to alter his lovely sister's moodiness.

"Here's to the most beautiful couple the world has ever known."

David and Salvatore clinked glasses and said in unison, "The most beautiful couple in the world!"

Angelo nodded his head and Patty said smiling, "Thank you, you're both very sweet."

"Hey," Salvatore said looking at his brother, *"Che cosa c'è che non va?"*

"Yeah...what's wrong?" David was appreciative that Salvatore's perceptiveness wasn't being affected by all the wine he had consumed, "Don't think that Salvatore and I haven't noticed how serious you guys have been throughout the whole dinner."

Patricia looked at Angelo and said, "Please darling, you tell them."

"Oh-oh," Salvatore interjected before his brother spoke.

"Everything is okay...everything is perfectly fine... it's just that," he took a deep breath,

"Patricia and I have to return to Firenze first thing tomorrow."

"Oh no," David moaned, "Just when we were starting to have such a good time."

"I am sincerely sorry David, but I must go for the family business. My father has called me because he needs my assistance with some very important and urgent matters. I have to go as soon as possible. There is no other choice. It is also time to make amends with my mother who has not spoken to me or Patricia since we eloped."

"Yes," Salvatore interjected again, "She was really 'pissed off' there was no grand wedding at the cathedral and a reception that would last at least a week."

"I don't blame her Salvatore. Angelo is her first born son and I'm certain your mother has dreamed of his wedding since he was a baby," Patty said extending her hand across the table to grasp her husband's arm.

Angelo looked over to David and said, "There is no reason for you guys not to stay at *Lago di Bracciano* as long as you wish…days…weeks…months."

"Years?" Salvatore asked in levity.

Angelo laughed, "Yes, little brother, you may stay for as many years as you like…but be careful…David might become bored if you stay at the lake for so long a time."

"They all laughed and Patty said, "I don't want to dampen your spirits, Poopsie, but you can't stay too much longer after Angelo and I leave."

"Why not?" David complained.

"Because Poopsie, it's time for you to go home, back to California. The family doesn't even know about my marriage, and I'm relying on you to tell them. Also, just like Angelo, you are the eldest male heir of the family, and you have responsibilities to attend, especially at the Vineyards."

"Maybe," David argued, "But Nanny and Poppa aren't even well into their seventies, and they're as healthy as anybody I know."

"California is your home, Poopsie, we can't *both* stay away forever. We're more than half-way through 1971. You must go back relatively soon."

"What about you?" David complained, "When will you come back and see your family?"

"David, your sister and I have been working on plans for the future," Angelo said. "We will both be coming to America within one year, maybe sooner if we are going to have a *bambino.* Patricia and I have already discussed the matter in great detail."

"We want our children to have dual citizenship," Patty added.

"Hey! What about me?" Salvatore shouted, "Can I come to America too?"

"I thought you wanted to stay for years, here at the lake, my little brother."

"Not for the rest of my life," Salvatore grumbled.

* * *

David was not thrilled with the prospect of leaving his lover so soon after they had just found each other, but he knew there was no other choice. He would be happy to see the family again, and he really did miss San Francisco and the Vineyards. *But,* Patricia had informed him that he must make an obligatory stopover in London to take a present for Magda and tell her about the marriage.

He was thrilled less than ever with the contemplation of having to see Magda one more time. There was comfort in the thought that he and Salvatore would one day be together again, but he certainly did not look forward to his stopover in London. Suddenly a shroud fell over David's world and he didn't want to face the dreary task that lay before him.

Patricia had foreseen her brother's reaction and thought it best to leave him alone with Salvatore. David hadn't said a word to her about his feelings toward Salvatore, but she sensed her little brother was deeply in love. She rose from the dinner table and Angelo instantly stood up.

"Well, boys," she said, "Angelo and I are asking you to pardon us from your company. I am ascending that majestic staircase, and I'm dragging my pulchritudinous lover to the boudoir."

"She is wrong!" Angelo shouted as he ran around the table and briskly swept Patty into his arms, "I will not be dragged; I will instead carry my most desirable love to our bed."

Patricia smiled broadly and placed her arms around Angelo's neck as he lifted her from her chair. He trotted from the dining room toward the staircase and David yelled out.

"Isn't she a little heavy for you to carry up the stairs?"

"She is lighter than feathers," Angelo shouted as he breezed up the steps with his lovely Patricia in his arms.

"What do you think, Salvatore," David said as he took another sip from his wine glass.

"I think I will be very sad when you leave me," Salvatore answered.

David reached for his cigarette case and offered one to Salvatore who shook his head negatively. David lighted one and took a quick puff.

"I know Salvatore," he said sadly smiling at his lover, "I will be sad as well, but let's not think about my departure. We'll see the married couple off tomorrow morning then you can show me around the lake. I know, let's have a very private picnic with good food, bread, cheese and wine. It will be fun!"

"Okay...okay...you win," Salvatore said. "We will not think about separation until much later. Tomorrow we will have a picnic and start a new day of vacation. We will play in the sun, eat in the shade, and make love for at least one more week...maybe two or three weeks... before you leave."

* * *

CHAPTER FOURTEEN

David felt grumpy after he boarded the plane for London. It wasn't easy seeing Salvatore's tear filled eyes at the boarding gate; and he knew the plane would be watched until it flew completely out of sight.

"I don't want to be doing this," David said under his breath as the Boeing 727 rose from the tarp at Michelangelo International Airport, "I don't want to be leaving Italy, and I do not want to see Magda."

The trip was uneventful and he was barely aware of the stewardesses who vied for his attention on the half empty flight. He didn't have any cocktails and had rejected other beverages and snacks that were offered. Depression and despondency were trying to settle into his psyche and he didn't know how to fight it.

He was thankful that Magda didn't know when he would be arriving in London. She believed that Patty and he would be stopping over when they left Italy on their way back to the States but she did not know that she would never see Patricia ever again.

The plane landed at Heathrow and David pushed himself through Customs. He hired a porter to take his luggage to the front of the terminal where he hired a taxi into town.

"*The Inverness Court Hotel*, Bayswater, please," David said to the driver.

David's room was simple, but comfortable with all the amenities he needed. He wanted to stay at this hotel only because Patricia had been here on her first visit to London. He was already feeling nostalgic for her guidance and loving warmth. He was going to be miserable without her special attentiveness to his emotional and spiritual needs.

His thoughts were interrupted by the telephone ringing in his room.

"Yes," he answered.

A female voice said, "Good afternoon, Mr. Wellington, you have a visitor here in the lobby. Would you like me to send him up?"

"Uh-h...no thank you...tell him I'll be down directly."

David needed time to think. She had said 'he', it was a *man*. Thank God it couldn't be Magda. Who was it? Salvatore didn't have enough time to follow so closely behind. Nobody in London knew he was here. He reminded himself again that it was a *man*.

He took the stairs since he was only on the second floor. He would undoubtedly be expected on the elevator, but the stairwell exited into the lobby on the opposite wall away from the lift. He might have a slight advantage of being able to see his male guest for an instant before having to speak.

He reached the bottom of the carpeted stairs and quietly stepped into the lobby. There was nobody there except a skinny black man who was leaning against a marble pillar and putting on a cigarette. He was startled by the sound of David's footstep and turned to see him face-to-face.

"Michael Smith!" David exclaimed trying to hide his horror at seeing this iniquitous creature again in his life, "What in the world are *you* doing here? How in the world did you know I was here?"

"Don't get excited, please don't be shocked," Michael said in a shaking voice. "I've been here everyday for the last two weeks waiting for you and Patricia to check-in. Magda has gone berserk! She had me terminated from employment at the Tate Museum. I've been staying at Sonja's place. I'm truly worried for my life, Magda wants to kill me!"

"Sit down Michael," David tried to act calmly pointing to a couple of Edwardian chairs in the hotel lobby, "What is this all about? Why were you fired from the Tate?"

"False accusations from her chummy female colleagues...she had them complain that I was harassing them...there are three of them with the same stupid story that I had pinched them on their ugly butts. You know it's not true David...it's a lie...but no one believes me, except Sonja."

"What does Sonja think about all this?" David asked.

"Sonja no longer speaks to Magda...they have disowned each other as sisters. They had stupid fights about many things, mostly about their childhood...I make up the least part of their feud. Sonja thinks that Magda has gone mad...she's over the brink."

"Where is Sonja right now?' David asked.

"She's not here in London; she opened an office in Birmingham and she's been staying there. She's grateful I'm keeping her flat in London now that I'm no longer working."

"Does Magda know you're living in Sonja's flat?"

"Yes she does, and she's been making me miserable by lurking around the neighborhood day and night. She telephones all the time…doesn't say a word…just heavy breathing."

"You're certain that it's Magda on the other end of the line?"

"It's Magda all right! I have to take the phone off the hook every night just so I can get some sleep. Sometimes I take it off the hook during the day. She also follows me everywhere I go…she's watched me come into this hotel every single day…she knows that you and your sister would be coming her here eventually."

"I came by myself," David said, "Patricia is still in Italy."

"I wish I was in Italy right now," Michael whimpered, "Right now I wish I was anywhere but here."

"It's not as bad as you think, Michael. Magda is not going to kill you."

* * *

David actually felt comfortable that Michael was not going to be annoying that evening. He had not even tried to touch David or make any sexual inferences; it actually turned into a somewhat pleasant evening and David was delighted to pick up the tab. Michael was grateful that there was no mention of the previous scene when they had first met.

David came to the conclusion that Michael really wasn't all that bad. It was obvious that he was very high strung and quite skittish, but there was a calmer and more rational side to him, especially when he was not drinking excessively. Michael showed David to a neighborhood pub that served decent food. It wasn't far from the Inverness Court so the guys opted for a walk back instead of hiring a taxi.

The night was slightly chilly, but not frigid as they strolled back to the hotel. David planned to have the front desk telephone for a taxi that would return Jack to Sonja's flat. They walked through the hushed Bayswater streets feeling warm and tranquil from the wine and lovely steak and kidney pie they had enjoyed at the little neighborhood pub.

Michael stopped suddenly and clenched his hand over David's arm.

"What's the matter, what's wrong, Michael?"

It was dark and David couldn't see the stark fear on Michael's face, "It's Magda!"

"Where?" David said, "I don't see anybody, the streets are empty."

"There!" Michael shrieked pointing down the street behind them.

David peered in the direction that Michael was pointing; he could just barely make out the shadow of a tenebrous vehicle moving lightless along the street. It seemed to be shifting from the street to the sidewalk as it continued forward motion toward the two men who stood frozen in place. The high beams surprised and temporarily blinded them. David now knew what it must feel like to be a deer caught in the headlights.

They heard the vehicle shift from first gear to second...and second to third gear...Michael screamed out "Jump...on the wall!"

David instinctively leaped on the four foot brick wall with a strong steel gated fence embedded in cement. He was able to grab on to two of the long metal shafts that protruded from the top of the wall, and pulled himself above the sidewalk. Michael struggled to do the same and David freed a hand to assist him to safety. The car actually scraped the side of the wall causing sparks to fly just inches from their feet.

They held tight to the heavy metal prongs of the fence above the brick barrier.

"That bitch...that fucking bitch...tried to kill us!" Michael exclaimed.

"I couldn't see anything," David asserted, "Are you sure that it was Magda?"

"Oh-ho...it was Magda all right...who else would try to kill you on your first night back in London?"

* * *

CHAPTER FIFTEEN

David's seven and a half hour flight on TWA from London to New York went speedily, probably because he slept most of the way. His short stopover in England had been mentally exhausting, but he was glad not to have seen Magda, at least personally, which undoubtedly would have made him even more tired.

'Thank God I was *spared* speaking with her,' David thought, 'and thank God I was probably *spared* my very life, much thanks to Michael.'

When David arrived at JFK International it was a mad house of people and activity. He still thought of this airport as *Idlewild*, even though it had been years since it had been renamed. Customs seemed to take forever, and after waiting in unconscionably long lines he found a porter to haul his luggage out to the taxi stands.

"Downtown...*Plaza Hotel*, please driver."

David had made up his mind to pamper himself in the Big Apple for a few days before heading out for California. He still hadn't made up his mind if he would go straight home to San Francisco or venture a stop in Los Angeles to see Hank. He knew that Hank would be 'chomping at the bit' to see him...but David wasn't quite certain that he wanted a reunion just yet...especially after his ardent and torrid affair with Salvatore.

He would have to think more fervently about his immediate plans for the future, and right now, New York seemed to be the perfect place for David's overactive mind. He was happy to be going to the Park Plaza Hotel where he had stayed many times throughout the years. The hotel on Fifth Avenue at Central Park was familiar and would provide an agreeable and convivial atmosphere for David who made new acquaintances so easily.

David loved New York, and he loved New Yorkers! This was the most cosmopolitan of all the cities that he knew, and it was always exciting and electrifying to be here. The energy level, the glamour, the food and the entertainment were unsurpassed in the entire world. He would immediately get the latest edition of *The New Yorker* and decide when he would attend the Metropolitan Opera, which Broadway shows he would see, what clubs he'd go to for great jazz, where he would shop, but most importantly, where he would eat. *Hello Big Apple!*

* * *

David was astonished at the amount of money he had gone through after only 5 days of enjoyment in Manhattan, 'I'd have to have billions of dollars to live here' he thought.

It was time to head to California, and he had decided definitely to fly straight to San Francisco. He wasn't in the mood for a tryst with Hank, at least not now, and he was emotionally exhausted.

He missed Patricia incredibly and he ached to see her. He had spoken with her only once since he'd left Italy, and that was an 1 ½ hour chat that he paid for along with the rest of his outrageously enormous bill at the Plaza. He was also somewhat apprehensive how he was going to break the news to the family of Patty's elopement and marriage to a man that nobody, yet, knew existed.

Nanny and Poppa would have no problem with the fact that their beautiful granddaughter had married Italian royalty. Richard would easily accept his daughter's choice of mates. It was Sylvia who would be the problem....she always took everything about her children to heart...she would be devastated that her daughter did not have the grandiose wedding that had been envisioned for many years. The bride's mother was going to be every bit as unhappy and upset as the groom's mother had been when her gorgeous son eloped.

"Just don't kill the messenger, please" David said aloud as he deplaned at SFO International.

It was more of a joy to be back in the Bay Area than he would ever have imagined. It was also a joy to arrive at an airport where he didn't have to suffer the agony of going through Customs. He went straight to the luggage claim area and gave his baggage tickets to a porter wearing a red cap.

"I'll need a taxi into the city," David said as he handed the porter a ten dollar bill and lighted a cigarette.

"Yes sir," the guy said eager to be of service, "Right away sir."

"I'll be sitting over there," David said indicating a row of padded waiting chairs that were lined up along the windows close to the exit that said ***Taxis***.

David sat down with his cigarette and watched the small parade of people who passed in front of him. This was one of the best travel days he had experienced in a long time. He was happy to be sitting here waiting for someone else to retrieve his luggage, and this time he was actually at home in San Francisco.

* * *

David was altogether jolted by Sylvia's reaction to Patty being married.

"Well, if that's what she wanted to do, it's her life," Sylvia had said blandly pretending to be unperturbed.

"Mom, I marvel at your attitude...I was really concerned that you would have been crestfallen and downcast that Patty didn't have a huge wedding here at home."

"Not in the least," Sylvia said coldly, "I'm certain Patricia didn't even think twice about what I may have wished...she simply did what she wanted to do."

"Don't pay too much attention to your mother's attitude," Richard said. "The real truth is she's not all that sentimental about weddings. We were married with another couple in a quick ceremony in Florida...both of us grooms were in uniform...you've seen the old photos of our wedding day."

"Yes that's right," said David, "you guys sort'a eloped too. You only had a couple of days before Dad went to the South Pacific."

"Our wedding wasn't anything like the stunt your sister just pulled...we were affected by the war," Sylvia responded tartly.

"Mom, you and Dad will love Angelo," he said trying to change the subject. "You can't imagine a more ideal son-in-law. He's unbelievably in love with Patty, and they're positively stunning together. It's truly a match made in heaven."

"Do they have any plans for coming to California soon," Richard asked hoping to erase the scowl on Sylvia's face.

"They've already decided to be here as soon as she gets pregnant; they want to make sure that all their children are born in the U.S." David said, "And I might add, that from observing Patty and Angelo, it won't be long before they'll be expecting a child."

* * *

David was eager to prove to his wealthy family that he could support himself. His goal was to look for employment in the city where he might find a little studio apartment and walk to work. His friend George lived in a really neat place on Jones Street just off Pine where all the apartments had built-in Murphy Beds and big bay windows. It'd be great if he could find a place like that in the same neighborhood of lower Nob Hill.

George's place was within easy walking distance of the Marine's Memorial Club and a few other places that David enjoyed going to from time to time. It would be wonderful to live independently with no responsibility other than getting to work on time. There were lots of different things he could do, but, of course, right now he wanted to find the job that would pay the most.

It was Richard who actually guided David to his first employment after college. His father had an acquaintance who owned an elite employment agency in San Mateo. David signed up praying that he wouldn't have to work somewhere on the Peninsula. He wanted to live, work and play in downtown San Francisco.

God seemed to answer his prayer. The name of the organization was Dun & Bradstreet, a prestigious credit clearing agency that was *not* in the financial district. It was located at 150 Hayes Street, right off Market, in a modern 3 story building. David's title was 'Business Analyst and Reporter,' and the company would be paying for his first 2 months of training. They were a very conservative company and required all male employees to wear white shirts with solid dark ties. David didn't mind the strict dress code regulation, he had tons of white shirts and dark ties.

He knew that he had been hired mainly on his good looks and his ability to write. The other two guys who had been selected had accounting and business degrees; but David's Liberal Arts Bachelor's Degree reflected several math courses included in his 3.85 grade point average transcript. He also had completed the M.A. courses in Speech and Drama.

The real deciding factor in landing the job was his answer to a question from the vice-president who sat on the interview panel of eight people. He had prompted David,

"Mr. Wellington, we would like to know just exactly what you expect out of life."

Of course, David had to lie, "I want a wife, three children, a German shepherd dog and a split level house with a station wagon parked in the driveway."

Six of the people on the panel laughed, including the vice-president of Dun & Bradstreet in San Francisco. It was at that moment David knew he had the job. He reported to work the following Monday morning.

Unfortunately, he was employed for less than two months when he became completely bored with the job.

* * *

David was headed down Bush Street coming up on Jones when he saw a parking place and impulsively pulled into it. He was less than half a block from George's apartment which was on Jones. He'd only seen George once since the return from Europe, and he felt this would be a good morning to stop by.

Patricia and David had first met George when they embarked on a probe into supernatural phenomena and attended the Golden Gate Spiritualist Church on Franklin Street at the corner of Clay near Lafayette Park. George Bellini was one of those who warmly greeted the siblings with a friendly and warm introduction. They knew immediately that this funny little man was extraordinarily intelligent and wise well beyond his thirty-something years of age. He looked identical to Wally Cox who starred in the 1950s television series *Mr. Peepers*. Patty and David both fell in love with him and cherished his friendship.

George was one of the most courteous, kindest, sweetest, least inoffensive people in the whole wide world. He was an invariable joy to be around and was worth at least, what Patty referred to as one LPM, or, one laugh per minute. He percolated cheerfulness and happiness with every breath, and his delightful jubilance was exceeded only by his ability to administer sage advice on the pitfalls and predicaments of life. This morning, in particular, David was anxious to speak with him.

George had his finger on the buzzer that unlocked the front door before David even got there. He was seen coming down Jones Street from George's big bay window on the 2nd floor. David ran up the stairs, he only took the elevator when he was carrying heavy packages or bulky items. He could see that George had left the apartment door to the hallway opened, so he ran right inside. George was busy spraying his many exotic ferns and plants with a fine mist of distilled water; the lack of chlorine and fluoride was good for their healthy appearance. The formula worked well, his plants were astounding.

"What's happening Kiddie? How's the job working out for you?"

George already apprehended there was a problem without David having to say a word.

"It's not working out and I'm miserable."

George put down the large atomizer he was using on the plants and said, "Come here Kiddie. Give me a hug."

The two men stood silently hugging each other. David allowed himself to be embraced for at least a full minute. He knew that his *rate of vibration* was being examined and probed by George's phenomenal intuition. They released their grip on each other and David flopped down in one of the two huge Regency chairs that proudly sat in the studio.

"Do you mind if I smoke," David asked holding up his cigarette case, "I know you gave them up."

"You know I don't mind at all, Kiddie. How about a nice cup of freshly brewed coffee? I just ground up some *Colombian* beans this morning?"

"A cup of your fresh coffee sounds terrific George."

George's studio apartment had a nice sized kitchen with a back door that led to a small balcony covered in a myriad of blooms and flowering plants. It was actually an extension of the rear fire escape.

The door was opened and David could see all the colorful blossoms and greenery from his seat in the studio. It was a gorgeous sunny morning, and the residents of San Francisco were enjoying it as much as George's blooms which were basking on his little porch.

"I had a strong feeling that I would see you today," George said as he poured boiling water over the filter of an antique Melitta decanter, "It's been much too long a time between visits."

"I've wanted to see you too, but with the new job and all, you know. I'm ostensibly working at this very moment. I was heading down Bush to the Financial District and I saw a parking place right on the corner. I guess it was meant for me to stop by here first."

"I guess it was meant for you to stop by," George affirmed with a knowing smile. He continued pouring hot water over the Columbian coffee as it slowly dripped sending out a tantalizing aroma.

"I spoke with Patty just a few days ago...of course she asked after you...I told her I'd only seen you once since I got back...that one Sunday when we went to brunch at *Gordon's*."

George laughed, "That was a fun day; I remember we went dancing at *Gold Street* after we ate."

"Maybe we can get together again this coming weekend?"

"Maybe," George answered, "Give me a call."

George set down a tray with Italian *biscotti*, and matching porcelain containers of rich cream and brown sugar. He brought in two large ceramic mugs and placed them on the table...he stepped back in the kitchen and collected the hot decanter of steaming coffee and filled each of their cups...he returned the pot to the kitchen and came back holding a small newspaper clipping.

"I've got something Kiddie that might interest you a great deal."

"What is it?" David asked taking the clipping from George's hand."

"It's an advertisement for a job."

"What job?" David asked unfolding the clipping.

"It's the first of its kind in the United States of America."

David looked at the bold title of the ad that George had circled.

'United Airlines is Hiring Male Flight Attendants.'

* * *

David had successful preliminary interviews with United Airlines, American Airlines, and Western Airlines. The only one that really interested him was Western because they were headquartered in Los Angeles, California. Western Airlines also had a major domicile at the San Francisco International Airport, and there was a good chance that he could be based out of his own home-town after completing training in L.A.

Even though United and American had recalled David for second interviews, he had no interest in being stationed in Chicago or Dallas.E ven if he couldn't get stationed immediately in San Francisco...Los Angeles wouldn't be all that bad...just a little over an hour back home by plane.

All of the airlines were frantically interviewing guys by the thousands, and Western was only hiring 3 male flight attendants that would go through training at LAX.

David was told that the guys would have to go through a series of interviews, at least six, or maybe seven. The next two sessions would be here in San Francisco, and the rest were in L.A.

He was very excited at the prospect of being one of the first three male *stewards* on an American carrier. Western flew as far north as Anchorage, Alaska, the Polar route east to London, south to Mexico City, and west to Hilo and Honolulu, Hawaii. If he could land this job life for David would be nearly perfect.

* * *

Everything in the whole world was going perfectly for David. He had been through a battery of eight different interviews with Western Airlines over a period of four weeks, and today he received telephone confirmation that he had been selected to begin the twelve weeks of Flight Attendant training in Los Angeles! His mind was a flowing current of euphoria! What elation, what blessedness, what ecstasy, what unmitigated joy!

Not only had he landed this dream job, but Patty was coming home today! She and Angelo were taking a TWA flight from London to New York where they would connect to a United flight from New York to San Francisco. In less than one hour they would be landing at SFO International. David had never been so excited in his entire life!

He had spoken with Patricia when she was in London a little less than a day ago, and he had confirmed all the information of their itinerary. She had also told her little brother she was bringing him a stupendously wonderful surprise. She didn't have to say anything more. He already knew that his sister was pregnant. He was to become '*Uncle David.*'

"Poopsie," she'd said over the phone, "Be prepared to hang on to your hat. You're going to blow your mind."

David knew that it was Patty and Angelo's plan all along to come to California when she got pregnant. This could be the only reason for her unexpected '*visit.*' He was also pretty certain that his sister and brother-in-law would be staying for a very long time. Most likely they'd make the Vineyards their headquarters and, maybe, fly to Italy once or twice a year to see Angelo's family. It also meant that Salvatore would be flying to America to meet his new little niece or nephew right after Patricia gave birth. David was thrilled!

He drove Richard's town car to the front of the air terminal and jumped out tossing the keys to a young man at Valet Parking, "I won't be any longer than an hour...meeting the United Flight from New York."

The attendant caught the keys and yelled, "No problem sir, I'll be here with your car when you get back."

David rushed inside the terminal and checked United's big board for arrivals.

"Damn," he said, it shows that they've already landed at Gate 2."

He hustled down the corridor and could see people were already deplaning from the jet way. He scurried to the front of the boarding area and strained to see if they were coming.

He looked all around the area to make sure he hadn't missed them...maybe they already went to baggage claim...there was no Customs to clear...they did that in New York.

It seemed to David that very few people were actually deplaning. This flight had been far from full. He continued to wait impatiently and was dumb struck when the pilots and stewardesses exited the plane. A ticket agent closed and locked the door to the jet way.

"That's it? Everybody's off?" David yelled to the agent.

There was a crowd of other people who were still waiting around the gate. The agent looked around and said loudly enough for everyone to hear, "That's it!"

There was a collective groan from those who were left standing and David dashed back down the corridor heading for Baggage Claim. He must have missed them and they were downstairs waiting for their luggage. He ran down the escalator and went straight to the carousel where they should have been. There were less than a dozen people waiting for bags from the New York flight. Patricia and Angelo were not among them.

David ran back up the escalator to the main terminal and fell into the shortest line at United's ticket counter. Maybe they had missed their flight...maybe their flight from London had been delayed for some reason...maybe they decided to stay in New York and Patty had called home after David had left for the airport.

"Your flight," David said as he approached the ticket agent at the counter, "Your United non-stop from New York that just arrived...my sister and her husband were supposed to be on it...they were connecting from a TWA flight in London...can you help me...can you give me any information."

"I'm sorry, I can't give you any information."

"Can't you tell me if they were on the passenger list for your flight?"

"Sorry, I can't give you any information here...you might want to check with TWA...they are the ones holding the original reservations and passenger name records if your sister started out from London."

David ran through the terminal to the TWA counters. He saw a crowd of people gathered around and recognized some of the same faces that had been waiting at the United gate where Patty and Angelo were supposed to arrive. His heart stopped for a moment.

He dashed back down the terminal to the pay telephones and selected one in a hurry.

He didn't have any change. His hands were trembling. He dialed '0' and then the number for home in Saint Francis Wood.

"This will be collect from David."

"One moment please..."

David was relieved to hear Richard's voice on the other end.

"I'll accept the charges, operator," he heard his dad say.

"Dad...Dad...I'm still at the airport...I don't know what's going on...they're freaking me out here.

"Come home," Richard said.

"But Dad..."

"Come home, now."

"Dad, you have to tell me...I need to know right now...I'm coming home, but I need to now right now."

"The plane went down over the Atlantic. No survivors are expected. Come home."

* * *

CHAPTER SIXTEEN

David's first instinct was to end his life when he learned that his precious sister was dead.

'What did I do that has brought such pain and total despair?' he thought. 'God had me to come into this world in the first place and now He wants to torture me. What am I guilty of having done to deserve such unbearable punishment? Is it because I loved my sister too much? Is it falling in love and knowing joy and happiness with men? Is it because I dearly loved and enjoyed life?'

He had never experienced complete and utter defeat. God had destroyed his world of felicity and happiness in one short phone call. He could not conceive how Providence would possibly permit such agonizing torture. For the only time in his life, David loathed his very existence.

* * *

He was lying on his bed in his room at his parent's home in Saint Francis Woods.

He heard the front doorbell ring as he reclined in a fetal position. He didn't care who or what was at the door. He hoped Brenda would stave off anyone who might interrupt his mourning. His thoughts wandered back through the last few days.

Sylvia was most likely still in bed because the doctors had put her under heavy sedation. She had been drugged from the first hour she found out about the death of her precious baby girl. She cried constantly during her waking hours and could not be comforted by anyone or anything. Even Richard, who had been a veritable paragon of strength for the entire family, could not console his bereaved wife.

David had at least stirred enough to go downstairs late during the nights and have a few bites of nourishment from the smorgasbord of food that flowed in daily from neighbors and friends. He had even sat down once with Richard while they silently ate a sandwich together. It had been five days since notification of the devastating catastrophe. Right now David just wanted to stay curled in his fetal ball and never move again.

David's father had been the only person who had offered any comfort.

"You know son that our life is very much like a vineyard, in order to be its best requires routine and discipline. If the vines are faithfully tended, tied and pruned when they are dormant, one grape vine can last for a hundred years. There are bad years for the vines with droughts, fires, and pests; but there are really good years after surviving those calamities. The vines need the love and care from people who have faith they will produce good fruit. The vines endure and prevail, and so do people who have faith and believe God will tend their needs with love and care. We don't have all the explanations to life on Earth, but we can have faith that we're in the hands of someone who knows the answers.

When we believe in God, than we believe there is a reason behind his actions. I know he loves us, tends us, and even prunes us for a purpose before he harvests us. I choose to believe that He was ready for your sister, and she's joyfully with Him now."

David's thoughts were interrupted by voices coming from downstairs. He tried to shut them out, turned over, and tightly closed his eyes. There was a light knock and he didn't move as someone opened his bedroom door and walked in toward his bed. He didn't roll over to see who it was until he felt a very gentle hand touch his shoulder. It was Sylvia.

He looked up into her red eyes and swollen face. She had a piece of paper in her hand.

"The night you went to the airport, there was a telephone call for you. Brenda answered the phone. It was a telegram. Brenda was upset and wouldn't take the message over the phone. She asked them to bring it in person and Western Union only now delivered the copy. I read it!" Her intonation was filled with disgust.

There was spite in Sylvia's voice as she threw the telegram on David's bed and left his room by slamming the door. David was annoyed that she had broken the sanctity of his privacy so hatefully. He picked up the crumpled message, it had been sent from London.

Arriving with Patricia and Angelo.
We will be uncles together in America.
Ti amo. Ti amo. Ti amo. Salvatore

Salvatore was with Patricia and Angelo when their plane went down! She was indeed pregnant, but the real surprise was that Salvatore would be arriving on the same flight!

David's anguish and grief reached a new level of despondency. He felt shattered and broken into a thousand splinters.

'Oh God, this is excessive obliteration of the soul!'

Sylvia gleaned *everything* from reading Salvatore's telegram. She knew that Patty was pregnant at the time of her death...she knew that there was a *gay* brother-in-law who was probably David's lover...and she knew they were all planning on living in California.

During this moment of extreme anguish, David made up his mind to attend the Flight Attendant training at Western Airlines. The program started next week and he had already accepted the position, signed a contract, and had a one way ticket to Los Angeles.

He could not stay in this house with Sylvia's recriminating martyrdom hanging over him like a thundercloud charged with contemptuous scorn. He knew now more than ever that his mother could not love him unconditionally. She could no longer even hide the fact that she would never accept David's homosexuality.

He had a feeling close to relief as he packed his travel bags. God and mother had both forsaken him; it was time to get on with his life. He would become one of America's very first male flight attendants...he would travel...he would meet new people...and somehow he might find a diversion or two in a pseudo life. It would be a life without the most precious people he'd ever known, and maybe, even a life without God.

David knew instinctively, if not intrinsically, that he couldn't go on without significant change in his attitudes and behaviors. Right now he did not care how that transformation would manifest itself; he could only think of immediate escape from his tormented spirit.

"Yeah," David said aloud, "If the Big Guy upstairs is punishing me for being a shallow, materialistic person...I'll show him how superficial and one-dimensional I really am...I plan on spending the rest of my life looking for gratification attached to no guilt. I'm leaving Saint Francis Woods behind for now and I'll stay at the Vineyards. I may even live with Nanny and Poppa John from now on.

* * *

CHAPTER SEVENTEEN

David had taken the last flight that Western Airlines had scheduled from San Francisco to Los Angeles. He would be checking in at the Century Hotel just before midnight. He had decided to take the latest flight possible thinking that perhaps he might be assigned to a room by himself.

The WAL Training Department had sent information that all newly hired Flight Attendants would be assigned a roommate upon arrival to LAX. David figured that since there were three men, one of the lucky guys might end up with a room by himself. He wasn't thrilled with the idea that he would have to share a bathroom with two other guys for the next 12 weeks...but he thought if the other men checked in before he did...they would end up being roommates and he would be the lucky one.

The plan worked perfectly. When David checked in at the front desk of the Century Hotel on Sepulveda Boulevard, he was assigned a room to himself.

The clerk said, "Looks like you're the lucky guy out of three, you have a room to yourself."

David discovered that besides the three men WAL had hired twenty-seven females which meant a total of thirty new hires would be in the graduating class in

November. The entire class would be living in sixteen rooms on the 3rd floor. David was the exception. He would be separated from the group and stay in his own private room on the 4th floor.

'How nice,' he thought as he took the elevator up to his floor.'

He knew that the new hires were supposed to congregate in the main convention room sharply at 7:30 A.M., or *0730 hrs*. He'd have to get use to telling hours and minutes in Military Time instead of Standard Time...that was really one of the lesser adjustments to make...the biggest adjustment was making sure *he was on time*. It would be a disaster to be late for any training meeting... that was apparent from the memorandum announcing their first meeting tomorrow morning...it stated in big bold letters *BE ON TIME*.

David quickly unpacked the clothes from his leather Gucci suit bag and the toiletries from his matching flight bag. He was glad that he traveled light with only a minimum of items. He had no idea about the socioeconomic status of the other two guys but he didn't want them to feel he was financially superior. There was a good likelihood that both the other guys were younger and just regular working Joes, and David didn't want any cause for resentment either before or after they all became colleagues.

He finished brushing his teeth, stripped off his clothes and jumped under the hotel's pristine sheets. David was used to a few moments of 'meditation' time when he crawled into bed; he had said prayers giving thanks and asked God to bless his family since he was a kid. He didn't do that anymore; he felt he had fallen out of favor with God; it was too painful to think of omitting

Patricia from his prayers. His mission in life right now was to think of the training that lay ahead. He still wasn't ready to accept Patty's and Angelo's death, or that of his beloved Salvatore. David knew that he was in denial about their violent demise crashing into the Atlantic Ocean on their way to America. He tried hard not to think about it.

Grandparents Nanny and Poppa John were, of course, upset because he had taken a job with the airlines, which meant he would be flying all the time. They couldn't wrap their minds around the idea that airplanes could ever possibly be safe after what had happened to their darling granddaughter. David's viewpoint was different... he figured that it was all in the hands of destiny...if he were fated to die violently there was nothing *anyone* or *anything* could do about it.

"Your number is up when your number is up," David said aloud.

He reached for the phone next to his bed and dialed the front desk, "This is David Wellington. Would you please give me a wake-up call at 6:00 A.M., uh... 0600 hours?"

* * *

The convention room was buzzing with activity when David made his appearance at 0700 hours. Tables had been set up in five perfect rows with a center aisle dividing each row into tables of three facing the front of the room. There was a name card at each seat with a place setting for breakfast which was being served from a grand buffet with a smorgasbord of eggs, bacon, sausages, pastries, tropical fruits and beverages. A small

card rested on a miniature stand on the center table...
COMPLEMENTS from MARRIOTT.

There were at least a dozen and a half girls standing around vigorously chatting and giggling. Most of them were quite attractive and two or three were wearing flight attendant uniforms. Only one girl was sitting alone, eating from a plate piled high with goodies from the buffet.

David made a surveillance of the situation and quickly found his professionally printed placard spelling out MR. DAVID WELLINGTON. There was also a professional nametag propped against a china plate with his name and the Western Airlines logo and insignia.

"Nice touch," David whispered to himself as he pinned the tag to his gray tweed sport coat.

He picked up his entree plate and headed for the food that was beckoning his appetite. It seemed like every female in the large room glanced in his direction as he served himself a hefty serving of scrambled eggs and threw on three strips of bacon, two sausage links, and a big fat Danish pastry bursting with blue berries. He walked back to his seat, put down his plate and picked up the coffee cup and saucer that had been set for him.

David walked briskly back to the table with hot and cold beverages and filled his cup from an urn with a sign designating *Kona Coffee.*

'This ought to be a treat,' David thought as he moved back to his location and sat down.

He looked around again and realized that he was the only male in the room. The other two male flight attendants-to-be apparently had not yet arrived. The time was 0715 hours and there was no indication that the eating and socializing was about to stop, so David dug into his breakfast and ate non-stop until he ran out of coffee. He rose from his seat to refill his cup and noticed that the big analog wall clock read 7:30 A.M.

David refilled his cup and returned to finish his Danish roll but someone had cleared his plates and utensils. Two pretty girls were seating themselves in the two empty spaces on his left side. He was glad to have a seat on the outside aisle of his table for three, and sitting in the sixth seat of the fourth row where he had a good view of the assembly as well as the front stage dais and podium which held the microphone.

The overall chatter decreased by several decibels and most of the participants were drifting toward their assigned tables. David did notice the back of a masculine head on the other side of the aisle seated in the center of the second row. The hair was ash blonde in a military cut and the guy was engaged in chatty conversation with a petite Asian girl sitting next to him.

David took another quick glance around the room and noticed the other male figure standing by the coffee urn pouring what was obviously his first cup of the morning. He wasn't any taller than 5'8" or 5'9", sturdy build with thick black hair. Suddenly a voice came over the microphone and David looked up to see a dainty little lady in her early thirties smiling broadly to welcome the assembly.

"Good morning," she said brightly, "and welcome to your first day of Flight Attendant training with Western Airlines. You should each have a blue folder before you on the table that contains an agenda for this first meeting and a calendar outlining your training schedule for the month of September."

David promptly leafed through the first pages in his folder behind the morning agenda and noted that they would blissfully be OFF half day on Saturdays and all day on Sundays. Tentatively and hopefully that would mean Saturday nights out on the town, and perhaps a Sunday or two spent peacefully with Hank. Later on in the training they would have a full weekend off; David decided he was eager to spend time with Hank.

After David's return from Europe, he had only been with Hank once, and that was a very short visit when Hank had come to San Francisco for a one day seminar at the U.C. Medical Center. They had shared a quiet dinner at a *Scoma's* on Fisherman's Wharf and then spent the night at their old haunt the Beresford Hotel. It had been a comfortable reunion with no discussion of love affairs that may have transpired on either side.

Hank found out about the tragedy with Patricia and her new husband when David cancelled their original plans for a weekend at Catalina. That was the last time that David had actually spoken with Hank who had also sent condolences to the Wellington family via postal service.

David knew that Hank understood the severity of grief and pain that was involved with the tragic scenario of his sister and her new spouse. Hank did not know that there was a third party involved, Salvatore, who was also lost in the terrible plane crash over the turbulent Atlantic Ocean. David wisely never shared the story of the love affair with his brother-in law's brother; even if he were asked, he would not know how to express the experiences and feelings that had evolved.

David also knew that he needed to put the past behind him; but he would still cherish the moments that had taken place during that beautiful time in Italy. The memories would always be alive for him, and the love would always remain with David's soul.

"If you will please turn to the page that outlines today's agenda, I'll give you a short synopsis of our activities for morning and this afternoon," he heard a voice interrupt his thoughts as the lady continued with her spiel.

"All of you will have to think of these first few days as basic training for following directions and taking orders from superiors. Please get to know just who is in WAL management and who is 'senior' to you in position. Outside of management everything is based on seniority, so get to know exactly who is senior to you, especially when you're on a flight. Right now, just starting out, you can expect that everyone you meet will automatically be your senior. You are at the bottom of the totem pole, so get used to it. Are there any questions about seniority?"

One of the girls at the front table raised her hand.

"Yes ma'am?"

A pretty girl with short brown hair asked, "How will seniority be determined among us in this class since we're all beginning employment at the same time?"

"Good question...we've given that a lot of thought and finally decided that seniority in this class will be based on age...the eldest in the class will be the most senior; perspicuously the youngest will be the most junior."

David felt an overwhelming sense of relief knowing that he was probably one of the oldest flight attendant trainees in the room. Everyone seemed to be looking around calculating and estimating who might be the most, or least senior. He wasn't totally certain how many different advantages he may have over the other trainees, but David knew that his seniority would definitely play in his favor.

The emcee for the opening ceremonies cleared her throat to get everyone's attention.

"Now I'm going to turn the microphone over to the big boss, Miss Tammy Dakota, who is the administrative director of Flight Attendant Training for Western Airlines. Please give her your full attention."

A slender stately lady wearing a Navy blue Castleberry knit suit with silver buttons and silver trim stepped up to the podium. She had on hooped silver earrings and matching bracelets that jangled when she moved her arms. She had short black hair and a very deep voice that reminded David of Lauren Bacall.

"I want to welcome each and every one of you to our Western Airlines family. This is a particularly exciting time to be joining our company. I look forward to feel personal pride for each of you when you graduate and are placed on the line. You should all understand that your first assignments will be '*on call*' which means that you will be married to your telephone for at least the first six months that you begin working; get used to the idea. Most likely it'll be more than a year before you can bid and hold a monthly block of flights and times at your seniority position. You will find out that bidding and holding a block largely depends on the city where you are based. Our most junior flight attendants are headquartered in Minneapolis-Saint Paul; and the most senior girls...sorry, I meant to say flight attendants...are based here in Los Angeles and San Francisco.

Tammy stopped for a moment and took a small sip of water from a paper cup that was obviously one of the same receptacles used for passengers on an aircraft.

"I do want to give you a little tip about bidding time which comes around every last week of the month. No matter what your seniority or your base, make certain that you always bid for a block of time, every month, *every* time without fail. Even if you are the most junior flight attendant in the company, be sure to bid for a block. Sometimes a little miracle occurs when there is a block left *unbid*, and that block could go to you. Even the worst block of time is better than having to remain 'on call' for the entire month."

She ran her index finger over her right eyebrow and continued, "If you follow our directions to the letter and learn *everything* verbatim, you will be successful and a welcome addition to this company. Your training staff is extremely capable and professional, but if you experience any problems that require special attention, my office hours are posted on the inside cover of the blue folder sitting in front of you. This is your time to keep your head screwed on tight, be organized, and get your shit together."

Every person in the room laughed jocosely, and no one laughed more heartily than David.

* * *

The morning continued with more introductions and information from all the instructors who would be working with the flight attendant trainees. They were *all female* instructors for the areas of training that would take place. These included such topics as food preparation, mixing drinks, serving techniques, over water training, first aid, and most importantly FAA Emergency Procedures. FAA training required taking separate comprehensive examinations leading to a specialized certification. There would also be lengthy sessions and training for 'make-up' application and personal appearance. David and his male counterparts would thankfully be exempt from those particular classes.

The morning went quickly and David was looking forward to all the aspects of training outlined for the newly hired employees. He knew that this was going to be a lot of fun and that he would enjoy every single day of work with all of his energetic colleagues; and he finally got the opportunity to meet the other two male employees after the lunch break.

Ronald Decker was also from California; David heard one of the girls say something about Salinas, California while talking about the other blond male flight attendant, and he assumed that she was referring to Ronald. He knew for certain that the third male, Robert Fields, was from Denver because he had overheard a conversation between him and two girls who were from Aspen and Vale, Colorado.

Ronald was definitely the more handsome of the other two guys; he was close to six foot tall, blond hair, bluish eyes, healthy ruddy complexion and masculine buff body with an *All American* look. Robert was shorter with black hair, brown eyes, washed-out complexion and a fit but stouter build. He had a pleasant face but overall he was average in appearance. David, however, was only comparing himself to these guys in one way, *seniority.* He didn't know their exact ages, but he knew he was the eldest. Hallelujah!

The three males finally met alone when they were all in the men's room during a short break from the afternoon meeting. The two others were standing at the urinal as David washed his hands with fragrant coconut soap provided by the Century Hotel.

"Did you see the tits on the babe from Seattle?" Robert said with gusto.

"I was too busy checking out that redhead from Minneapolis, not only tits but what a face! She's gorgeous; I'll bet she could make a fortune as a model," Ronald said.

"Yeah, makes you wonder why she's bothering with this flight attendant job."

"She's from Minnesota," David interjected, "Give her time here in Los Angeles and someone from Hollywood might discover her."

All three guys laughed as they exited the rest-room and strolled toward the meeting room.

"Hey," Ronald said, "Let's get together when they cut us loose this evening and go have a drink at the bar. We need to get to know each other better since we're the only guys around here, and we may as well start tonight before the training gets too intense."

"If you ask me it's too intense already, especially with all these gals to lust after. Sounds like a good idea to me though; if they let us out of training after dinner we should hook up for a beer or two," Robert agreed.

"Count me in," David said. "I'm not a beer drinker but I'm sure I can find an adult beverage suitable to my taste."

"Good," Robert said, "It'll give us a chance to talk."

David wondered why Ronald looked somewhat bewildered after his comment about drinking adult beverages instead of beer.

* * *

The first days of training went by as fast as marbles going down a sliding board. The weekend did not materialize the way David had hoped; it was instead spent studying for the first big examination which was to be taken Monday morning. The new hires had to memorize all the city codes and airports that Western served in addition to the aircraft that was used on their routes. He thought there was a lot of other extraneous information to learn that would be much more useful to a pilot or reservation agent, but his was not the reason why.

He was particularly happy to have a room to himself because he didn't like distractions when he studied. Both of the other guys did their homework with both television and radio blaring, and both of them chain smoked as they studied. David had been in their room just once to exchange some notes, and determined that neither of the other guys was in any way scholarly, not by a long shot. They were also untidy.

* * *

It was on a Tuesday, the third week of training when David and a dozen other flight attendants, including Ronald, were in line for a buffet lunch that was being served in the hotel's dining room. They were filling their plates with grilled chicken, roast beef, ham and various fresh fruits and vegetables while conversing about the morning's class familiarizing them with emergency equipment on the Boeing 737 aircraft.

David was ahead of Ronald in the lunch line with just one girl separating the two guys. She was chatting with Ronald and David heard her ask, "Did I understand that you were in the Air Force before getting hired by Western?"

"Yup," Ronald answered, "I wasn't a pilot, I was with the 52nd Equipment Maintenance Squadron at Spangdahlem Air Force Base in Germany."

David suddenly and clearly remembered hearing that voice.

'I'm in the Air Force...I'm not a pilot... I'm with the 52nd Equipment Maintenance Squadron at Spangdahlem Air Force Base near Trier, Germany. I have ten months of duty left before I go home.'

David stopped moving along the line and froze with a ladle of rice pilaf in his hand; he looked directly at Ronald and said, "Amsterdam!"

Ronald's face turned a bright crimson red and he pretended he hadn't heard the remark.

David quickly changed the subject and turned to the girl next to him, "Didn't you say you're family was from Salt Lake City? I've never been to Salt Lake, everybody says that Park City is the place to ski, I've always wanted to ski there."

Ronald quickly picked up on David's cue and continued down the buffet line as though he'd never heard the word 'Amsterdam.' It had just slipped out of David's mouth when Ronald said he had been stationed in Germany with the Air Force. The memory of their tryst at the Park Hotel in Amsterdam came swirling back to his mind...their chance meeting at the DOK... the song 'San Francisco,'...the Heineken Beer... the nightcap at the hotel bar...their brief but hot encounter in David's room.

He knew that Ronald was remembering everything as well, and it was most likely he'd be receiving a visitor tonight in his room at the Century Hotel.

* * *

Western Airlines was headquartered in Los Angeles with five other pilot and flight attendant domiciles in San Francisco, Seattle, Salt Lake City, Denver and

Minneapolis. The new hires were informed that there would be positions opening at the bases in Los Angeles, San Francisco and Denver and Minneapolis. Those were the cities growing with more daily flights and connecting flights to each other and Hawaii and Alaska. David learned that less than 10% of the entire United States population had ever flown on a commercial air line; a statistic that would dramatically change within the next decade.

Working for a major airline was an invigorating livelihood for all the employees of the company. It didn't matter if you were a mechanic, reservation or ticket agent, pilot or baggage and cargo handler, there were plenty of interline travel perks for all. Their own company included health, dental, retirement and credit union benefits. David was going to be in the right place, at the right time. He couldn't be more pleased. He just hoped that his first base assignment wth Western would be in his hometown of San Francisco.

He understood that San Francisco was *'everybody's favorite city'* but it was especially David's personal inspiration. He loved to travel and have new adventures and experiences. He loved to meet new people and learn about new places, but he always loved to come home to his city by the bay. There were times when he felt insecure about being away from his city; he felt incomplete and had an empty sensation that his mind and body lacked some curious nutrient, and he had to be back by the bay that he loved.

David also thought that recognizing and remembering Ronald Decker had to be an act of Providence. He knew that it was Ronald's goal to be as discreet as possible about the secret the two guys shared. Their brief encounter in Amsterdam would remain undisclosed to any of their new professional colleagues at Western Airlines.

David was, however, delighted to think that he and Ronald might become great friends and share wonderful new experiences going through the this training together. It even occurred to David that they both might get based in San Francisco and maybe find a lovely apartment to rent. It was a fact that they would both be 'on-call' for the first year of employment. Both of them would often be away from home and at odd times and days of the month. It would provide a modicum of stability if they shared a place together.

David also entertained the thought of living with a handsome discriminating sex buddy who was naturally masculine and discerning. Ronald was not exactly the intellectual type, but he was obviously circumspect and insightful. It could fun getting to know him, and it would be great living and working with a man of similar sexual and social sentiments. Maybe...just maybe...life would be somewhat pleasant again.

* * *

It was 2230 hours and David was leafing through his notes in the Flight Attendant manual when a knock came on the door of his hotel room. He jumped up from the desk and reached for the knob. Ronald popped in and swerved around to push David against the door and kiss him enthusiastically.

"Just like the old times in Amsterdam," he said running his fingers through David's hair.

David laughed lightly and shook Ronald's hand off his head. He stepped back and held him tightly at arms length.

"I can't believe it's you, I haven't been able to think of anything else but our meeting in Amsterdam since I recognized you at lunch this afternoon."

"I know," Ronald stated emphatically, "me too. I can't believe that we've hooked up again here after nearly two years. What a riot!"

"I hope I wasn't too blatant when I hollered out Amsterdam."

"Oh no," Randy said, "It just caught me off guard, and nobody paid attention except you and me. My face must of got real red for a minute or two...but I picked up on how you changed the conversation...it helped me to a quick recovery."

"Come on in...sit down...let's get comfortable," David said guiding Ronald to the small sofa sitting under the window.

They both sat and unconsciously placed an arm on the back of the divan. David realized that he and Ronald were firmly grasping each other's arm as they quietly spoke.

"You look really good," Ronald said, "You are one handsome dude."

"So are you." David said as he squeezed Ronald's firm arm..

"Were you studying when I came in?"

"I was leafing through the manual wondering if you might come up for a visit."

"Well, here I am. I needed to get out of that room. It's so stuffy and full of smoke. Your room is cool and smells fresh and clean. Robert smokes like a chimney and throws things around like a pig. There are Snicker's wrappers and boxer shorts all over the place. Your room is military neat and orderly."

"You're always welcome to study up here at night. I very rarely smoke in the room."

"Yeah, I noticed; I think I've only seen you with a cigarette once, or maybe twice at most. A lot of the girls smoke except for that little group from Salt Lake. Somebody told me that Mormons don't smoke or drink, but they do fuck like rabbits."

David laughed, "I think that I've heard something similar."

Ronald stared intently at David's face, "Look buddy, I'm not too good at expressing myself when it comes to conversation and all, but I have to tell you that it's obvious you're from a high class background. You're so fine in every way. You look like a Hollywood movie star and you talk like you were educated at one of those exclusive universities in England. You have fine manners and you've been well raised. I want to be your close friend if you can put up with an ordinary guy like me."

David smiled broadly and stood up...Ronald did the same...the two men embraced in a big warm hug.

"Thanks man," Ronald sighed, "This is going to be good."

"Yes," David answered with a sigh. "Will you be missed if you stay a while longer?"

"Yeah, one of those smart gals from Minneapolis is coming over to quiz us on the Boeing 707 for tomorrow's test. I'd love to get you naked under those sheets," Ronald said nodding toward the bed, "but it's probably best to play it cool; I should get back now."

"I'm sure we can figure out a time for some fun and relaxation in the near future." David answered as he kissed Ronald goodnight at the door.

* * *

David was not 'chomping at the bit' to hop in the sack with Ronald, but he could easily have sex with his old buddy again. Ronald seemed much more interested in establishing a friendly relationship than an emotional involvement, and that would be just fine, too. David was less driven toward sex since the deaths of his sister, and his former devotee and lover, Salvatore. He was, however, prepared to continue his affair with Hank, and the coming weekend they were scheduled a meeting right here at the Century Hotel.

The new flight attendants were all looking forward to their first full weekend off and almost everyone was going home to their respective families. In fact, David was probably going to be the only member of his class who remained at the hotel for the weekend. Everybody else was taking advantage of free passes and flying back to their city of origin. The only other exception was three or four girls from Seattle who were spending the weekend at the home of a gal from Los Angeles who lived in Beverley Hills.

David knew that Ronald would be taking a shuttle to visit with his family in Fresno. He was grateful, especially now, that Ronald and Hank would not cross paths just yet.

'I may never have the occasion to introduce Hank to Ronald,' David thought, 'especially if we don't get assigned to the same domicile. I think I'll let this ride until I know just where the chips will fall. Hank and Ronald don't have to know about each other at this juncture in time. Besides, I'm really looking forward to the weekend with Hank. I'm in his home-town and I think I'll encourage him to take the lead on everything.'

* * *

The weekend came quickly and Hank came early. David had just completed his shower around 0700 hours and the phone rang...it was Hank calling from the lobby... he sounded very chipper.

"Come on down, we're going to breakfast."

"I'm on my way," David answered as he zipped up his white cargo pants and buttoned his light blue Aloha shirt with green palms.

David scuttled down the elevator and found Hank chatting with the young male clerk at the front desk. They were talking about Jaguars...a conversation undoubtedly prompted by a sparkling brand new 1973 XKE convertible sitting in front of the entrance to the hotel. David felt a small tinge of pride as he approached the desk and Hank winked at him.

"Good morning," David said, "I'm glad to see that you're also wearing a Hawaiian style shirt, that's a real sharp green."

"I'm wearing a Hawaiian shirt...I'd go with you guys... but I have to work, darn it all," said the young man behind the desk.

"Maybe next time," Hank said, "I'll bring the sedan so we can all fit in the car more comfortably."

Hank and David glided through the door and into the convertible.

"This is really nice," David said as he buckled his seat belt, "beautiful shade of gold."

"Yeah, I really like it." Hank said, "I've always wanted one of these cars."

"Where are we going to have breakfast?" David asked, not really caring where they went.

"I thought we'd drive down the coast to Laguna Beach and spend most of the day down there. You told me you've never been there and I think you'll enjoy the area. Laguna is sort of like Sausalito in that it's an artist's community with galleries, boutique shops, restaurants and bars."

"It feels good to be going somewhere with you on this gorgeous day. I needed a break from all the rigorous training we've been going through."

"How's that going?" Hank asked, "Are you finding it a little bit stressful at times?"

"Oh, no, stressful, but it can be pretty tedious. We have to be on guard all the time about what we say, what we do, how we act...everybody is under microscopic scrutiny...and three of the girls have already been washed out within in the first three weeks."

"What did they do to deserve being fired?"

"Two of them walked into class two minutes late."

"Wow! That seems pretty harsh. Do you suppose there was any other reason?"

"I'm not sure," David said, "The two of them were from Denver, and they were roommates. Administration may have used them to make an example of the importance of punctuality in the industry. We know that one flunked every quiz we've had so far, so it wasn't a big surprise when she was cut from the crew. She was from San Francisco."

"Did you know her personally?" Hank asked.

"No, I've never met any of the others except for Ronald." David wanted to kick himself for letting that slip out.

"Do you mean that you knew one of the other two male flight attendants before you guys began training? Is he from San Francisco?"

"No...I mean, uh, yes..." David stumbled in his speech, "I mean no, he is not from San Francisco, and yes, I met him a couple years ago when I was in Europe."

"Well, what a coincidence that you guys would meet up again here in Los Angeles."

"Yes," said David now resigned to telling Hank part of the story.

"We met at a popular gay bar in Amsterdam, the D.O.K. Ronald was in the Air Force stationed in Germany at Spangdahlem Air Force Base. He and a couple of straight buddies from his base were on a three day pass. They didn't know about Ronald. It was his last night when I met him at the bar. We had an 'American' reunion and got drunk on Heineken beer...they only serve beer at the D.O.K....we had a couple of nightcaps at the Park Hotel where I was staying, then Ronald had to get back to his buddies who were staying at the American Hotel. They all had to be back on base that next morning. I'm not sure if they drove or flew back."

"Wow, what a coincidence," Hank said again.

"Yes, "David said, "It was a brief meeting. We just recognized each other the day before yesterday."

"How'd that come about?" Hank asked curiously.

"Oh, Ronald mentioned that he had been stationed in Germany and it dawned on me who he was...all I had to say was 'Amsterdam'...we were at lunch among other members of our class and he immediately turned red...I immediately changed the subject. We've only had a couple minutes alone since then...but we both remember our former introduction."

Hank said for the third time, 'What an amazing coincidence!"

* * *

David really enjoyed riding down California Highway #1 along the coast. The air was perfect, the sky was azure blue and the water was solid navy. Hank had a batch of cassettes in the glove compartment...most of them were classical...some jazz and blues.

David selected Dinah Washington...she was one of his very favorites since high school.

"This is the jazziest rendition of Blue Skies ever recorded!" David exclaimed.

> *Blue skies smilin' at me*
> *Nothin' but blue skies do I see*
> *Bluebirds singin' a song*
> *Nothin' but bluebirds all day long*

> *Never saw the sun shinin' so bright*
> *Never saw things goin' so right*
> *Noticing the days hurrying by*
> *When you're in love, my how they fly*

Hank took Interstate 110 to Long Beach where they picked up the Pacific Coast Hwy. #1.

They wound along the coast through Huntington Beach, Newport Beach and Laguna Beach. When they arrived in Laguna David liked the surroundings immediately. The community was teeming with little boutique shops and art galleries everywhere. The majority of them, as well as the restaurants, seemed first class to David who felt great!

* * *

On the return drive back to LAX David and Hank enjoyed a spectacular Pacific Coast sunset replete with bursting brilliant colors that changed with every mile they rode. The vista transformed through stages of hues in yellow, gold, orange, lavender blues and finally deep purple. By the time they reached the Century Hotel the sky was totally black.

David presumed that he would not be alone that night. Hank had purchased a decorative ceramic jar for replanting one of his favorite ferns. He bought it at an iconic store called the *Laguna Coast Pottery*. When they had opened the trunk to safely secure the piece David couldn't help noticing that Hank's duffel bag was already aboard. He wasn't sure exactly how he felt about a sexual interlude that night, but he certainly couldn't complain if this handsome masculine Adonis shared his bed for the night.

Hank wordlessly pulled into the hotel's reception drive and gave an attendant the car keys. He hopped out to retrieve a parking stub and popped open the trunk to grab his bag.

"I've got something special for us in this old duffel bag," Hank announced proudly as he guided David through the door to the main lobby.

"Is it something to eat or drink?" David asked nonchalantly as they took the elevator up to the fourth floor.

"As soon as we get to your room, call down for a bottle of tonic, limes and a bucket of ice."

David felt very comfortable being with Hank. It was as though he sensed that David wasn't exactly the same person since the untimely death of his only sibling. Hank couldn't fathom the depth of David's grief...no one could...

but he was aware that David's life had been changed forever.

The two men had only wine with their elaborate late brunch at the iconic *Little Shrimp* restaurant in Laguna Beach. Neither of them felt particularly hungry, but they were both ready to settle into the bottle of Bombay gin that Hank had tucked in his duffel bag. David called room service for the tonic water and a few embellishments such as canapés, fruit, cheese and nuts. He also contacted the front desk to find out what good movie they might be able to view in their room.

David said to the clerk on duty, "Would you hang on just a minute?"

He put his hand over the receiver and turned to Hank, "Have you seen '*Who's Afraid of Virginia Woolf*?' Liz Taylor and Richard Burton? It won a lot of Academy Awards?"

"No, I've never seen it...sounds good to me...go ahead and order it."

David lifted his hand and said, "That's our ticket for tonight...but we're not quite ready to see it...maybe in about an hour or so...okay...I'll phone you when we're ready."

He put down the phone and said, "We're all set for our movie, and the accoutrement for the gin is on its way."

"Great," Hank said as he lit a cigarette and sat down in one of the two comfortable chairs in David's room. "I always wanted to see that movie...I'm surprised the hotel can show it so soon after its release...it's only been a few years."

"1967 to be exact," David added.

"Have you previously seen it?" Hank asked taking a drag from his cigarette.

"Oh, yes," David answered. "I saw it with Patricia when it first came out, and I can't wait to see it again. You know, I met Elizabeth Taylor once, in person."

"No, you never told me," Hank said as he put out his cigarette, "How did that happen?"

"It's no big deal...it happened when we were in London...she was at a cocktail party that David Niven was giving in the suite next to ours at the Hilton. It was pretty uneventful, but at least I can say I met Elizabeth Taylor."

The conversation was interrupted by the buzzer announcing the arrival of room service. Hank hopped up and opened the door as the server wheeled in a cart filled with food, ice and all the goodies they needed for a good time. Hank tipped the bellboy and took over preparation of their first drink for a relaxed evening.

Both men stretched out side by side on the bed propped up with two cushions from the single sofa in the room. When the movie started Hank replenished their drinks and put a bowl of salted nuts between them. Three or four times he reached over and stroked David's knee. The gesture was very reassuring for both of them. David especially was drifting into a comfortable zone of soothing contentment.

They became absorbed in the film and Hank kept their glasses full of gin and tonic. By the end of the movie David was completely relaxed and could sense a growing erection. Hank placed his hand strategically on David's waist and played with the belt buckle of his now bulging cargo pants. The credits for the movie faded and the television screen went blank

"Let's get rid of the clothes," Hank suggested.

David stripped completely naked in a matter of seconds. Hank did the same except for his white jockey shorts. David had decided that he was going to let Hank take the lead in their love-making. Without a word being spoken Hank did just that.

It was evident to David that Hank had gained remarkable experience in his sexual techniques since their very first meeting; his apparent goal tonight was to service David orally. The objective was reached quickly. David released what seemed like months of stress and anxiousness into Hank's obliging warm mouth.

David looked down on Hank's chiseled face and body. He was holding David's virility deep in his throat still savoring the moment. Both men closed their eyes and breathed deeply. Neither of their bodies moved. They both lay there in a relaxed state of euphoria.

David thought about what had just happened...he thought about how much Hank must care for him...how much Hank had wanted to please him...how much Hank had seem to enjoy the act of servicing him. David's mental reflection again caused a stirring physical response. Hank began gently, so very gently massaging with his moist warm mouth. He had not relinquished David's delicious pulsating organ since the first explosive discharge.

'This will be a first for me,' David thought, 'back to back ejaculations...oh yeah!'

Hank seemed to be as excited as David as he quietly moaned approval of the now rigid masculinity in his throat. His entire body moved in cadence with every downward thrust. David knew there would be no hesitation on his part for a second orgasmic ejaculation.

"Here it comes," David whispered softly.

Hank made a long slow groan as he swallowed the second massive advancement of seminal discharge. This time around was as delectable as the previous release from David's responsive body.

Hank adeptly jumped from the bed and said, "Don't move an inch, I'll be right back."

He went to the bathroom and David could hear running water. Hank returned with a warm wet washcloth and a towel. As he approached the bed David reached out and touched the crotch of Hank's damp underwear.

"Is that your chaos I detect? Did you..."

"Yes," Hank interrupted as he sat on the edge of the bed and delicately cleansed the private parts of David's body, "I boiled over the second time you turned the corner."

"I hope it was as good for you as it was for me." David asserted.

"It was *at least* as good," Hank said leaning over and touching David's lips gently with his mouth.

The next morning Hank took David to a luxurious outdoor brunch in Marina Del Rey. The weather and the food were in harmony to perfection. David downed three Ramos Fizzes before he put one bite of food in his mouth, and then he ate non-stop for almost two hours.

"It's one of Nature's unexplained mysteries," Hank said shaking his head.

"What's that?" David asked as he devoured another marzipan Danish pastry and washed it down with black coffee.

"Your intake of calories and the shape of your body... from all accounts that I've seen... you should be about one hundred pounds heavier than you are."

For the first time since his sister had died David guffawed loudly. "Yes...yes...I admit it openly...I am an h-o-g... *pig*. I just hope I'm not embarrassing you in public."

Hank laughed as well and offered David a cigarette hoping it might slow down his eating.

"Don't you have some sort of a weight restriction now that you're working as a flight attendant?"

"Yes," David answered, "Our weight must remain in healthful proportion to our height."

"Who determines that?" Hank asked.

"Our supervisors will check our weight every month and go by the recommended proportions outlined from *your* American Medical Association. Someone of my height cannot weigh more than one hundred ninety pounds or less than one-hundred fifty five."

"You weigh about one-seventy or one seventy-five?"

"Two days ago I weighed in at one seventy-three with my clothes on."

"Looks like you have nothing to worry about, have another pastry," Hank said pushing the tray toward David.

The two men laughed again, and not for the last time that day. They spent the rest of Sunday afternoon enjoying each others company. It was once again dark when Hank drove his Jaguar back to the Century Hotel. David would have been glad to have Hank stay another night, but they both had to be up early and it was probably a good idea for them to rest before beginning another rigorous week.

* * *

David returned to a freshly cleaned room that held no evidence of the night before. Everything had been cleared away or tidied...bed had clean linens and bathroom was restocked with fresh towels and washcloths. He plopped down in the most comfortable chair and lit a cigarette. He wanted to take a moment for reflection.

He was well into Western's Flight Attendant training and he was totally confident of successfully finishing the program. Once again he took time to look at his life. He found himself analyzing his existence much more than he had ever done previously. Maybe it was a sign that he was maturing, or maybe he was still bitterly wounded by Patricia's death and somewhat afraid of the future. Either way, he knew there were subtle changes taking place in his character.

David had never dreamed he would feel insecure, but since the deaths of Patty, Angelo and Salvatore, he was definitely in touch with his own mortality. He had always felt bold and confident in all his interactions within the world. He always felt that he had been personally blessed by God in all things; but when the deadly accident occurred he felt that he had been betrayed and abandoned by the Almighty.

David thought silently 'I guess I'm angry with the Big Guy upstairs, and that's a scary place to be. I've felt loved by Jesus as far back as I can remember, but I don't think I'll ever understand why this happened. I need to be realistic and to take control of my own life. If I ever expect to find happiness again I'll have to create my own euphoria in spite of the negative interference from outside sources such as my mother.'

'It's disconcerting and intimidating to think that God might be my adversary, but, He did put up a roadblock to my felicity and joy in life. Grief can be a disabling affliction. I have to learn to fight and overcome it! I absolutely refuse to spend life in dispirited gloom and depression. I don't want to believe that God has taken my loved ones because He was displeased with my promiscuity. Doesn't He know it is punishment enough that He appointed Sylvia as the earthly agent of harassment regarding my homosexuality?'

* * *

Flight Attendant training was almost completed. Today he had very expertly passed the overwater exercises and was now qualified for all the flights to Mexico, Hawaii and Alaska. Not all the new hires were interested in becoming qualified for overwater flights. Many were content with overland continental routes. David was qualified for everything!

He was still in his swimming trunks with a towel around his neck and scuffled across the lobby in a pair of thongs when he heard his name.

"Mr. Wellington...David Wellington...here at the front desk," an attractive Latino man was waving from behind the counter.

"Yes," David said approaching the desk. "There is a package here for you."

"Do you know from whom?"

The clerk reached around to David's mail bin and retrieved a small professionally wrapped box.

"It looks like it came from some medical clinic in Huntington Beach."

"Thanks," David said, "I know who sent it."

Hank had sent him a present. 'I was just thinking about him and he sent a present,' David thought. 'It's almost as though he knew that today was a special milestone in my flight attendant training. Most of those girls seemed terrified about qualifying for overwater, and I actually enjoyed jumping in and out of the life raft and swimming around with the guys. We even found time for a few impressive dives off the board.'

"I wonder what's in the package," David said aloud examining it in the elevator. "He wouldn't be sending a ring...it looks about the size for a watch...I'll bet it's a watch! I'm going to shower, clean up for dinner, and relax with a cigarette while I telephone Hank and open it. It's just like he knew I qualified for overwater today; he really is intuitive."

David had already passed the test for conversational Spanish, an additional qualification for which a handful of the new hires had applied. It was mostly for those flight attendants who were to be based on the West Coast. David's propensity for languages encouraged him to be fully qualified to work on Western's flights to Mexico.

The last two hurdles for the newly hired employees were to work on their first flights and then take a comprehensive final examination. The trainers lovingly dubbed the first flight working as their 'Bippy' flight. They were each to work on non-stop flights to Hawaii, Seattle, Denver, and Minneapolis. They were assigned various flights in twos and threes from their class. They would be under the direct supervision of the senior flight attendant on their trip and the new-hires were expected to assist in all food and beverage service.

David was not in the least concerned about either of the final events, either the Bibby flight or the their final examination. Most of the flight attendants thought of them as concluding obstacles. Finally, he would be flying and enjoying his new career in earnest. He could also think about a new life free from his mother's exaggerated suffering and martyr-like attitude. Relief was in sight! He turned on the radio next to his chair on a lamp table and uncannily heard Jimmy Cliff's song.

> *I can see clearly now the rain is gone.*
> *I can see no obstacles in my way.*
> *Gone are the dark clouds that had me blind.*
> *It's gonna be a bright (bright)*
> *bright (bright) sunshiny day.*
> *It's gonna be a bright (bright)*
> *bright (bright) sunshiny day.*

David didn't find time to open Hank's package until much later that night. Ronald, Robert and three of the girls came laughing and pounding on his door while the song played. They were there to celebrate their qualification for the overwater trips. The 'Bibby' flight and the final examination were the only hurdles left and the revelers were walking to a steak house not far from their hotel on Century Boulevard to party!

It was almost midnight when David got back to his hotel room. The message light on his phone was blinking. He called the front desk to find it was Hank who had phoned several times. There was a number to call and the message time didn't matter ; David was to call *immediately* on his return.

As the number was ringing David panicked for a moment. 'The package, what did I do with the package?'

Too late, Hank picked up the phone on the second ring. "David?"

"Yes, hi Hank, sorry to telephone so late; I just got back from a little celebration with some of the flight attendants from my class."

"Did you get the package I sent," Hank said with urgency in his voice.

"Yes, I got it earlier this evening, but I was surrounded by people before I had time to open it. I just got back and called you first thing. I still haven't opened it."

"Good," Hank said with a sigh of relief, I'm glad you have it in your possession. It's medication I want you to take."

"Medication?' David said trying not too sound disappointed, "What kind of medication?"

"Antibiotic...penicillin actually...take three everyday... staring one tonight...finish the package. I wasn't absolutely certain that there was a problem until the day before yesterday. The first time I felt a mild burn urinating was the Sunday I was with you.

David couldn't help laughing, "You mean to tell me you have gonorrhea?"

"That's exactly what I'm telling you and it's nothing to laugh about. This is a serious matter."

"Of course, I'm sorry," David said covering his mouth to keep from laughing again. "It's just that I had no idea that you sent me penicillin."

"I hope you're not disappointed but it's imperative that you start taking it immediately."

"Sure Hank...you're the doctor...but..."

"But what?" Hank sounded official.

"I don't believe that we did anything that could have put me at risk. If you remember I was never exposed to the private parts of your body, you wore your shorts during sex."

"That doesn't matter. We have to be certain and play it safe."

"Sure Hank...like I said you're the doctor...I've never had any social disease except crabs once in my Freshman year at college. Does it hurt very much to have...what... you have?"

"It's not very pleasant, so please open the package and start on the penicillin tonight. I'll call you in a couple of days"

"Yes sir," David said and placed the receiver back in its cradle.

"Shit!" he said aloud.

'I'm no doctor but I know that Hank didn't get the 'clap' by jerking off with a buddy. It had to have been through anal sex with some dude. Just the idea of anal sex repulses me! Now I find out that the man *I was* falling in love with, the same man I *might* have spent my life with, had anal sex with some dude. I have no intention of taking this penicillin. I'll save it for a rainy day like the next time my tonsils flare-up,' David thought as he turned down the sheets of his bed.

* * *

CHAPTER EIGHTEEN

For his 'Bibby Trip' David was assigned an evening flight from LAX to SEA along with the only flight attendant trainee who was his senior. Jeannie was calm, mature and basically quiet. David thought she was a promising candidate to be one of the best in the business.

Their flight time from Los Angeles to Seattle was supposed to be around two and a half hours, but circumstances caused the plane to stay in the air much longer. They were scheduled to leave at 1935 hours and their Boeing 707 departed right on schedule.

The flight was not filled which benefited David and Jeannie with passenger seats instead of jump-seats for take-off and landing. There were five regular flight attendants, two in first class and three in coach. Because she was senior to David, Jeannie worked with the first class passengers and David worked in coach.

The lead flight attendant was a pretty black girl named Donna. She and Tina worked first class and Tammy, Cheryl and Sue were in back with David. Donna, unfortunately, was suffering from head cold symptoms and had to constantly blow her nose. David was glad to work in coach class away from the germs.

Everyone was wonderfully supportive to the two new hires for their 'Bibby' flight. The pilots were especially solicitous and hospitable toward David who was greeted warmly as the first male flight attendant on this Western Airlines flight. He knew he was going to enjoy his new career.

Minutes after take-off David was diligently preparing a beverage cart with all the trimmings for distributing drinks along with Lombardi Champagne for any passenger who wanted it. No one knew of his connection to the winery, and he was determined not to tell. Free champagne for all adult passengers was one of Western's great selling points along with other special hall-marks such as leg-space. '*When you fly coach on WAL your legs go first*,' which accurately described leg-space for passengers in coach class who enjoyed the same leg space as those in first class.

Tammy and Cheryl began beverage service from the front of coach and David started with his cart from the back. Sue remained in the galley and began food preparation for everyone's dinner. There was a choice of entrees, fried chicken breasts or pot roast, and the passengers were pretty much split in half by their decisions. Sue confided in David that there would be more than a half dozen meals left and he would have his choice.

"You mean we get to eat when we work?" David had asked.

"Oh, sure," Sue answered, "if any meals are left they belong to us. We almost always get to eat on dinner flights where Marriott usually overstocks with food. Tonight you shall dine! The only tiny drawback is that we're not supposed to eat in the main cabin; we have to sit on one of the jump-seats or stand in the galley. We usually take turns, it always works out well."

David guided his beverage cart into the aisle and before he could ask the first passengers for their preference he froze to the sound of bells. One bell meant that passengers could unbuckle but must remain seated' until otherwise advised,...two bells meant 'all is well to unbuckle and move about the cabin freely,'...three bells signaled that one of the flight attendants wanted to converse with the cockpit, or vice versa...and four bells meant 'emergency, walk to the cockpit calmly for instructions from the Captain.'

David counted one bell, two bells, three bells, four bells! Oh, no! It can't be a real emergency, not on a 'Bibby' flight, not David's first time working as a flight attendant.

The other flight attendants heard the same alert because they left their stations and were heading for the cockpit. When David got there Jeannie and Tina were already standing outside the cockpit door. Tina calmly said "We don't know a thing except Donna is being briefed by the Captain. Tammy, Cheryl and Sue return to your posts and continue the beverage service. David, you stay here with me and Jeannie and you can report anything we hear from Donna."

Jeannie looked at David and whispered, "Do you believe this is happening on our very first flight?"

"I've been flying for over five years and this is the first time I ever heard four bells."

"Hopefully it's not too serious," David said. "Our plane is flying smoothly and nothing seems wrong with the engines."

The cockpit door flew open and Donna came out of the cockpit looking wide-eyed and serious. "I just got the germs scared right out of me."

David thought she looked a little ashen in skin color. He knew that this was no time to panic and he gave his full attention to her. She beckoned them to follow her into the first class galley where she drew the curtain for privacy.

"We've got ourselves a situation. Right after take-off the landing gear on the nose didn't retract. There are supposed to be back-up strategies, but nothing works."

David said, "The first system is electronic, then there is a pneumatic system, and if that fails there's supposed to be a manual crank to retract the gear by hand."

"You remember your training well," Donna said. "When the first two systems failed both the Captain and co-pilot couldn't move the gear manually even an inch. They really don't know the exact position of the landing gear; that wheel might be halfway up or halfway down."

"Sounds like an emergency landing to me," David said.

"You got that right," Donna replied. The Captain has orders from SEA-TAC to keep the plane in the air to burn off excess fuel before we attempt landing. Meanwhile, we're not to breathe a word of this to the passengers. We'll finish beverage, dinner and coffee service and then the Captain will let us know what to do after that."

"Aye-aye ma'am," David said with a salute, "Thanks for the update Donna, good job!

I'll let the girls in the back know what's happening."

Donna waited for a moment until David was gone and she turned to Jeannie and Tina,

"I'm really going to like working with that young man, there's something comforting about having him on this flight."

"Oh yeah," Jeannie agreed, "He's really special. He's been a standout in our class, and everybody, and I do mean everybody, likes him the best. The other two guys are okay, but they sure don't have David's brains or personality."

"What about his good looks?" Tina wanted to know, "Are either of the other men half as good-looking? I think he's one of the most handsome men I've ever seen."

"I'll agree with you there," Donna said, "He's really, really hot!"

"Robert, the girls call him Robbie, and Ronald, aka Ronnie, are very handsome men. I suppose it's a matter of taste but I prefer David's classical good looks. The other two are more like the average All-American Joes."

"Can't get much better looking than David, or much nicer," Donna said.

* * *

David headed back to the coach galley with the last of the dinner trays in his hand. He really wasn't hungry but thought it wise to eat. He downed the meat from both pot roast and chicken breast trays hoping to store a little protein for the emergency to come.

Just as he finished eating, standing up, Donna appeared at his galley with an update.

"The Captain will be making an announcement that our landing at SEA-TAC will be delayed due to a slight mechanical problem. Actually, he's going to keep us in the air as long as possible in order to burn off any excess fuel. He said even though it's raining hard, they're foaming the emergency runway for our landing. Nobody knows how that will go, so we need to plan for evacuation as soon as the plane stops."

"Do we need to say anything else to the passengers or will the Captain take care of that?' David asked.

"We'll let the Captain take care of the details; our job will be to keep the passengers calm and safe. David, you and Jeannie will sit in the two empty first class seats you used for take-off. Just remember your training... head between your knees with a pillow, etc., and you'll be fine. Also remain in your seat until the Captain says otherwise, than be the first up to start the evacuation immediately."

Donna went back to first class and a few moments later the Captain's voice came across the intercom. He explained that there would be a delay as they circled Seattle airport in order to delete fuel before attempting an emergency landing. He also asked the passengers to remain seated unless there was an urgent need to use the restrooms. They were to extinguish all cigarettes and the no smoking sign would remain on for the rest of the flight. Before he was finished with the announcement half the people crowded into the center aisle and lined up for the lavatories at the rear of the airplane.

The passengers were also told that it would be necessary for women who were wearing high heeled shoes to remove their footwear which might provide an additional hazard to the slides used for disembarking. High heels would be collected and placed in the lavatories before landing. The passengers were also informed to remain calm during the evacuation and follow all instructions from the flight attendants.

At the conclusion of the Captain's announcement Donna's voice came over the intercom,

"Ladies and Gentlemen, the Captain has informed us that we will be in the air for an indeterminate amount of time. We will use this opportunity to prepare for an emergency landing. Please clear the area around your seats of any loose objects and secure small personal items in your pockets. Ladies...we will be collecting purses and high heeled shoes to temporarily store in the lavatories for landing. We will also be reviewing the emergency exits nearest to your seats that you will use after we land. Please remain calm and orderly and I'm confident that we'll all get through this safely. Thank you for your cooperation."

The cabin buzzed loudly with conversation from the passengers. David let the girls Tammy, Cheryl and Sue collect the ladies' shoes and purses. While they were working through the cabin, Jeannie came back from first class and drew the curtain in the galley where David was clearing loose items and locking them in the metal cabinets. She smiled nervously and spoke lowly and quickly.

"Captain said that it's raining hard at the airport, and unfortunately there's a lot of gusty wind. The emergency crews will be lined along the runway with fire-trucks, ambulances and other vehicles. They have decided that they will foam the runway as an additional precaution."

"Won't the wind and rain wash away all the foam?" David asked.

"I don't know," Jeannie laughed nervously, "I'm just glad they're doing everything possible to save us from burning up when we land. The rain might be a blessing in disguise. Captain said there'd be more than one-hundred emergency vehicles around...I'm praying that will be enough to rescue us. I'll see you at our seats up front."

David hadn't thought about prayer, but right now it sounded like a good idea. Maybe if Patricia and the guys had been given advance notice to pray, they would still be in the world. His mind starting racing with multifarious thoughts and images; he wondered if Patty knew she was going to die. From all accounts regarding the TWA crash, there was no warning. Fragments of the plane were found along with a few body parts like hands and feet which might indicate an explosion, possibly planted by some crazy terrorist.

David also thought about his remaining family; his dad Richard would spend the rest of life trying to bring comfort and solace to his inconsolable wife, Sylvia. David suddenly felt great love and compassion for his father, and then his thoughts turned to Nanny and Poppa John. All the hopes and plans for the future of the Lombardi Winery would disappear if David died; Sylvia had no personal interest in overseeing the vineyards. Her only real concern was her life in Saint Francis Woods with her loving husband. David wondered if Sylvia might even be relieved if she no longer had to deal with her gay son.

Nanny and Poppa loved their daughter, but well understood that they, along with the vineyards, were far from being a priority in Sylvia's life. Their hopes and dreams for the future of Lombardi Wines rested squarely on David's shoulders. He felt the same love and compassion for his grandparents as he did his father. He had always imagined taking care of all his family at the vineyards when they reached the last of their golden years, even Sylvia.

'It's time to pray for the first time after a long self-imposed hiatus from God', David thought to himself.

His thought was interrupted by Donna's appearance in the galley where he was working.

"It's time for you to go to your designated seat up front, Sweetie. Just make a quick seatbelt check as you walk through the cabin. The Captain will take charge for now and give instructions over the intercom."

"Okay Donna, good job, thanks for all the support."

"Hope to see you after we land," she said hesitantly.

David walked slowly through the cabin toward his seat at the first class bulkhead. Jeannie was already seated next to the window and David buckled in on the aisle seat next to her. She handed him a pillow that she had ready. The Captain's voice came calmly over the system, and the lights went out with the exception of a dim glow at the emergency exits.

"Ladies and gentlemen, we're preparing for our landing now. When your eyes become accustomed to the dimmed lights, please take note of the exit you will be using after you are given the order to evacuate. The flight attendants will guide you in a calm and steady manner. You can anticipate a wet landing and exit because the rain is coming down pretty steadily. Once you reach the tarmac there will be special crews to conduct you to transportation that is along the runway. There will be no other announcements."

The cabin was silent except for a small female voice coming from behind somewhere in the tourist section.

"Help me please. I need help please."

David quickly unbuckled and found his way toward the back trying to locate the voice.

"Right here, please."

He stopped at the aisle seat of an older lady that he had noticed earlier when serving dinner.

David knelt down beside her seat and calmly said, "What can I do to assist you, ma'am?"

"I have to pee," the little lady said in a strained voice, "really bad,"

"I'm sorry ma'am, there's nothing we can do; the lavatories are closed and locked. I must encourage you to wet your panties, don't hesitate to find relief while sitting in your seat, it'll be okay in this emergency situation."

"Thank you," she said in a small squeaky voice.

David returned to his spot and once again buckled his seat belt. Jeannie was resting her head on the pillow she held between her legs. She turned and looked wide-eyed at David.

"Everything okay?" she asked.

David leaned toward her and said in a stage whisper, "I had to tell her to pee in her panties."

Jeannie had to stifle a giggle, "I remember that from flight attendant training." She allowed herself to snicker a little. "In an emergency tell them to pee in their pants."

David let out a diminutive laugh and said, "I never imagined I'd have to say that to a little old lady, I always pictured telling it to a little old man."

Jeannine smothered her laughter in the pillow on her lap. David suddenly felt like laughing out loud, but he controlled the urge.

They both felt the plane surge downward and everybody knew it wouldn't be long now. Jeannie looked out the window and David watched over her shoulder. He could tell that it was raining hard and then he saw a string of flashing lights below the plane. It touched the tarmac and everyone held their breath. David could make out fire trucks and what looked like ambulances as their craft slid along its path.

The landing seemed to take forever and then as the plane slowed everyone could feel the nose dipping lower. David knew it was caused by the nose gear not being properly in place and he could tell that the plane was beginning to skid. There was a loud mechanical sound and he looked out the window to see the lights swirling around in a circle. The plane looped around once, twice, three times, slower and slower each time. They finally came to a stop and David heard one bell.

"Let's go," David said as he headed to the right hand forward emergency exit that he and Jeannie were supposed to cover. Donna and Tina were already evacuating first class passengers from the left, Tina's shrill voice could be heard shouting "Jump and sit...jump and sit...jump and sit as each person approached the door where the slide was deployed.

David opened the right door with no problem, and the rain and wind immediately rushed over his handsome face and lithe body. There were only four passengers left from first class who approached the door. David guided each one by the shoulder and hollered "Jump... sit...jump...sit...jump...sit."

Jeannine magically appeared with a small line of passengers from coach and guided them calmly one by one to David's door. "Jump...sit...jump...sit...jump...sit." He was soaked to the skin from the cold rain lashing at his body, "Jump...sit...jump...sit...jump...sit."

Abruptly and suddenly there were no passengers left to evacuate. The Captain and the first officer came from the cockpit. The Captain went to the left forward exit and hollered for Tina to jump. At the same time the first officer came up to David and almost quietly spoke the words "It's time to go David."

With no hesitation David jumped on the slide and sailed downward into the strong arms of two men who seemed big as mountains. "Good work, son," one of them said as they both easily lifted David to his feet.

David turned to watch Jeannie fly down the slide and then the first officer right behind her. A small band of firemen guided them to a shuttle with a female driver. The three airline employees were the only ones in this vehicle. Apparently the others had already been picked up. The driver shouted "You 'duckies' sit tight and hold on," as she stepped on the gas and drove away from the plane.

David tried his best to see what was happening and couldn't make out very much through the wet steamy window of the shuttle. He saw trucks with lights flashing through the wind and rain and one or two figures dashing around in the night. He was annoyed that the driver of their shuttle had the heat on full blast inside their van and the air was stifling and foul smelling.

The vehicle finally stopped at an outside door under one of the ramps at the Seattle airport. David, the first officer and Jeannie were ushered through the door, down a long bleak hallway, and into a small room with a big conference table where they sat down. The Captain and the rest of the crew from their flight were already seated. They looked drained and exhausted.

In less than a minute two people, a woman and a man came through the door. "Oh, thank God you made it!" the woman said. "We've been praying for you guys all night. I'm Cynthia Miller...call me Cindy...I'm Director of Customer Service here at SEA-TAC for Western...this is Charley my assistant," she indicated to the little sheepish fellow who had followed her through the door.

"There will be a de-briefing in the morning...not too early...I think it is set for ten thirty... we have rooms for each of you at the Airport Hilton...Charley and I will escort you to the hotel shuttle in just a minute. We've made all the arrangements for everyone of you guys... charge anything you want to your room...it's all taken care of. You'll get a wake-up call from either me or Charley around 0900 hours...you'll be shuttled back to the airport in time for the meeting. I'm sure you must have a lot of questions...but it can all wait until after you've rested. Just think of this as an R.O.N., remain overnight assignment, in Seattle."

Dave felt a wave of relief wash over his entire body. He was suddenly depleted of energy and couldn't wait until his head hit the pillow. He had a lot of questions... what was the condition of the plane they were on... was their traumatic event on the news...had all the passengers evacuated without injury...did the trainers and classmates in Los Angeles know what happened to them...when would they be flying back to LAX?

'This woman is absolutely right,' David thought. 'My questions will all be answered in the morning...right now I want a warm shower, a brandy, and clean linen sheets...I wonder if I'm too tired to eat."

* * *

David and Jeannie were in first class seats flying back to Los Angeles on the two-thirty afternoon flight from Seattle. They both felt tired and they didn't know what to expect when they arrived back at LAX. By the time their flight landed their training class would be over. Today was supposed to be the dreaded final examination, and they had missed it.

When the two arrived at LAX there was a ticket agent waiting with a message. They were to report directly to the large conference room at their hotel.

"What do you suppose they're going to do with us?" David asked calmly.

"I believe," Jeannie answered calmly, "I really believe they're going to make us take the final examination. It was scheduled for this morning in the conference room so we already know we missed it. Today was also supposed to be the day we bid on openings at the various bases, and we missed that too."

"That's right," David said, "I forgot all about that. Everybody's supposed to be leaving tomorrow to their assigned domicile. I'm not worried about having missed the bidding part; I'm sure Tammy saw to that for both of us. She knows that you're number one in seniority and that I'm number two; she also knows that if there is only one opening in LAX, you would want it, and everybody knows that I'd be the first to bid San Francisco."

"That's right," Jeannie agreed, "I'm positive that Tammy took care of us there; it's just that I don't want to have to take that dog-gone final exam."

"If we have to, we will." David said. "But I think you're wrong... they're not going to make us take that final...especially after what we've been through. The test is mostly on emergency procedures, and we've been through enough to teach the damn class what it's really all about."

When they arrived at the Century Hotel David and Jeannie dropped off their luggage with one of the bellboys and walked straight to the conference room. The doors to the room were closed and the two returning flight attendants looked at each other and shrugged. David tried the door and held it opened for Jeannie.

They were met with resounding cheers and applause. Their entire class and all the instructors were gathered giving a roaring standing ovation for just the two of them. David was truly surprised and maybe even a little embarrassed. There were a couple of guys with cameras taking pictures as they entered. Tammy was standing in front of the group clapping her hands. She beckoned for the two to come toward her.

She hugged Jeannie first, and then she wrapped her arms tightly around David and kissed him on the cheek. The entire room cheered. The noise was deafening. Tammy indicated for everyone to sit down, including Jeannie and David. There were two chairs of honor that had been placed for them in front of the group.

"Okay," Tammy said, "Everybody settle down... welcome back Jeannie and David...I wish we were able to give you more of a hero's welcome...you two really deserve it."

David noticed Ronald sitting toward the back of the group...he was gesturing wildly trying to communicate something specifically to David. David could only shrug his shoulders and turned his attention back to Tammy.

"The first thing I want to say is that I took the liberty of submitting bids for your home bases. Jeannie, you and sixteen others from your class will be based here at LAX...and David you and eight others from the class are going to San Francisco. What Ronnie has been trying to communicate to you from the back is that he and Bobby both got SFO; and yes, you heard me correctly, from now on Ronald will be Ronnie, Robert will be Bobby."

David and Jeannie laughed out loud and David said, "I hope my name hasn't changed to Davy."

Everyone in the room laughed along, including Tammy who said, "No need to worry, you'll still be known as David."

"Meanwhile, the good news is that you two will not take the final examination. In fact, I'm sure that you guys know enough about emergency procedures to last until recurrent training which is a year from now."

Jeannie patted David on the knee and said, "You called that one right."

Tammy said, "I think that David had a pretty good idea that we weren't going make you guys take that test. Now to get on with the rest of the evening; we'll all meet in the Oak Room restaurant in about one hour thirty minutes for a final dinner celebration. So that gives you time to freshen up before we reconvene. I presume that the rest of you will hang around in the bar before time to 'chow-down.' You're all dismissed."

* * *

David and Jeannie scurried out behind the rest of the group to retrieve their luggage from the bellboy and head upstairs to change. David was grateful that he didn't have a test to take, and it also dawned on him that his flight attendant training was over. He was ready to celebrate! He was going to take a quick shower and change into a fresh pair of slacks and one of his favorite Hawaiian shirts.

He took the elevator to the fourth floor and hurried down the hall to his room. It was a pleasure to be back and find everything neat and clean. He walked through the door and stripped off all his clothes leaving them in a heap by the door. He went naked into the bathroom and started the shower. He looked in the mirror and decided to eliminate his five o'clock shadow with a quick shave from his Norelco razor. He was excited.

Just as David stepped out of the shower and was drying himself, there was a knock on his door. He wrapped the towel around his waist and stepped over

the pile of clothes still lying on the floor. It was Ronald...
now Ronnie...standing there smiling broadly.

"May I come in," he asked politely.

"Sure, just try not to step on my uniform," David said
indicating the pile of clothes lying on the floor.

Ronnie stepped over the pile saying "Wow, I've never
known you to be so messy. You'll have to change some
of your habits if we're going to be 'roomies' together in
San Francisco."

"Whatever you say goes for me Ronnie."

"I say we have plenty of time for a little fun before
we go downstairs."

Ronnie pulled off David's towel and dropped to his
knees.

* * *

CHAPTER NINETEEN

Ronald, now known as *Ronnie* and Robert, now *Bobby*, flew up together to San Francisco on the same Saturday afternoon flight. David wanted to take them straight to the Vineyards, but it would have been too impractical for them to be on call sitting in Sonoma. It was just a little too far from the Vineyards to SFO International Airport.

He had phoned home in Saint Francis Woods just prior to their flight hoping to hear Richard's voice on the other end. His Dad didn't answer, fortunately, neither did Sylvia. It was Brenda who picked up the phone.

"David Wellington, where are you calling from," she'd asked, "your parents aren't here."

He explained that he was calling from Los Angeles and was bringing two colleagues with him from Western. They would be on reserve call for work beginning at eight the next morning. They'd be staying at the Wellington home for a few weeks, maybe a month, until they found places to live in the city. Both guys should have guestrooms with access to the home telephone lines. They would work out other details when they got there.

"Where did the folks go today?" David had asked.

He was happy to hear, "Oh they're in San Diego for the weekend. They flew down for shopping and the football game day after tomorrow. Raiders are playing the Chargers, and your parents won't be coming back until sometime Tuesday afternoon after the Monday night game. I'm happy to fix dinner for you guys...what would you like to eat?"

"Don't bother with that, Brenda, I'll take them out somewhere like Villa D'este or the Gold Mirror. Just have their rooms ready and I'll take care of the rest. See you in a couple hours."

"Do you want me to pick you guys up at the airport? I can bring your dad's town-car."

"No, we'll grab a cab into the city, you have plenty enough to do at the house."

* * *

The guys arrived at SFO around 1400 hours, took a taxi and were riding up the drive to the Wellington mansion by 1515 hours. David rode in front with the driver and the two other guys sat in the backseat.

"Wow!" Bobby said as they approached the house.

"O-o-o-oh, and, ah-h-h-h!" Ronnie wailed.

David cracked a grin and said, "The nice thing is that we have the place to ourselves until Tuesday. The folks are down in San Diego for the Monday night Raider game with the Chargers."

"That's going to be a good game," said Bobby, "I just hope I'm near a television when the game starts.

"Who knows where we'll be...you might be in Hawaii or Alaska or even back in Denver," Randy stated.

"Yeah, or we might be right in San Francisco waiting by the telephone," David said.

"Well it's good to know that it's just a quick cab-ride to the airport...what'd take...twenty minutes...and gee...I feel like we're out in the country some where instead of the city of San Francisco," Ronnie said as he got out of the cab.

"I don't think anyone who works at Western has such a fabulous place...not even Kirk Kerkorian."

"I'm sure that Kerkorian must have three or four places at least as nice as this," David said. "That guy is a billionaire loaded down with money. My dad is just a salaried employee at Lockheed Missiles and Space in Sunnyvale."

"He must have quite a job," Ronnie said looking up at the Wellington mansion.

Brenda had the front door opened before the guys got to it. The two poodles rushed out and went crazy jumping around David. He stooped over and picked one up in each arm.

"This one is Zachary...and this one is Bogey...they're brothers."

"These little guys sure missed you...and so did I... put them down so I can give you a big hug," said Brenda.

"I thought you said your mom was in San Diego," Bobby said.

Brenda let go of David and laughed heartily, "Hi guys, I'm Brenda, I just work for the family...I've got your rooms all ready...if you need anything just let me know... just tap on my door...when I stay here I sleep in the little guest house just outside the kitchen...David will show you where it is. David, why don't you show your guests upstairs...I would be happy to show off my cooking for the guys...there are some nice steaks...or I can run to the store and get fresh seafood for cioppino."

"No thanks Brenda, we'll have cocktails here at home and probably just stroll over to Villa D'este for dinner."

"Oh, Villa D'este, you guys are in for a treat! I'll call and let them know you're coming; remember it's Saturday night."

"Thanks Brenda. Tell them about seven thirty, that'll give us plenty of time for cocktails before we walk over."

"Would you like some of my savory little hors d'oeuvres for your happy hour?"

"Sure, Brenda, but please don't go overboard, just something light because we want to enjoy our dinner. We'll be back downstairs in about forty-five minutes...you guys grab your stuff and follow me...and Brenda, there's no need for you to stay tonight. I'll clean up after happy hour."

中 中 中

Even though he didn't relish the thought of being with Sylvia, David was actually glad to be back in his home. He knew that she would be on her best behavior in front of his airline colleagues. 'The trick is never to be alone with her...always be with someone whether it's a colleague or a family member,' David thought. 'Sylvia won't get on my case in front of guests or family like Dad or Nanny and Poppa John.'

David began to feel more and more relaxed about being in his home...after all he knew that he would eventually inherit this property...he'd even seen the will and knew that Richard left it to the last surviving family member. If Richard Wellington were to die first, the property went to Sylvia, and if she died it went equally divided to the siblings. David thought he would lovingly and willingly give his half to his Patricia if she could somehow return to this world.

The Wellington family bedrooms were all located on the second story around the west side of the house. The four large guestrooms with private baths were on the east side. The two sections were connected by a long open hallway that looked down on the main rooms. A magnificent banister that ran the entire length of the hall ended in matching curved staircases on both ends of the mansion. Brenda had seen to it that David's guests each occupied corner rooms separated by two other guestrooms and an astonishing skylight of intricate beveled stained glass.

David was walking along the connecting hallway with both Zachary and Bogey right on his heels. He stopped at Ronnie's room first and found the door open. The two poodles immediately ran into the room and jumped on top of the bed. Ronnie was standing at a full length mirror combing his hair.

"No you don't, that's not allowed in this house unless you're invited."

Ronnie turned around with comb still in hand and said, "You mean I have to ask permission to comb my hair?"

David laughed cheerfully, "Of course not partner. I was talking to the dogs. They're not allowed on anybody's bed unless invited."

"Oh-h-h," Ronnie said sitting down on the bed scratching both poodles behind the ears. "These little guys are always invited on my bed, and so is their master."

David laughed again, "Thanks, I'll remember that."

"Hey! Why do you call me partner...partner?"

"I don't know," David answered, "You remind me of George Peppard, in the 1960 movies 'Home from the

Hill,' standing there combing your hair. It just seems like I should call you partner."

Ronnie laughed brightly, "You sure know a lot about movies and you sure know how to make a guy feel good, partner."

They both laughed and Bobby appeared at the door. "What's going on? What's so funny?

What's all the laughter about?"

"We were just chuckling about the way Ronnie looks when he combs his hair."

"I've laughed the whole time I watched him do that for the last twelve weeks of training."

All three guys chortled as the dogs danced around on top of Ronnie's bed.

"Who's ready for a well earned drink?" David asked.

"Me!"

"I am!"

"Good, then you guys follow us downstairs and I'll show you the bar."

"The dogs drink too?" Bobby asked.

"You'd be surprised what my dogs do at happy hour."

* * *

The three male flight attendants from Western Airlines enjoyed cocktails in the Wellington mansion and then strolled the four and a half blocks to the restaurant. They laughed and relived incidents from their recent weeks of training. David studied Bobby over the course of their dinner and came to the conclusion he didn't like the dude.

Bobby, a.k.a. Robert Fields wasn't bad looking and he presented himself with a modicum of charm...but David thought that there was something sneaky about him...he was polite and mannerly but there was also something in his personality that seemed contrived and possibly deceptive. Bobby talked about girls a little too much, always making reference to their tits, asses, sexiness, etc. David didn't care one way or the other if this guy was truthfully straight or gay; he simply did not like him.

When they returned to the house David noted that Brenda's jeep was gone. They entered through the kitchen door and were greeted warmly by Zach and Bogey. Ronnie picked up Bogey and David was compelled to pick up the other poodle. He also took noticed that neither of the dogs instinctively did not interact with Bobby who had just announced that he was immediately retiring to his room.

"Before you go upstairs, let me tell you guys about the telephones in your rooms. There are three buttons that represent three lines. The first button is your personal line, and the number is written on the telephone. When you call scheduling tonight before you go to sleep, that's the number to give them. Tomorrow when you're ready to come downstairs just remind me and I'll route your line so you can answer downstairs if you get a call."

"Hoa," Bobby yelled, "you've thought of everything. Thanks again for accommodating us, and special thanks for that fantastic meal at Villa D'Este. It was delicious! Many, many thanks and I hope scheduling doesn't call too early in the morning. Good night."

Bobby headed for the main hall and toward the east wing staircase. Ronnie looked at David and shrugged his shoulders. "I'm not ready to sleep yet. Can I help you clean-up from our happy hour?"

"Thanks for asking," David said, "But it looks like Brenda already did that before she left. I'll tell you what we can do...we can have a nightcap and leave the mess for her to clean up in the morning."

"Heh-heh-heh, sounds good to me! I'll have whatever you're drinking."

"How about I pop a bottle of *Lombardi's Cold Duck*?" David asked heading for one of the two massive refrigerators in the kitchen? "We can sit right here at the counter and be comfortable."

"I like Cold Duck...don't we use Lombardi's champagne on our flights?"

"Yeah, we sure do."

"I've got something to ask you, David."

"Sure...shoot!" David said as he opened the bottle with a pop and poured the wine into matching champagne glasses."

"Are you related to the people from Lombardi Winery in some way?

David nearly choked on his first swallow. "How did you find out? Who told you?"

Ronnie turned a little red, "Bobby told me."

"Bobby? How in the world does Bobby know?"

"He said it heard it from the guy who works in the lobby of the Century Hotel...you know...the one who always wears Hawaiian Aloha shirts."

"Son of a gun! How did he find out? I wonder why he would tell Bobby of all people."

"I guess you had some classy hot gentleman visiting the hotel when the rest of us had left for the weekend. He mentioned your family was involved with Lombardi Winery. The hotel employee also told Bobby that your man drove a bitch'in gold Jaguar convertible."

"Son of a bitch!" David exclaimed. 'Why would he share all that with Bobby?"

"Uh, I thought you might have picked up on the fact that Bobby and the dude from the hotel were having a fling. You did know that they're both gay."

"No, I didn't pick up on that...in fact...I didn't pay much attention to either one of those guys. I only know that Hank talked to the hotel man for a few minutes that weekend while waiting for me to come downstairs."

"I hope you're not mad or pissed off."

"No...not really...I'm just taken back a little since I never mentioned it to anyone who works at Western. Do you suppose Bobby shot his mouth off to anyone else?"

"I can't say for sure," Ronnie answered, "But I know he thinks your family affiliation with Lombardi Wines is probably the reason you got the job."

"What I do know for certain is that nobody in the entire hiring process at WAL had a clue that Lombardi Vineyards belonged to my grandparents. I also know something else for certain...I can never...I will never... trust Bobby Fields for the rest of my life."

* * *

The following morning David was in the kitchen when Ronnie appeared fully dressed in uniform carrying his suitcase.

"I thought I saw a line light up about a half hour ago."

"Yeah," Ronnie said, "It was scheduling. I'm flying to Vegas on the ten o'clock flight. They said I would probably dead-head back to SFO. They'll let me know when I get there. My first assignment and I only work half a trip. Bobby got called out earlier this morning... he did go to Denver on a R.O.N., *remain overnight*. I need to call a cab."

"Take my Alpine, it's in the third garage," David said pushing a set of car keys toward his friend, "It's all gassed up and ready to go."

"Are you sure? I don't mind grabbing a taxi, I've got plenty of time and scheduling might send me somewhere else overnight from Vegas."

"No problem, there are two other vehicles I can drive. I know my little car will stay safe in the WAL employee lot. Hang on to the keys and use it as long as you're staying here."

"Wow, what a buddy you are! I was thinking about going down to Fresno on my day off and pick up my old blue Chevy."

"There'll be plenty of time for that later. You and I can look for a place to live around town, somewhere nice, on our first day off...that is...if you still want me for a roommate."

Ronnie laughed, "I can't think of anyone in the world I'd rather have for a 'roomie.'

"Good," David said, "I feel exactly the same way about you."

Just as David made his comment the telephone rang. "Guess who that's gott'a be?"

David picked up the phone...it was Scheduling from WAL...there was an opening to fill for the noon flight to Hawaii.

"Oh boy," David said excitedly, "This will be my first trip to paradise. Pardon me partner, I have to run upstairs and put on my Hawaiian shirt. Have a great first workday!"

* * *

David quickly changed into his Hawaiian uniform which consisted of one very colorful shirt and pale blue cotton slacks. He liked the shirt that had been selected for the guys to wear on flights to Hawaii, but he wasn't crazy about the pants. They had been treated with some type of fire retardant and they made his legs itch.

He threw his overnight kit into the WAL suitcase. It contained razor, toothbrush, comb and Old Spice aftershave. He thought for a moment of taking another set of clothes, but decided he would buy some new things in Honolulu. The only other article of clothing he packed was a pair of Navy swim trunks. He was determined to spend lots of time in the warm waters off Waikiki Beach.

Brenda was coming into the house just as David was leaving. "I'm off to Hawaii for my first assignment! According to Scheduling I should be back tomorrow night around nineteen hundred hours...seven o'clock. I didn't have time to give the puppies their morning treats...both the other guys are out on flights...Ronnie will probably be back later today."

"Have a good flight; stay safe!" Brenda yelled as David ran around to the garages and opened the second door where Patricia's Mercedes, Big Red, was parked. He knew that if she were still alive she would be happy for her little brother. 'I miss her so much,' he thought.

David zipped down the 101 Freeway to the Burlingame exit and drove straight to Western's employee lot at their building and hangar that sat a mile north of the passenger terminal. There was a shuttle every fifteen minutes that ran from the building to the airport and he had plenty of time before 'checking in' with Scheduling. He was supposed to call from a telephone in the Flight Attendant lounge downstairs in the main terminal.

Western was the only major carrier to have a permanent domicile for both pilots and flight attendants in San Francisco. All the office space below the walkway under the north terminal belonged to Western. Two partitions at the end of the terminal were the only exception; those belonged to TWA.

Western's offices included one for the Manager of In-Flight Services Harry Laughlin.

Second in command was Manager of Stewardesses (now to be known as Flight Attendants) Jennifer Hamlet, and there were four offices for her each of her Assistant Managers, Margo, Doris, Sally and Jane. Margo was the prettiest and the most personable. She had previously worked for Pan American Airways as a sales representative. Doris, Sally and Jane were former stewardesses with Western with Jane being the first black female to have a management position within the company.

David arrived at the airport with his disarming smile and a nod to everyone he encountered. His first duty was to use the phone in the Flight Attendant Lounge and check-in on the hotline to Scheduling. There were about a dozen female flight attendants, none of whom he recognized, sitting or standing around gabbing with each other. They all went silent when he walked through the doorway.

"Good morning," he said cheerfully trying to make eye contact with everyone. Almost everybody acknowledged his greeting.

"This is the telephone for scheduling?" David asked rhetorically pointing to the only phone in the room.

"Today's my first assignment, guess where I'm going," he said indicating his Aloha shirt.

"It's not going to be Hawaii," muttered a much older unattractive flight attendant wearing the muumuu style uniform for a flight to Honolulu. "Pardon me," she continued as she rudely pushed David aside and took the telephone from his hand.

"I'm here," she said into the phone, "I've made it in time for the flight, and I think there's someone here that needs to talk to you." She handed the phone to David and disappeared as quickly as she entered.

David's heart sank as he spoke into the phone, "Hi Scheduling, this is David Wellington, I guess I'm not going to Hawaii today."

* * *

David learned several important lessons his first morning on the job. First he learned to expect the unexpected as long as he was a Flight Attendant on Reserve. Second he became enlightened regarding the temperament of many of the senior female flight attendants; they could be insufferable bitches. He also became aware of the importance to prepare for all contingencies in respect to his uniform.

Scheduling had David sit around the Flight Attendant lounge until they got notice a couple hours later of an opening on a flight to Minneapolis-St. Paul. It was December and David had no other clothing except the Hawaiian shirt and cotton slacks he was wearing. There was nothing else in his suitcase aside from the pair of swimming trunks he had hurriedly thrown in with his small toiletries case. 'What else can go wrong?' David thought.

Working the flight wasn't actually all that bad; most of the crew were sympathetic about David's *misassignment*, including the pilots in the cockpit. A few passengers commented on his light uniform; some of the people thought he might be a sales representative reminding everyone that Western also flew to Hawaii. He worked hard with his female colleagues and impressed them with his quickness and willingness to assist.

When the flight landed it was late at night and the jet-way was cold. He and the crew walked toward the front of the terminal where they were to meet the shuttle to their motel. Everyone was bundled in a winter coat, except David. When they walked outside to the shuttle pick-up stop the driver was not there. David's teeth began to clatter and rap against each other almost immediately. He looked up and saw a brightly lit sign that displayed fourteen degrees Fahrenheit.

"You better wait inside, son," the Captain advised, "I'll signal to you from here when the shuttle arrives."

"Tha...tha...thanks," David yammered as he slipped back into the terminal.

He couldn't keep his teeth from clamoring for the next ten minutes. It was past midnight and the terminal was virtually empty except for one Western ticket agent and a couple of janitors cleaning the floor. David found a place to sit where he could keep the crew in sight. They were talking and laughing when the Captain waved to indicate the shuttle was arriving.

David stood up, grabbed his suitcase, took a deep breath and jogged outside into the icy night air. The driver hopped out and began to assist the crew with their luggage placing it at the back of the van. David waited patiently for the driver who finally turned around and with a surprised look said, "Who are you? Where's the other girl?"

"I'm Da...Da...David...Well...Well...Wellington."

"He's our first male flight attendant," the Captain offered cheerfully.

"I'm sorry sir, but nobody told us. We don't have any place for him to stay. We're all filled up and overbooked. As it is, you and the first officer have to share a room with twin beds. The only other bed is in the girl's room."

"Don't wo...worry, I...I...I'll work some...some... something out with sch...scheduling."

David picked up his suitcase and trotted back toward the terminal.

"Sorry buddy," the driver shouted.

'Screw you,' David thought as he went through the terminal door, teeth still chattering.

He walked over to the lone ticket agent and asked, "Where is the fli...fli...flight a...a...attendant lou...lou... lounge?"

"I was wondering who was with our crew from SFO. You must be one of the three new males Western hired. I heard all three of you new guys are based in San Francisco. Hey man, you must be cold!"

David took a deep breathe, "Ye...ye...yes I am."

The agent put up a sign that read 'Back in 15 Minutes' and said, "Follow me, I'll walk you down there."

The concerned ticket agent escorted David directly to the phone in the dinghy lounge that smelled strongly of stale cigarette smoke.

"There's the phone with hotline to scheduling; I'll be right back. If you leave the lounge for any reason, and want back in, the code is 4441."

David immediately picked up the phone, "Hi this is David Wellington checking in; it seems that no one made a reservation for me to stay in Minneapolis. I'm cold, tired and would appreciate a hot shower and some clean sheets."

"Oh, David, this is Amy at scheduling. It looks like someone on day shift didn't do their job...stay on the line...I'm putting you on hold for a minute."

David kept the phone to his ear and was too nervous to even sit down. The ticket agent reappeared with hot chocolate, a blanket, a pillow and an unlined raincoat with the WAL logo stamped on the back. He dropped the items on a moth eaten sofa and handed the hot chocolate to David.

"I wish it were something stronger; you could probably use a warm brandy."

David took a long look at the male ticket agent who wasn't exactly handsome but he was masculine with a pleasant face and a nice body.

"I'm grateful for all your concern," David said softly, "what's your name?"

"Bill...Bill Brady...I wish I could do something more to help you," he said blushing slightly.

David switched the phone to his left ear and extended his right hand, "Glad to meet you Bill, I'm David Wellington, your newest best friend."

David looked into Bill's eyes and knew that this Western Ticket Agent was interested in him sexually. At that moment a security guard buzzed himself into the lounge and David felt relieved.

"Hey Bill...what's going on...I saw the light under the door and just came in to check it out."

"Hey Jim, this is our new male flight attendant, David, and it looks like he might be stranded here at the airport tonight."

"Bummer," said the guard, "let me know if I can do anything to help out. See you upstairs later Bill."

"Thanks Jim...see you."

David changed phone position again and said "Yes Amy, I'm still here...okay...all right...The Coach Inn... should I take a taxi...okay...thank you."

David hung up the phone and looked at Bill who was shaking his head and rolling his eyes, "Oh no, not the Coach Inn; that's the worst motel in Minneapolis."

"Beggars can't be choosers."

"They said they're sending a shuttle for you?"

"Yes, she said to wait outside now...they're supposed to be sending a driver right away. You don't mind if I take the raincoat with me."

"Don't rush, that place is a good thirty minute drive from the airport and those people aren't very reliable. Some of our flight crews used to stay there years ago and they named the shuttle the 'Roach Coach'. I guess that tells you something about the place. Don't worry about the coat, it's yours to keep."

David laughed nervously, "Thanks! Just as long as they have hot water at the motel; I want to get in the shower first thing."

* * *

Bill, the ticket agent, was exactly right, the Roach Coach was unreliable. David had been standing outside for more than a half hour and there wasn't a vehicle moving anywhere in sight. His teeth were clattering worse than ever, and he felt zero warmth from the shell of a raincoat he was wearing. He looked up at the time and temperature; it read **1:45** A.M. **9** degrees Fahrenheit.

"Br-r-r," he said aloud, "this is ridiculous."

He picked up his suitcase and trotted back into the terminal. It was absolutely empty and it looked like Bill might have gone home, and then he suddenly appeared at the far end of Western's ticket counter.

"Hey Pal! You're still here; I thought you were long gone. What happened?"

"No...no...nothing   hap...hap...happened.   No...no... body came."

"Good grief...you must be frozen by now...do you want me to make you something hot to drink? I get off in a few minutes at 0200. Nobody will be around here again until 0600."

David took two deep breaths and answered, "No thanks B...Bill, you've done plenty enough for me a... already. I'm heading downstairs and curl up with that blanket and pillow you left for me. I'm supposed to work the 0930 flight back to San Francisco; I'll just sleep downstairs until then."

"Sounds like a sensible idea at this point...take care David...remember the code is 4441. Get some rest and have a safe trip home."

David went straight to the Men's Room downstairs next to the lounge to relieve himself. The coldness of his hand startled him as he unzipped at the urinal. He went to the sink and allowed the water to run for nearly ten minutes before it got Luke-warm. Even if he couldn't take a shower, it really felt good to thoroughly wash the hands.

He buzzed himself back into the dreary lounge and threw his body on the old beaten-up sofa. It stunk. He was still wearing the WAL raincoat and he didn't bother to take it or his shoes off. He tossed the blanket on his body and put his head on the fresh passenger pillow that Bill had provided for him. "This pillow and my hands are the only clean things on this sofa," he said aloud.

David fell into an immediate deep and dreamless sleep. He didn't hear Bill buzz back into the lounge or know that there was fresh hot chocolate and another blanket. He didn't feel Bill run his fingers gently through his hair or place the blanket over his tired body. He didn't see the illumination of affection and admiration in Bill's eyes. He just slept.

* * *

The return flight to SFO was full, and David still felt tired. Fortunately, he was with the same crew that had left him at the airport the night before. He was also fortunate enough to shave, brush his teeth and splash on a little Old Spice. It was hard to tell that his Hawaiian shirt was wrinkled because of the fussy pattern of palms and lotus blossoms. His slacks were just slightly smudged but not too noticeably.

Once he got into the routine of food and beverage service the flight went quickly. All the flight crew thought that David was a really good sport. The girls that worked with him also unanimously agreed that it he should complain to management about Western's Flight Attendant Scheduling in Los Angeles.

He had no intention of complaining, but he was seriously considering quitting. He knew that nobody in management would appreciate a whining novice employee who was on probation for the next six months. He also knew it would make the ultimate statement if he walked off the job and never looked back. He'd have to think it over.

The flight landed at SFO International at 1330 hours that afternoon. David said good-bye and thanks to the Captain and his co-pilot and then walked with the girls downstairs to dutifully check in with scheduling. He found out that he was not on-call again until 1400 hours the next afternoon. He had twenty-four hours to think things over.

* * *

It was around two-thirty in the afternoon when David drove up the drive to his home in Saint Francis Woods. Brenda must have picked up Sylvia and Richard with the Town-car because it was still in the driveway. He put Patty's Mercedes into the garage, noticed that his Alpine was gone, and ran into the kitchen. Nobody was there, but he heard the vacuum cleaner running in the downstairs hall. Brenda caught sight of David and indicated by pointing that everybody else must be upstairs.

He took the west staircase to the master bedroom and tapped lightly on the door before entering. He could see Sylvia lying on the bed probably feigning sleep with her left arm dramatically flung across her forehead. Richard appeared from the alcove office which adjoined the main room. David met him halfway for a big warm bear hug.

"Go Raiders!" Richard whispered in his ear.

"That's right," David said in a stage whisper, "What was the score?"

"Raider's...thirty-five...Chargers...twenty. Let's go to your room and I'll tell you all about it."

They stepped into the hall and David asked, "Did you get to meet either of the guys who are staying here?"

"Yes, we met Ronnie this morning when we got back from San Diego. He'd been called out on a flight to Hawaii from where you just returned by the looks of your uniform. It also looks like you really got a workout."

David groaned, "I'll tell you all about it later. So, you didn't get a chance to meet Bobby?"

"No, and apparently we have to forgo that privilege, at least for now. Ronnie said that he moved in with one of the girls from Western; I think he said she was from San Mateo, or maybe it was Menlo Park. She picked him up here very early this morning. I don't know about Bobby, but Ronnie seems to be a really upfront and sincere guy."

"I thought you'd like him. Did he tell you that he's former Air Force?"

"Yes, we spoke briefly about that. Your mother seems to like him as well."

"What's happening with Mom? Is she sick?"

"Oh no, she's just resting a little. She didn't get much sleep at the hotel last night; some of our Raider fans from Oakland were a little loud and wild with their partying. They let everybody in the hotel know why they were celebrating. I'm going to wake Sylvia in a little while to get dressed. We're going to the Memorial Club for happy hour and *your* choice of restaurants if you'd like to join us."

"I accept the invitation! I think there's time for a short nap before we go."

* * *

Happy Hour at the club was pleasantly congenial. David was glad to hear details of the Raider-Charger game in San Diego, and his parents were sincerely interested in his account of incidents at Western Airlines. David opted to go to *The White Elephant* for dinner. It was almost directly across from the club on Sutter Street.

"It looks as though I'm going to be driving home tonight," Sylvia stated bluntly.

"Why do you mean, Mother?"

"If we're dining at the White Elephant my meaning is that you men are certain to drink Pimm's Cups and you never seem to know when to stop."

"Pimm's Cup is one of my favorite drinks in the world and that's one of the main reasons I selected The White Elephant."

"What's another reason?" Richard asked trying to keep the conversation on a bright note.

"Well," David said, "Aside from the impeccable British waiters it's an occasion for me to have rack of lamb; which you and Mom don't like and *never* eat at home."

"Oh come on, young man...I can't even count the times that I've grilled tender little lamb loins when the rest of the family had steaks or pork chops. Right now, let's head for the restaurant, we should start moving...I'd like to get home in time for seven or eight hours sleep...I have a doctor's appointment at Kaiser in the morning."

"What's the scoop about that Dad?"

"A routine six month checkup...there's no concern... just a checkup."

* * *

David ran into the house wearing a clean Hawaiian uniform. Sylvia was sitting at the captain's table drinking a cup of coffee in the sun room next to the kitchen.

"Good morning Mom. I just put my suitcase in the car. Guess where scheduling assigned me to go?"

"So, I guess this means you've decided not to quit after the first calamity you suffered when they assigned you to Hawaii."

"Yes...and more than that...I'll be gone for three days...this one's the best assignment at Western...there is a fifty-three hour layover in Honolulu! It'll be like going on vacation.

Where's Dad, did he leave for work already?"

"If you remember, he had a medical appointment at Kaiser this morning. He's stopping at the facility in South San Francisco for his biannual checkup."

"Oh yeah, in all the excitement I forgot. Please be sure to tell him about my trip and give him my love."

"Of course, you be careful and don't party too much in Hawaii," Sylvia stated as she turned her cheek upward for David to kiss.

"Tell Ronnie where I am when he gets back. I have to fly...literally." David kissed her cheek and laughed.

"Try not to drive too fast; I'm sure you have plenty of time."

"See you Mom," he said picking up a poodle in each arm and allowing them to kiss his face. He placed the dogs together on the chair next to Sylvia, and jogged out the door.

* * *

David jumped out of Western's Employee Shuttle, sprinted through the terminal, and dashed down the stairway to the flight attendant lounge. He was surprised to see Ronnie sitting alone having a cigarette.

"Hey partner," Ronnie said putting out the smoke in an ashtray and standing up.

The two men started to shake hands, looked around, and hugged.

"We probably shouldn't have done that Ronnie said as he sat down again, "There's a surveillance camera up on the ceiling in the corner. Sit down partner and let's catch up on a few things. I see you're on your way to Hawaii."

"Yes," David said as he walked to the hotline telephone to check in with scheduling, "It's a fifty three hour layover."

"Whew! Whew!" Ronnie whistled, "Some people get all the luck!"

"What's happening with you?"

"I just finished the roundtrip early bird to Vegas, again. I'm waiting for a one way to Salt Lake and deadhead back to SFO, then I'm not on call again until tomorrow morning."

"How are things going at the house?"

"I met your parents...really high class folks... they're just like you...they know how to make a guy feel comfortable. Bobby was really dumb to leave your set-up."

"Is there a chance that you'll be off for the weekend?"

"It's looking real good for all day Saturday and all day Sunday."

"For me, too, Ronnie. Maybe we can find time for me to show you around San Francisco and meet my friend George, whom I told you about, and maybe a few others."

"Sounds like a plan Partner."

Just then the door to the lounge buzzed and a beautiful woman with a Vidal Sassoon haircut (and wearing an outrageously tasteful designer's dress in a filmy blue fabric) entered the room. She was very poised and had a gorgeous smile; she reminded David of his sister Patricia.

"Hello gentlemen, welcome to Western. I'm Margo Curtis, Flight Attendant Supervisor, and you must be Ronnie," she said pointing to him, and then she pointed to David, "and you are David."

"How'd you know who was who?" Ronnie said.

"It's simple, I know that David is assigned to Hawaii this morning and he's dressed in his aloha uniform. I'm check-riding that flight for quality service."

"Oh, oh," Ronnie said, "David will have to be on his best behavior."

"No need for concern David," she said almost tenderly, "I'll be in First Class with two very senior flight attendants and you are assigned to Coach. I'll make it a point to come back and chat with you in the galley while the movie is on right after lunch."

"I'd like that," David answered, "and I'm very pleased to meet you. You're supervisor for Bobby; have you met him?"

"Yes, I've met Bobby, but haven't had a chance to see him work."

"Gee whiz, some guys get all the luck. Sure wish you were my supervisor," Ronnie said.

Marge smiled again. David was certain that she had heard similar compliments often.

"Ronnie, I can tell you now that you will get along very well with your own supervisor. Have you had the opportunity to meet Jane?"

"No not yet."

"Her office is right next to mine just down the hallway. I know she's there now, if you come down I'll be happy to introduce you."

"Just give me a minute to wash my hands and comb my hair and I'll be right there. If it's okay with you I'll stop by your office first."

"It's okay Ronnie, mine is the last office on the left. David...I'll see you on the plane. You'll need to be at Gate #2 about fifteen minutes from now," she said indicating the large clock on the wall.

"Yes ma'am, looking forward to seeing you on the flight later."

Margo glided through the room and out the door.

"She looks like a model or something," Ronnie sighed.

"Oh yeah," she's a rare beauty," David agreed.

* * *

David worked very hard accomplishing his flight attendant duties on his first trip to Hawaii. The only negative moments were at the beginning of the flight while their plane was taxiing during announcements. The number one senior employee from SFO, also coincidently named Brenda, kept referring to flight attendants as *stewardesses*.

"Your *stewardesses* are demonstrating how to wear your life vest...your *stewardess* will be happy to assist you with seat belts...your *stewardess* will begin a beverage service shortly after take-off...your *stewardess*...your *stewardess*...your *stewardess*."

David knew that Brenda was perfectly aware of her faux pas and she did her best to use the word stewardess at every opportunity. The passengers giggled and laughed and pointed at David every time she emphasized the word. He made everybody laugh all the more when he squinted his eyes, shook his head and smiled broadly each time the word was spoken. He was going to show that he was a good sport and knew how to play along.

Immediately after take-off, while the Captain still had the seat-belt light illuminated, David saw Margo carefully making her way toward the back of the airplane straight to his jump-seat. He unbuckled and stood up as she beckoned him to the far rear galley of the Boeing 720B craft and pulled the curtain.

"I'm so sorry you had to suffer through that during the safety procedure announcement. I've spoken with Brenda who unfortunately was having fun embarrassing you. I'm certain she won't do it again."

"Oh, it doesn't matter that much. I know exactly how to remind her. I'll simply pin her tits to the cockpit door."

Just as David made the statement one of the other flight attendants pulled the curtain to the galley. It was obvious she overheard his last sentence. Her eyebrows shot up so high David thought they might fly right off her face.

Margo went into convulsive laughter and said, "Oh David...David...I'm speechless!"

* * *

The rest of the flight went very smoothly. In fact, while everyone was watching the film '*West World*' starring Yul Brynner, David was summoned to first class where Marge had him sit in the empty seat next to her. Brenda immediately came out of the galley with a sumptuous sundae of exotic ice creams with chopped Macadamia nuts and melted marsh mellow and warm chocolate syrup.

For just a moment he prepared himself to receive it smashed in his face or have it dumped in his lap.

Brenda said in a matter of fact voice, "Peace offering," as she adroitly pulled down the tray in front of David's seat.

"Wow!" David said, "Peace and thanks, this almost looks too good to eat."

"I want you to know that I heard about your comment regarding my female anatomical features," she took a deep breath and extended her bosoms. "Thanks for the warning, but I am now reprogrammed to use only the term 'Flight Attendant.'

Margo and Brenda both laughed hard...but not as hard as David.

* * *

After a glorious two days of swimming, eating, drinking and tanning with the crew in Honolulu, David's return trip to the mainland was more fun than he could have imagined.

The plane was about half empty in coach and Brenda persuaded her regular partner to exchange duties with David so he could experience working first class where they were only four passengers.

As the plane left the gate in Honolulu she handed David the microphone. "You can make the safety procedures announcements; that way there won't be any slip-ups and I won't have to worry about my tits getting pinned to the cockpit door."

He wished that Margo had been on his return flight, but she had returned to San Francisco on the same day she had arrived in Honolulu. Even though she wasn't his supervisor he would have liked to show off his skills. He had the passengers in stitches with his down to earth announcements, and he skillfully mixed drinks, sliced roast beef in the aisle directly from the cart and catered to every need and whim of the happy people in first class. It was an excellent trip.

Later that evening, when they arrived at SFO International, David said fond alohas to the Captain and crew, and even got a hug from Brenda. He verified with Scheduling that he had the weekend off and would not be on call until 1000 hours Monday morning. He didn't for a moment consider that bad news awaited his arrival in Saint Francis Wood.

* * *

CHAPTER TWENTY

David didn't imagine his heart could ever be broken again after the death of his sister; he was wrong. Finding out that his father had terminal liver cancer took him into a quiet state of mourning. He knew that he would have to fight hard not to show a hint of sadness to Richard; and he didn't relish the prospect of having to deal with Sylvia's martyrdom,

Once again in his life, David felt abandoned and betrayed by God. Living in the world would never again deliver the joy he had known growing up with his beloved family. In a matter of months his attempt to recover felicity in life was devastatingly thwarted by this heinous news. Why was God being so cruel? Why was existence turning into a nightmare for David Wellington?

"I'm still going to fight this depression," David said aloud, "Somehow I'm going to enjoy life even if it kills me!"

* * *

Richard Wellington was always a hero and he played his part lovingly with wit and charm. He was well aware of the desolation his diagnosis had caused for Sylvia, but he was really more concerned for the damage it would do to his young son's life. His biggest concern was that David would be disillusioned with his own personal happiness and God.

Richard understood David perfectly and knew that his son's spiritual needs and libido were intertwined like a fragile and delicate mechanism. He knew that Patricia's untimely death had impacted David permanently and he had prayed for his son's emotional recovery. He wished with all his heart that he could keep disappointment and pain from ever entering David's life, but he knew that wasn't going to happen. David's best chance of dealing with life successfully would have to be the ability to rely on God.

Richard knocked lightly on David's bedroom door. "Yeah, come in." He was lying on the bed fully dressed except for shoes. Zachary and Bogey jumped up on the bed and began licking his face and ears. "I was just resting a little."

"It looks to me like you spent the entire night sleeping on top of the bed in your clothes."

"Yeah, I guess I did. It's not the first time; I rested comfortably."

"If you get off the bed and come downstairs I'll make you a sensational breakfast starting with a Ramos Fizz."

David immediately jumped up and said "I'm putting on my slippers."

Richard went down the stairway followed by the two dogs and David. It looked as though everything was ready to start the show. The Captain's table in the sun room was set with breakfast china, the aroma of gourmet coffee was in the air, the blender and ingredients for the fizzes were on the counter, and the waffle iron was hot. Richard started the blender.

"We can have a fizz before I start the waffles. You have your choice of bacon, ham, or sausage," he said pouring the perfect gin fizzes. "You can have all three if you like. Salute!"

David clinked glasses with his Dad, "*Salute-ta mi papa.*"

"Let's sit at the table."

"Sure," David answered.

They sat down at the Captain's table and David took another gulp of his drink.

"Slow down, son, I don't want to hop up every five minutes to make another one."

David laughed, "Sorry Dad...you're right...I need to slow down on a lot of things...but this is the best Ramos Fizz I've ever put in my mouth."

"You say that every time I make one for you."

They both sat quietly for a moment and the dogs rested at their feet. Bogey was pushed up against Richard and Zachary had his head on David's foot, using it for a pillow. David took another small sip of his drink and noticed his Dad staring.

"Dad, I can't ever remember you staring at me like you are right now."

Richard smiled and kept on staring, "I'm just studying your eyes. They are so very wonderfully green."

David laughed, "You're the one in the family with the beautiful eyes, Dad, sparkling slate blue granite."

"There's something I'd like to talk over with you this morning son."

"Sure Dad...let 'her' rip...you know you can talk to me about anything."

"I'll get right to the point. You know there's no hope for me to get rid of this cancer. You and I both know that it's up to the Big Guy however long it goes. My major concern is for your happiness. I don't believe that you're going to be a flight attendant the rest of your life, but it's a good start. Western is a good company with good benefits and plenty of opportunity for advancement into management, reservations, sales, or training. I'd like to know that you will find security and happiness with your work."

"Sure Dad...you always told us it didn't matter what kind of work we did...just make sure we're the best at doing it...but I think that the Big Guy has directed me to make some decisions. Western is a great company, but family comes first. Things are going to get a little rough around here and I'm not going to bail out on my family when they do."

Richard smiled, "I was also going to say it's probably a good idea for you to move to your own place. I think that Ronnie might be a great roommate for you. Right now it might also be best to lease somewhere in town; a little later you can think of buying property, it's always a good investment in this city."

"Dad," David interrupted, "Slow down! You're not going to get rid of me! I am your only son and now the only living off spring you have. It's true that I've been selfish in my youth only thinking of my own pleasure, but my life had to change at some point, and it looks like I'm at that point."

Richard laughed, "You know I'm not trying to get rid of you son. I only believe that it's important for you to make your own way in life. You're wrong about being selfish, no one can accuse you of selfishness. We've all been proud of you and the way you deal with the world. You sister often said the world needs more just like you. I know nothing I can say will change your mind about whether you stay with Western or go from Western, and the same is true regarding your home here. I know you will make your own decisions. You have been blessed with wonderful legacies from both sides of your family. You can choose whatever you like, and we will all support you."

David looked intently into his father's august face, "I've made up my mind to quit Western forthwith and spend quality time with my father. You're right, Dad, nothing you can say will change my mind. My destiny is not to continue the search for gratification and self satisfaction. My mission is to take care of my family."

David watched tears well up in his father's sparkling blue eyes. "I guess there's nothing more to discuss, except, remember to stay wise in your choices. Don't get carried away by the world; your soul needs quiet and rest just like your body. I know that you're not on the best terms with God right now, but...he'll never abandon you...you belong to him. You became his before you were born and then went from the cradle to the Baptismal Font. Trust in him in all things and you'll never go wrong."

David knew that his father was one hundred percent correct, but he wasn't ready to reconcile with the Big Guy just yet. God was throwing too many staggering curves and fast balls for David's soul to find any peace and quiet. Right now he felt like Job in the Old Testament... Job who lost everything...health, love, money and his most important family members.

David wasn't going to pursue a religious conversation with his dad. There wasn't time to be concerned with devotional matters. God had circumscribed Richard's life with cancer, and David wanted to make every day count for his father.

"I'm glad that my friend Ronnie is here right now to act as liaison between me and Western Airlines. I'm going to have him turn in my badge and resignation so I don't have to make face-to-face explanations. Later on I'll help Ronnie find a place of his own in the city. Until he finds a place I'd like him to stay here, if that's all right with you and Mom."

Ronnie appeared at the doorway of the sunroom right on cue, "Did I hear my name mentioned?"

"You sure did, sir," Richard said getting up and shaking Ronnie's hand. "How'd you like a Ramos Fizz to start your day?"

* * *

"We're finally going to find a place for you to live today, Ronnie, and I know just where to begin our search. Prepare yourself to meet George Bellini!"

"You don't think we should call first?" Ronnie said as David raced along Market Street in Big Red.

"Oh, heavens no...I have a strong feeling he knows we're on the way to see him. I've told you a little bit about him; he's the one who has psychic abilities. He's responsible for me becoming a flight attendant; he's also the one to help you find the right place to live."

"Sounds like a far-out dude, take me to him!"

Once again David was lucky finding a place to park just half a block from George's studio apartment. They parked and hurried along Jones Street to his building. *Once again* the front door miraculously buzzed open even before David could ring George's studio.

"What did I tell you? He knows we're here already," David said as he took two steps at a time up to the apartment.

George was waiting in the opened doorway to his studio.

"You guys are right on time; I just finished making coffee and I have some fabulous cookies that Paula made. You remember her David; she lives in the studio just above mine."

"Of course, she's a very good friend of yours. She is well?"

"Oh yes...there was a small personal problem...but it's all gone now."

David wondered for a moment if it might have been some bad vibration or pesky poltergeist that George had exorcized from Paula who was a confirmed Spiritualist.

"This is Ronnie; he's the one I've been telling you about over the phone. Well, here he is in person."

"Oh yes...it is a complete pleasure to meet you Ronnie...and welcome to San Francisco."

"Thanks," Ronnie said smiling and extending his hand.

"Oh no, kiddie...no handshake...you're family now," George said giving Ronnie a hug.

Ronnie blushed slightly, "Sit down, make yourself at home."

"Thanks," Ronnie said, "I really like your place; it looks like you have a botanical garden on your fire escape."

George looked at Ronnie approvingly and said, "We're going to get along just fine; are you guys ready for some coffee? By the way David, have you heard from Hank lately?"

David exhaled heavily, "We'll need to talk about that later."

George smiled knowingly "No urgency, I have a pretty good idea what's going on."

George brought out two mugs and his matching containers of cream and organic brown sugar; he went back to the kitchen and collected the glass decanter of hot coffee. After filling their cups he returned the decanter to the kitchen and came out again holding a small piece of folded paper.

"What's this? Ronnie asked as George handed him the note.

"It's the address of a lovely Victorian apartment in Buena Vista Heights on Buena Vista East, right across from Buena Vista Park. As soon as you guys finish your coffee we could drive up there and look it over. The landlord, a friend of mine, Charles, will be waiting to show Ronnie the place; I'd enjoy riding up there with you guys if you can make room in the car. Charlie said the view is absolutely inspirational."

"There's plenty of room in the car." David said, "We brought Big Red, the Mercedes. We won't be able to stay for very long. I want to get back to my dad right away; I know you guys understand. In fact, would you mind if I drop myself off back in Saint Francis Woods? You guys can have the car for the rest of the day and just take your time."

* * *

CHAPTER TWENTY ONE

David was in the stables at the Vineyards saddling Majestic Genius, long overdue for some extended exercise. A wave of nostalgia passed through him as it always did when he thought of riding the steed so much beloved by Patricia. He felt a closer bond than ever with the poodles and this magnificent horse. It was as though all the animals who had known Patty sensed her brother's pain. They missed her too.

The phone in the tack room rang and David called to Larry, one of the stable hands, "Would you pick that up for me?"

"No problem Mr. Wellington."

In a minute the boy appeared in the doorway, "It was Leonardo at the house Mr. Wellington, he said that you have a visitor, and you need to go up there right away."

"Thanks Larry...and Larry...it's David...not Mr. Wellington...would you guys please finish saddling Majestic for me? I'm still going to ride after I get rid of whoever's here."

"Sure thing mister...I mean...David."

"Thanks."

David walked swiftly toward the house wondering who could be stopping in for a visit. Everyone knew that

Nanny and Poppa John Lombardi had died over a year ago and that he was the only family member alive from both families. The Lombardi estate was no longer a center for contrived visits from distant cousins or freeloaders to enjoy five star food and board. Everyone knew David was no longer the *playboy of the western world*.

As he approached the south side of the mansion he saw a brand new gold El Dorado gleaming in the driveway. It had California plates and a bumper sticker that read *University of California, Berkeley.* 'Who in the heck could this be?' David thought..

Leonardo met him at the hallway door. "Who is it?" David whispered.

Leonardo shrugged his shoulders, "He's an old friend of yours and your sister; that's all he said. He's in the main room."

David walked slowly down the hall into the main room. There was a tall male with clean cut hair which was obviously professionally cut. His back was turned to David. He was looking at an original oil painting by Nicolas De Corsi. It was of an old church in Italy, perched high on a hill with a winding road overlooking the roiling Mediterranean sea.

The man looking at the painting turned around and smiled familiarly, "David," he said. Just as he spoke the two poodles ran into the room and began jumping all around the man's legs. He squatted to pet them "I remember you guys...Zachary...and Bogey."

At the mention of their names the dogs began wildly licking the handsome face.

"Steve, I hardly recognized you with the haircut and the suit. Looks to me like you've gone yuppie after all those years of being a hippy in San Jose." David walked over and gave him a bear hug.

"I saw your El Dorado in the drive. Are you now affiliated with Berkeley in some way?"

"How'd you guess? I'm an Assistant Professor of Art...I teach art history and a couple of practicum classes...also working on my doctorate to become a department associate."

"That's fantastic, Steve, you look absolutely terrific; more handsome than ever. The establishment certainly becomes you."

"Thanks...thank you. You look handsome as ever except maybe a bit thinner."

"That's what a steady diet of anxiety, grief and stress will do. It's all over now; I'll tell you all about it someday. Of course, we all still drink a little wine out here in the Vineyards. Will you have some with me?" David asked slipping behind the large cherry wood bar and raising a bottle of Lombardi's Beaujolais.

"You bet...I'd be honored to share some with you... anytime."

"I'll bet you have a beautiful wife and started a family at this point in your life," David said as he stopped uncorking the wine long enough to point to Stephen's ring finger."

"Oh, no," Steve said, "I just wear this to discourage all those sweet little co-eds from attacking me at the university. I never got married, David, and I probably never will."

"Oh?" David said handing Steve a glass of wine.

The two guys clinked glasses and said in unison 'salute-tah.'

"You remember!" David said enthusiastically.

"Of course, that's one of the first things Patty taught me when we first met. I remember everything David. I also remember that magnificent cherry wood bar you're standing behind used to sit in your house in Saint Francis Woods. It was a favorite of your dad."

"You have a sharp eye."

"David...I'm an artist...remember?"

"Do you live in Berkeley now that you're working at the University?"

"Yes, I have a small bachelor's pad just within walking distance of the Art Department."

"Sounds great Steve; it's good to see you so...so... settled?"

"Yeah, I guess you could say I'm settled. I've wanted to come to see you for a long time. I still stay in touch with Nancy who's married now and lives in the East Bay. She told me about your mom and dad both passing away."

"Yes, I got an invitation to Nancy's wedding. I didn't go. I think I was busy that week burying my Nanny or Poppa John; I don't remember which one. They died within two days of each other."

"I'm so sorry, I know. Nancy has told me most of what you've been through losing your dad and grandfather, and then losing your Nanny and your mom. You've had much more than your share of grief and sadness. I don't know how you're even still standing."

David laughed, "I'm still here; I guess I haven't dissolved. I don't want to proselytize but it was God who ultimately saved me. It took me long enough to realize, but He's the one who stood by my side and guided me through all the turmoil. The last years have been a blur, mostly because of my denial in Providence. During that time I lost all my family members and many of my friends. After they were all gone I woke up one morning and remembered Jesus. I had been fooling myself to believe that God was my enemy."

"I know that you and Patty didn't broadcast your faith but you two were raised to believe that *God is Love*. I always marveled at that and wonder if I'd have turned out differently if my family had been more religious."

"I think you turned out pretty well, Stephen," David smiled.

"I like it when you call me Stephen; Patty...Patricia... almost always called me Stephen. I miss her so much." He began to cry.

"I'm sorry David. I never expected to do this; I didn't expect this to happen." He sobbed.

David quickly came around from behind the bar and held Stephen in his arms. He continued to cry with his face on David's shoulder. David gently patted him on the back of his head. Smiling ever so slightly David closed his own eyes until Stephen sniffed deeply and took a deep breath.

"I'm sorry David; I'm really sorry. I am the one who should be strong for you. I'm embarrassed; I should be going now."

"No, wait! Please sit down a minute. I want you to stay a little longer. Please."

Stephen sat on a nearby Victorian loveseat and David sat next to him. Their knees were touching as David put a hand on Stephen's shoulder. They looked solemnly at each other.

"This is good Stephen. You wanted to see me and I'm so glad to see you. You have questions you want to ask...questions about Patricia...and I have answers for you. I want to talk with you about her. I want to tell you about our time in Europe...her marriage...her life...her plans for the future. I also want to tell you about myself. I want to talk about my disappointments in love...my brief career in the airline industry...and how I've grown up a little more since you last knew me. I don't want to talk about these things right now...today...but I do want to talk about them. Will you come back soon? Maybe you and I can..."

David didn't have the opportunity to finish his sentence; Stephen had leaned over and kissed him. It wasn't a passionate kiss...it was a loving brotherly kiss...a seal of attestation and unconditional consent between two men joined by a mutual destiny.

* * *

David headed back down to the stables. With the assistance of another strong employee Larry had brought Majestic Genius out in front of the stalls. The two men were using all their strength to hold the horse down. When David drew close he patted the stallion on the nose, took the reins from Larry and jumped on a polished English saddle. Majestic reared high showing his spirit and David smiled broadly.

He shouted "We'll be back in a couple hours," and they rode off at a lively trot.

David guided Majestic to a favorite trail that wound up the wooded mountain directly behind the Lombardi estate. The smell of the Sonoma forest fell fully on his face as they galloped and glided up the trail. The wind rushing through his hair gave David a feeling he hadn't experienced in a long time.

A little more than thirty minutes later David came to their destination and dismounted. He didn't have to tie Majestic's reins to anything... the horse showed no intention of leaving his side...not only out of loyalty but also because of David's jeans pocket bulging with sugar cubes.

David looked down on *his* Vineyards...*his* palace...*his* winery. Once again he had a feeling of real contentment and pride.

"Thanks be to God," he shouted aloud, "for everything!"

David allowed his mind to wander back remembering many happy moments in his life.

He remembered his father laughing,

'I hereby declare that you *are* grown up, son!'

He thought of Sylvia the night she met Hank at the Marine's Memorial Club,

'Welcome to San Francisco, you have a fine tour guide.'

He thought of that Sunday afternoon when Hank said,

'Egad, I didn't give you my phone number...call me at the clinic tomorrow morning.'

He thought of his Poppa John saying,

'*I'ma* think *dat'a I'ma* glad to see my grandson.'

He remembered Nanny on that same day,

'I like to get up to hug my favorite grandson.'

He remembered Sonya and Magda and Patty yelling,

'Long live King David.'

He thought of Angelo carrying his sister up the stairs shouting,

'She is lighter than feathers!'

He remembered Salvatore,

'We will play in the sun, eat in the shade, and make love...'

David smiled again. He looked up at the sky and reflected on the puffy white clouds coming inland off the Pacific Ocean. He placed his arm under the head of Patty's horse and tilted its stately head toward the sky.

"Look Poopsie....it's a good omen, there's enough blue to cover *three* Dutchmen,"

Majestic neighed softly and fondly nuzzled his master's shoulder.

*And the Lord turned the captivity of Job, when he prayed for his friends: also the Lord gave Job twice as much as he had before. So the Lord blessed the latter end of **Job** more than his beginning:*

Job 42:12

THE END

Printed in the United States
By Bookmasters